The Russians have conquered the US without firing a shot. Feodor Zalinsky sits in the White House. Colonel Gregor Rostovitch is in charge of putting down the single public act of defiance against the Soviet occupation—an impotent student protest in the Middle West. He does so with chilling efficiency. A reign of terror against the Jews begins. America, in shock and despair, settles into passive acceptance—until . . .

A black cab driver named Frank,

Hewlitt, a White House interpreter,

Haymarket, a former Chief of Naval Operations,

an incredibly brave and beautiful woman,

and one fully operational nuclear submarine,

provide the raw material for the most daring, brilliant and secretive force of freedom fighters in the world!

THE FIRST TEAM

"Compares favorably with such top-rate brink-of-disaster novels as SEVEN DAYS IN MAY, FAIL-SAFE, and NIGHT OF CAMP DAVID . . . Few writers can carry off a fast-paced adventure fantasy with the verve and professionalism of John Ball!" *—San Antonio Express*

"SUSPENSE AT ITS BEST!" *—Miami Herald*

THE FIRST TEAM

Books by John Ball

The Van
The Kiwi Target
A Killing in the Market
Rescue Mission
The Fourteenth Point
The First Team
Phase Three Alert
The Murder Children
The Winds of Mitamura
Mark One: The Dummy
Miss One Thousand Spring Blossoms

Virgil Tibbs Mysteries
Five Pieces of Jade
Eyes of the Buddha
Then Came Violence
Singapore

Chief Jack Tallon Crime Novels
Police Chief
Trouble for Tallon
Chief Tallon and the S.O.R.

THE FIRST TEAM

John Ball

SPEAKING VOLUMES, LLC
NAPLES, FLORIDA
2014

The First Team

ISBN 978-1-61232-992-5

For PAT, a small return for the months of hushed patience, the many cups of hot cocoa quietly put at my elbow and for inspiration when I needed it most.

AUTHOR'S NOTE

The preparation of this book has been materially assisted by many of the officers and men of the United States Navy. More than fifty individual specialists took the time and trouble to help. Their number properly begins with Rear Admiral Edwin S. Miller, and includes, in particular, Commander Harry Padgett, whose resourcefulness was apparently inexhaustible; Lieutenant Alcide Mann, whose expertise was matched only by his hospitality; and Yeoman First Class Austin T. Jordan, who proved particularly talented at unearthing the answers to difficult and complicated questions.

An especial message of gratitude goes to the officers and men of the U.S.S. *Canberra* (CAG-2) who did the author the very signal honor of electing him a permanent honorary member of the crew.

Sincere thanks are also tendered to Mr. Harry Spitzer and to Mr. Jack Dinsfriend for supplying needed information from their special areas of knowledge.

Thank you, gentlemen, one and all.

John Ball

CHAPTER ONE

When the alarm rang Hewlitt stayed in bed for a minute or two wondering if he should get up at all. The clock had not awakened him; he had been lying for some time with his eyes wide open, staring at the plaster ceiling that hung above his head. He had been a slave of the efficient little electric clock for so long that the idea of being able to ignore it had a certain hypnotic fascination. Then, carefully, he listened. Outside, through the open window of his bedroom, he could hear the familiar traffic noises; they told him that for the moment, at least, people were doing what they had always done.

Still he lay quietly, waiting. Then he caught the faint aroma of fresh bread from the Georgetown bakery close by. That settled it; things were at least normal enough that he would have to get out of bed without any more delay.

As he shaved he attempted to sort things out in his mind and formulate a plan of action for each of the several possibilities which he might have to face within the next two or three hours. Because he did not have enough in the way of hard facts to go on, he ended up with nothing except the awareness that in his line of work being late on the job was normally unthinkable. He wondered if he still had a job at all. Then he reasoned very simply that the only way to find out was to go and see.

The automatic coffee maker that he had turned on showed a glowing red light. He unwrapped a Danish sweet roll, dropped a cube of sugar into an empty cup, and sat down to breakfast. His watch told him that he was substantially on schedule. As he ate he took note of the continuing thumping caused by automobile tires as they ran over the edge of the irregular manhole cover in front of the apartment building. He knew the sound so well it transmitted a certain sense of satisfaction, like the grasp and feel of a familiar object. He wondered, then, if Frank would be there as usual to drive him to work. He seemed to be finding satisfaction in trivialities; they occupied his mind and kept him from focusing on the bigger things which would confront him all too soon.

When he had finished and was ready to go, he glanced through the window and saw that Frank was waiting for him as always. He was parked at the curb, sitting behind the wheel of his five-year-old taxi, a veteran survivor of the Washington traffic. If Frank were to get a new cab it would disrupt things even more, Hewlitt decided as he made his way out. He climbed in and spoke his usual greeting.

"Where to?" Frank asked.

That was the first break—the first thing that was out of its usual pattern. For more than three years Frank had driven him almost every weekday morning to the same address—and sometimes on weekends too when he had been needed.

Hewlitt's first reaction was to strengthen his own confidence by snapping back a little tersely, but he thought better of it almost at once. Frank was a pillar of reliability, and clearly he too was concerned. "The same as always," Hewlitt said, "at least for the time being."

Frank nodded, then he slipped his cab into gear and began to thread his way into the pattern of the flowing traffic.

As the minutes passed, Hewlitt noted that if there were any other signs of change, they were well hidden. When they paused for a light an electronic parts store had a sign out announcing its annual sale. In the dusty window bare speakers gaped like forlorn souls in some sort of mechanical purgatory, naked and defenseless without mountings to hold them decently enclosed or amplifiers to give them life.

When they moved forward once more Hewlitt noticed one or two shops which were still closed when they should have been open, but they were too few in number to be conclusive. He sat back in the seat and tried once more to set the pattern of his mind so that he would remain calm, but still be prepared for whatever circumstances he might have to face. Then Frank caught his attention. "You still planning to go to your office?" he asked.

Hewlitt leaned forward and matched his own voice to Frank's. "Why not?"

The driver's powerful shoulders rose once and then fell. "Things might be different," he said. "You might just walk right into a lotta trouble."

"I thought of that," Hewlitt said, "but what choice have I got?"

Frank waited until they were free of other cars. "This old hack don't look too good, but it runs just fine," he began. "I take care of it myself. We could load up with some gas, most of the stations are still open, and plain get the hell outa here. I know a few places."

"Down south?"

"In the mountains."

Hewlitt realized what the offer meant. "They could find us," he warned. "That could be very serious for you—if they thought we were trying to run away."

Frank became a trifle more urgent. "Don't worry about that. I can take care o' myself. If it comes to that, I can always say that you hired me to drive you there. That would put the monkey on you, but don't sweat it, I'm pretty good in the hills. They couldn't find us that easy."

For a moment it was a temptation and Hewlitt rapidly weighed the factors involved. Then he shook his head. "If you'll feel safer that way, then you go," he said. "Believe this, I wish that I could go with you and I'd trust you completely if I did. But I'm going to take a chance because it might just work out better that way."

Frank considered that. "I figure I know what you mean. In a way it makes sense. But if you need some help, you know where to come."

Hewlitt reached out and for a moment laid his hand on Frank's shoulder. "I won't forget. And it goes both ways, you can depend on that."

The cab turned into Pennsylvania Avenue. For the rest of the ride neither man spoke; they had said all that they had to say to each other. When Frank pulled up in front of the entrance to the West Wing of the White House, Hewlitt climbed out as he always did and then passed over a folded bill. "For tomorrow, too," he said.

"Gotcha." Frank pushed the money into his shirt pocket without looking at it and then drove away.

Automatically Hewlitt produced his identification. The men who guarded the entrance knew him well, but the rule had been inflexible for some time—everyone had to produce identification and an authorization card, every time, without any exceptions. The check-in process remained unchanged; his presence was duly noted as he passed inside and went to his small office in the basement, not too far from the communication room. On the way there he was tensely alert for any indications of change in what should have been a charged atmosphere, but things seemed deceptively placid. The few other persons whom he encountered nodded to him and then went on about their own separate businesses; there was no unnecessary communication, no evidence of camaraderie.

In a sense his role here was a minor one, but he had no illusions that he would escape whatever lay ahead. If he had entertained that idea for even a moment, the appearance of of his office would have awakened him to the truth. Two things were different, minor things that were significant. First, the usual pile of papers and documents which normally lay on his desk each morning for him to read and translate was not there. And, secondly, the modest, unimportant picture that someone had stuck on his wall a few months previously once more showed its familiar face.

There seemed no work for him to do; he felt like someone returning from a long vacation to find that his desk had been cleaned out and the familiar trappings of his employment removed. The picture told the same story in different language. It was a routine publicity photograph, in color, of the Polar Aircraft Corporation's latest fighter, the supersonic *Ramrod*. A press representative had passed out several of the framed prints, one of which had ended up on the wall of Hewlitt's office. He had let it remain there because the photographer had done an amazingly good job; the sleek dynamic lines of the plane and its almost unbelievably small wings had been captured in a picture which was both the portrait of an aircraft and an abstract composition. Even within the boundaries of the neat black frame the fighter seemed about to leap forward with uncontrolled raw power. Later, when the news tickers began to beat out the relentless facts about its disappointing performance and mechanical problems, he had one day turned the picture face to the wall. Everyone knew, of course, what the picture was and the blank side had been a silent, effective rebuke. Now it was before him once more, the aircraft appearing so full of promise and so invincible in combat. He had been told to look at it, or so it seemed to him, and he did not like it at all.

He decided it would be best to leave the picture as it was and sat down in front of his desk. In the lower left-hand drawer he had a pile of material for review when time would permit. Time permitted now; carefully he removed it and put it in place where the regular morning's input should have been. From the center drawer he took out a yellow legal-sized, ruled pad and prepared to make notes.

For some reason his mind turned back to *Uncle Tom's Cabin*. He had never read the book, but he remembered the frequent allusions to Eliza, or whatever her name was, and her escape across the broken ice. That was the way he felt now; he was trying to cross a river without being able to see the far shore. He could only leap from one convenient piece of ice to another, knowing that any chosen foothold could prove false and plunge him into dark waters. The work before him was an ice cake—something he could utilize for the moment to keep his head above water.

As he began to note down the salient facts he was gleaning from the pile of technical and semitechnical material, he tried to fight down the feeling that much of what he had done in the past had been disregarded, as the radar warning had been before the attack on Pearl Harbor. People did not like to receive unwelcome information and often looked for a way out—such as ignoring it altogether. That was the key word—ignore. They wouldn't ignore it anymore.

His work was interrupted when a colleague paused in the open doorway to his office. The two men simply looked at each other a moment before Hewlitt spoke. "Is he here?" he asked.

The man in the doorway nodded; after that he was gone. Hewlitt felt a slight flare of anger, then he forced himself to think logically and to banish the danger of emotionalism. The responsibility clearly lay in many different areas, more important ones, and his piece of the puzzle had been at best small and unimportant in comparison with all the others. After he had fixed that idea in his mind, he felt a little better.

The phone on his desk rang. He picked it up with deliberate calm and spoke his name. "Come to the cabinet room at ten-fifteen," he was told by a secretarial voice. "We're to get some kind of a briefing."

Hewlitt acknowledged and hung up. Now some of the uncertainty was about to be resolved; for that he was grateful. First of all he wanted information, as much of it as he could get. After that he would decide which cake of ice he would leap to next. He turned back to his work, suppressing the prickling sense of alarm which kept trying to germinate in his mind. If he kept his head, he knew, he couldn't help but come out better in the end.

At six minutes after ten by his Rolex watch he got to his feet, locked his notes inside his desk, and slipped a small memo pad into his coat pocket. With a strange, almost chilly sense of calm he went up the stairs and headed toward the portico. The short walk in the open air supported him and gave him the feeling that God was still in his heaven no matter how much his human creatures had managed to foul up things on the planet Earth.

By contrast the atmosphere in the cabinet room was tight. In times of crisis this chamber had seen men of high capability, and some of far less than that, gather to confer, but it had always been in an aura of problems shared. Now, Hewlitt sensed, it was a clear case of every man for himself. He counted thirty-two people, all of whom he knew more or less well, including five women who had about them the common look of confidential secretaries who could be trusted to keep classified information inviolate. There was very little movement or conversation; everyone simply stood and waited in an aura of strained and counterfeit patience.

Without preamble or ceremony a man came into the room and immediately froze the air by his presence. He was not an imposing figure; he did not stand more than five feet seven or eight and he was distinctly tubby. The plain blue suit he wore was without any pretensions; it was indifferently cut of very ordinary material and there were flecks of what might have been dandruff on the shoulders.

The man's walk had in it a slight suggestion of a waddle; his body moved visibly from side to side like that of a laborer on his way home after a day of physical toil. His face was broad, a trifle coarse, and expressionless. His nose was flattened in the Slavic manner, but it was entirely overshadowed by his eyes, which were charged with hostility and suspicion. He was a peasant, Hewlitt decided, but it was far too early to know whether that was good or bad.

The man stopped, looked about him, and said, "You will all sit down. If there is not enough numbers of chairs, look for more and bring them in."

There was no mistaking the tone—it was an order. At the same time it was to a degree reasonable. There were different reactions; all five of the women went out, perhaps because they were used to providing extra chairs when they were needed. Some of the men went with them. Hewlitt did not; he chose a chair conveniently at hand and sat down, aware that he had done what he had been directed to do but that he had not allowed himself to be used as an errand boy. People who sat down in this room were not expected to carry in their own chairs, despite the tradition that retiring cabinet members took their chairs with them when they left. But not in their own hands.

There was an interval of awkwardness as chairs were carried and rolled in through the doorway by people who were not too accustomed to doing this for themselves. During it Hewlitt reflected on the intonation of the words the man had spoken and examined them in the light of his special knowledge. The eastern European accent had been unmistakable and the grammar had been visibly inaccurate, but the fluency had been reasonably good. In all probability the man considered that he spoke English very well. It hit Hewlitt suddenly that perhaps this occasion was a strain on the man also and that his acquired language capability had suffered as a consequence. That reminded him of something he had learned in the translation business—not to read nuances into the words of people who had less than a perfect command of the language they were using. Or expect these same people to grasp subtleties they could not understand. He sat calmly, his legs crossed, waiting for the next move.

The room quieted down as people found their places and

settled themselves in uncertain expectation. Hewlitt remained motionless, taking inventory of who was present and who was not. The people who surrounded him were largely GS-11's, with a few higher and a scattering lower. It was a meeting of the office staff, those who did the paper work, processed the mail, and kept the business end of the establishment going. None of them was on a policy-making level, which was probably a good sign.

When it was quiet enough, the man was ready to speak once more. He stood at the head of the table, still an unimposing figure, but with the advantage of head height over his listeners. "My name is Zalinsky," he said. "If it is necessary that we speak, you will address me as 'Mr. Zalinsky' only. It is allowed no exceptions."

He paused for a moment and tipped his head far back to one side as though he were trying to remove some sort of small muscle cramp from his neck. "I am here to do work which has already begun. I know that you ask each one what will happen to you. If you follow the orders you receive, and perform your work as told to you, there will not be too much of change. That is, for you there will not be too much immediate change; otherwise there will be many changes. If you have not already found out, you will soon learn that much which you have been doing in the past was very wrong. It will not be wrong any longer. I will say this to you: the easier you accept what will be done, the more willingly you perform the duties which will be to you given, the easier it will be for you and all of your friends.

"But!"

With that single word his voice became a bark, a declaration of iron authority without mercy or flexibility.

"If any one of you, in any way at all, attempts to"—he searched for a word and found it—"impede, you will be dealt with immediately and drastically. There will be no playacting; you will accept and obey. If you do this, it is possible that you will also learn. That would be very good for you."

He stopped deliberately, waiting a long moment to see if anyone present would dare to challenge him. Facing him there were only silent people, sitting very still, waiting for him to go on.

It seemed to Hewlitt that the man was gaining courage

from his own words, then he looked again and changed his mind. Zalinsky might be an absurdly out-of-place figure in the White House, but his narrow suspicious eyes gave no hint of softness behind them. In appearance he might look like a Slavic version of a small-time salesman of limited ability, but the man who wore the nondescript suit had a toughness which needed no bolstering by listening to the sound of his own voice. The momentary judgment had been an error; Hewlitt resolved immediately to draw no more such hasty and dangerous conclusions.

"Because you come from a soft society where you have been enjoying ridiculous luxuries at the cruel expense of the masses, you now believe that what has happened to you all is a bad dream, that it will go away in a few days of time."

Again his voice hardened and the muscles of his jaw became tense. "It will not be gone—ever. Your militarists, your imperialist warmongers dared to challenge us, we who have the force of all the people behind us. We were patient for a long time. We demonstrated what we could accomplish, but you would not heed the warning. You refused to learn. Because you had never been defeated, not until the determined revolutionary people of Vietnam rose up and made you ridiculous before all the world. Even then you tried to pretend that you had not been defeated, that our skillful propanganda had not eaten the heart out of your will fight. You were reduced to confusion and indecision while we grew stronger because of our unshakable determination."

It was at that point that Hewlitt sensed that the man before him was delivering a prepared speech, one which had been written for him. The change in grammar was obvious, and so was the way in which he spoke the words. Hewlitt did not alter the expression on his face, but hidden deep within himself he found a minute ray of hope. This man was not infallible, nor were the people who had sent him here.

"There will now be work for all of you to do in rebuilding this country as you will be taught to do. You will follow orders absolutely; there is no other way. If you do not, you know what to expect."

He is repeating himself, Hewlitt thought.

Zalinsky looked up. "You have here an interpreter who is fluent in my language. Where is the man Hewlitt?"

It was not a question—it was a demand. Hewlitt raised his hand just enough to identify himself, then he put it down again. He was watching his own every move now with meticulous care—what he did, what he might say, even the shape of his secret thoughts. He could not afford even one mistake and he did not intend to commit any.

"You will wait until I send for you in your office," Zalinsky said. "I will give work to you. Do you understand?"

Hewlitt had never doubted for a moment that somehow this absurd nightmare would be swept aside, that the United States as he knew it would emerge triumphant, and that this untidy little man would be dealt with one way or another. He saw at that precise moment a minute opportunity to launch the counterattack; without thinking further he took it.

"Yes, sir," he said, only loudly enough to be heard clearly. He kept the tone of his voice totally respectful.

He looked up to find himself staring into the man's rigidly hostile eyes. *"What did I tell you?"* Zalinsky demanded.

Hewlitt swallowed hard. "Yes, Mr. Zalinsky," he said.

For a second or two there was total silence. Once more Zalinsky stared through Hewlitt, his face clamped in a hard mask. "You will make no more mistakes," he directed.

There were no more challenges, none whatsoever. Satisfied, Zalinsky pulled down the edges of his coat, waited until he was fully ready, and then said curtly, "You will go."

CHAPTER TWO

Back in the confines of his small office Hewlitt faced up to the fact that what he had been accepting as a nightmare had been resolved into harsh reality. Up until now he had never really believed the things that had happened; it had always seemed that in some miraculous way everything would be set right in time for a triumphant finish. But there had been no triumph, just as there had been no long-range supersonic bombers, no intensive radar surveillance, no stockpiles of needed materiel.

He drew a deep breath, held it, and then let it out slowly as he remembered once more to keep his emotions under control. If ever in his life he had need of his self-possession it was now; he had no way of knowing what demands might be made upon it even before the day was out.

He looked at the pile of work he had begun and decided against putting any more effort into it. He could not think of any possible good his notes would be to anyone, including himself. For a moment he felt bitter frustration; he had put in long years of intense work learning a very difficult language to the point where he could read and understand intricate technical manuals and other involved material. All that was by the board now unless, perhaps, this language of the conquerors would become a compulsory means of communication. In that event he would have a long head start, but he could not see how it could possibly do him any good except to spare him some additional labor.

He forced himself to be logical. Because of the peculiar nature of his work and its sensitive environment, he knew much more than had ever appeared in the newspapers or in the television analyses with which the nation had been deluged during the past months. He leaned back in his chair, deliberately shut his eyes, and began to retrace in his mind some of the things that had made the difference. He did not want to do this, but he felt that he must. He forced his mind to sort out and play back the salient facts that he had stored there, facts which he had tried to ignore because they were unpleasant and because the conclusions toward which they had pointed had been unacceptable.

Unacceptable then, but now reality.

He was not certain where it had all begun, but the Marc Orberg draft case offered a good starting point. That had opened the door to much that had followed.

Marc Orberg had separated himself from the conglomeration of other folk singers by walking stark naked onto the stage of Town Hall in New York to begin his announced concert. He had stood there, holding his twelve-string guitar by his side, until the shock had bounded and rebounded from the walls and the audience had been hushed. Then in his familiar voice he had spoken into the microphone.

"All right, you all know me or you wouldn't have come here to hear me sing—right?"

There had been some response to that, some of the sounds of agreement.

"And you all know that I'm a man, just like all my other fellowmen all around the world—right?"

That had generated a heartier response. "Right."

"Well I'm not ashamed of it; the time to be ashamed is when you're not a man—or a woman. *So why pretend?*"

A small uproar had answered that, and in it there had been many feminine shrieks of approval.

"Now let the cops come in here and arrest me if they dare. They can't, and you know they can't." He had stopped deliberately then and had casually strummed the opening chords of the black rock song that had first made him famous. "A lot of people have stood on this stage, all dressed up to make them look like something they weren't. Or to hide what they were. Well they'll all remember the day that Marc Orberg came here because in what I do, and in what I am, and in what I sing, I've got nothing to hide." Then he had gone on with his concert.

It had been an explosive occasion, there had been no denying that, and overnight Orberg recordings had leaped to the head of the charts. An album cover, which had been prepared in advance to show him as he had appeared in the formal old New York recital hall, had been put on sale over the loud protests of many PTA's, church groups, and so-called citizens' committees. It had been permitted nevertheless in most of the larger cities. Some dealers had been hesitant to display it, but they all had to carry it, and it set a new record for reaching two million in sales in an almost unbelievably short time.

It was at that point that Marc Orberg's draft board had reclassified him 1-A. They had done so reluctantly because the Army very definitely didn't want him, but too many voices had been demanding to know why he was escaping service when so many others were being compelled to go. Orberg had been perfectly aware of his position and knew almost without question that he would have been refused on whatever grounds might have been convenient. But he had exactly what he wanted and he captitalized on it with outstanding ingenuity.

On the day that he had formally reported and refused induction, it had taken the police more than three hours to clear the area and make the arrest that could not be avoided. Through his attorneys Orberg had challenged the whole structure of the draft mechanism on the basis that it was discriminatory and forced those who were inducted to enter a world of corruption and expediency. The case had been before the appeals court when a military scandal, small but sharply pointed, had erupted on the front pages of all but the farthest right newspapers. That had given new meaning to Orberg's argument, and despite his well-known politics, a few editorial writers had dared to support him.

One of them reversed himself rather dramatically on the day after the decision was handed down:

> Because of our precious traditions of full freedom of religion and of conscience we have been moving steadily toward less oppression of unpopular points of view, and a greater constitutional equality for all men.
>
> But in the exercise and protection of our hard-won freedoms, it is possible for us to forget from time to time the discipline which our forefathers imposed upon themselves in order to win for us the things which we enjoy today.
>
> The decision just handed down from the federal bench, that the entire structure of the military draft, as it is now organized, is unconstitutional, must be received by some of us as a blow. It is now no longer a matter of personal

liberty, but rather a question of how long and how far we will choose to go in lowering our defenses until, in terms of effective performance, they will cease to exist.

The editorial had been read by some people, but it had passed little noticed in the barrage of reports about celebrations in the streets by young people in every major city. Many of the demonstrations had been relatively orderly, others had gotten far out of hand, and the one in San Francisco, at which Marc Orberg had appeared personally, had been a disaster. The governor had been forced to call in troops and the aftermath of the wild affair had gone on for another three days.

Eventually the draft mechanism had been reestablished, but it had taken time and the watered-down version which had finally been enacted into law provided so many loopholes that only the semi-literate sons of the notably poor had needed to concern themselves that they might be required to serve their country. When the pay and other inducements for military service had been upgraded an increased number of volunteers had appeared, but the Navy had still been forced to report that it had only fifty-two per cent of its basically required manpower. The Marine Corps had been down to forty-six percent while the Army had gone on record only as requiring "many more men who are ambitious to learn trade and technical skills."

The result of all of this had been, in part, to make Orberg a national hero to a good segment of the fifteen-to-twenty-five age bracket. He had stopped singing then except for infrequent recording sessions and had turned instead to becoming one of the heads of the protest movement.

That had been one factor, and whatever the right and justice of it, it had seriously weakened the whole military establishment, both in numbers and in prestige. The very words "military establishment" had become an anathema to many people. After the Orberg decision the antimilitary camp had become intensely active; it had sponsored protest movements, speeches, demonstrations, and appeals. By sheer force of rhetoric it had created the illusion that the great majority of the population was with it until a significant number of congressmen began to believe that it might be true. Shortly thereafter, the armed forces had been substantially cut back. The time had seemed right; there had been loud calls for economy and the Department of Defense had had no visible role to play other than to maintain a posture of readiness. Furthermore, the international situation had been giving every appearance of simmering down during the several preceding months until the unexpected challenge had come with lightning speed and total surprise. Obviously those on the other side had been reading von Clausewitz.

Hewlitt remembered next Senator Solomon Fitzhugh, the Midwesterner who had successfully parlayed his biblical name and its connotations of great wisdom into four succesive terms in the United States Senate and eventually the chairmanship of one of its most powerful committees. The Fitzhugh committee had created a private hell for the State Department through its relentless probing into certain secret commitments which had been entered into with the President's full knowledge and approval, but which had not been made public for well-established reasons. The senator himself had been vastly irritated that he had not been made privy to all that was going on and he had sought to take revenge through the power of his office. That had been the springboard which had launched some notably heated testimony.

One of the high points of the committee hearings had been the appearance of Admiral Barney Haymarket. The former Chief of Naval Operations had been in retirement for more than two years when he had been summoned once more to come back and be heard on the hill. In the nourishing light of publicity Fitzhugh had pounded away and the admiral had parried him with the expert technique of one who had faced congressional committees many times before. The admiral had maintained that since he was no longer part of the military establishment, the only information he was qualified to give was largely of a historical nature. Fitzhugh had refused to buy that, of course, and the battle had been joined.

"Admiral Haymarket, I'm going to ask you a point-blank question," Fitzhugh had said when the afternoon had been well advanced. "Isn't it true that during the time you were in the Navy, while you were occupying a position of very high responsibility, you had knowledge of certain secret international agreements which could, under some circumstances, bear on the posture of our fighting ships at sea?"

"To some degree, yes."

"Now we're getting somewhere. All right, admiral, now let's have a closer look at some of these agreements. Do we have any still secret naval commitments, never mind what they are, or what their terms call for, in Southeast Asia? Wait a minute, that's too broad for what I want to get at. Let me put it this way: have we at present any under-the-table naval agreements with the Republic of China? I mean Taiwan."

The admiral had taken his time in answering. "There are some very clear mutual commitments which have been approved by the Congress. I have no knowledge of any recent additions, classified or otherwise, which may have been entered into since my retirement."

"Never mind what may have taken place very recently, I'm asking you about secret agreements which were entered into, or were in force, during the time that you were running the Navy. That's what we're interested in, because these secret treaties that were never submitted to or seen by the Congress may still be tying us hand and foot right now. Now I'm asking you again, do we have, or have we had, any such secret commitments with Formosa?"

"Formosa is not a nation, sir."

"All right, then, Taiwan. Or the Republic of China. Call it anything you like."

The admiral had looked him squarely in the eye. "Senator, with your permission, sir, I would prefer not to discuss the subject further."

Fitzhugh had visibly bristled at that; he had leaned forward and pounded one closed fist endwise against the table before him. "Well you damn well are going to discuss it! You know the penalties for contempt of Congress; I'm warning you that you are skating on very thin ice over that pit right now."

Haymarket had still kept his self-possession with no sign of his sometimes celebrated temper. "I am perfectly aware of the penalties for contempt of Congress, senator, but if the President has chosen to place any confidences with me, it would be totally impossible for me to violate them."

"I'm not interested in the President's confidence, Admiral

Haymarket, but I am damn interested in knowing if we are going to have to send American boys to fight and die for the sake of some corrupt, crumbling Asian government. We did that once and it was the greatest mistake that we ever made."

Haymarket had remained silent.

"Now look here, admiral, let's quit this horsing around," Fitzhugh had said. "You know and I know that all of this is going to come out into the open, it's going to have to, and there's no point in holding back. So let's get to it here and now."

The admiral had the reputation for being an outspoken man with considerable eloquence at his disposal whenever he needed it. But he still remained silent.

"You haven't said anything," Fitzhugh had stated.

"You haven't asked me anything, sir."

"All right, I'll ask you something. Are you going to tell us whether or not we have any secret agreements which might affect the Navy with the Republic of China?"

"In answer to your question, sir, no."

Fitzhugh had lost his temper then and it had been seen on a million or more television screens from coast to coast. "Dammit, let me get one thing across to you: we're not staging a puppet show here! I'm going to get the answers to these questions, and do whatever else is best for the good of the country. Is that plain enough?"

That was when Haymarket had given him his famous answer. "If that is your splendid purpose, sir, have you thought of cutting your throat?"

Two things had saved the admiral after that—the four stars that he had earned and the favorable editorial response to his remarks that had tidal-waved across the country. Fitzhugh was sensitive to publicity and for him to have taken revenge on a near national hero would have been inadvisable.

Hewlitt decided not to think any more about Fitzhugh despite the fact that at the most recent election he had been returned by a narrow majority to his seat in the Senate and to the privileges of his seniority. One good thing at least, Hewlitt thought, was that instead of six more years of Fitzhugh, he was probably all washed up and done with right now. As things stood, a current seat in the United States Congress had very little real meaning.

"Busy?"

The question startled Hewlitt. He looked toward the door of his office and then relaxed. "Come in, Bob," he said.

The young Air Force major who responded gave Hewlitt a moment of satisfaction. His uniform was sharply creased, his grooming was immaculate, and the neat rows of ribbons testified to his competence. He was at that moment an assurance that not everything had fallen apart.

"You heard about the briefing," Hewlitt declared.

The major nodded. "Verbatim, I believe." He put one hand behind his ear and lifted his eyebrows in inquiry.

In response Hewlitt shook his head. "As far as I know," he added cautiously.

The Air Force officer was satisfied. "I very much doubt that they could have bugged this place as yet," he said, "though undoubtedly they will."

"I understand that it can be done quite rapidly," Hewlitt said. "Sometimes in just a few minutes."

"True, but you have to have access to the premises for that length of time. I've done some checking and so far the regular security staff has been on the job without interruption. Are you willing to chance it?"

"Go ahead."

"All right. Pardon my speaking softly, but I don't want to close the door for obvious reasons. We took it on the chin as we never have before, but it doesn't have to be the end of the road."

Hewlitt nodded.

"You are in a particularly strong position with your job and your language capability. Also, if you'll forgive me, I've had a look at the file on you in the Pentagon and, as you must know, it's damned good."

"What can I do?" Hewlitt asked.

"For the immediate present, nothing, other than to keep your eyes and ears open. We're down, but there are still some of us who don't think that it has to be for the count. Without going into details right now, you must know that there are some secret reserves tucked away here and there."

"I never doubted it."

"Good. For now, let's leave it that the ball game isn't over yet. The question is, do you want to play?"

"Doesn't everybody?"

"No, I'm afraid not. And if the threats we have heard are serious, it could be a dangerous business. There are a lot who have the feeling that somehow it will work out all right, and they don't want to stick their necks out."

"Then they couldn't be much help."

"Exactly. Then here is the picture as of this moment. I'll be contacting you—me and no one else, is that clear?"

Hewlitt nodded once more.

"Good. For the time being, no matter what, don't talk to anyone else. If someone does try to contact you, let me know about it as soon as you can. A lot of people may want to help, but right now we're going to have to exclude the amateurs. You know why."

As soon as the major had left Hewlitt renewed his firm resolve to trust no one without first taking every precaution and considering all of the known facts with the utmost care. Impulsive judgments could not be tolerated any longer.

Major Robert Landers was a graduate of the Aerospace Astronaut and Test Pilots School at Edwards Air Force Base. He had top secret and cryptographic clearances; there was a high probability that he had Q clearance also, but there was no safe way to check on that now. He had been selected for White House duty only after intensive screening which eliminated any possibility of conflicts of interest, homosexuality, or anything else that might compromise his usefulness or tempt him to betray extraordinary trust or responsibility. He was, in short, a career officer who had been gung ho Air Force from the first day that he had walked into the Academy and who had repeatedly demonstrated that he had what it took.

Negative evidence: none whatsoever.

Verdict: highly reliable. Probably totally reliable, but that level was reserved in Hewlitt's mind; he did not propose to award it to anyone until that person had proved himself all over again under the conditions which prevailed now. With the rules all changed, it might mean that it would be necessary to field a whole new first team.

Hewlitt looked at his watch and saw that it was time for

lunch. Zalinsky had told him to stand by, but he had not told him that he couldn't go out to eat. A careful second thought made it very clear that Zalinsky would not be likely to discuss minor points of semantics; he had been told to stand by and it was highly prudent for him to do just that. With that thought fixed in his mind he picked up his phone and ordered his lunch sent in.

CHAPTER THREE

Hewlitt sat in his office for the rest of the day waiting for a summons, but he received no messages of any kind. That in itself was highly unusual; normally his phone was reasonably busy and a day during which he was not called in for consultation was rare. Not that his opinions or judgments were that highly respected at thirty-two, but his language capability was. The questions usually revolved around what might be the implications and nuances of specific material which he had translated. Now the silence was disturbing.

When the normal working hours were over Hewlitt considered carefully whether he should remain overtime, as he had so often done. Zalinsky had told him to wait, but his manner of speaking had not implied that he would necessarily be wanted the same day. The decision was partly made for him when he noted that everyone else was going home. He solved the problem by arranging to be one of the last to leave. Just before going out he put a slip of paper on his desk with his home telephone number on it. It was on file, of course, but by doing that he at least indicated that he would be available if Zalinsky chose to summon him back. Satisfied that he had taken the best path, he went out through the gate and over to Frank's cab, which was waiting for him in its usual spot. He climbed in, but refrained from saying anything until the vehicle was well out into the stream of traffic. He was still holding his peace when Frank asked over his shoulder, "How did it go?"

"I honestly don't know," Hewlitt answered. "That's the real truth."

"Did you see this guy, you know the one . . . ?"

"Yes, I saw him—briefly."

Frank abruptly changed the subject. "That was a twenty you gave me this morning. Make a mistake?"

"No. I wasn't sure what might happen next and I thought that you might need it—that's all."

"That's what I thought." Frank turned his full attention to his driving and maneuvered his way proficiently, and illegally, out of a traffic bind. "The cops, they ain't writing any tickets today," he volunteered. "If you knock a guy down you might get one, otherwise most anything goes."

"How is it working out?" Hewlitt asked.

"All right, I guess. Just as soon as we get more by ourselves, I'd like to talk to you a little."

That called for another decision; Hewlitt weighed the odds and then, somewhat against his better judgment, committed himself. "Frank, I think you'd better be careful. You know how all of this happened; we let our defenses down. We talked a little too much, trusted too many of the wrong people. And they bugged us more than we ever dreamed that they could. They listened in on everything. This cab, for instance, it could be bugged right now."

"Not likely," Frank said.

"Of course not, but that's what we thought about a lot of other things and we were caught dead asleep."

Frank nodded, the back of his thick neck creasing and uncreasing. "I know what you mean, they had bugs in every can in town. Funny how when a guy goes to the john he figures that somehow he's got more privacy. But did I ever tell you 'bout Davy Jones? Not the guy in the ocean, another one."

"I don't think so."

"Davy's a good friend of mine and he's a genius with electronics, that man is. He built himself a little box with a light on it and some batteries inside. He keeps it in his car. Anytime any cop shines a radar signal at him, that little red light goes on—just like that."

As he stopped to untangle another traffic problem Hewlitt carefully refrained from telling him that radar detectors were not new, there would be no point in it. When they were again free of the congestion Frank went on.

"Yesterday I went to see Davy to find out if he had any more news. He's got radio equipment that he built himself and he can talk all over the world. He's got his little place next to the garage where I do my work. I had this hack in, tunin' her up just in case we might be going down to the mountains like I suggested. After I talked to Davy he came out and while I had the car up on the rack he went over it. He knows I carry you every day and how you work in the White House. When he got through he said that the cab was O.K.—no bugs. It was locked in the garage last night and I been in it ever since."

That was evidence of a sort, despite the fact that Hewlitt had never heard of Davy Jones before and wasn't inclined to trust him too much. When it was added to the fact that Frank's cab would have a very low-priority interest to the enemy it resulted in a reasonably safe conclusion that the vehicle had not been tapped. The big remaining caution now was Frank. Hewlitt had known the man for years, but that did not constitute a security clearance. Far from it—and that too had been vividly brought home. The United States had not been defeated as much as it had been betrayed.

"What happened today?" Hewlitt asked. "Did you see anything or pick up any news?"

Frank nodded again. "All day long, the planes they been coming in. Big turboprops, freighters, even some supersonic stuff—all from the other side. At National, Dulles, Andrews, all over the place. They had it all planned out; I took an air controller home and he told me they had it so well organized he could have stayed in bed. Most regular air traffic was cut off except for a few flights. It was all their stuff, full of men, troops, a lot of equipment. We just let them come in, but I guess there ain't much we can do about it now."

That made Hewlitt flush, and it took him a few seconds to recover his composure. "Not right now, anyway. Anything else?"

"Lots of stuff on the radio. All about the same, telling us to keep on with our regular jobs for a while, not to do anything out of the ordinary, and to remember that if we get in the way, or try anything, we'll be 'dealt with.' Maybe I can pick it up now if you want to hear it." He leaned over to turn on the set.

"Not now," Hewlett said. "I'd rather talk to you. How threatening were they?"

"Mighty damn threatening, take it from me. There was nothing polite about it—get out of line and right now you get shot—that was about the size of it. Listen to that fifty times over and you begin to believe it. It's been on TV too, I hear. I can see it, the people are runnin' scared."

"I can't blame them too much."

Frank lifted his shoulders as he had in the morning and let them fall. "I'm no hero, but I was in the Marines once."

"I didn't know that."

"Nothin' to talk about. But I still hate to see us just lie down and play dead. You'd think that somebody'd do somethin'."

"It's pretty early in the game," Hewlitt said carefully.

Frank pulled up to the curb in front of Hewlitt's place. No one was visibly within earshot. "Sure, but that's a good time to score some points if you can, ain't it?" he asked. Then he changed his tone. "Never mind about the fare, you've got a lot in the bank yet."

For a long time after he had let himself into his apartment Hewlitt sat in the gathering darkness. He had a little more data to go on now, but there was nothing even approaching a clear picture in his mind. He had tried to think before; now in surroundings which were more personally his own he tried again, with strengthened determination.

First he had the uncomfortable knowledge that he had been named at the briefing and had been told to hold himself in readiness. Since he was only one of the many on the White House staff, he accepted the conclusion that it was his language capability which had made him stand out. He remembered Frank's statement that there had been a heavy influx of aircraft bearing troops and other personnel. He could talk to them, give them instructions if need be, read their communications. All this might make him useful as an errand boy. His nature rebelled against that kind of an assignment, but his good sense told him that it would be far better to survive in such a capacity than to accept a possibly severe alternative. He did not draw the alternative out of the shadows, he simply acknowledged to himself that it would be totally unacceptable and left it at that.

There was one possible advantage to such a position—he would to some degree at least know what was going on and if Bob Landers got something started, his position could be a useful one. He did not expect Landers to work any miracles, but he was a highly resourceful man. If there were enough more like him, and if they did have resources hidden away, there was always the possibility that something could be done.

He was interrupted when a newspaper was shoved under his door. It was thin and, Hewlitt decided, frightened. Probably the editors should have been praised for getting out anything at all; it was hardly a time to be taking a position on public issues, or even to be distributing factual information which the new masters of the country would prefer not to have broadcast. The front page was a curious mixture of "safe" news items and an obvious, massive restraint. Traffic accidents received a half column. The weather report was expanded to several times its normal size. One cautious, careful item did state that a steady inflow of air traffic "from overseas" had been landed at the principal Washington airports. But there was no indication whatever of the pay loads that had been carried.

Quickly Hewlitt leafed through the paper to check on certain specific things. The editorial page was missing entirely and there was no reference to its absence. The sports page was relatively normal; some big-league games had been played and the scores and team standings were reported as always.

The financial section had been reduced to a half page with the remainder of the space occupied by contract ads which had been booked some time ago. The lead item announced, in cautiously controlled language, that the directors of the New York and American stock exchanges had decided to close their floors for an indefinite period. Almost as a gesture of defiance the final prices of a selected few stocks were given; General Motors headed the list at 18⅝.

The rest of the financial news was skimpy and had an aura of the unreal. A few belated reports of earnings during the last quarter were published dutifully in the usual place. The only other major item was a fairly lengthy follow-up story on the collapse of Polar Aircraft from a high of 167½ toward a bottom which had not been found. When trading had stopped it had stood at 22¾ and there had been no buyers. In an insert box it was reported that Seymour Brown, the industrialist who controlled Polar, was still in Washington where he had been summoned to testify before the military preparedness subcommittee. The hearings were not now expected to take place.

From what Hewlitt knew, that was just as well. It would have probably ended up as a far juicier and more revealing fracas than the Bobby Baker scandal had been. Now Brown would get off, as he would have anyway.

Boxed prominently on page three was the official statement that had been on the radio throughout the day. It was harsh, unyielding, and totally specific. In essence it said, "Do what you're told and nothing else. Stay in line or take the consequences." The type was strong and bold, a hard border set it off. But, Hewlitt noted, it was on page three. It belonged on page one. Perhaps that was a little bit of defiance on the part of the editor too; he had run it, he had run it prominently, but the front page of his paper was his to control and no one else's.

By the time he had finished reading, Hewlitt was beginning to feel hunger. He had no real desire for any of the things he had stocked on his shelves or in his refrigerator; he wanted to go out, to have at least that much freedom of movement while he could enjoy it. A steak, he decided, would be inappropriate; he didn't want one. Then he remembered a small Chinese place where he ate occasionally. It was only four blocks away and he decided to walk.

When he pushed open the door the restaurant was still relatively empty, as he had hoped it would be. He could not remember ever having been there when the place had been even moderately full. How it managed to stay open he did not know, unless it was the late hours and the many bowls of noodles that it served long after other cafés were dark and still. He chose a booth where he liked to sit simply because of the framed needle painting that decorated it. Something about the scene and the colors used touched him; he always felt better when he could sit and look at it.

When a waiter shuffled up with a pot of tea and a glass of water, Hewlitt ordered without looking at the menu. Then he simply sat there, one hand closed into a fist, the other wrapped around it. Presently a bowl of hot soup was set in front of him. He picked up the porcelain spoon and felt the pleasant sensation as the hot liquid ran down his throat. He finished it all and then looked at the several well-filled bowls which had been placed on the table. He ate a full plateful of food and then helped himself to more, washing it all down with cup after small cup of hot tea.

When he had finished he picked up the check and took his time walking toward the front where the cash register was next to a modest display of packaged teas, fortune cookies tied up in small bundles, and boxes of almond cakes. He paid for his dinner with a sense of gratitude for the fact that the restaurant was an island, apparently immune to the events which went on outside its door.

"You haven't been in for a while."

Hewlitt looked up and recognized the man who had just taken his money. He was a young Chinese dressed in a severely plain dark suit and a simple black tie.

"No, I guess not." He wasn't sure what he was supposed to say.

Although no one was close by and the nearer tables were all empty, the Chinese dropped his voice until he was barely audible. "I have the impression that you work in the White House."

The alarm bell rang, silently but sharply, in Hewlitt's mind. He thought very rapidly before he answered. "At present I do." That committed him to nothing and supplied only public information.

"Let us know if we can help," the Chinese said. "We're Americans too, you know." His face gave no hint of the words he had just spoken.

When Hewlitt arrived at the West Wing Entrance the following morning, the familiar security people were still on hand, but there were now also others. Their clothes, and the set of their faces, betrayed them immediately for who and what they were. They were taking over, and there was no room for the least doubt. The one who looked at Hewlitt's credentials was surrounded by an almost visible cloud of hostility. His narrow eyes were hard and cold, he was a machine that had somehow mistakenly been born a human being and who was determined to correct that error. Hewlitt maintained a stony silence until he was waved through with a minimum gesture. He had been allowed in, but it was made clear that the license he had been given did not extend beyond that bare fact.

He went to his office soberly, wondering what the day

would bring—trying to anticipate and then having to admit to himself that he could not do so. The appearance of Zalinsky had misled him a little; that such a comic opera character had been sent to administer the United States of America did not speak very highly of the capabilities of those who had dispatched him—or so it had seemed. Now the atmosphere was very different; the reality was beginning to take shape.

When he reached his office he found himself face-to-face with the same frustration that had plagued him the day before; he had nothing to do except to translate old material for the benefit of decision makers who were no longer in a position to decide anything except when they would have to go to the bathroom. He had a sudden urge to escape, to go somewhere far away, where this monstrous thing which was taking place in Washington, D.C., would be far removed and impotent. He remembered Frank and his offer, but before he could even review it in his mind his sense of reality told him that it would be futile. Possibly he might have gotten away with it the day before, but now he had been pointed to and told to stay. The faces he had seen at the portal that morning had told him that he was trapped. He looked up at the picture of the *Ramrod* fighter and for a brief moment his jaw tightened in frustration.

He did not choose to do any translating that morning. He had a typewriter available, but whatever he wrote would be read by cold unfriendly eyes and he did not want to give them even that limited satisfaction. On the back of his desk he had a few reference books and one or two others that he had put there to read when he might have the chance. He picked one of them out, adjusted the lamp on his desk, and prepared himself to concentrate.

He had been reading for a little more than an hour when he was sharply interrupted. Without ceremony or any respect whatever for his privacy, two men came into his office. They were not the same ones who had been on the gate, but they had been stamped out by the same machine—hard, insensitive briquets of men, fashioned for utility purposes only. Before Hewlitt could adjust himself to their sudden appearance, one of them, with a flip of his hand, gestured him to his feet.

Hewlitt drew breath to speak, but then the strong sense

of caution that had been growing within him like an onrushing tide told him to keep his mouth shut. In his own language the man who had motioned him up said, "We will search your office."

There was no use pretending that he didn't understand—it would be a futile gesture and he had resolved that there would be no more of those. From thère on in everything, no matter how small or unimportant, would have to be made to count. He waved his own hand in an equally economical gesture giving them free access to his limited cubicle.

As they went through his desk he saw that they were thorough, they took nothing for granted. He had given up smoking; when they found an old package of cigarettes in his desk they emptied out the contents and checked for anything that might be concealed inside. When they had finished with the desk and had examined the few fixtures, the leader of the two motioned to Hewlitt to turn around.

There was no choice but to comply. Hating it intensely, he permitted himself to be searched. The hands were steely that prodded his body, that even felt up into the crotch of his trousers. Rage began to mount in him and he had to fight hard with himself to force it down.

When the ordeal was over, there was a pause while the man who had searched Hewlitt consulted a notebook. "You are an expert in the art of karate," he declared.

Hewlitt found a bit of savage satisfaction in proving him wrong. "No," he answered. "That is a Robert Hewlitt. I don't know him—I've seen his name in the papers."

The man wrote. "Your name is not Robert?"

"No, it isn't."

Another note went into the book, then the writer spoke to his companion. "He has no weapons," he said, and there was almost a suggestion of contempt in his tone.

The hell I haven't, Hewlitt thought. I'm not your karate expert, but I have a brain in my head that you can't feel or take apart to see what's inside. And you are a numbskull lout because you speak like a peasant and you're not even comfortable in your own language.

That was what went on in his mind. But externally, on his face, he betrayed nothing. His insides were knotted and his spirit cried for action, but he knew that for the moment he could do nothing.

CHAPTER FOUR

It was all that Hewlitt could do to keep his voice civil as he ordered his lunch over the telephone. Each minute that had passed since the invasion of his office had contributed to a slowly mounting rage that was building up within him. He discovered that in spite of himself his hands were clenching and unclenching as though they could not stand the inaction.

To attempt anything, he knew, would be useless. Worse than that, if it did not destroy him, it would cancel out any possible chance he might have to do something really effective at some time in the future. He told himself that he would undoubtedly have to face much worse, probably very soon, and that above all he would have to remain in possession of himself.

The food, when it came, did nothing to assuage his blackening mood; he ate mechanically while his mind raced ahead, planning things that he might do, whetting itself to seize every opportunity, no matter how minute, to begin the counterattack. He had only one solid thing to hold onto at that moment: the very brief conversation he had had with Bob Landers. That had told him that he was not alone, that there were others, and that there was hope. Hope. He had never known how magical that word was before.

To ease his frustration he turned back to the book he had been studying. It was thin comfort, but it might yield something that he could make use of and his mind, like his physical body, thirsted for action.

The summons came when he was not expecting it—a little after two when he had his mind well geared into the studying he was attempting to do. He was called on the phone as he had been before; this time the female voice seemed almost apologetic. "Mr. Hewlitt, Mr. Zalinsky would like you to report to him immediately in the Oval Office. Bring paper and pencil." As the line went dead Hewlitt sensed that she had wanted to say something more, but that she had not dared.

Reaching into his desk with a forced calm, he took out two pencils and a long, yellow ruled legal pad. This time he wanted to write everything down, although it would probably be unnecessary. He owed his exceptional language capability in part to his mnemonically trained mind; no one had total recall, but there were times when he could come close, and that ability had been highly useful to him in the past. The idea stabbed him that this might be a weapon, a small talent that might not be known or reported in his dossier. He took two or three deliberate deep breaths to steady himself and then went to keep his appointment.

He was ushered in without ceremony. As he entered and looked at the man who was sitting behind a desk that had belonged to three Presidents, he blocked out of his mind the idea that this was an impostor. He looked a little more formidable now—not because of the chair he was occupying, but because his physical imperfections were less visible and any uncertainty there had been in his manner the previous day was now apparently gone.

Zalinsky looked at him and said without emotion, "You will sit down."

"Yes, Mr. Zalinsky."

The man from overseas leaned back and contemplated him. "In which language do you wish to speak?" he asked.

"Entirely as you wish, it makes no difference."

Was Zalinsky trying to woo him with that minor concession of courtesy? He did not have time to decide.

Zalinsky picked up a folder from the top of the desk. "I have read the files about you," he said in English, "yours and ours. Why are you not married?"

Instantly Hewlitt knew that the answer might be in the confidential personnel evaluation which was in Zalinsky's hand; therefore the best tactic would be to tell the truth. "I wanted to be," he said. "I expected to be. Then something intervened which was not of my choice. After that I decided to play the field for a while."

"You are not then a homosexual?"

"I am not." This time he let hardness come into his voice, as would be expected of him.

Zalinsky noted it as Hewlitt knew that he would. "It will do you no good to become angry, no good whatever. You are, I know, at the moment with anger because you were searched this morning. It will happen many times again."

Hewlitt managed to say nothing.

"I will now speak with plainness," Zalinsky said, "because it is my wish. Before we are making occupation here we made a choice of certain people for usefulness and you are one of them. You understand why."

"Because I am familiar with the operation of the White House and I speak your language perfectly."

"Perfectly you do not, but you are confessed to be very good. I have now massive work to do and insufficient time so I will come directly to the edge. I can make use of you if you will undertake to obey what I tell you. Loyalty I do not expect and would not belief if you pretended it. Obedience, yes. I have staffing of my own people, but many of them have not been here before. You are muchly traveled through this country; as you say—you know your way."

Hewlitt nodded.

"It is not that you will be my assistant," Zalinsky went on. "I will not allow that. You will have certain necessary permits to your convenience . . . what is the word I want?"

"Advantage," Hewlitt supplied.

"Correct—advantage. This is not a . . ."

"Bribe."

Zalinsky stiffened slightly. "I have the acquaintance of that word," he said.

"I expect that you would." Hewlitt hated himself the moment the words were out of his mouth; he had been unable to resist the temptation to be glib. He looked at Zalinsky and was almost terrified by the penetrating look in the man's eyes.

"After this, you will not correct me unless I made a definite ask—is that clear?"

Hewlitt retreated rapidly. "Yes, Mr. Zalinsky."

"I will then trial you at this new function. You will keep yourself where you are at the same office for the same times of day. If I demand you in the evening, you will be called."

"Do you wish me to always be at home, sir?" It was a gamble, because if the man answered "yes," he would be all but a prisoner in his apartment. He took the chance because a "no" would carry with it automatic permission to be out as much as he liked; it would lift the cloud he had lived under the night before.

"No. Except that I may tell you."

Hewlitt nodded again to indicate that the arrangement was agreeable with him. He was minutely careful to be entirely respectful this time; another ill-advised outburst could be the end of everything.

"Once more," Zalinsky said. "You have read in the paper the instruction to the people of this country?"

"Yes, Mr. Zalinsky."

The man behind the desk leaned forward and planted his elbows firmly. "Believe this," he said. "For the people at large it is a warning—for you it is much more. You comprehend this?"

"Fully, Mr. Zalinsky." It was a tiny thing, but he might be able to "Mr. Zalinsky" him to death. He had asked for it—he would get it.

"It is good. You are intelligent, we know this. Do as instructed and you will be to your advantage. *But!*"

That same trick again!

"If you for any moments at all believe that you can betray us I will be without bending. You will pay the price at once. Is this clear to you?"

Hewlitt's blood froze but he did not allow his face to betray him. "Yes, Mr. Zalinsky."

"It is good. Do not believe that you can fool us, it is impossible. You are children at this; we have just taught this to you. From this hard lesson—learn!"

Hewlitt opened his mouth to say, "Yes, Mr. Zalinsky," but thought better of it in time. "I will," he answered instead.

"Good," Zalinsky said. "You will go."

Hewlitt went back to his office, his mind full of the interview he had just had. On the surface it appeared not too bad; for the time being at least his life could continue relatively undisturbed. His only continuing frustration was the lack of anything significant to do. He ached for action, but there was nothing immediately available except to continue with his reading and to wait for a communication of some kind from Landers. He had a considerable degree of confidence now in the young Air Force major; his experience in Washington was limited, but in his strictly military capacity his performance had been superb.

He returned to his book and tried to apply himself in order to make the time pass if nothing else. Through pure determination he succeeded; he was so deeply engrossed he was hardly aware of it when Landers did come quietly into his office. The officer held a magazine in his hand, which suggested that his visit was a casual one.

Hewlitt came to and motioned toward a chair. Landers ignored it, preferring to stand next to the desk. "I just came by to return your magazine," he said. "I think you were right, the piece on the Alaskan Air Command was probably written by an Air Force man under another name. But it was carefully done and under other circumstances I'd say that it didn't do us any harm at all."

Hewlitt had never seen or heard of the magazine before, but he responded promptly. "I thought that you ought to see it," he said. He was rewarded when the major nodded almost imperceptibly to show his approval.

Hewlitt felt a light flush of satisfaction; he looked up, lifting his eyebrows slightly, to see if Landers had more to say to him.

"Have you received any orders yet?" the major asked.

"Nothing definite."

"Me either. I'm sure that Mr. Zalinsky will send for me when he wants me. I'm practicing the 'mister' since he so definitely wants it that way. You remember."

Hewlitt nodded. "I do. Thanks for the magazine."

As soon as Landers had left Hewlitt played the conversation back in his mind. The major had been ultracautious, assuming that the office had been wired. The need for security had been drilled deep into everyone who had been assigned to the White House, now that preparation was about to pay off in a new way.

Hewlitt forced himself to continue his reading for a while just in case, through some devilish technique, he had been placed under visual observation. When he had allowed enough time to pass he put the book down, stretched his limbs without getting out of his chair and then picked up the magazine. It was elementary that Landers had left it for some reason; it only remained to find out what the reason was.

The solution was so simple that Hewlitt felt he had been cheated out of an opportunity to use his brain. He turned to the story on Alaska and there found a bit of flimsy inserted in the pages. The message on it was brief: *Be home at 19:30 tonight.*

Hewlitt continued to turn the pages, wondering if it was actually possible that he was under observation and trying to decide if the enemy would consider a full-time watch over him worthwhile. His judgment told him that it was most unlikely. A bug, quite possibly yes, but an optical device was almost impossible. He played it safe nonetheless. First he opened the center drawer of his desk and propped the magazine open on it. Then he spread the pages until the bit of paper fell out and dropped down on top of the pencils and other material he kept at hand.

He was sure that no one was watching, but it was a rehearsal. The time might well come when he would have to do something like this under scrutiny and he wanted to know how. After some time he put the magazine down and made a pretext of straightening out the contents of the drawer. While he was doing so he contrived to roll the flimsy into a tiny ball. When his pretended housekeeping was finished he took out a roll of Life Savers, peeled open the package, and put one of the candy discs into his mouth. With it went the message. He was not entirely satisfied with the way that he had performed the maneuver, but he felt sure that if anyone had been watching he would not have noticed anything amiss.

His mind was too full to talk to Frank on the way home; he was grateful that the Negro driver understood this and left him alone. When he was back in his apartment he showered and stepped on the scale. He had gained one pound, but the reading was not entirely accurate and if the added weight was there he would have it off before morning. He ate lightly while he watched the TV news program that he found most reliable at that hour. The announcer had almost nothing to say; it was obvious to Hewlitt that he had been muzzled and was trying to walk a tightrope in the dark. Somehow, with the practiced skill of a professional, he managed to stay on the air for fifteen minutes without reporting anything beyond neighborhood fires and a shake-up in the staff of Georgetown University. It was totally sterile, but Hewlitt was quite accustomed to hearing newscasts which included none of the real events of the day because the facts were classified and had not been made public. However, there had always been something to talk about before; tonight the evidence of enforced, near-total restraint had been blatant. Perhaps the announcer had intended it that way—as a warning. It could have been his way of fighting back; if so, that made him another member of the team.

Almost on the minute of seven-thirty Hewlitt's doorbell rang. When he answered it Landers was there in civilian clothes with two girls, both of whom Hewlitt recognized as being on the White House staff. "Hi," the major said, "you didn't forget, did you?"

"Of course not." Hewlitt picked up his cue smoothly this time while he evaluated his two unexpected guests. One of them was a Barbara somebody who was probably Landers' date, since she was considerably the more attractive of the two. She was a raven brunette who had sense enough to wear her striking hair long, something which accentuated the ripe, rich promise of her body. As she walked in, her motions were quietly potent, and Hewlitt appreciated them to the full.

The other girl he knew by sight, but if he had heard her name, he could not remember it now. She was somewhat smaller, auburn-haired and built along less dramatic lines. But she had a sense of possession about her and also a visible aura of restraint. She was attractive enough, Hewlitt decided, and she probably danced very well.

"I've got the car outside," Landers said. "So far, at least, we can have all the gas we want, so we might as well take a drive."

"I'd like that," Barbara said. She would probably like a lot of things, Hewlitt thought; and Landers was a man to be envied.

He excused himself long enough to put on a sports coat and check that his wallet was adequately filled, then joined the others. Not for a moment did he believe that this was intended purely as a social engagement; Landers' opening remark had established that. The girls would be cleared in the normal sense, but whether they were qualified to play in the dangerous game that Landers had proposed was open to serious question. Until he know a great deal more than he did at the moment, the only course open to him was to keep his mouth firmly shut.

Landers' car was a sleek convertible of precisely the right caliber to fit with his job, as well as his reputation acquired when he had been a totally efficient, almost nerveless test pilot at Edwards Air Force Base in the Mohave Desert. Hewlitt was the last to climb in; he was surprised, and pleased, to find that the place reserved for him was in the back seat next to Barbara. He settled himself, smiled agreeably at his companion, and then tried his best to suggest that he had nothing on his mind but the pleasures of the evening that lay ahead.

They crossed the Potomac into Virginia and then headed westward toward the low mountains which were still faintly visible. The conversation was limited; once they were more or less by themselves there was no attempt on the part of any of them to pretend a relaxation that they did not feel.

When the twilight had gathered halfway into night, Landers pulled the car over to the side of the road. He stopped the engine and then turned around in his seat so that he could talk to the others without raising his voice.

"First of all," he said without preamble, "if anyone comes by and wants to know what we're doing here, we're deciding where we'd like to go to dinner. We can talk safely here. I went over the car very carefully after work tonight with a bug detector. Even if it were wired in some way, we're well beyond the range of the best equipment we have and I don't believe that theirs is any better. In fact, I know it isn't. Do you girls know Mr. Hewlitt and what he does?"

"Yes, of course," Barbara said. Her voice was calm and very businesslike. Hewlitt understood that she spoke for them both.

"Hew," Landers said, "both of these girls hold top secret

and beyond. They're not civilians; Barbara is in the Air Force, Mary is in the Army but works for the Agency. They've been handling highly sensitive material for some time and you can trust them absolutely."

"Good," Hewlitt said. He was not able to rid himself entirely of a feeling that as a breed, females had trouble keeping their mouths shut, but he knew that there were exceptions and that some of the best agents that the CIA had were women.

As Landers continued, his voice too became quiet and unemotional, but there was no questioning his seriousness. "We are organizing ourselves according to their system—because it works. It was all set up some time ago, and we know what we are going to do. I've been assigned to be the leader of our cell. You know how it works: I'll be your one and only contact with the rest of the organization. If anything happens to me, then you will be contacted by someone else, who will identify himself. Clear so far?"

Silence answered his words, which Hewlitt highly approved.

"You understand that the cell system doesn't mean that you aren't totally trusted. But when we get going on a larger scale there will be a lot of people involved and we could take in a bad apple. If we do, he or she can blow the cell, but no more; the rest of the organization will be protected."

"That's only sensible," the girl in front said. "I think every intelligence organization uses some variation of the same plan."

"Thanks, Mary. I've been instructed to go over certain rules with you, although you know them already. First, whatever you pick up you feed to me only; in turn I'll keep you informed as much as I can about what's going on—you'll just have to trust me in this. Try never to write anything down. I had to break that rule today, which reminds me—you got rid of that note, I take it?" He looked at Hewlitt.

"Of course."

"This is elementary, but don't trust anyone, no matter who it is, without checking with me first. If I need to, I can check with the person who is controlling me and so on as far as is necessary. For example, I won't send you any messages by persons you don't know personally to be with us."

Barbara leaned forward a little. "I think we're wasting time, Bob," she said. "We all know this very well."

Landers changed the tone of his voice. "Of course you do. I'm following my orders and I believe in them, because this is damn serious business. Now I want to tell you something else: the three of you were all preselected some time ago when our planners saw possible trouble ahead and set up the organization at that time. I didn't just pick you up off the top of my head. You've been checked in ways that you wouldn't believe, with the result that we feel that we can trust you completely and that you can trust each other. They've been particularly careful because this will be one of the key cells in the country."

"Will we have meetings?" Hewlitt asked.

"I think so, but that's something that hasn't been worked out yet. Perhaps you might undertake to teach us their language. That might be an effective cover."

"I don't think so," Hewlitt answered. "These people know that we hate their guts and despise them for what they've done to us. For us to pretend to be learning their language now would be too cooperative to be believed. It would imply that we expect them to be here a long time and no American, no real one, that is, will admit to that right now."

"He's right," Mary said. She did not elaborate.

Landers agreed. "I haven't anything else in mind, but I'll think about it and check with my controller. You think too, unless someone has an idea right now."

There was no response.

"Then that's that. I'll find a way to get in touch with each of you after something has been decided. One more item: if anything happens to me, the person who will take over will be identified by the name Asher. It could be a man or a woman. If that person is eliminated, the code name is known at the top levels and someone else will be assigned to take his place. He will use the same ID. Now let's go through the motions of getting something to eat."

He started the engine and moved the car back onto the main part of the road. For a moment Hewlitt wondered if they ought to go back and erase the tire marks on the shoulder where they had parked, then he dismissed the idea as unnecessary—if it came to that they had a simple explanation that would hold up.

Midway through the next morning Hewlitt was in a much heartened frame of mind. Not even the fact that the security guards at the West Gate were now all from the enemy's camp upset him unduly, because he was convinced, or very nearly so, that as soon as things got properly organized the return to sanity would be under way. He had no doubt that American ability and ingenuity would in some way manage to reverse the disasters of the past few weeks despite the overwhelming military pressure that the enemy had been able to bring to bear. The underground, once it got going, would be able to work unimpeded with no Fitzhughs to get in the way. Even the inertia of forced inaction which now pervaded his office could not dampen the determined optimism which charged his whole being.

Then a man came in.

He was one of the enemy, a structure of human flesh and bone in a poorly designed and badly worn uniform, but inflated with the confidence of total victory. He was a soldier, conspicuously armed and with the attitude that the weapon holstered on his hip gave him total authority. His face was anonymous in its frozen expressionlessness of military conformity. It was his pride that he was one unit in a conquering army.

He entered Hewlitt's small office holding a few sheets of paper. When he spoke it was with the voice of a not too intelligent NCO dispensing a minor order to a mechanical subordinate. "You will take this and translate it into English at once," he directed in his own language. He thrust the document at Hewlitt and then left without ceremony.

Before Hewlitt read the material he had been given he evaluated the handwriting. It was moderately good, an educated person's work, but he doubted that it was Zalinsky's. He had no good reason for that conclusion, simply the feeling that it had been done by someone else. The paper was from the regular White House supply; to make sure he held it up against the lamp on his desk and checked the watermark. That minute fact upset him—they had no right, no bloody right whatever, to invade the supply closets and take government property for their own use.

When he read the text he found that it was for a speech to be delivered by some unnamed individual at a time and place not specified. It was brusk, overbearing, and rock-hard in its content. Again, it was a warning and a directive of things to be done. In particular it laid out a familiar communist tactic—that every listener could protect himself only by acting as a listening post and reporting immediately to those in charge any deviations from the rules which had been set down. As Hewlitt turned the pages a certain sense of hopelessness fought for lebensraum within his mind. The document was totally uncompromising; the enemy maintained an inflexible posture.

He fed paper into his typewriter, setting up for two carbon copies. Then he typed in a title which might apply and began the translation into English. It pleased him to make it as literal as possible by putting all of the harsh intransigence of the original into his rendition. He wanted it to be that way; perhaps it would help to educate a little more some of the members of Congress who had been maintaining, right up to the moment that the first surprise blow had fallen, that negotiation and concession over a protracted period would resolve all differences. Too strong a military posture, they had argued, would only antagonize the other side. They had been sincere, and because many of them were reasonable men they could not conceive that others could or would be any different.

They knew now.

When he had finished his work Hewlitt read over the translation and was satisfied with it. It would grate on the nerves of those who heard or read it, which was what he wanted it to do. In that way the firmness and resolve of the American public, or whatever part of it was destined to endure these words, might be stiffened a little. At the same time the translation was totally accurate; there could be no question of his having reshaped the text in any way.

He laid the work out on his desk and collated the sheets. The original and one carbon he clipped together to be delivered or called for, the second carbon he put into a manila folder and placed it carefully in full view on the top of his desk.

That was on Wednesday. For the rest of that day, and for the rest of the working week, he was ignored. The translation he had made was picked up sometime overnight from his desk; the carbon in the folder was left undisturbed. Otherwise no one came to see him, he received no messages, and he had no contact with Landers. Outside the office his life was almost equally uneventful. He was already accustomed to the steady inflow of aircraft from overseas, augmented now by many of MAC's heavy airlifters. He did not know whether they were being flown by Air Force crews acting under orders or by the enemy, but the steady flood of men and materiel continued around the clock. It had been a popular impression for some time that the enemy had not understood the full implications of airlift—that illusion, too, was now dispelled.

Frank passed on to him the rumor that the ships were on the way. According to the reports that the cabdriver had heard, they would make port all up and down the East Coast. There was one ugly piece of news which, if it was true, was grimly foreboding. Somewhere in the Carolinas a union official had dared to speak out. He had said something to the effect that if the enemy put into the port where he was in charge, the members of his local would not unload the ships; they would have to provide their own men. According to the rumor, he had been taken outside and shot against the wall of his own office, summarily and without the least question of a trial or hearing.

On Friday night Senator Fitzhugh, with permission, made a television address to the nation. He read visibly from a prepared manuscript and seldom looked up from the paper before him into the eye of the camera. He appealed for moderation and restraint. Humanity, he declared, would always prevail; the Dark Ages and the torture chambers of the Inquisition had long since been banished forever and were impossible of revival. Already, he continued, he had been in touch with several of the enemy leaders who under happier circumstances had been his personal friends. He had served the nation for many years, he reminded his audience, and he intended to continue doing so now. Congress was not in session, but he had been elected to represent the people and that mandate was still upon him. He would inform everyone soon of the progress which he had been able to achieve.

On Saturday night Marc Orberg had appeared. The usual setting for a spectacular was missing. Instead, he sat on a high stool before a simple background and sang a program of the songs which had first brought him to national fame. He was undeniably good, and despite his reputation the way in which he presented his material was effective.

When he had finished singing, he made a short speech. In sharp contrast to his usual style, he spoke with restraint and even a measure of dignity. As Hewlitt listened and watched, he found it hard to believe that this was the same man who was a national symbol of violence and militancy. His appearance and manner contrasted almost irreconcilably with his one-time conviction for attempting to throw acid into a policeman's face.

Orberg's speech was his own; Hewlit knew that because the enemy could never have shaped it into the same idiom or made the same effective use of colloquialisms. There was no denying the cleverness of the man or his skill in handling his audience; he was a professional all the way.

> For more than two hundred years we have lived here in this country, or on this land, under one system of government. During this time we have made enormous technical progress, but our society has been steadily going down the chute. Finally we lost a war. So here we stand now, with our rivers polluted, our land ruined in the dust bowls and strip mining areas, and our people hopelessly divided. Millions of us lost our life savings in the stock market to professional speculators while the mortgages on our homes go on and on, that is, if we're lucky enough to have a home. A lot of us don't, and a lot more of us have to live in ghettos because our skins are black or we're Jews, or just because we like to do our own thing the way we want—without hurting anyone else.
>
> Now it's different. We're defeated and we're going to be living under a different system from now on. Well, maybe it isn't so bad. The Japanese were terrified when MacArthur came, but now they know that he brought with him the best turnaround that the country ever had. It could be that a year from now all of us will be glad as hell that this has happened. Anyhow, no more computers stuffing bills into your mailboxes every month and no more going to court

because the baby got sick and you couldn't make all your payments last month. So hang loose and see what happens, you might be real surprised. Maybe this is the best thing that has ever happened to us too.

When the show was over, Hewlitt sat back and thought about what he had seen and heard. The man could have convinced thousands, perhaps even millions, that there was no real need for concern. Unfortunately, they'd find out the truth soon enough. Or would they? It was a hard question. He doubted that the news services would be carrying the story, if it was true, about the union agent down South. Or whatever other things like that might be going on.

He had no real plans for the weekend; when it came he simply went home, called up a girl he knew moderately well, and with her took in a show. It was a war picture with the inevitable triumph of the Allied armed forces over the Wehrmacht. Once more the Nazis strutted across the screen and once more they met their downfall at the hands of the invincible Americans and their allies. He took the girl home, where they sat and had a drink or two before they made love and he went back to his apartment.

Apart from that limited excursion Hewlitt stayed close to home in the hope that Landers would call. He found it reasonable to assume that quiet private meetings were being held in secret all over the country. How even the best intended and motivated people would succeed, when the armed forces with all of their massive power had failed, was a question he did not permit himself to consider.

When Monday morning came he was almost glad to return to work, for despite everything that had happened and was continuing to happen, he was confident that Landers would contact him shortly. At the West Entrance the guards were still all foreign. Hewlitt checked through and allowed his person to be patted in various places before he made his way down to his office. He did not know very much about intelligence operations, but he did know that the search he had just submitted to would never embarrass any properly equipped operator who had a mission to accomplish. He dropped two books he had brought with him onto the top of his desk, noted that everything appeared to be untouched, and sat down with the feeling that this new week held promise, even if any action would be very limited at this stage of the game.

Oddly enough, the morning passed with no contact with any other person at all. None of the enemy intruded into his area, no one came in, the phone did not ring. He could not detect any change in the atmosphere, but that was not conclusive, since he could do precious little detecting while he sat alone and undisturbed in his cubicle. And he was prudent enough not to instigate anything on his own.

He was summoned to the Oval Office shortly after two-thirty. Zalinsky had on a different suit, a brown creation that showed signs of a slightly higher quality level. Otherwise he had not changed in the least; his manner was still exactly as it had been before.

"You will sit down," he directed as Hewlitt came into the room. Hewlitt sat and occupied himself in looking for any visible changes in the famous office. A few personal mementos of the President's had been removed, but nothing had been put in their places. If Zalinsky had a family, there were no pictures to give evidence of it anywhere. The man from overseas still appeared to be exactly what he was—a usurper in the office of the President of the United States. Where the President himself was Hewlitt did not know; he had been spirited away in time and the secret of his whereabouts was well kept. For a moment Hewlitt wondered if he would become the active head of the underground, then he decided that that was highly unlikely. The President was an honest and honorable man, but he owed his high office to a series of political events which had been unpredictable and which had left him at the last moment as the only acceptable candidate. He lacked a firm power of decision, which was one of the contributing reasons for the nation's downfall. He had not believed intelligence reports which had proven to be accurate and in his honest attempt to heed the voices of all the people he had delayed too long.

"You made translation of the document that was sent to you," Zalinsky said suddenly. "It was very strict. It has been read by experts and they agree that you made it very hard."

Hewlitt nodded his agreement. "That was the tone in which the original was written. When I translate I do more than just go word by word from one language to the other;

I also include the feeling of the original and the inner sense that it intends to convey."

Zalinsky grunted, but said nothing. Then he twisted in his chair as though he could not accustom himself to its adjustments and looked at Hewlitt once more. "You know Amy Thornbush," he said, making it a declaration.

Hewlitt shook his head. "I can't place her," he answered.

"You know Robert Landers." He did not get the name quite right, but Hewlitt understood.

"Yes, I know Major Landers."

"Give me your opinion of him."

That was highly dangerous ground; Hewlitt walked it carefully. "Major Landers is an outstanding officer; his record is brilliant."

"He is a fool," Zalinsky said. "An idiot fool. I myself told you that you are children in some things, but you unbelieve this." He leaned forward and became rigid with controlled anger. "You have heard, and seen, the warning given to you in all of the papers and radio stations."

"Yes."

"Landers did not obey. Like a little child, he tried to oppose us."

It seemed to Hewlitt that the blood had turned cold inside his body. He did not dare to show undue interest in what Zalinsky was saying, but he was desperately anxious to learn to what extent Landers had been compromised—and how.

"What did he do?" Hewlitt asked.

Zalinsky bored through him for one quick moment. "If I tell you that, I would become a bigger fool than he is. You will come."

As Zalinsky rose Hewlitt followed him out of the room with his mind spinning. He could not doubt any longer that Bob Landers had been blown, but he could not imagine that careful, experienced officer being as foolish as Zalinsky had depicted him. Worse, if Landers had been found out, how about the two girls and himself? His thoughts refused to sort themselves out in order; the only thing that he was certain of was that the alarm bells were ringing inside his brain and that he was for the moment highly uncertain as to what he should do next.

Zalinsky led the way outside to the South Lawn. They

had advanced only a few paces when Zalinsky stopped and turned around, facing the executive mansion. Dutifully Hewlitt did the same, waiting for the next cue that he might receive. He looked at Zalinsky, but the administrator simply stood there as though he was communicating with himself and did not choose to be disturbed.

Hewlitt watched him, waiting, until he realized that they were no longer alone. He turned to discover two more of the enemy, wooden-faced uniformed troops who now made up the security guard for the White House. Between them was Bob Landers, his eyes fixed straight forward, his smartly tailored uniform seeming now only to hang from his body. Hewlitt was shocked by his appearance. Clearly he had been through some kind of concentrated hell—for a few hours or for several days—there was no way of telling.

"You will talk to him," Zalinsky said.

Holding himself in the tightest grip of which he was capable, Hewlitt walked the few steps to where Landers stood and tried to read whatever was written on his face. "What happened, Bob?" he asked.

"I disobeyed an order," Landers answered. "I tried to contact some of my old Air Force buddies."

"What's wrong with that?" He was doing his desperate best to give Landers an opening, to learn whatever he could before they took him away.

"I wanted to fight back," the major answered. "They didn't like that. So now I am to die for my country."

"No!" Hewlitt could not help himself; the word was out of his mouth before he knew what he was saying.

Landers looked at him and his intelligence penetrated through the fog of whatever ghastly experience he had been through. "Good-bye, Hewlitt," he said. "Nice to have met you."

By the grace of God Hewlitt understood; Bob Landers was denying any close association. In a way that answered one question.

Zalinsky spoke to the guards in his own language. Upon receiving his order they led Landers up to the wall and turned him around. The man on his left drew his pistol from its holster, held it directly against the major's head, and pulled the trigger.

The sharp report of the gun blasted through the air of the

presidential garden. As Hewlitt stood frozen he saw Landers' knees unlock; then as his body slumped to the ground, a blackened hole in the side of his head became obscenely visible.

Hewlitt's arms quivered at his sides; his hands knotted into straining fists. He wanted to lunge forward and yank out the life of the loathsome guard with his bare hands. He forced himself to look again and saw the corpse of what had seconds before been an intelligent, dedicated human being lying like a broken, bloodied doll, the bright command pilot's wings still, unknowingly, proudly reflecting the sunlight.

For a blinding moment Hewlitt thought that he could get to Zalinsky before either of the guards could interfere. Violent rage stormed through him, seized him, screaming for action regardless of consequences. He crouched to spring, to leap and break the vile creature's neck with one mighty yank of its head, but at that instant Zalinsky stepped back and out of range.

"Learn from that!" He hurled the words at Hewlitt. "He is not the first. There will be many more before you learn, but learn you will!"

His eyes blazed as he stood there, watching the shock pass through Hewlitt's body. "We are the masters, forget it not for one moment." Venom reeked from every word. "You will go!"

CHAPTER FIVE

The hardest decision that Hewlitt could recall ever having had to make was to go to work the next morning. For a long and nearly sleepless night he had lain in his bed, living over and over again the hideous scene he had been forced to witness on the White House lawn. Often he found it difficult to believe that it had actually occurred; it seemed a dreadful nightmare that the dawn would at last dispel.

During the first hours of daylight he thought the problem out. If he went to work, he stood a good chance of being dealt with in the same manner as Bob Landers, and he had no desire to have his brains blown out by some animal on two feet with the intellect of a cretin. The risk was definitely there, because he was a member of Landers' little organization, even though his role so far had been an entirely passive one.

He visualized the possible scene in the Oval Office: Zalinsky would say to him, "Were you a member of his organization?" If he were to answer *no* and Zalinsky knew better, as he very will might by now, that would be it—then and there.

If he admitted to it, it would be pure suicide. If he tried to vacillate by saying that he had been approached but had not agreed to participate, it would not only be cowardly, but also it would in all probability totally wreck the White House cell. It was worse than Hobson's choice; he had nowhere to go at all.

If he simply did not show up, his personal situation would be bad and his usefulness to the organization would be over. Considerations of personal risk retreated when he remembered again that sight he had seen on the South Lawn: Landers' cadaver lying there with the sick ooze coming from the hole in his skull. The abiding concern now was to find a way to counterattack. He knew then that he was going to go to work; he got up and went into the bathroom to shave.

For the rest of the working week he was left strictly alone. After the first few hours had passed the suspense grew less; then he began to wonder if Zalinsky was waiting for him to make some sort of move. The obvious counter to this was to do nothing, particularly since he now had no contact and no assigned mission to perform. He spent the time in his office reading; it kept his mind busy and was as good an occupation as any for the time being.

As the time passed, he did not drop his guard. With his nerves at concert pitch his temper with himself became short as he tried to carry on under the almost intolerable strain.

Late on Friday afternoon his phone rang. His heart jumped at the sound, fear he could not control began to edge through his body as he picked up the instrument. "Hewlitt," he said.

"This is Barbara." Her voice recalled her at once—her face, her shining black hair.

"Yes."

"I've been thinking," she said, "about the suggestion you made the other day."

He picked up her lead at once. "I remember."

"Well, the way that things are, and after what's happened, it doesn't seem to make much difference anymore. I guess that we might as well have a little fun while we can."

"Good," he answered her. "I feel very much the same way. How about after work tonight? We could have dinner . . ."

"As good a time as any, I guess." The line went dead.

He hoped, almost fervently, that the call marked the beginning he had been waiting for. He remembered the risk, but he thrust that thought aside; there would be no point in trying to exist like a vegetable. If he couldn't be around at the finish some others would be. And they might remember his name.

When his watch at last told him that he was free to go, he locked his desk just to give them trouble opening it, wrote "T.G.I.F." on his calendar pad, and felt for a few moments that he was again the master of his own destiny.

As he made his way toward the West Gate he realized that he didn't know the girl's last name and had no idea where she lived. It didn't matter; what he did know was that Landers had vouched for her and that was enough.

She was waiting for him outside, wrapped in a coat which to some degree concealed her succulent figure, but not the striking black hair. For an instant he wished that the rendezvous was a real one; Barbara in bed was something sensational to contemplate.

As he approached her she nodded slightly in recognition. He walked up and asked, "Did you bring a car?"

"A cab would be better, I think." He liked her voice and the way she spoke. She kept it from being a demand or an order; it was a suggestion he could override if he wanted to.

Frank was there waiting; without explanation Hewlitt put her inside, climbed in himself, and then asked, "Where to?"

"Drive out toward Maryland," Barbara said. "I'll show you where."

Obediently Frank started up and headed out in a northwesterly direction. The usual Friday after-work traffic was far heavier than normal; there had been rumors all week of a severe gasoline rationing program to come, coupled with that was the apparent desire of all who could to get out of a city that promised nothing but greater disaster to follow. Following Barbara's occasional directions Frank worked his cab slowly through the almost impossible congestion until they reached the state line. A half mile farther on she stopped him before a good-sized shopping center and indicated to Hewlitt that she wanted to get out.

He asked no questions. He handed her out of the cab and reached in to pay the bill, but Frank nodded with his head that he was to come to the other side. Hewlitt walked around the car and then leaned in. Frank took the bill which he offered and then asked, "Did I take you back to your place tonight, or what?"

Hewlitt appreciated that; he was a good man and clearly he was willing to take a chance if he was asked to do so.

"No," he answered. "If anybody asks you, I had a young lady with me—they'll know that anyway. You took us over to the Maryland side and dropped us off somewhere around here. You may not remember exactly."

"That's no joke in this traffic," Frank said. "Then that's how it is. You be wanting me later?"

"Maybe, but right now I can't say."

With his change Frank handed him a card; it stated with proper formality TAXI and in one corner FRANK JORDAN. At the other corner was a telephone number.

Hewlitt put the change and the card in his wallet together, spoke his thanks, and rejoined Barbara, who was waiting silently for his return. When the cab was gone she led him casually past the stores which were still putting up a brave show of carrying on the usual way of life. The window displays were as bright as ever; from the record mart hard rock music came surging out of the door. It was America on any Friday night, on this one pretending as best it could that nothing had happened.

The real estate office was well back toward the rear and behind a row of other shops which depended much more on eye appeal for their trade. Barbara walked in the door with the kind of familiarity which implies an established relationship and leaned on the railing before the one occupied desk.

The woman seated there was short, solidly built, and had white pudgy fingers. Her hair was cascaded up into an artificial arrangement which made claims that her body could not fulfill. Vermillion lipstick accentuated the lines worn into her face; the eyebrow makeup was an anachronism which had been applied twenty years too late in her life. A certain hardness emanated from her; it told of the years that she had spent earning her own way, of the disappointments she had had, of the few pleasures that had come her way. It told also of a hard-gotten bank balance that was her security against the fate that life had prepared for her, and that she would guard it with her life's blood. She was a businesswoman.

She looked up, offered a mechanical, commercially approved smile, and asked, "May I help you?"

"This is the gentleman," Barbara said. There was no emotion in her voice, the heavy restraint she had maintained since Hewlitt had picked her up remained intact.

"Oh, yes, of course." The woman got up, crossed to the wall behind her, and surveyed a board hung with keys. After some scrutiny she took down a set from one of the hooks, checked the tag, and then brought it back to the counter. "This is really a very nice place," she said. "It's not too far from here; you can walk if you want to. Take your time looking it over; if you don't want to see it tonight you can go in the morning, just so long as I get the keys back by noon."

"That's fine," Barbara said. She dropped the keys into her purse, gave Hewlitt an unexpected half smile, and led the way out. When they were by themselves she turned and said, "There's a little restaurant here, if you like Chinese food."

His mind was confused as he nodded. He was prepared to follow any clue that she gave him, but the tone of her initial invitation over the telephone, plus the business of the keys, had him slightly off balance. They were a long way from the White House now and there was no visible need for play acting. Despite this, her mood and actions appeared to be directed along a single pathway which gave him a strong feeling that he was simply along for the ride.

They ate together in a small but quite attractive little restaurant which clearly outclassed the one which Hewlitt occasionally visited near his home. It was much newer, the menus were less thumbworn, and the decor was more subtly conceived. The food, as far as he could tell, was the same. They sat in a booth making conversation which had little shape and definition. They spoke to each other from time to time, exchanging bits of trivia, but saying nothing. Hewlitt enjoyed Barbara's company, but the occasion was too heavily overshadowed for it to be anything more than a surface pleasure. He realized that there were many things he would have liked to have said to her if the circumstances had been less strained. This time he was entirely following her lead; she had started this game and until he knew what the rules were he was content to wait.

Barbara excused herself while he was paying the bill; he wondered if she had gone to telephone. She rejoined him promptly enough to dispel that notion and then led the way outside. When they were by themselves once more she turned and asked, "Would you like to go and look at the house now?"

"Fine," he answered. He still did not know what she really had in mind. There was an obvious explanation and he considered it carefully: they had met semisocially and, while he did not regard himself as anything exceptional as a potential lover, it could be that her purely animal instincts called for masculine company. Under such circumstances she might well prefer someone who could be relied upon to keep his mouth shut. It was doubtful if she was concerned with protecting what once would have been called her reputation; too many girls regarded that consideration as archaic and too many men no longer desired a spotless virgin for a bride. But when a girl who carried the responsibilities that she undoubtedly did chose to relax, she would have good reason to want a companion she could trust.

It took them almost fifteen minutes to reach the house. It appeared to be a quiet ordinary one which had had the good sense to be neither conspicuously better or worse than its contemporaries in the immediate neighborhood. It sat a little back on the lot; a short straight driveway led up to the garage. Two or three sun-faded throwaway newspapers before the front door suggested that no one had been in or out for at least a day or two.

Without glancing either way to see if anyone was watching, Barbara fitted the key into the lock and opened the door enough to pass inside. As Hewlitt followed, the slight mustiness of the air told him that despite the furniture in place the house was unoccupied. Barbara dropped her coat onto a chair, glanced at him, and said, "You take the upstairs."

He knew precisely what she meant. He went through the small second floor carefully, opening all of the closet doors, and for a finale checked the panel covering the crawl hole which gave access to the small space between the ceiling and the rafters. It was tightly shut, and when he attempted to move it, a fine sifting of dust told him that it had not been disturbed in some time. Brushing himself off he went back downstairs, noting the undistinguished furniture, the commonplace prints of bug-eyed children which adorned the living room, and two pieces of bric-a-brac which depicted a leaping gazelle and a Japanese geisha girl in the best traditions of lower Broadway. Whoever lived here, or had done so, had been contented with an installment payment decor and had picked out the objets d'art at a price of a dollar or two each.

As Barbara returned to the living room Hewlitt put the tips of his thumb and first finger together and raised his hand for her to see it.

"You were thorough?" she asked.

He nodded. "All the closets, under the beds, the shower stall, the attic entry, behind all of the doors. Did I miss anything?"

She sat down on one end of the low-priced davenport and the tension visibly eased out of her. "I'm sure you didn't," she answered, and her voice was eloquent with relief. "Come over and sit down. Now we can talk."

Hewlitt sat beside her. "Who lives here?" he asked.

"I don't know, but it doesn't matter. These houses come on and off the rental market all the time. The woman in the real estate office used to be with the Agency; she still helps out now and then. It's simply impossible for them to bug every house in Washington and then listen in on all of them, so when some perfectly ordinary people move out, we use the premises."

"How long has this been going on?" Hewlitt asked.

"Not too long, only since we discovered how much listening in was being done all over town. When they get onto this trick, we'll use something else."

"I understand. Now let's get down to cases; you wanted to see me."

Barbara shifted her position and folded her legs up underneath herself.

"Yes. First, did you hear what happened to Bob Landers?"

"I was there; I saw it."

She brushed a hand through the air. "I don't mean that. Captain Scott, who's more or less an Air Force messenger boy between the White House and the Pentagon, asked to see Zalinsky. He got in. When he did he asked if Mr. Z minded what he did with the body. He was told that it didn't make the slightest difference; he could do with it as he liked."

"Scott was a little nervy," Hewlitt commented.

Barbara nodded. "He was. He took the body to a mortuary and had Bob properly laid out. The next day he got some people from the Navy and some others, and made some fast arrangements—I don't know just how. Anyhow, they took

Bob to Arlington and buried him there, military honors and all."

Hewlitt felt a surge of admiration for the men who had done that even while he was evaluating the risk that they had taken. "Is Scott one of our people?"

"Not so far as I know, but he'll bear looking into. Now let's get serious for a minute. Answer me point-blank—are you Asher?"

"No, positively not. Are you?"

The moment he said it he realized the absurdity of the question, but once more his mouth had been faster than his brain.

Barbara ignored the slip. "I've checked with Mary; she hadn't been contacted either. So as far as we know, there's just the three of us."

"Let me tell you what I think," Hewlitt said. "Since this organization has been set up for some time, I don't believe that we should trust anyone—no matter who—until Asher appears on the scene. Somebody gave Bob away. He looked pretty bad just before . . ." He stopped to reshape his words. "I'm sure they put him through hell before he was shot, and God only knows whether he was able to keep his mouth shut or not."

"Did he look as though he'd been drugged?" Barbara asked.

"No."

"Then we'll have to go on the assumption that he was able to protect us. If not . . ." She shrugged her shoulders and let them fall. "I agree with you absolutely that we trust nobody—take nobody in—until we are contacted in some way by Asher. If after a month nothing has happened, then we can talk about it again."

"That long?" Hewlitt asked.

Barbara nodded. "I know a little more about this sort of thing than you do, at least I think I do. Impatience is one of the worst enemies."

"One month, then," Hewlitt agreed. "I hope it isn't that long."

"If you hear," Barbara continued, "let me know. Invite me to lunch and suggest an Italian restaurant if you've met him, a Chinese one if you've heard in some way."

"Fine."

"Two more things: first, don't contact Mary; that's to prevent too obvious a connection between the three of us. Don't underestimate her either; she's a very bright girl and knows how not to let it show."

"All right." He was a little frustrated that she had no more concrete news for him. "What's the other thing?"

"This is my idea pure and simple, but until we get orders to the contrary, I suggest that you become my visible boyfriend. I just got rid of one, so it's all right. That will cover any contacts we make."

"I'd been thinking of the same thing," Hewlitt said. "To be sure that I understand the ground rules, just how far does this, or is this, likely to go?"

Barbara looked at him. "That's up to you," she said. "Just don't take too much for granted, that's all."

On Monday morning Zalinsky sent for him. This time he welcomed it; if he was to be confronted with a question about Landers he wanted it over and done with. Any kind of action was preferable to the inertia he had been enduring. He took pad and pencils and presented himself, feeling for the first time that he could face this man unafraid.

When he had been admitted Zalinsky waved him to a chair. He was again wearing the poorly cut suit he had had on during his first day at the White House and Hewlitt noted it; the President seldom wore the same suit twice in one month.

"Today we will converse in my language," Zalinsky said.

"Very well," Hewlitt answered. The idiom he used suggested that he had given his consent. Zalinsky noted it and looked up, but he made no comment.

"You are now extremely displeased with me," Zalinsky went on in his own tongue, "because of the execution of Major Landers. He was your friend—I know. By the way, what does T.G.I.F. mean?"

"Thank God It's Friday." Hewlitt switched to English, as he had to.

"I see. I have no desire whatever to enlist your sympathy, I have no need of it, but do you know why I ordered the execution of your friend Landers so promptly?"

Hewlitt saw the trap: if he gave any indication that he was aware of Landers' underground activities he would condemn himself with the same breath. He allowed a suggestion of suppressed rage to show momentarily on his face. "I have no idea whatsoever. Furthermore, he was a very outstanding man. You destroyed . . ." He stopped as though he were incapable of going on.

Zalinsky put his fingers together. "I told you that he was a fool—that was true. Like Don Quixote he wanted to fight the world when he was defeated hopelessly before he began. But he was a soldier who would not surrender; you should have had more of them."

"And for this you ordered him shot," Hewlitt said. He was totally unafraid now. When Zalinsky spoke his own language some of his crudity disappeared and he gave ample evidence of being an educated man. Hewlitt realized fully that he spoke Zalinsky's language far better than Zalinsky spoke his.

"That is correct," Zalinsky continued. "You will recall that I told you you were children at this game; you should take note of that fact. We became aware of the fact that Landers, your friend, was engaged in a reckless attempt to annoy us against our specific warnings to the contrary. My security people, who are not as stupid as their sometimes commonplace faces might suggest, reported this to me and also to their headquarters at home. Major Landers was inconclusively questioned after which I ordered his immediate execution. These instructions were carried out approximately one hour before I received orders to ship him back at once under close guard for complete interrogation in my country. The outcome would have been the same, but if you possess the intelligence that I suspect that you do, you will see that I spared him a great deal. A very great deal; many men would have prayed to God, if they had one, to be allowed to shoot themselves rather than to undergo professional interrogation such as we are able to administer."

Hewlitt's legs began to shake slightly; he had to make a massive effort to control them.

"Now to the business at hand," Zalinsky went on. "I wish to have you arrange for me what you call a press conference for ten o'clock tomorrow morning. It is absolutely your responsibility that only the people who should be there are admitted. I will permit no questions. All personnel who come, male or female, will be searched; if any attempt is made on my life by any member of the press group, they will all pay equally for that offense. These facts you will make clear in advance."

"Yes, Mr. Zalinsky," Hewlitt said.

"Good. I trust you enjoy the company of Miss Barbara Stoneham."

"Very much so." As far as he knew, he did not turn a hair.

"Then that will be all. Hereafter, when possible, we will speak in English. I require the added practice."

"Yes, Mr. Zalinsky." He rose and left the room.

Although it was not normally his job, Hewlitt arranged the press conference as he had been directed with the aid of Cedric Culp, who, up until a few weeks previously, had been the President's press secretary. Three members of the regular White House corps, all male, refused to attend when the requirement of submitting to a personal search was made known to them. Of those who did come, many had their first direct contact with the wooden-faced, hard-handed security personnel whom Zalinsky had brought with him. Sharp resentment tightened the atmosphere; no one regarded it as a joke.

Several minutes before the scheduled time the conference room was already well filled and strangely still. The usual little conversational groups did not form, and there was none of the normal stir which had always preceded even the most important of the President's meetings with the press. Because he had been directed to call this conference, Hewlitt had taken advantage of the implied permission to be there himself. As he stood to one side now he thought that it was like a jury in a courtroom, except that this time the roles were reversed and those present were here to listen to the pronouncement of their own fates.

Three minutes late Zalinsky made his appearance. He entered without any pretext of formality, his face set in a stiff pattern which denied the least hint of cordiality. In his left hand he carried a sheaf of papers. With his slightly awkward walk he crossed to the podium which had been set up for him. The presidential seal had, of course, been removed, so that only the bare wood faced those who were seated before him. Zalinsky's suit was the better of the two

Hewlitt had seen, but it had not been pressed for the occasion. As he took his place before the microphones the room remained as it had been—almost totally quiet.

He surveyed his audience without any display of emotion, then he picked up the first sheet of the papers he had brought in and began to read.

"My name is Zalinsky. If at any time you have occasion to speak to me, you will address me as 'Mr. Zalinsky' and in no other manner. I am here to administer this country along the lines of policy which was decided from long ago. I will now explain to you what some of this policy is."

He stopped and took a drink of water. Hewlitt noted it carefully; it could be an indication of nervousness before an audience and he was meticulously collecting every possible weakness of the man that he could detect. The words that Zalinsky had just delivered were obviously not his own, a fact which he also considered worth cataloguing.

"The conquest of your country," Zalinsky continued to read, "was begun several years ago. Into this place we sent our agents, and they in turn were able to get many of your people to act for us. Some knew it and many did not. While you argued we planned and helped you to argue more. Always we planned for surprise. Our propaganda over the whole world was very effective; yours was pitiful."

He looked around the room after that, but got no reaction whatever.

"In your newspapers your cartoon people drew the pictures we wanted—not always, but often enough to be of great value to us. We made slogans: you laughed at slogans, but on your Madison Avenue you hired people to make slogans for you about cigarettes and other things. Your slogans sold more cigarettes, our slogans conquered your country. So do not try to make slogans against us—we are better at it than you are.

"It is important that I tell you now something that was not made public two years ago because at that time it had not happened. You had a big Air Force with many planes. But they were getting old and you needed new ones. With our agents we learned that your McDonnell Douglas company had a very good design; we are building it now. Also your Boeing company made a good design. But you did not buy these planes because a Mr. Seymour Brown also had an airplane which was a very poor design, but he had much influence. With great force of pressure he influenced your Congress, and because we knew that it was a very bad plane, we were glad to help. I shall not tell you to whom he paid money, but to many other people he gave gifts, arranged things, supplied very loving girl friends. Of lobby people he had many with also much money to spend. Because of this you bought his airplane and he made a great deal of money in your Wall Street."

Hewlitt was not sure, but he thought he detected a possible hesitation before Zalinsky continued.

"I now announce for you certain policies which become fact immediately. You will abide by them; if you do not, we will not trouble with you, you will be removed permanently. This has already begun to happen; some of you know this. It will surprise you that we do not intend to ruin your country; instead we intend to, and will, improve it greatly. You will be much happier that we have come. Not all of you, but most.

"You are each to continue the work you do until directed otherwise. You will not strike. We will shortly decide the payment wage for each job, and that you will receive. From this you will pay no income tax, as that is a capitalist invention against the masses. We will take taxes, yes, but in different ways.

"All laws you now obey you will continue to follow until we tell you what is different.

"There will be no naked dancing by women in public places.

"All tobacco and beverages of alcohol are forbidden unless bought from our own stores which will be ready very shortly.

"No person will buy more than two pairs of shoes in each year. Our people need shoes.

"Our security police will be obeyed at all times and no one will speak against them."

It was definite this time. Hewlitt clearly saw him stop and take a fresh grip on himself. Not because he was tired, clearly he wasn't; but the pause was unmistakable.

"Beginning very shortly, all people known as Jews will be

barred from public office, from teaching, and from certain other places we will designate."

An electric shock, unseen but violent, paralyzed the room. Images of Adolf Hitler and the horrors of the Third Reich seemed to burst into being. Hewlitt stared at Zalinsky, but this time no emotion whatever could be read on his broad features.

The administrator picked up his papers and left the stage. Hewlitt did not know his own emotions; he had not had time to respond to any as he looked quickly about him. The press people were leaving as rapidly as possible, but they were not speaking to each other; it was more of an emergency evacuation with every man for himself.

Hewlitt swallowed hard and tried to find reality. He had known within himself that something drastic was bound to happen, but he had never dreamed of this. The first clear and coherent thought which came to him was in the form of a question: he wondered if black-haired Barbara Stoneham was Jewish.

He walked back to his office slowly, trying to think—to sort things out in his mind. The questions which confused him were not moral or ethical; he was concerned as to what would happen next—and after that. He walked into his office hardly aware that his phone was ringing.

He picked it up mechanically and said, "Yes?"

A female, mature voice he did not know wasted no time. "Mr. Hewlitt, did you arrange this press conference?"

"Yes."

"Then will you come over to first aid right away, please." That was all.

On the table in the small medical facility a man was lying on his back. He was breathing steadily and deeply, his eyes were open, but his mind seemed to have left his body. An efficient-looking middle-aged nurse Hewlitt had never seen before spoke to him without bothering with formalities. "I think you'd better call his paper, Mr. Hewlitt, or his home, and get some help. He's in shock. No danger, but he should be moved from here as soon as possible."

"Who is he?" Hewlitt asked.

A man in the room, whom Hewlitt had been aware of but had not looked at directly, answered the question. "Sol

Horowitz of UPI. He's had a bad heart for years." He stopped, looked at Hewlitt, and realized that he was not one of the enemy. But his voice was still bitter when he spoke. "He was in Dachau when the Army came through and rescued him. All the rest of his family died there."

CHAPTER SIX

After the incredible news of defeat, which was still disbelieved in many parts of the country where the reality had not yet sunk in, the impact of Zalinsky's announcement was dulled. It was extensively reported by every form of the news media, but it did not arouse a great reaction. In the minds of millions of Americans the impossible and unthinkable had already taken place; after that nothing that followed in the wake very much mattered. The national illusion of being and having the best of everything had been broken, and that calamity totally overshadowed everything else.

As Hewlitt rode home that night he discussed the matter openly with Frank. The idea of listening devices everywhere was beginning to wear thin, plus which the subject did not compromise the fledgling underground organization in any way. Hewlitt was having thoughts about that too. All that he had to go on was Bob Landers' statement that such a thing existed, but he could very well have put it that way in order to generate at least some initial enthusiasm within his own little group—to build "morale." It could very well be that later on Landers would have formed other little groups and thus might have brought his "organization" into actual being.

"You're in the White House," Frank said. "Can't you do something about it? Not much, maybe, but something."

Hewlitt shifted the subject to a safer tack. "Frank, I've been as confused as everybody else. Right now I haven't a clear idea of what I ought to do. I don't want to clear out of here, even the way things are. I don't know where I'd go."

"Switzerland is supposed to be a pretty nice place. And they keep out of wars and that sort of thing."

"Yes, but we can't all go there. We just kept out of a war, and lost it by default."

"I carry Senator Fitzhugh every now and then," Frank offered as he edged his way into a traffic circle. "He still thinks that we did the right thing. He told me that at least we can live with our consciences."

"And with our enemies. I don't imagine that he likes that too much."

Frank dropped his voice to the confidential level. "I'll tell you something about that: he thinks that he's going to fix everything in a few days. He knows all the higher-ups overseas face to face, and he's confident that he can be a one-man peace mission to put things back the way they were, more or less. Then he's gonna run for President."

"He hasn't a hope in hell," Hewlitt said.

"He thinks he can do it." Frank took the cab around a corner.

"Where do you get all this?" Hewlitt asked.

"I carry a lot of people. And you'd be surprised what they tell taxi drivers. Ask my advice and everything. This afternoon I had a young girl in trouble. She just got in and asked me to take her where she could get a safe abortion."

"What did you do?"

Frank half-turned until he could partially look over his shoulder. "In your business there's a lot of things you can't talk about. On some things I keep my mouth shut too."

Hewlitt appreciated that; if a few others had had the same attitude, it might have made an appreciable difference.

As he read the detailed reports of Zalinsky's announcement for the second time, Marc Orberg found it difficult to contain his elation. His life, at that point, satisfied him enormously until it seemed to him that he had nothing more to ask of God or man.

Everything, absolutely everything, was the way he wanted it now. He looked about him simply in order to savor the great success that was his, success that his enemies despised, which made it sweeter still. The entire penthouse suite was strikingly decorated in crimson, black, and stark white. Great dramatic globules of color carved the walls into a Brobdingnagian jigsaw puzzle. The vastly oversized, ultrasoft lounge davenport displayed its black and white zebra stripes at the focal point of the room; scattered around it were huge, almost shapeless upholstered chairs done in dead black and a white imitation of angora fur. The carpeting, laid over a triple pad, was the most brilliant red the manufacturer had been able to achieve; the pile was more than an inch and a half thick.

Opposite the entrance doorway the wild ballet of colors gave way to white once more in order to provide a background for a display on the wall of the famous Marc Orberg album covers. Mixed in the pattern, like brass rings awaiting the patrons of a merry-go-round, were six gold-colored records made in metal; symbols of a sale of one million copies or more. In a corner of the ceiling a small spotlight illuminated the display with an artful circle of light.

On the opposite wall was an heroic, larger-than-life-size portrait of Orberg himself, standing hands on hips, accentuating the taut, sinewy hardness of his body. He wore a suede leather shirt laced loosely up the front, a wide belt to define his lean middle, and jeans which fitted him with near skintightness. The outline of his groin was clearly visible. The photograph radiated a fierce pride of masculinity, a restlessness, an unsuppressed urge for action, the knowledge of conquest achieved while most others of his own age had barely seized hold of their graduation diplomas.

Off the spectacular living room there was a dimly lighted alcove with an elaborately-carved Chinese bar. Close to it was the seldom closed door of the single bedroom, the electric blue carpet defining its twenty-five-foot-square area. The two walls opposite doorway were almost entirely of glass, giving a spectacular view of the city spread out below. The bed itself was circular, almost ten feet in diameter, and set on a slightly raised dais where another concealed spotlight bathed it in deep violet light when the shades were drawn. Several pieces of striking abstract art dramatized one wall; on the fourth a huge sumi-emural suggested romance and courtship in ancient Japan. The entire effect was sybaritically luxurious with a strong sense of detachment from any other world that might exist elsewhere.

Marc Orberg had had it designed and executed exactly as he wanted it for two specific purposes: to satisfy his own incessant craving for the exotic and to offer an unparalleled setting for a continual variety of sexual experiences.

Although he was only twenty-six, he had been enjoying the pleasures of women for more than a decade. With the great surge in his popularity he had discovered that conquests became absurdly easy; he had only to make an announced personal appearance and hundreds of females would fight for the right to be closest to him when he emerged from the stage door. Through his narrow-framed, uniformly successful business manager, Nat Friedman, he had seen to it that the word got out how any girl who wanted to could bring herself to his attention. All she had to do was to write her name, age, and telephone number on a small slip of paper and fold it to less than an inch square. Whenever Orberg made his way from a theater or concert hall to his waiting car, he would hold out his hands and accept the slips of paper placed in them. When his hands were filled, he would stuff the results into the pockets of his jacket and collect more. When he was asked the purpose of this, he always replied that it was so he could send them Christmas cards.

Only Nat knew that in this midst of plenty Orberg had a method for marking the slips he chose to select; as he gathered them in he would press the edge of his thumbnail into the offering of any face that caught his eye, or any figure that triggered his imagination.

Once he had erred; Nat had phoned a twenty-two-year-old (or so she had described herself) where the indentation had been particularly deep, made in all probability by the girl herself while she had been desperately waiting for the opportunity to offer herself. Marc had said, "Get me a woman," which differed from his more usual request for a girl; following instructions Nat had chosen the twenty-two-year-old who properly answered the description. The usual tactful phone call had as almost always been successful and within an hour the subject presented herself. She proved to be plain, somewhat overweight, and adorned with practical glasses. Orberg was at first in a concealed rage of frustration, but when the girl had gotten her clothes off, her body had been riper than he had expected and the resulting experience far beyond his expectations. For some time he had avoided repeating himself, but for this particular person he had broken his rule not once, but four separate times. There was no form of sexual gratification that she was not prepared to offer to her idol, and that in itself was a considerable improvement over the often frightened, tightly thrilled youngsters who had described themselves in writing as eighteen and who were hesitantly willing to be laid, but nothing more. After a while these little virgins began to annoy him and he looked for more capable companionship.

The conquest of the United States he did not expect to hurt his popularity in the least. If the people who had taken over knew anything at all about the country, they would know what he had been doing for them. They had talked together often enough in Cuba, Hanoi, and Moscow; they had praised his good work and had promised him that when the day came he would not be forgotten. That was all right as far as it went; he would decide later on whether he wanted to cooperate with them or not. He had done the TV stint for them simply as an exercise in virtuosity; after building an enormous reputation as a dynamic leader of violent protest, after becoming the number one law-defying rebel symbol of the hard left, it had given him great satisfaction to put on the character of the inherently wholesome-after-all young man and con the whole damn country into believing in him. He could do anything to them that he wanted to, he had proven that; and they couldn't do anything to him. They had been trying for years but his popularity in his own generation was too great.

For the lack of anything else to do he picked up a guitar, checked that it was reasonably in tune, and then turned on a tape recorder. He had several of them built in so that when he wanted one it would be available. The concealed one in the bedroom had produced some rare moments of interesting listening, but that did not concern him now. He was about to turn on what had been described once by a reviewer as his "outstanding talents as a composer."

He seated himself on the edge of the zebra-striped lounge and picked purposelessly at the strings. He let his fingers do as they liked, searching for a possible bit of novel rhythm. He was only a rudimentary musician; his great talent lay in his way of manipulating audiences. His singing voice was only passable, but with it he could do remarkable bits of histrionics whenever he liked.

He decided to concentrate on what he was doing; he did not feel like composing very often and if he got something good right now, it could be another million-copy record. With no more income tax to pay, that would be a sweet addition to the considerable fortune Nat had already managed to stash away for him. He would never have to work again as long as he lived, which suited him precisely. He had never worked at all in the strict sense of the word; his personal appearances were only fun to him. The lack of experience in this area did not trouble him.

He had it! Somehow his fingers had traced out a little rhythmic pattern, first slowly, then faster, which had a beat to it. He leaned forward and plucked it out again: ti—da—de—dum; ti-da-di-dum. Ti—da—di—dum; ti-da-di-dum. He had a vague feeling that he might have heard it before someplace, but so what. He began to seek out words in his mind, then a pawky idea hit him. It would be a simple song about the farm on which he had grown up. Or so the song would say. He would be homesick for the farm. For the wind-polished twin hills to the north, for the little triangle of woods down in the hollow by the stream. And the old well in the yard. The old well—that would make the navel. How long, he wondered, would it be before the saps woke up to what he was really singing about.

An hour later he had it down on tape. When the pieces were all assembled, and he had added several other little touches to his liking, he started the tape once more and did the whole thing straight through. It took him two minutes and twenty-five seconds, enough for a forty-five single, or if he had to, he could add another verse.

When he had finished, he stretched out on his back, his arms thrown high, letting his head roll slowly from side to side in an exercise of pure animal delight. Inaction was beginning to weigh on him and he craved some of the excitement on which he thrived. He had promised to be the first to greet and welcome the invaders on American soil; he wondered if he should do something about that. He could go and call on that clown Zalinsky in Washington, but it might be better just to let him wait.

Zalinsky sent for Hewlitt at fourteen minutes after three. This time it was not by telephone. The messenger who had brought him the speech to translate appeared without warning at the door of the office, his broad face as wooden as ever. For a sharp instant Hewlitt wondered if the sudden arrival of the soldier meant that the time had come for him to be taken out on the South Lawn for the ending of his life. Then he received his instructions. He picked up pad and pencils and went to face the man who had summoned him.

One change in the office Hewlitt noticed at once—the framed portrait of a Slavic-looking foreign officer hung on the wall. As he noted it he made a quick decision not to enquire about it.

He sat down without being invited this time and waited to see what was in the wind. He could feel that he was less tight now, that his nerves were not as taut.

Zalinsky looked up from his work, studied Hewlitt for a moment, and then spoke. "You have for some time not been doing work to earn your pay."

Hewlitt refused to be put on the defensive. "I have been available," he answered.

"But you have done nothing."

"The President and the Department of State kept me quite busy." He kept his voice quiet and factual.

"So you blame me."

Hewlitt decided not to press his luck any further. "When you have had a chance to become more familiar here, Mr. Zalinsky, you will probably have a greater need and use for the White House staff."

Zalinsky pondered for a moment and then decided to break it off. "I have now an announcement for you," he said. "The days you have been enjoying of nothing doing are over. You will move at once to the office just outside this one. There you will keep watch to the people who come and go. For this I select you because you can talk to my own people."

"You mean that I will be your appointment secretary."

Zalinsky showed him a palm. "Such names we do not employ in my country and I will not hire them here. If you wish a name, you will be watchdog. I will state to you who it is I wish to see. If others arrive, you will advise me and reverse those who I do not wish to allow. You understand?"

"Yes, Mr. Zalinsky."

"It is good. Later I may wish you to do other things as I become aware of your abilities. I now say one thing more: do not try to make manipulations against what it is that I wish."

Hewlitt ventured a probe. "If you believe that I will do that, why are you giving me this job?"

Zalinsky hardened for a moment, then Hewlitt thought he saw him relax. "It is not necessary that we discuss this. Only I warn you—do not get away from the line. That will get you nowhere, and it will get you there with rapidity."

Hewlitt's mind was racing. The stakes were being raised, he saw that clearly, and he responded to it. "I'll start moving my office immediately, Mr. Zalinsky," he said. "Understand what I say when I tell you that I am no mind reader and you will have to tell me what your program is each day."

"It is not necessary to instruct me in the elementary," Zalinsky responded. "Mind readers they perhaps possess in Tibet; you are not of this breed. You will be told."

"Yes, Mr. Zalinsky."

"You will go."

As he cleaned out his desk and prepared to assume his new duties, Hewlitt was still unable to sort out all of his emotions. One, however, stood out—a subdued sort of elation. He felt as though he had been sitting on the bench as a substitute and now was being sent into the big game. He would henceforth be seeing Zalinsky constantly and the invisible battle would be joined for certain. Could he take the measure of the man? He did not know, but he knew that he was going to try.

Admiral Barney Haymarket was in civilian clothes, but that fact did not diminish the aura of his rank in the least. While not a word had been said on the subject by anyone, it was tacitly understood that the "retired" which had been attached after his name some time previously had been withdrawn. How valid this premise was remained a fact known to a very few people. As was the standard practice with all retired top officers, he had been briefed on a daily basis ever since he had stepped down as Chief of Naval Operations. He had gone through the motions of accepting a job as chairman of the board of a leading civilian company, one which did not directly supply the military establishment, and then apparently had settled down to the usual routine of occasional public appearances and the accepting of appropriate awards from such suitable organizations as the National Conference of Christians and Jews.

Late in the previous administration, while he still had been wearing the four stars on his shoulder boards, he had been summoned for a very private conference with the President. It had been unusual in that only the two of them had been together. When the coffee cups had been set down and the door firmly closed, the President had spoken his mind.

"Barney, I don't need to tell you that I don't like the look of things at all. I don't think that any man who has ever sat here was really happy, but you know what the score is."

"I do, Mr. President, and believe me, I don't like it either."

"All right, then, let me give you this: in my judgment we are on a course which could conceivably lead to the first military defeat in our history."

"I agree, sir, that is my conclusion also."

"Then we don't need to waste time in rhetoric." The shadow of his heavy responsibilities had crossed the President's face. "Suppose now, Barney, that Fitzhugh and the others like him make their point, have it their way, and we more or less tear down our military structure. After that we take a pasting. Where do we go from there?"

The admiral had leaned forward to deposit cigar ashes in a tray before he had given his answer. "We would have two alternatives then: either we swallow it and do what we're told for the indefinite future, or else we go underground and fight back one way or another."

"Do you think that could work?"

"Mr. President, as I see it we would have to try. If we take it on the chin, then there's nobody left and the commies will have what Napoleon, Hitler, and all the rest were denied—total world domination. And you know, sir, how they play the game. Personally I'd rather fight back and lose my life in the attempt than to knuckle down to their way of doing things. You know the reports we've been getting for years about the horrors the Chicoms have been dishing out. I've seen pictures, Mr. President, that damn near made me vomit, and I don't have a weak stomach."

The President had considered that in the light of his decision.

"Barney, I'm going to give you a job. It's a tough one, but you are the man for it. Your term as CNO will be over in five months; I want you to retire and go through all the motions of returning to civilian life. But what I really want you to do is to get together with a team of your own choosing, military, civilian, or both, and put together a plan for just such a resistance operation in the event of our defeat. I'll see that it's financed and also that you get whomever and whatever you want. But it has got to be totally secure; I'd suggest a special clearance level for anyone who even knows of the plan's existence."

"Mr. President, don't we have something like this already?"

"Yes, but not to my satisfaction. I'm going to keep the other plan going, if for no other reason than to cover up what you'll be doing. Not even the joint chiefs are going to know about this unless you approve it first. And I'm going to give you a deadline: I have a pretty good idea who my successor is going to be and I don't at this moment have too much confidence in him."

"I know the man you mean, sir," the admiral had said, "and once more I agree with your conclusion. I don't question his integrity, but in plain language he lacks guts."

"That he does. So you have until I step down to get the job done. After that I can't promise you a thing; so you'd better stash away whatever you'll need now. Let me know how you're getting on. Do you trust Colonel Gifford?"

"Totally."

"Then I'll see that he makes BG more or less immediately to give him a little more muscle and turn him over to you. He's one of the most resourceful men I've ever met. I'll set him up with a cover job and let him be the liaison man between us."

At that point the admiral had gotten to his feet. "Time's a wastin', Mr. President, and I have an awful lot to do. I'll send you my requisitions, personnel and otherwise, through Gifford. Have you a suggestion for a code name?"

The President had looked out of the window for a few moments while he thought. "Politics aside, there's one American I've always admired tremendously. He was way ahead of his time and I'm not sure that he isn't ahead of us right now. Thomas Jefferson."

"Tom Jefferson it is, then, sir." He had shaken hands and left. As he had climbed into his waiting staff car with the starred plate out front, his mind had already been busy planning, considering, sifting, and projecting.

All that had been a while ago, but not a long enough while for Barney Haymarket to accomplish everything that he would have liked to have done. Ten years would not have been enough, but he had put first things first and he had been helped by some of the best planning brains the country had had available. As a result he had been able to stuff enough aces up his sleeve to be in a position of some strength, although it was pitiful when compared with the total military posture of the enemy who now stood on the nation's shores.

As he walked into the command post he had provided for the operation which would now go into effect, he knew that it was totally secure from any kind of eavesdropping activity. Delicate electronic devices in duplicate monitored the premises with a ceaseless vigil. For a bare moment he looked at General Gifford and the few others who had assembled at his bidding and who were waiting for him, on their feet, around a plain, functional table.

"Sit down, gentlemen," he invited. "It's time to put Tommy Jefferson to work."

Some thirty-nine hours later the body of retired Admiral Barney Haymarket, one of the most colorful and efficient Chiefs of Naval Operations that the service had ever known, was found in the wreckage of his car where it had gone off the road during a heavy night rainstorm in the Rocky Mountains.

As he went through the motions of installing himself in his new office, Hewlitt kept forgetting where he wanted to put things because of the many thoughts which were seething in his brain. He was beginning to awake to an uncomfortable realization, and he did not like it at all. He was thirty-two years old, by any reasonable calculation his life was at least one-third over, and he had never as yet made a conscious decision as to what he wanted to do or what he hoped ultimately to accomplish.

His collegiate career had been appropriately distinguished, particularly since he had been born with a quick ear and a gift for languages. He had studied for a year abroad; after that the suggestion had been gently made to him that now that his education in the formal sense had been concluded, it was time for him to go to work. It pained him now to realize that he had not made a decision then either—he had simply taken the path of least resistance. A job had been available in the State Department, it had been offered to him, and he had accepted it. Every move he had made after that had been decided for him. While up until a few weeks ago most of his various friends had agreed that he had "made good," he was now beginning to be conscious of the fact that all he had really done was go where he had been pushed.

He adjusted the reading light on the desk and set his typewriter where it would be conveniently at his elbow. Now, he knew, from that minute forward he would have to lead a very different life. He would be right under Zalinsky's nose, his every word and action subject to scrutiny and analysis. He could play it two ways: he could do as he was told and keep his nose clean, or he could go for higher stakes with his life on the line. That was a helluva lot different, he thought, from being on the collegiate tennis team, where a victory or a defeat meant very little when you came right down to it.

As he put a supply of freshly sharpened pencils into the center desk drawer, he wondered just how much chance he would have of accomplishing anything if he *did* elect to try to fight back. The entire American military establishment had been overcome by swift, brilliant, almost bloodless action. Billions of dollars in defense preparation had proven ineffective. Now he proposed to try to reverse that outcome with a team which so far consisted of two stenographically skilled, reasonably willing girls. Bob Landers had tried it and Bob Landers had lost his life within a matter of days.

But, dammit, that kind of defeatist attitude was what had beaten the country in the first place! It had not been overcome on the field of battle or by warfare at sea, it had been outmaneuvered from without and within. Leftist subversion and the attitudes of people like Fitzhugh, the peace-at-any-price boys, had caused the military to be in an understaffed, demoralized posture when the enemy had hit. Hewlitt was not a militarist, and he had never served in any branch of the armed services. But now his spirit cried for action. Bitterly he knew that it was too late; he should have felt that way before instead of filling out his deferment papers as he had done. Of course if this disaster had not overtaken the country, a military career would not have appealed to him at all.

When his desk was finally in order, he sat down to think. He didn't want to leave things as they were—he wanted for the first time in his life to make a decision—probably the most important one he would ever face. He had to make it to establish his own self-respect. He was aware that his position was unique in the country; he was sitting at the nerve center of Zalinsky's administration, that meant that he would be in an invaluable position to help any bona fide underground movement. It also meant that he would be exposed to far greater jeopardy than would be the case almost anywhere else.

He was startled when he looked up and found Zalinsky himself at his elbow. Without thinking, he rose to his feet. "You have of everything you need?" he was asked.

"Everything, Mr. Zalinsky. As far as I know now."

"It is good. You will soon become very busy. When I wish to call you, what is the name you employ?"

Hewlitt thought rapidly, but he could not find the words he needed. "My friends call me 'Hew,' " he said. He was reluctant to put Zalinsky in that category.

"But that is not your initial name."

"No, my first name is Raleigh; I never use it."

Zalinsky considered the information. "I have not yet the fullest awareness of this country, but that name I have never heard before."

"Our family is distantly related to the Raleighs of Virginia. When I was born, my mother evidently decided to make me the connecting link. So she gave me that name."

"It was a bad idea," Zalinsky said.

Hewlitt nodded. "I agree; I don't like it either."

"So there is one thing about which we are not enemies." With that Zalinsky disappeared into the Oval Office.

Perhaps the man had been trying to be friendly, but Hewlitt doubted it; more likely it had been an invitation to him to let his guard down.

Then, quite simply, he made his decision; he would fight back. He was in it all the way—to do the best that he could. A surge of fierce pride took hold of him; he was not doing now merely what was expected of him, he was not reacting automatically, he was undertaking something with his eyes open, on his own initiative, and God willing, they would know that he had been in the battle before it was through.

A man from the enemy was approaching his desk; this time Hewlitt carefully catalogued him in his mind. Age about fifty-five, five feet ten, weight one eighty, face moderately intelligent, uniform better fitted, an officer. "Yes?" he asked.

"I am told that you speak our language." The voice, educated but cool.

"Yes, I do." He switched effortlessly into the other tongue.

"I have some instructions to give you. I am Major Barlov, commander of the security detail for this headquarters."

Hewlitt started to say, "Pleased to meet you," automatically, then he caught himself. He spoke his own name and then waited.

"I am informed that you are to be in charge of appointments and visitors for Mr. Zalinsky. Therefore you will be required to vouch for each person who applies to be admitted. That is to say, you will be called upon to confirm that he has an appointment and that Mr. Zalinsky has consented to see him. Each visitor will be searched. This is to be explained beforehand to save additional trouble for my men."

"How about women?" Hewlitt asked.

"The same thing, but I do not believe that Mr. Zalinsky will have much time for any women. The point is, no one is to enter that office until we have given permission. Is that very clear to you?"

"Perfectly."

"One more thing: I am specifically warning you against taking advantage of your position. You are never to walk in on Mr. Zalinsky without his prior knowledge. And you are never to carry anything, such as a letter opener, which could be used as a weapon. If any attempt is made upon Mr. Zalinsky, you will protect him with your life; if you fail to do this, you will be regarded as part of the attempt. That is all for the present." The major nodded, turned on his heel and walked away.

It seemed to Hewlitt that precious few Americans would be asking for appointments to see Zalinsky—if they knew what was good for them. It was like calling on the Turkish sultans in the old days; give the slightest displeasure and your head was served up in the middle of a big platter, then and there. Zalinsky had already ordered one execution, which had been immediately carried out; the man was as trustworthy as a cobra and Hewlitt did not intend to forget that fact for a moment.

However, one American who clearly was not afraid to face the administrator called that same morning; the office of Senator Solomon Fitzhugh came on the line. The senator wanted to know, via his secretary, when it would be most convenient for Mr. Zalinsky to see him.

"Put him on," Hewlitt said, and waited.

In a few moments the senator's well-known voice came to him over the wire. "To whom am I speaking?"

"This is Hewlitt, senator. Raleigh Hewlitt."

"Do I know you?"

"No, sir, we've never met. I've been on the White House staff for some time as a language specialist; now Mr. Zalinsky has assigned me this job."

"You're an American, then."

"Absolutely, senator. I understand that you want to see Mr. Zalinsky."

"That is correct, yes."

"Hold the line, sir, and I'll see what I can do."

For the first time he made contact with the administrator without having been summoned first; he pressed the intercom button and the man inside answered almost at once. "Mr. Zalinsky," Hewlitt said, "I have Senator Solomon Fitzhugh on the line. You know of him?"

"You are wishing to insult me?"

"Of course not, sir. Senator Fitzhugh would like to know what time it would be most convenient for you to see him today."

"I have no wish to see him," Zalinsky answered, and hung up.

Hewlitt turned to the other phone. "I'm sorry, senator, Mr. Zalinsky has just informed me that he has no time available."

"Tomorrow, then."

"Senator, I regret this very much, but he made it clear that he didn't wish to see you at all. Might I suggest a letter, sir."

"No you may not, Mr. Raleigh, or whatever your name is. He can't treat me this way and he knows it, I know his boss too well. I intend to see Zalinsky in the immediate future and you can give him that message for me!" The line abruptly went dead.

Hewlitt typed up a memo slip. *Mr. Zalinsky: Senator Fitzhugh was very upset by your decision. He asked me to inform you that he intends to see you in the immediate future.* He added his initials and then put it aside; he would decide later whether to deliver it or not. If it got Fitzhugh into trouble, it would be the senator's own fault for not waking up to the realities.

Ever since it had been forcefully, and ruthlessly, reorganized by the enemy, the Pentagon complex had been like a graveyard. The few people who remained on the job were largely clerks who were familiar with the files and a small number of junior officers whose level of responsibility had been limited.

One of the first of the enemy's planes that had set down at Andrews Air Force Base had contained the Pentagon Reorganization Team and it had gone to work immediately with a vengeance. The initial occupying forces had had the buildings blocked off, and when the team arrived it was equipped with full sets of plans showing every office and facility together with its function or purpose. Supposedly secret information was found to have been hopelessly compromised, with the likelihood that some of the people who had cried "security" the loudest had been responsible.

Office by office, section by section, the Pentagon and adjacent buildings had been gone through. Some secret files had already been burned, some safety precautions had proven effective, but still a vast accumulation of data had fallen into enemy hands—enough to amount to uncounted tons of paper. When the job had been completed a few individuals had been selected to stay on while the enemy's sentries constantly patrolled the corridors, likely to appear anywhere at any time to be sure that no one did anything other than what he had been specifically directed. Stunned, the skeleton staff of the Pentagon did the enemy's bidding and silently prayed for help.

Things were therefore in order, by the enemy's standards, when a very hard-faced man whose pudgy nose and squared-off jaw revealed his Slavic origin entered the Bureau of Naval Personnel with a pass which was immediately respected at the entrance. Once inside the building he did not require any direction; he walked rapidly to the precise area he desired and entered an office where the records for flag officers were stored.

A thin, nervous-appearing yeoman in white uniform took one quick look at his visitor and got to his feet as rapidly as he was able.

"The file on Admiral Haymarket," the man demanded, his almost brutally direct voice matching the cold hostilty of his face and the demanding tension in his body.

"The admiral is retired," the yeoman stammered.

The visitor jerked his arm back, then whipped it forward, smashing his palm across the face of the slender young sailor. The yeoman went reeling and fell, his body sliding several inches after it hit the floor. Silently he picked himself up and, avoiding looking at the man who had hit him, went to a row of filing cabinets, searched briefly, and extracted a folder.

Before he could turn around it was yanked out of his hand. It was a very thick service record, but the intruder had no interest in the accumulation of promotions, citations, and awards of decorations that it contained. He opened it from the back, found what he wanted, and extracted a regulation fingerprint card. Holding it in one hand he threw the rest of the papers with savage force across the room so that they were scattered widely among the desks and chairs. After that he stalked out.

At almost precisely the same time, in a small town in the western half of Colorado, the local mortuary had an unexpected visitor at a quite early hour. For a moment or two the manager who answered the door was concerned that the obviously foreign gentleman who had rung the bell was in a very upset frame of mind. He was quickly disillusioned; in poor, but understandable English, the visitor stated, "I wish to see a body."

The manager was politely considerate. "I'm very sorry, sir, but our slumber rooms have not been prepared as yet. If you could return . . ." He stopped when he saw the look on the face of the man to whom he was speaking; for the first time he grasped that this was one of the enemy.

The man quickly pushed his way inside and looked once about him. "Where is the workroom?" he demanded.

Despite his mounting concern, the manager immediately became firm. "That is impossible, sir, the state law prohibits it. No one is ever allowed—" A hand against his chest pushed him aside, then the unwelcome visitor began opening doors and peering inside. He discovered a showroom with several empty open coffins on display, a small chapel, and then the door he wanted. Although there was a firmly-worded notice posted on it, without hesitation he opened it and went inside.

The embalmer at work looked up, startled, and knew in a moment what the intruder was. He was a veteran of the Vietnam conflict and he had seen that kind of man before. He also knew which of the four bodies in the room would most likely be of interest to him.

The cadaver of Admiral Haymarket lay covered by a sheet; the nature of his fatal injuries had dictated a closed coffin service from the beginning. Close by the body, leaning against the wall, was a fine enlarged portrait of the admiral showing him at the height of his career; the impressive array of decorations above his left breast pocket matched by the neat row of four stars displayed on the right side of his collar. It was intended for display next to the sealed coffin and the flowers which would be placed around it so that those who came to pay their last respects would feel the presence of the man they had come to honor. The portrait had been flown in from Coronado and had been delivered only a short time previously.

The intruder pulled the sheet off the body. He looked at it for a moment and then began to change color; the embalmer waited to see if he would keel over.

After a few seconds the man recovered himself somewhat and pulled an ink pad and a thin piece of coated cardboard from his coat pocket. Proceeding with a duty he knew that he had to complete, he pressed the stiff fingers of the corpse against the ink pad and then, somewhat clumsily, pushed their cold tips onto the paper. He did it methodically; when he was not satisfied with the results from the right hand, he did the distasteful task once more to be sure. When he had finished he turned quickly away from the disfigured body and left the room as rapidly as he was able. Once outside of the funeral home he took a deep breath or two of fresh air, then jumped into a Mercedes-Benz sports car which was waiting at the curb and drove off with an abrupt, angry burst of speed.

Some seven hours later the fingerprints he had taken were delivered to the dignified Washington building which before the war had been the conqueror's embassy. Because the premises were known to be totally secure, and were readily available, they had been taken over by the secret police—so designated only to distinguish them from the regular authorities. They were anything but secret and derived much of their strength from the combination of awe and terror in which they were held in their own homeland.

In his office Colonel Rostovitch received the prints from Colorado. He adjusted the light on his desk for close work and then placed under it the fingerprint card he had obtained personally that same morning at the Pentagon. With the aid of a magnifying glass he compared the two sets of prints; he was not an expert, but in this instance he did not need to be. There was no doubt whatever; despite the inadequacy of the work done in Colorado, the two sets were clearly identical.

When the day was at last over and he was able to escape from the confines of his new job, Hewlitt congratulated himself that he had come through unscarred. He had, on this day at least, done everything that had been asked of him and had risked nothing. It would probably be a week or two before he could begin to probe for the cause of Bob Landers' betrayal. By that time they might have him down as an ordinary employee prepared to do as he was directed and no more. That would suit his own plans perfectly.

He made his way out past the enemy's security men and climbed into Frank's cab with a sense of relief. He had a compelling desire to go somewhere away from the city where he could think his own thoughts or enjoy the simple luxury of talking to someone without having to feel that every word he spoke was being weighed and every idea he expressed judged.

"You look tired," Frank said when they were well out into the traffic.

"I am," Hewlitt admitted. "It's a strain."

Frank appeared to consider that answer as he edged his way into position for a turn. When he had completed it he seemed ready to say something, but before any words came out he evidently changed his mind.

"What is it?" Hewlitt asked.

"Well, maybe I shouldn't," Frank said.

"Go ahead, it's all right."

The muscular man behind the wheel still hesitated, then decided to try his luck. "I was just wonderin' if you'd care to do me a real big favor."

"If I can. Are you short on cash?"

Frank raised a hand and waved that off. "Nothin' like that. You've heard me tell you about my friend Davy Jones—the electronics guy. Well, I've told him about you, working in the White House and all that, and he'd sure like to meet you."

"I'd be glad to."

Frank half-turned to show his appreciation, then his driving took over his full attention for the next two or three minutes. When he had broken out into the clear once more, he reopened the conversation. "Davy's giving a little party tonight," he said. "He's got a big old house where you can let your hair down and enjoy yourself a little without havin' to worry that someone's listening all the time. Just five or six guys. We was wondering if you'd like to stop by for a little while. I've known you long enough to know that you aren't concerned with color. There'll be plenty of beer, Scotch, whatever you like, and one of the guys has got some nice film of pretty girls with no clothes on. You haven't got anything against that, have you?"

"Hell no," Hewlitt answered. For no good reason he thought of Barbara.

"Care to come?"

"How about for a little while? I've got some other things to do too."

Frank turned his head and nodded. "How about if I pick you up a little after eight?"

"Fine."

Having committed himself, Hewlitt remained silent for the rest of the trip. Once inside his apartment he showered, dressed in informal sports clothes, and turned on the news. He had no desire to go out for dinner; instead he chose a packaged meal from the stock he kept in his refrigerator and put it in the oven.

While the food heated he watched the news and gained nothing from it. The principal item was an obituary of Admiral Haymarket; with the aid of film clips his career was retraced without any reference to the disaster which had overtaken the Navy, and the rest of the armed forces, as well as everyone else. The enemy probably wouldn't like it, but it was presented in such a way that it would be difficult to take exception to anything that had been said. Hewlitt took careful note and decided that there might be a contact worth making at the Washington station that had produced the program.

When his doorbell rang at eight-fifteen Frank was there, turned out as he had never seen him before, in well-cut sports clothes, very much the man about town. For just a moment Hewlitt wondered if the ladies who were to entertain would all be on film or not.

The cab, as usual, was outside. Frank ushered him in back and dropped the flag as he was pulling away from the curb. "That's just for show," he explained, "in case somebody gets nosy."

Twenty minutes later they pulled up in front of a rambling old house in a neighborhood which was living on its memories. As he climbed out, Hewlitt noted the preponderance of Negro faces in the vicinity.

The man who admitted them was unusually tall, very slender, and urbane; a pencil-line mustache set off his features.

"Davy," Frank said, "meet Mr. Hewlitt."

The tall Negro smiled his welcome and held out his hand.

"Please come in," he invited. "I'm very glad you could make it. Frank has told me about you many times."

Hewlitt liked him. He expressed his pleasure as he shook hands and followed his host inside. "Frank tells me that you're an electronics expert," he said.

"Expert is a rather strong word, Mr. Hewlitt," Jones said. "I make my living fixing radio and TV sets, and do a little dabbling on the side. One thing: after what's been going on, you might like to know that this house is free of listening devices—I can guarantee that."

"Good," Hewlitt acknowledged. He followed Jones down a short hallway and into a living room where four more men, all Negro and all moderately well dressed, were gathered. He was introduced around and offered a drink by a volunteer bartender. He would have been a little more comfortable if he had not been the only Caucasian present, but the warmth of his welcome was evident and he responded to it.

Someone turned on a stereo and presently the voice of a blues singer filled the room. Drink in hand, Frank rejoined him and led him to a corner where they could talk. "Mr. Hewlitt . . ." he began.

"My friends call me 'Hew.' "

Despite his complexion, Frank appeared to flush slightly. "Thanks, I really appreciate that, Hew. I'm Asher."

CHAPTER SEVEN

The initial crews of workmen who were brought in to blast out the underground headquarters for Thomas Jefferson were told, by means of some carefully planted rumors, that they were preparing a storage area for nuclear weapons. The need for strict secrecy was stressed and observed; the job was done with almost no leakage of information. Those who came after them understood that the facility was to be a supersecret alternate command post for NORAD, to be ready in case anything happened to the well-known installation near Colorado Springs. The men who installed the living quarters and all of the complex communications equipment were also worthy of the trust reposed in them; when they left the isolated mountain area the local people knew only that something had been going on. Since there were many classified defense projects in that part of the country, very little interest or discussion was generated. And since the visible traffic to and from the facility was very limited, it was assumed from the start that it was not of major importance.

From the beginning Admiral Haymarket had applied some ideas of his own toward maintaining the secrecy of the project. In the entire Pentagon there was not one scrap of paper which supplied any information whatsoever concerning Thomas Jefferson. The necessary communications facilities were both inconspicuous and protected by fail-safe, auto-destruct devices set to function the moment that the equipment was opened or a call attempted without first dialing a code number known, just prior to the start of the surprise conflict, to four men. The funding was handled by the President himself with dollars which were never knowingly appropriated for the purpose by the Congress.

During the time that the headquarters had been under

construction the admiral had been busy reviewing the records of hundreds of individuals in whom he had had a preliminary interest. He weeded ruthlessly, not always following the guidelines which had been in use for some time to decide who would be trustworthy and who not. In particular he chose one newsman whose capabilities were extraordinary and through General Gifford approached him about serving his country without giving the least indication as to what the duty would entail, where it would be located, or the duration of the time involved. Shortly after that conference had been held the editorial employees of a major national publication were told that one of their colleagues had been diagnosed as having a serious lung condition; there was genuine concern and sincere regret when he left for Arizona and an indefinite period of recuperation. Not long after his departure the word filtered through that his illness had worsened to the point where he was being kept in absolute quiet without visitors or communications by mail. Eventually some Christmas cards were sent to him, but none were received in return.

The admiral also knew of, and got, a former Marine major who had been mustered out of service when he recovered from battle injuries incurred in Vietnam with part of his left hand missing. A retired industrialist quietly disappeared from the golf club where he had been spending much of his time; it was understood that he had interested himself in some mineral resources project located in northern Alaska.

An Air Force search and rescue pilot whose physical bravery and devotion to duty were legendary was relieved of his command and assigned to "classified duty"; his colleagues knew better than to ask where he had gone.

The most spectacular addition to the team the admiral was so carefully assembling was a circus performer whose death-defying high dives had terrified spectators throughout Europe and America. The admiral had had to go to the President himself to get him since the Central Intelligence Agency had had no intention of relinquishing one of its best men.

When they were finally assembled, they constituted the best that the nation had available. Gradually, other personnel were selected to support them and to carry out the field operations they would direct, if such action became necessary. To these other people the invisible men who constituted the heart and brains of Thomas Jefferson were known by a code name of their own invention. The admiral liked it and adopted it officially; from that time forward they were called the First Team.

As the admiral had watched the inauguration of the new President on television he had given silent thanks for the foresight of the man who was being replaced. The new President, he had felt with reasonable confidence, would go along with what had already been established, but it was quite doubtful that he would have been willing to fund and develop something like Tom Jefferson on his own initiative.

It had not been long after that that the President had been compelled to flee Washington and, invisibly, the First Team had moved to the center of the stage.

The thought of what they were up against was in every member's mind as the team met around the functional conference table on the same day that the funeral services for Admiral Haymarket had been held earlier, by permission of the occupying forces, in Arlington National Cemetery. It was a grim and sober time; so much so that the very walls seemed to reflect back the gravity which pervaded the room.

One minute before the time at which the meeting was formally scheduled to begin, the door to the residential section opened and Admiral Haymarket entered the room. He sat down briskly at the head of the table, rested his forearms on the top, and nodded his greetings. "We seem to be off to a good start," he said. "Every report I've had on our initial effort has been most encouraging."

"Yes, sir," the Marine major said. "The operational team that handled it did a first-rate job."

"Let's have a brief account," the admiral said. "All of us can stand to hear a little good news."

The major addressed the table generally. "The body was defrosted and prepared as planned. It was a little gruesome at the time, but the way in which Dr. Heise smashed in the face with the duplicate steering wheel was a work of art. The accident, I understand, went off perfectly except for the fact that there was no fire; we were rather hoping for one."

"Couldn't you have arranged that?" the circus performer asked.

"Yes, but not without an element of risk; it's difficult to do without leaving some evidence on the scene. We decided against it."

The retired industrialist made a note. "I'll look into that," he said. "We ought to be able to develop something."

"Fine," the admiral commented. "Go on, Ted."

The major continued. "Our study of Rostovitch indicates that he never takes anything at face value, and he didn't this time. He went to the Bureau of Naval Personnel personally, don't ask me why, and picked up the fingerprint card we had planted there. I've had a good report on that."

The search and rescue pilot, who wore the Air Force Cross ribbon on his uniform, raised his hand.

"Yes, Henry," the admiral said.

"When you laid out the ground rules, you stated that we were expected to bring up every doubt that arose in our minds."

"Right."

"Two questions: first, is there any likelihood that they might exhume the body?"

"If they do," the major said, "I believe that it will withstand any examination they might give it; it was very carefully selected. We have a set of dental charts planted, too, in case they go that route."

"All right, I'll accept that. Second question: admiral, at this moment how many people outside of this room know that you are still alive?"

"The President knows; I am in contact with him. The operational team that staged the accident knows; that was unavoidable. Other persons within our organization know because they have to. And my wife knows. I've been married to her for more than thirty years and her discretion is absolute. She's had lots of practice."

The former reporter spoke up. "I saw a little of your funeral on TV—they didn't allow much of it on the air. She wept very convincingly; I was deeply moved."

"She was an actress," the admiral said, "and a damn good one, before I married her. Any more questions?"

There were none.

"All right. Gentlemen, as to our campaign plans: we have not had adequate time since this department was established to prepare for all contingencies. During this past week I have been reviewing everything that we do have and all of the other possibilities that suggested themselves. Until someone comes up with something better, I'm in favor of going ahead with Low Blow. Against the background of the present situation, it's the best bet that we've got."

There was silence.

"Any comments?" the admiral asked.

"We'd be putting a lot of our eggs into one basket," the industrialist said, "but it's one hell of a basket."

"Can we do it in such a way that if it gets shot down, the whole show won't be compromised?" the circus performer asked.

"Yes," Haymarket answered.

"I'll buy it," the Marine major said. He ran the fingers of his remaining hand through his closely cropped hair as though the sitting still irked him.

Admiral Haymarket looked around the table, but no one else had a comment or a question. "Then I take it that for the present, at least, we are in agreement. Let's get the machinery going, because it's going to take a while and it will be as tricky as all get out."

The industrialist nodded, a solemn bean pole of a man in contrast to the very muscular circus performer who sat next to him. "Those things can't be rushed," he agreed.

The admiral had one more thing to say. "In any kind of warfare you have to expect casualties; we've had a bad loss right at the begining. Bob Landers, whom some of you knew, I'm sure, was spotted, interrogated, and then shot on the White House lawn. The best information I can get indicates that he didn't talk, but even if he did he couldn't have blown more than his own immediate local contacts. We've been watching them and so far they seem to be all right—although it could be a cat-and-mouse game to draw us in. I've had a contact made. There was an element of risk, but I was banking on Landers as I knew him. The White House is very important to us if we can establish a reliable listening post on the inside."

"How was Landers found out?" the high diver asked.

"I don't know yet," Haymarket answered. "One of my best people is looking into it. I just hope that no anxious amateurs get in his way."

Senator Solomon Fitzhugh sat alone in the solemn quiet of his office, long after everyone else had gone, struggling with his inner conscience and a heavy secret with which he was burdened. Despite the fact that it was decidedly painful to him, he was carefully retracing in his mind the events which, when strung out like crows sitting on a fence, had conspired to put him in his present dilemma. The starting point, he knew, lay in his own character and convictions. There were certain things in which he believed so implicitly that he had never had cause to question them before; foremost among these was the unshakable belief that war is hell. He held this so deeply that it had overshadowed and influenced his entire legislative career. If he could keep the nation out of armed conflict, no matter what the price, he was going to do it. If human life was beyond all value, then the preserving of large amounts of it would be of incalculable worth. "Blessed are the peacemakers, for they shall inherit the earth."

There was one possible excuse for warfare, and that was when you were actually invaded and had to fight on your own soil to defend your own womenfolk and children. However, the simple fact was that if everyone followed the same principles that he did, there would be no invasions and no one would ever have to fight to defend his homeland.

His mind would not let him evade the responsibility of what came next; it took him overseas in swift retrospect and to the capital of the nation which had so ruthlessly and shockingly overcome the United States of America. Although his trip had been presumably a private one, and he had been accompanied by his family, it had not been viewed in that light upon his arrival. He had been accorded all of the protocol formality which he might have expected had he been there officially on behalf of the government as the designated representative of the President. He had been taken to see many things, he had been wined and dined, and he had been given a private meeting with the premier himself.

The American embassy had been a little disturbed by

that, but the senator had held the firm conviction in his mind that he could talk to any man on earth without fear, for his conscience had been clear.

The private conference with the premier had been in many ways a vindication of the principles upon which he stood. He relived it again now. Once more he was back in the warm informal room. In the middle was the table beautifully set with delicacies and three bottles of the one alcoholic beverage that he genuinely enjoyed. The premier himself was pouring the drinks; as they sat down together, apart from some language difficulties of a very minor sort they might have been two men of goodwill meeting anywhere in the world on a topic of common interest. Although the premier's command of English was incomplete, he spoke it well enough to make an interpreter unnecessary, a factor which helped to establish an aura of private mutual understanding.

It literally never occurred to the senator that the premises might be equipped with any kind of a listening device or that the words he spoke informally could be fed into a sensitive tape recorder.

The premier raised his glass. "To your visit to our country," he said.

"Thank you, sir," the senator responded, "and to the pleasure of being here."

"In these few private moments which we are having to share with each other," the premier continued, "there are many things we can to say."

"I agree, sir," Fitzhugh said. "But I must remind you that I am only one of one hundred senators, and the Senate itself is far from being the final authority in the legislative process."

The premier gave him a shrewd look. "What you say, it is true, but the reality—it is different. From the one hundred senators you are one of the most important. You have, what is it . . . ?"

"Seniority?"

"Yes, that is the word. We do not use it here. In fact, I will go further: your career, we have watched it for some time. I welcome you now as an important senator. I expect to welcome you before long another way—as the President of the United States."

Fitzhugh flushed—he could not help it. To every elected official of the government above a certain level that thought of the White House was at times unavoidable. Fitzhugh knew that he lacked the glamor sometimes thought necessary for the big job, but experience and sober counsel, plus his known dedication to keep the nation out of war, could have a tremendous voter appeal in times of stress and trial. "Keep our boys at home," could well be his campaign slogan. If he were to be called to that highest office, he would serve with unswerving devotion to duty, and there would truly be peace in his time.

The premier drew up a chair and sat down. With the care which befitted the dignity that might come to him, the senator also sat down and prepared to listen and to speak.

All that had followed he could not remember in total detail, only that he had upheld some specific ideas concerning which he had long been on the public record, and in turn the premier had been surprisingly frank about some of the internal matters within his own country. At one point he even had asked Fitzhugh for his advice and appeared to take deep note of the possible solution which had been presented to him. When at last they rose, the premier had made one final remark. "About our talk together I ask that you remember most one thing: there is no conflict between us simply because with different systems we are engaged. You do not desire our territory—we know this, it is elementary. And also you look first at the map of my country and you will then no problem have in believing that we are not desiring yours."

That had been a totally practical statement, and a delineation of policy which upheld every thesis that the senator had supported for years. He had shaken hands warmly with the premier and they had drunk a final toast together before the private conference was concluded.

From that meeting Fitzhugh had gone home with his last doubts dispelled and a reenforced dedication to the work which lay before him.

At sixty-two years of age he sat in his chair, the sharp memories still acid-fresh in his mind, trying to make the pieces fit together as he wanted them to. Political expediency, the need to hold his own job against a tidal wave of internal opposition, could explain the premier's astonishing change of attitude. The harsh, belligerent statements being made now simply did not fit with the man he had met and talked to in such a close and candid relationship. The refusal of Zalinsky to see him was a pinprick, brought on because the ridiculous administrator presently occupying the White House hadn't been told about the personal relationship between his premier and the man who had proposed to call on him. When he did find out, it would be an altogether different matter.

Then through the senator's sagging body an electric current of realization suddenly took hold; he physically responded and sat up straighter in his chair. All at once, in a sudden flash of inspiration, he saw the whole thing, he gulped in a deep lungful of air and marveled that it had taken him so long. His hands tightened, his jaw muscles started to work, and a fresh supply of adrenalin began to feed into his bloodstream. As the truth dawned, in its fresh strong light everything that had been troubling him so much stood clearly revealed. It all fitted together and it was right, as he knew it had to be. For the first time he understood what the premier had meant when he had said that he expected to welcome his senatorial guest back as President of the United States. Because now it could very well be.

He was so completely elated by his discovery of the truth that even the knowledge of his almost certain elevation to the presidency became secondary. The United States was not in any danger—it had never been. The premier was a man of great political sagacity; the whole world was aware of that. When he had taken office he had inherited a vast military machine, one which had been built up with almost ruthless singleness of purpose at the harsh expense of the civilian economy. And, most important, many of the men who had put the premier into power had been responsible for the almost intolerable burden of military costs.

That situation could not continue indefinitely, as the premier knew very well. Yet if he were to begin reducing the armed forces, as Fitzhugh himself had done, his supporters would have removed him without ceremony and installed someone else who would be more responsive to their wishes. Militarists were the same the world over.

Therefore the premier had made one of the boldest and

most astute political moves in world history. He had had his strategists map out the stunning surprise campaign which had brought down the United States literally before the Air Force planes could get off the ground or the ground combat units brought into effective action. Some people had died on both sides, but compared to the staggering toll a real world conflict would have entailed, losses had been slight. That eliminated the superpower against which the enormous military machine the premier controlled had been aimed. With the United States no longer in a provocative military posture, the need for the premier's armed might disappeared. The premier had been entirely truthful when he had said that his country did not desire to take over millions of square miles in America; the enormous territories he already controlled could supply all of his present and future needs for as far as any man could forecast.

The conquest of the United States had simply been a brilliant move to deny his own military establishment any further right to exist.

Japan had been conquered by the United States in a long and bloody conflict with intense hatreds generated on both sides. Yet after the peace had been signed, Japan had forged rapidly ahead in far better condition that if it had not been defeated in the first place. Now Japan and the United States were friendly powers, granted that restrictions had to be imposed to curtail low-priced imports from the Far East from entering the United States in sufficient quantity to compete effectively with the products of America's far more advanced economy.

The war, such as it had been, was over. Zalinsky was a brief stopgap and nothing more—a futile figurehead. After war comes peace, the inevitable meeting of the two sides to agree upon the terms of settlement. The President of the United States had, for all practical purposes, abandoned his office. Furthermore, he had never met the premier. But Senator Fitzhugh, who sometimes liked to think of himself in the third person, had. He was in Washington, and what was far more important, he was the undisputed leader of the peace movement in the United States government.

Then he knew. Within a few days time he would be sum-
premier again in Europe or even on American soil—it made
moned to speak for his country, for he alone knew the truth

as it had just been revealed to him. He might meet the no difference. Between them the artificial dispute would be settled with a proper show of mutual negotiation. The premier would emerge as the man who had conquered America and his position would be unassailable before his own people. He would sweep the militarists out, reduce his armed forces to token units, and get on with the rehabilitation and development of his civilian economy.

As the peacemaker, Fitzhugh knew, he himself would return home in triumph, revealed as the one man who had been right all along. After that his call to his country's highest office would be all but automatic. Solomon Fitzhugh, President of the United States. It had a fine ring to it, a ring of rightness.

Only one thing troubled him after that. When he had seen the premier for the first time he had hesitated to bring up the conspicuous anti-Semitic policies of his government—it had been at that time an internal matter affecting the premier's country only and an intrusion by an outsider might have destroyed the fine rapport which had been established.

The singling out of the Jews worried Fitzhugh. If it went on too long it could have serious consequences. On his next conference with the premier, whether it would be slightly awkward or not, he would have to bring it up. His only son was dating a Jewish girl, and while a marriage undoubtedly would not take place, she was a very nice young person, well-behaved, and deserved his protection.

For the past several weeks Hewlitt had had a growing sense of unreality. The Billiken in his mentality told him that there was no one named Zalinsky in the White House—that no such person would even be admitted to the grounds, and that the cloak and dagger atmosphere into which he had been casually wandering was a celluloid creation as unreal as the monsters in an amusement park go-cart ride.

But the fact remained that he was in a very real house, surrounded by actual people despite their difference in ethnic background, and that a code word he had been anxious to hear had just been spoken to him with unmistakable clarity.

The pieces were all there—it was the total that came out wrong.

Asher was an ancient name, one of the twelve tribes of Israel, but it was not common. The man before him was Asher, he had announced that, but he did not fit the image of Asher as he should have been.

Hewlitt looked at his glass to see how much he had drunk of his cocktail. "That's an unusual name," he said, sparring for time and more data.

"I thought that you might have heard it before," Frank answered.

Hewlitt saw the opening and took it. "I have, but I'm trying to remember where."

Frank took his time, sipping his drink with apparent concern. "Maybe from Major Landers," he said.

That, Hewlitt knew, was conclusive. That fact that he had known Frank for more than two years made it difficult to accept him in this new light; by logic and rights it should have been someone who normally would have been at a reasonably important echelon of the government.

"Forgive me," he said. "You surprised me, that's all."

Frank smiled. "Understood, Mr. Hewlitt, I don't blame you a bit. Take your time if you'd like."

"How did all this come about?" Hewlitt asked.

"Well, you remember my telling you that I had been a Marine once. I was well treated in the service and I liked the work. The way the cards came out I was assigned to intelligence and they found out that even if I didn't have much brains, at least I could keep my mouth shut."

He stopped to wave his glass in greeting at a newcomer who had just entered the room, then went back to his topic.

"It's a funny thing about cabdrivers, people almost never pay them any attention. They don't look at them, they don't remember their names, and sometimes they don't even know that they're there. And they always let you know where they're going, they have to do that. Remember that I told you too how people sometimes talk to cabdrivers when they're alone and ask them all sorts of things. An' one very important thing: a cabby in his hack can be anywhere at almost any time without people wonderin'. Night or day, a guy driving a cab isn't questioned; maybe he's on a call, or just dropped off a fare someplace. An' if he shows up when you want a ride, you don't ask him how he came to be there."

"Let me get this straight," Hewlitt said. "Are you a real taxi driver or aren't you? If not, you had me fooled."

"Oh, I'm real enough all right as far as it goes. When I'm not needed I hack like everybody else. But when they want me, I'm on call."

"How do you manage to pick up the right passengers, for example . . ."

Frank took a little more of his drink. "I don't think we need to get into all o' that," he said. "I'll give you a for instance: suppose I'm to pick up a certain guy at the Mayflower. A couple of the other guys are there too, just in case. I get in line, but not too far forward. Then just before the subject comes out, some of our people step up and take the hacks ahead of me. That's one way. But like I said, you don't need to worry about all that. The point is, there's work to be done now."

Hewlitt took a long pull at his own drink. "Do you believe Davy's statement that this house is completely safe?" he asked.

"Bank on it, Davy is one of the boys—which is one reason you're here tonight. An' this isn't an ordinary house—it belongs to the Agency. It's been fixed up with a lot of hidden equipment so that if anyone monkeys with it, we know it right away."

"Does Davy actually live here?"

"Yep, and he makes sure that things are in order. Like me he's got protective coloration, so not many people are willing to believe that he's bright. You can take it from me that he is."

Hewlitt felt a developing sense of interest, even excitement. He believed what he had been told, and he had heard enough to be convinced that Frank was all he claimed to be. He had wanted action; now there were greatly improved prospects of getting it. He had always liked Frank; already he began to feel a certain kinship with him despite the differences in their backgrounds.

"What do I do now?" he asked.

"I was just comin' to that," Frank said. "I've got some orders for you. From up above. Major Landers told you that there's an organization."

"Yes, but for a while I wondered about it."

"You can stop wonderin'. There's a real good one and

it's run by pros; they know exactly what they're doin'. Are you ready?"

"Go."

"All right. First off, you aren't to do anything on your own, no matter how good it looks to you at the time. Bob Landers did and he fell inta a trap. You know what happened."

"Do you know what it was?"

"Right now, no, but we found out that he walked into a setup. So don't do nothin' on your own, nothin' at all. Until you get the word from me."

"If anything happens to you?"

"You'll be contacted. And when it's the right guy, you'll know for sure. If there's any doubt, any at all, don't bite."

"O.K."

"Next, no matter how good somebody looks, don't do any recruiting, leave that to us; most of the people we want are already picked and set up. Some of 'em know it; some don't yet."

"What can I do?"

"Several things. First, keep datin' Barbara—that's important. An' it shouldn't be too hard to take."

"Not at all."

"Good enough, she's a real smart girl. What we want you most for right now is a listenin' post. You got that new job right next to Mr. Z and we want to keep you there. So keep your nose real clean; do what he says. Sure as hell they're goin' to push somethin' under your nose; don't try to run with the ball, but don't play stupid either, 'cause they know you aren't. Just try to imagine that you're strictly on your own, against them, but a little scared because of the Landers thing. If you play stupid, they'll be on to you right then."

That was good advice and Hewlitt knew it.

"Whatever comes your way," Frank continued, "you pass on to me, or if you can't, give it to Barbara. Mostly, though, she and Mary will be feeding you. You know what the word 'control' means in this business?"

"Vaguely."

"Well, I'm your control, which means that I give the orders, I pick up your info and, if it comes to that, I look after you if I can. Nobody else, not even Davy, if I go under. If that happens, hang on tight and someone'll get to you. Right now you can trust Barbara, Mary, Davy, and me, later you'll get a couple more."

"It sounds as though I'm going to be the cell leader."

"No, Barbara is, but you're the contact man because it's a lot easier than to have me seein' a white girl all the time. She's got the experience, so she calls the signals, but you work with me."

"How do we do that?"

"You follow my lead. Never talk to me, no matter what, unless I ask you first if Barbara's given in yet. If'n I do, that means that it's safe. Because of the way we had to set this up, Barbara knows who I am; we've worked together before. But the others don't and you die before you tell 'em, you got that?"

Hewlitt digested the words. "Clearly," he answered. He was beginning to believe in this man.

"All right," Frank said. He rose to his feet and Hewlitt got up with him. "Don't be surprised," Frank said when they were standing together, "if Barbara and her friend move in here after a little while."

"In this neighborhood?"

"About the best place for it," Frank answered. "We're goin' to turn this into a real nice whorehouse."

CHAPTER EIGHT

The following thirty days were the most traumatic in the history of the United States of America. It had faced disaster, civil war, and Pearl Harbor—even the divisive agony of the Vietnam war—but never before the galling indignity of defeat. The belief that had persisted at first—that the country would somehow extricate itself from its unexpected, awkward embarrassment, died under a series of events which fell like hammer blows throughout every part of the nation. Each day dozens of flights from overseas terminated at major airports with pay loads of up to four hundred of the enemy—troops, administrators, censors, secret police, and even scientists to take over existing plants and facilities. In a few places people resisted; they were ruthlessly pushed aside and were lucky if they escaped with their lives. Some did not.

It came as a bitter shock to most Americans when a swift and tight control was clamped on all forms of news dissemination. This was something almost impossible for a free people to understand, even for those comparative few who had visited East Berlin and had had to surrender every scrap of paper which might bear tidings of the West before being permitted to pass into the Communist-controlled portion of the city. Such isolation might be the unfortunate lot of certain other peoples, but it had been inconceivable that it could happen to the citizens of the greatest nation on earth.

The news vacuum was filled by an undisciplined mass of rumors which scurried back and forth like a maze of molecular particles. Some were cautious, but most were fearful, wild, irrational, frightful, uncertain, terrifying, fanciful, and at times distorted beyond any hope of reality. In mid-America the report was rife that the granaries would be rapidly emptied for shipment of their contents overseas and that severe rationing would face the American public during the winter to come.

The news blackout was followed by sharp restrictions on travel; flights from one part of the country to another were permitted only after specific permission had been granted for each individual trip. The commercial airlines reduced their schedules to the minimum, but the larger aircraft still flew half empty. Enemy uniforms began to appear everywhere while the now controlled radio and television stations constantly warned that any attempt whatsoever to impede the actions of the men who wore them would be severely punished.

For the first time in living memory Americans were forced to keep their women at home and out of sight. It all became part of the larger picture, the still incredible circumstance that the nation had been defeated—that an aggressor had been able to impose his will by force of arms, and that the decimated military of the United States had not been equal to the challenge. It had happened before in world history to many different countries and peoples, but never to the land of the free and the home of the brave, the land of Patrick Henry, of Ethan Allen, Thomas Jefferson, John Hancock, Abraham Lincoln, Theodore Roosevelt, and Harry S. Truman. The nation desperately wanted a leader who could do something about all this, but no such man appeared. The President was somewhere out of sight for his own protection and safety, but in the cold gray light of this disastrous dawn he was seen revealed as a choice of political expediency, adequate to do a satisfactory job, but far from the man that the country so urgently needed.

In a few places individual Americans remembered the time that a retired admiral had had his say before a congressional committee, but he was dead. The citizens of the United States had only one choice open to them, and that was to do as they were told.

Of all the Americans in this plight, those who had the greatest cause for concern were Jewish. Some few of them who still bore tattooed numbers on their forearms were bitter to the point of denouncing life itself and asked their God what they had ever done in their history as a people to deserve this deadly final blow. Some found no answer and quietly took their own lives; double suicides by elderly couples whose children had married and moved away passed unnoticed by the limited, tightly censored, daily press.

There were others who viewed the new policy as a heaven-sent opportunity to escape from the grasp of a vicious enemy known to be anti-Semitic long before the beginning of the period of goodwill which had immediately preceded the sudden outbreak of the war.

At Kennedy International Airport the employees of the largest American overseas airline were doing their best to handle the tide of passengers. Yiddish-speaking personnel were pressed into emergency service when it was discovered that many of those going abroad had never learned the English language.

Most of the passengers booking during the first thirty days were only too glad to leave behind a country which had suddenly shifted from one where certain restrictions still existed in a few areas to one wherein anyone born a Jew might well be in growing peril of his life.

In the hastily constructed lounge for departing refugees the scene brought back memories of train terminals during World War II. People slept, babies cried, mothers changed diapers without worrying whether they and their infants were on public view or not. Some complained and a few demanded; the majority simply waited for the opportunity to climb on board an aircraft, occasionally feeling again the slight bulge on their persons where they had their extra money concealed. As far as was known, no one had as yet been subject to search.

Threading their way through the several hundred waiting people were three individuals in a little group who were trying their best to make a systematic circuit of the whole area. Very little attention was paid to them; those who were nearby sensed that they were not Jewish and in view of the circumstances which prevailed, slightly resented their presence. Despite the fact that all of the people who were ticketed for overseas were leaving on their own volition, a tight sense of suppressed misery could almost be felt in the air. They were going, but they were not happy, even those who had relatives waiting to greet them and make them feel welcome. Some few of them had relatives waiting ready to tell them that they were not wanted and that

God only knew how they were to be taken care of or housed.

The public address system came on with the announcement that the 747 was still in the hands of maintenance and hopefully would be released within the hour. The announcement created little stir. Despite the fact that scheduled airline operations had been cut back to a bare minimum, the aircraft shortage was drastic because of the enemy's appropriation of almost all of the long-range equipment.

Mrs. Sarah Rappaport eyed the cruising trio and hoped that she would not be disturbed by its members, whatever it was that they were doing. She was fully occupied, in her mind at least, by taking care of little David, aged seven, and Marsha, who was two. She was booked for the flight out on the urgent advice of her husband who, heaven knew, was a genius. From a humble beginning in the Bronx he had moved ahead so fast on Wall Street that he was already in the research department of one of the biggest brokerage houses in the country. Danny Rappaport was smart, everyone who knew him agreed on that, and when Danny had told her that the sooner she got out of the country with the kids the better, she had had no choice but to follow his direction. She did not wish to leave; she wanted to remain to enjoy the rich, if strictly Jewish, social life that she was enjoying on a neighborhood level. The money that Danny was beginning to make had elevated her position somewhat and she was human and feminine enough to like it. Now it all had to be thrown away because the government had fouled things up again. With a Jewish President, maybe, it wouldn't have happened; he would have been smarter.

Over the transatlantic telephone Danny had made all of the arrangements. Old Morris Rappaport had not been too enthusiastic, but he had reluctantly agreed to look after Sarah and the children until Danny could join them. Danny would stay as long as he felt he could despite the fact that the market was all but closed down; he was making money giving advice to people and as long as he could do that he was going to stay on the job. No, he had told old Morris, he wasn't taking any chances, it was just that every day he could stay on the street he would make that much more money, and in view of the uncertainty ahead, every bit of it might be needed to tide them over until they could come back safely once more. Then, if he had enough left, he would consider opening his own firm.

"Pardon me."

Sarah looked up and stiffened a little; the three people were beside her and since the man had spoken, she could not ignore them.

"What is it?" she asked. She looked at the man and decided that he was not bright. His straw-colored hair was brushed back in a way that a clever businessman would have avoided; the open features of his face were not smooth and urbane like her Danny. His suit was ready-made and had cost only about sixty-five dollars. He was a schlemiel.

"I'm Reverend Jones," the man said, "from the Church of the Little Shepherd. This is my wife Doris and our son Greg."

Mrs. Rappaport took a single searching look at the Reverend Mr. Jones' wife and decided that you get what you pay for. "So what are you wanting?"

"We're here to help if we can." He motioned toward the tray of sandwiches his wife was carrying. "If you're hungry, please help yourself. Greg has some coffee. It isn't as hot as it was, but it's still warm if you'd like some."

"How much does it cost?"

"It's free—please take what you want."

Her deeply rooted suspicion of strangers purporting to offer something for nothing seized hold of Mrs. Rappaport and warned her; if she took anything she would have to pay for it one way or another—they might even force her to listen while they read to her from the New Testament. Nobody gave anything away for free. If he had been a rabbi she would have believed in him, but a minister—no.

She shook her head that she wanted none of it and turned her attention back to her children. These people could do as they liked. She, her Danny, and their children had been virtually cast out. Hatred of the injustice swelled within her and she slammed her mind shut as an act of pure self-defense.

For all of his visible lack of sophistication, the Reverend Mr. Jones understood and led his small family to the next group of refugees. This time it was a man and a woman with a single small girl who looked up at him with deep sad eyes. He repeated his little speech of introduction while his wife held out the tray of sandwiches.

"Is your church doing this, reverend," the man asked, "or is it the airline?"

"It's our church. We're not too far away and we wanted to help if we could."

The man stood up and shook hands with the minister. "I'm Jack Bornstein, reverend. My wife Hazel, and Molly."

The Jones family acknowledged the Bornsteins while Greg took his cue and poured out two cups of lukewarm coffee.

"You know, this is damn decent of you," Bornstein said. "Our position is rather awkward at the moment because of our religious faith, and a helping hand like this is certainly appreciated."

"That's what we're here for," Jones responded. "It isn't a matter of religion, it's simply human decency. You've been hit by a misfortune that's not your fault, so this is little enough."

Bornstein chose a sandwich. "We're going to England if we can until this thing blows over," he said. "We thought of Israel, but if we went there Molly would have to learn Hebrew and they might indoctrinate her more than we would like. In England she can at least speak her own language."

Jones nodded. "That's a wise decision, I think. I've never been there, but we were Welsh originally, so I feel we have some roots there."

Bornstein looked around the large lobby and seemed to be forming some conclusion in his mind. "Let me ask you something," he said. "From your viewpoint, how long do you think that this thing is going to last?"

"That's terribly hard to say," the minister replied. "I don't have any special sources of information. It might be as much as a year—I really don't know. These people are so hard to understand. The next thing, they may shut down all of the houses of worship. If they do, then I don't know how I'll support my family. My work doesn't pay very much, but it's enough for us, and the ministry is what I want. I guess I could become a teacher."

Bornstein laughed. "You came pretty close; I'm in education myself—or I was. But get on with your good work. If we meet again, and I hope that we do, well . . ." He did not finish the sentence; he could not find the words he wanted. Once more the men shook hands before the Reverend Mr. Jones and his little family continued on their slow rounds of the lounge.

Some forty minutes later there was a brief but disturbing scene. At the far end of the lounge a man jumped to his feet, exclaimed something in a loud voice, and then viciously slammed one of the last of the free sandwiches into the Reverend Mr. Jones' face. The boy Greg doubled his fists and jumped forward to do battle, but his father restrained him. The minister inhaled a very deep breath and then regained control of himself as he let it out slowly. "Come on, son," he said. "Forgive him. It was our fault; we should have known better than to bring any ham."

His complexion red, but his head high, he quietly walked out, followed by his enraged, frustrated son, and his patient wife who was openly in tears.

At the Hunters Point Naval Shipyard the nuclear-powered *Poseidon*-firing submarine, the U.S.S. *Ramon Magsaysay*, lay in her berth, a warship of enormous sophistication and firepower, in the hands of the enemy.

She was brand new, commissioned, but not yet the veteran of even a single tour of duty at sea. The *Magsaysay* was richly loaded with classified materiel and had a nuclear power plant which the enemy would find highly informative when the original work of occupation had been completed and attention could be turned to the milking of the vast American industrial capacity. Meanwhile she was under heavy guard and totally devoid of any of the provisions which would be essential for her to go to sea. Guarded as she was, and stripped of all of her essential supplies, she was as helpless as though she had been embalmed in some gigantic cube of transparent plastic.

With a certain sadistic satisfaction it pleased the enemy to allow three or four junior officers without submarine experience to maintain the pretext that she was still in United States hands. The sharp frustration of fighting men in being forced to pretend on powerless watches, on the deck of an impotent ship which had cost the United States multiple millions to construct, afforded amusement to the commander assigned by the enemy to control and oversee the former United States defense facility. Americans, he knew, were basically inept, granting that they had a flair for technology and had had the extraordinary good fortune to be able to put men on the moon before anyone else. A precious lot of good it would do them now.

The *Magsaysay* was the first of a new, ultra-advanced series which had proven too much even for the people who had designed and built her; the shakedown sea tests had turned up a multitude of problems which it would have taken six months to put in order if the Americans had been left alone to do the job by themselves. They would fix her all right, but they would put her in shape to join the already mighty fleet that had helped to bring about their swift downfall.

As soon as the *Magsaysay* was finally ready she would be sailed away to her new destiny, but not before she had been renamed. And the new name she would be given would not please the Americans, not one little bit.

At shortly after eight-thirty on a Monday morning, while low-lying fog still obscured much of the local area, a workman who clearly disliked his assignment applied for a pass at the main gate. His qualifications as a technician were limited, but he possessed sufficient ability to do the electrical repair and modification work for which he had been recruited from one of the suppliers of the *Magsaysay*'s equipment. He was precisely the type and kind of man the new chief of security for the naval facility wanted—resentful, but frightened enough to obey orders without question to save his own skin; capable of doing the work expected of him, but not advanced enough to do any dangerous improvising. He was kept waiting an hour and a half while he was checked out and his background verified. After that he was made to strip to the skin and both his person and clothing were thoroughly searched.

When the routine had been completed he was assigned a number, given a biting two-minute lecture on the penalty for the slightest infraction of the rules and shown the muzzle of a gun, in order that he would be fully impressed with what he was being told. He grew red and cringed at the same time, which was the psychologically desirable reaction; the security chief who had watched the process through a one-way mirror signaled that he was to be admitted. By phone the chief of the guards on board the *Magsaysay* was told to expect him.

Obviously uncomfortable, the middle-aged man started out to find the ship, inquired twice for directions, and at last located her berth. He crossed the brow onto her deck and was intercepted by a lieutenant junior grade, who had the mock position of being the Officer of the Day.

"Who are you?" the OD demanded. He was fighting his own private war; whatever they did to him, and to the ship under his feet, he was an officer of the United States Navy and he was damn well going to show every enemy son-of-a-bitch who might be watching how such a man conducted himself.

The workman dug his credentials out of his pocket and showed them. "Summers," he said.

The lieutenant scanned the pass and the letter of authorization, wondering to himself as he did so how an American, any American, could so lower himself as to help the enemy take over the property of the United States government. "All right," he said, with cold contempt.

"How do I get in?" Summers asked. The lieutenant pointed toward the hatch, not wanting to speak unless he had to.

Summers took the direction without comment, put the papers away, and then painfully climbed down through the indicated opening.

Operation Low Blow had begun.

In his cell at the federal penitentiary at Leavenworth, Kansas, Erskine Wattles, black ultramilitant, was desperately impatient. He had fought and fought hard for this day and he was anxious for his reward.

The people who had now taken over the country *had* to know who he was and where he was to be found. He had met with them or their representatives on many occasions; they had given him much encouragement and some money. They had also promised him, in a rather vague manner, that if he helped in certain directions, he would rise to a position of great power and importance. Power had been the magic word; he had savored it and hung onto it, and dreamed of the day when he would be mighty in the land.

To symbolize the new power that would be his he rose to his feet and looked about his narrow cell with the feeling that he was a great man whose very thoughts would burst the walls that held him captive. He strode the two or three steps permitted him by the stones and the bars, then turned and strode the other way, trying to ignore the blood-boiling frustration of the limited space at his disposal. In the upper bunk he saw the inert back of his cellmate, an unimaginative rapist who had gotten horny and dragged a thirteen-year-old girl across a state line. He was stupid, and despite the fact that he was black, Wattles hated him.

He did not want to take hold of the bars to feel his own strength, because to do that would be to acknowledge their existence and the fact that they held him prisoner. He would *not* be kept in prison; every minute of his time was vitally important to his future plans. And for every bit of time that he was held back, those who had put him here would pay with their life's blood when he became dictator.

No one but a black man could run the country, and he knew that he had been chosen. He was the leader; he had proven that the first time he had organized a celebration in honor of the anniversary of the death of the black traitor to his people, Martin Luther King. He had made a speech that had rocked the whole nation that day, and they surely knew who he was after that.

With the Weathermen he had helped to lead the attack on the colleges and universities; he alone had closed a campus of the University of California for weeks and had kept hundreds of advanced degree candidates from graduating. At the time of his proposed induction into the armed forces he had provoked and led a riot which had put more than thirty people into the hospital, a lot of them pigs. He loved that word—pigs—he had shouted it, screamed it, made it synonymous in the minds of most of the black people for any kind of policeman or any member of the armed forces.

He had been in all of the big ones—the Watts riot, the Chicago Democratic convention, the peace marches, the campus blow-offs. The only man who had been ahead of him, and that was because he was a big name singer, was Orberg. But Orberg had never had the nerve in court to leap onto the bench and punch a federal judge's face with his thumbs out and hard enough to blind him permanently in one eye. He and he alone had been able to do that. And every sick pig in the country had been afraid of the name of Wattles that day and they were still afraid. Because he was coming out now and when he hit the street, the whole world was going to be his.

His sharp lawyer, a Jew named Wolpert, had gotten him out on bail for another appeal. Wolpert had pleaded that his client had been under the effect of drugs, to which he had been addicted for years, and therefore was a sick man. Because his lawyer had told him to, he, Erskine Wattles, had hung his head and playacted, and had gotten out on bail that a lot of protesters had put up because he was their great hero.

He had had it made then except for the lousy Korean pig. Who in hell expects a Korean to be on an airplane anyway! His gun had scared every lily white bastard to death and they were already over the water on the way to Cuba when the Korean pig had had to go to the can. He had let him, and for thanks the pig had jumped him with his goddamned karate or something, mocking the authority of his gun, and the pilot had turned back toward the mainland.

Mao had said that power came from the barrel of a gun, and he knew that that was right, only the frigging Korean pig that he had been nice to had betrayed him. And now he was in this goddamned hole, waiting to get out and dying every minute that he wasn't out and tasting the power that he had been promised. For a month the pigs had been eating dirt and nobody had come for him yet. When they did, he'd show them who was the big man! He rushed to the bars of his cell, grabbed them hard in his powerful hands, and yelled at the top of his lungs, "PIGS! PIGS! PIGS!"

During the month that he had been on his new job Hewlitt had learned a great deal. With the initial shock of the conquest over and dissipated, the remaining members of the White House staff had settled down to what was substantially a waiting game. Cedric Culp, the former press aide of the President, was now doing the same job for Zalinsky; in addition he was an active member of the underground cell. Both Barbara and Mary remained on the roster, and there were now three others. The orders routed through Frank had been specific: wait. Pick up any available information, report it through channels, but take no individual actions without direction. All of them had played the game exactly that way, but Hewlitt could not help wondering from time to time how much his colleagues would be influenced if they knew that the directions which he was faithfully passing on to them were being routed through a Negro taxicab driver.

However, if it seemed hard to credit at times, that was all to the good, because it would confuse the enemy even more. "Protective coloration" was the phrase that Frank had used, and it was valid.

The one most encouraging thing was the knowledge that something *was* being done. Hewlitt was satisfied as to that. You had to believe in something, he told himself, and wondered if the day would come when Frank's invisible boss would establish a direct contact.

The intercom light went on, indicating that Zalinsky wished to see him. He picked up paper and pencil as always, if for no other reason than to cover the fact of his well-trained memory, and went into the Oval Office. Zalinsky worked with his coat off a good part of the time now, and while Hewlitt was not privy to much that crossed the administrator's desk, he was aware from the man's general manner that not everything was going as he would have liked.

"Sit down," Zalinsky said.

"Yes, Mr. Zalinsky." He sat in the usual place and waited.

The administrator looked at him. "Why for is it that always you say the same thing to me?"

"Because that was your order," Hewlitt answered. "You said that you were to be addressed in no other way. Major Barlov said it too."

Zalinsky brushed a hand through the air. "It will be changed, I am not so anxious that I hear the sound of my own name all the time. I do not like it that much."

Hewlitt debated his next question before he put it, but he wanted to measure the reaction. "Speaking of names, do you have a first name? You must, but no one seems to know what it is."

"It is Feodor," Zalinsky said, "but, like you, I do not use it. I now ask you something: you read our language, you must have read some of our propaganda."

"A lot of it. It was my job."

"But you are not yet convinced that we are right?"

"No."

"Why not?"

"Because your system doesn't work."

"It worked well enough that we won the war."

"You won it," Hewlitt said, "by deceit."

Zalinsky smiled. "That is part of the system."

"I shall remember that," Hewlitt told him. "You wanted to see me."

Zalinsky moved his hands on the top of his desk. "I have an embarrassment," he said. "It is because of your Senator Fitzhugh. You are knowing him?"

"I have never met the senator," Hewlitt said.

Zalinsky ignored the response. "The senator, he is a fool. He has now written a letter to our premier that is a nuisance to him. This Fitzhugh, he proposes to make peace for the United States."

"On his own?" Hewlitt asked.

"I do not understand."

"I mean, does he propose to make peace all by himself? Does he mean to speak for the President and the whole country?"

"President you have not," Zalinsky said. "He has made himself absent and I sit here in his place. But yes, it is that Fitzhugh sees himself that he is now the person to speak for the country."

"I doubt that," Hewlitt said.

Zalinsky leaned back. "It is good that you say that, because it is that I wish you to see him. I do not want to having him here, I have no time for him. But you go, you explain."

"Explain what, Mr. Zalinsky?"

"You have not stupidness, you should understand. This Senator Fitzhugh, he believes that he remains a fragment of the government. He does not understand that he is now nothing. He is allowed that he sits in his office, but he is playing with shadows."

"What you want me to do is to tell him that he's through."

"Exactness. Also, please explain to him that he was granted interview because we wanted him to make a bigger face, as say the Chinese, and become reelected. That is absolutely all."

Hewlitt pressed his lips together and thought for a moment. "If you want me to talk to him, Mr. Zalinsky, I will—of course. I suspect that it will make him . . . I mean, it will break him up completely."

"It is overdue that he think badly of himself. Please to do this."

Hewlitt made an unnecessary note on the pad before him. "I'll call the senator immediately for an appointment," he said. "He will probably keep me waiting for a day or two; it's usual."

Zalinsky shrugged. "Only please to make it clear to him that he is not to annoy our premier with any more letters. If he does, we may have to take his toys away from him."

"I'll make it clear," Hewlitt promised.

He was on his way from his office to the West Gate when a man he did not know fell in step beside him. He was a youngish type in Air Force uniform. He wore the twin bars of a captain, a rank of minimum importance in the military environment of Washington. "You're Hewlitt, I believe," he said.

Hewlitt looked at his unexpected companion and nodded.

"I'm Phil Scott," the captain said. "Please, may I come by and see you about six-thirty? I know where."

"O.K.," Hewlitt said. He lifted his left arm, looked at the dial of his watch, and gave the exact time as he had it to the captain. Scott took off his own watch and made a pretext of resetting it. They went through the check-out gate one behind the other, then Hewlitt climbed into Frank's waiting cab and was driven out into the traffic as usual. He did not look behind him to see what the captain had done or where he had gone.

Frank bent down and turned on the radio, keeping the volume reasonably low. "Might be something on the news," he explained. "I'm kinda lookin'."

"Good," Hewlitt said.

"Your girl friend come through yet?" Frank asked.

"I want to ask about an Air Force captain," Hewlitt said. "His name is Scott, Phil Scott. I don't know him, although I've seen him around once or twice. He came up to me just as I was leaving and asked to see me this evening at six-thirty. He said that he knew where I lived."

Frank guided the car through an intersection. "Don't know him offhand, but I'll try and find out. If he's comin' by at six-thirty, that looks like dinner, doesn't it?"

"Yes, I guess so, unless it's a short visit over a drink."

Frank devoted himself to his driving for a minute or two. "You know that Chinese restaurant near where you live?"

"Sure, I eat there every now and then."

"Suppose you go there to eat tonight if he's with you. If I find out anythin' in time, I'll get word to you."

"You could phone me," Hewlitt suggested. "Tell me that you may not be able to pick me up in the morning if anything's wrong. If not, give me any other kind of message."

"O.K. If I find out anythin' in time; it's pretty short and I may not be able to get hold o' my boss."

"Do what you can," Hewlitt said. "I'll play it cozy in the meanwhile."

"That's the word," Frank said. The news broadcast began, but if there was any significant item on the air, Hewlitt did not recognize it as such. When they pulled up in front of his apartment Frank spoke a formal good night and drove away.

His guest arrived within two minutes of the appointed time. Hewlitt welcomed him and gestured toward his small portable bar. Captain Scott, still in uniform and immaculately so, bent instead over the stereo component equipment installed at one end of the room. "I'm interested in this stuff," he said. "Could I hear it play?"

"Of course." Before Hewlitt could turn on the set himself Scott did so. The sound came on at once, the Tchaikovsky Fourth Symphony in the middle of the second movement. Scott set the volume at a slightly uncomfortably high level, but one which did reveal the system at its best. Then he spoke quietly to Hewlitt. "That's the best cover that I know for listening devices," he said. "After what happened to us, I don't take any chances anywhere."

"Don't blame you," Hewlitt agreed. He made two drinks

at his small bar and placed one of them in his guest's hand. "What can I do for you?" he asked.

Scott sampled his drink and approved of it. "Before that, let me introduce myself a little more. I'm simply an Air Force type a little like Bob Landers was, only not so much so—I'll never be as good a man as he was."

Hewlitt's mnemonic memory functioned and a near-forgotten item came back to him. "I think I know you—aren't you the officer who claimed Bob's body and arranged for burial in Arlington?"

"That's right," Scott said. "I think they'd have left him there to rot. Anyhow, he rated Arlington as much as anyone, and that's where he is. It wasn't a solo operation, though, I had a lot of help from some other guys."

"I'm glad to buy you a drink," Hewlitt responded. "How about having dinner with me? There's a little Chinese place near here—not the greatest, but the food's not bad and there's quite a bit of privacy. I doubt like hell that it's bugged."

"Probably not," Scott agreed. "Percentagewise, it wouldn't be worth it. But let it be a dutch treat; I'd like it better that way."

The symphony paused in midflight as the movement ended and a few seconds of silence followed while the announcer turned over the record. Then the familiar work resumed once more.

"You're still wearing your uniform," Hewlitt said. "Do you think that's a good idea?"

"Damn right. In the first place, no one's told me not to, either them or my military superiors. Secondly, we're in a time of war."

"Technically, the war's over." Hewlitt probed carefully.

"Not for me it isn't. We haven't officially surrendered, and unless I'm completely off, we're not going to. Maybe you think that I'm a dreamer, but old Ho Chi Minh, who's roasting somewhere in hell right now, beat the French and even gave us a hard time in a limited action."

"Yes, but he had both communist China and Russia behind him at the time."

"True, but what were his resources otherwise? We've got resources, and I'd like to think that we have some people with brains and spirit."

Hewlitt looked across the room to where a clock rested on the mantel. "How about getting something to eat?" he proposed. "We can talk better sitting down. The place is usually pretty uncrowded at this hour, we ought to be able to be strictly by ourselves."

"Fine, let's go. I haven't had any Chinese food in months."

Hewlitt lingered for another two or three minutes hoping that his phone would ring, but it remained inert. Then he ushered his guest out and fell in beside him for the short walk to the restaurant. By unexpressed common consent, they kept their conversation entirely neutral.

They were received upon arrival by the same quiet headwaiter who, without being asked, showed them to a booth which offered a maximum of privacy. He put down two menus, wished them a pleasant dinner, and left without further comment.

They were well into their meal before Scott brought up the thing that was on his mind. "Look," he began, "I'm going on the assumption, and I consider it a damn safe one, that you're a solid citizen. I have the word that you were tapped by Zalinsky to sit at his right hand, but that you never bent an inch in his direction."

"I've tried not to," Hewlitt said.

"All right. Now just for the sake of argument, suppose that a bunch of Americans who don't have any ax to grind apart from the fact that they are loyal to their country and what it used to stand for were to try to organize something. How would you feel about that?"

Hewlitt already knew what he was going to say when that question came. "I'd certainly wish them well; that goes without saying. At the same time I'd have to regard it as a damn dangerous game. Basically we can't get away from one thing: we had our whole Air Force, plus the Army, the Navy, and the Marine Corps. With all of this, and our whole industrial capacity completely at our disposal, we took a licking. How can we hope to reverse all that by, say, an underground guerrilla organization?"

Scott was thoughtful. "We weren't licked, Hew, you know that; we were tricked. The Orberg decision took away the power of the draft while all kinds of people kept telling us that patriotism was out of date and that we were fools to salute when the flag went by. Remember Wattles, the black militant? He eventually went to prison, but not for his basic crime—trying to tear down his own nation. And there was old stonehead—Fitzhugh. Perhaps we had too much freedom—and we abused it. Abused it enough to con ourselves right out of our security; all that they did was to take advantage of our weakness. Granted that they helped it along with their undermining, bugging, and all that."

"It's your thought, then, that if an underground were to be organized, it would be able to operate without all of these drawbacks?"

"Of course, but that's only a small part of it. We've got an immense country here and a couple of hundred million people who don't like the way that things have turned out. They're bound to do something eventually."

Hewlitt pushed his plate aside. "I've got to agree with that," he said. "Only I'm afraid that they could get terribly hurt in the process."

"True," Scott responded. "Probably a lot of people would be shot as Bob Landers was, but that's the price we're stuck with for having let our guard down."

He stopped when the waiter approached the booth. The man cleared away the used dishes, wiped the table, and set down a fresh pot of tea. In front of each of them he put a tiny plate with a fortune cookie and then withdrew.

Hewlitt had used the time to think. He had no intention of revealing to Scott even by the vaguest hint that such an organization did, in fact, exist, but he did not know how to break off the conversation without committing himself in one way or another. He poured himself some fresh tea. As Scott did the same he broke open his fortune cookie and extracted the tiny slip of paper which promised to reveal his destiny. In red typewritten characters he read: *Do not trust. Believe dangerous. Asher.*

CHAPTER NINE

From the day that his supposed death had been made public, Admiral Barney Haymarket had been by his own order a literal prisoner in the underground complex of Thomas Jefferson. He longed to go outside, to walk for an hour through the rough mountain country, to drink in the beauty of the sky, the land, and the air; but remote as the region was, the chance existed that he might encounter someone who would recognize him or wonder who he was and what he was doing there. That minimal risk could be avoided at a cost; without a second thought the admiral paid the price. He was asking, and would ask, far more of others.

As a substitute he paid a daily visit to the little gymnasium which had been set up, took a rubdown, and, if he had time, spent a few minutes with a putter and two or three golf balls on the carpet in his quarters. The admiral had never done anything by halves; he applied that principle in working to improve his game. Each night he slept six or seven hours if the situation permitted; the rest of the time he was on duty, turning the full scope of his abilities onto the fiendishly difficult problem with which he was confronted. It was characteristic of him that he did not allow it to oppress him; he remained alert and confident, a skilled commander engaged professionally in the greatest campaign of his career.

At the admiral's expressed wish the other members of the First Team also remained close to the operating base. He wanted an absolute minimum of traffic of any kind to and from the facility; when the time came to move he would approve it, until then secrecy had to remain as close to absolute as possible.

He had been extraordinarily careful about that. The blasting crews who had made the original excavation had also prepared several others which had been subsequently listed as "abandoned." A massive amount of paperwork had been prepared and planted in the classified files to indicate that the entire job had been part of another canceled project, given up after millions had been invested in its development. There were even more than two hundred letters on file in case anyone authorized or in a position to do so decided to go through all of the correspondence. Not far from the concealed entrance there was a landing strip made of natural materials and so artfully concealed that an unsuspecting hunter could walk right across it without being aware that it was there.

The entrance itself was camouflaged as an abandoned mine shaft crudely boarded up and with a warning sign which, while apparently badly weather-beaten, was still clearly legible. There were also some loose strands of barbed wire to discourage the inquisitive. If anyone persisted beyond this point, delicate and invisible electronic equipment would report his presence immediately.

At the morning conference which he had called the admiral was, as always, brisk, efficient, and confident. "All right, gentlemen," he began when everyone was present, "it's time to compare notes. Stan, you first."

Stanley Cumberland, the retired industrialist, wore an alleged sports jacket which had been conservatively cut to fit his narrow, six-foot-three frame. His lean, austere features suggested the Great Stone Face; there were those who had paid dearly for the privilege of learning that they were part of the equipment of one of the greatest poker players in recorded history. Not on visible display was a brilliant intelligence coupled with a profound knowledge of mechanics and ways of getting things done. Few people would have dared to call him Stan; the admiral did and Cumberland felt honored.

"Operation Low Blow is on schedule," Cumberland reported. "They are watching the *Magsaysay* very closely but we are watching them."

"Good," the admiral said. "How about the supply problem?"

"We're working on that. The first job was to find a suitable vessel; we finally have one. She is a great big, lumbering old fishing craft designed to go to sea and to stay out there for long periods of time. I'm sure you know, sir, that the fishing industry is not being interfered with in any way —at least not until now. When the Nazis were in control of Europe they permitted fishing operations even out of the French ports opposite the channel for the sake of the food produced. I suspect that for the next six months, at least, fishing operations will be allowed to continue. After that we won't be concerned."

"How about getting the necessary quantities of supplies?" the Marine major asked. "It may be a little tough getting our hands on what we'll need without attracting attention."

"That's being attended to," Cumberland answered him. "We were able to get hold of a very good man in the ship supply field. He has laid out a plan of action and will put it into operation as soon as we're ready."

The former high diver, whose muscular development was the envy of all present, was also carefully weighing the factors involved. "Where is our fishing vessel home ported?" he asked.

"At the moment San Pedro, but when we have completed taking her over she will be able to show up almost anywhere that there's a fish market without any questions being raised. If we have to, we can shift the price structure a little to make San Francisco her obvious destination."

The admiral smiled his approval of that. "A little manipulation of that kind may be right in order. Next, turning to the *Magsaysay* herself, let's have a crew report."

Major Theodore Pappas, USMC, responded. He opened a folder in front of him with his good hand and then spoke in a clear, decisive voice. "As of the present moment we have fourteen men aboard her under Chief Summers. They've been able to create enough feeling of personality conflicts to provide the atmosphere that we want." He looked around the table for a moment. "I can assure you, gentlemen, that they are among the best that the Navy has got and that's mighty damn good. None of them are tattooed and they have been given special indoctrination in avoiding Navy or sea-going language. When one of the top ratings hit his head on a hatch, he had the presence of mind to curse at the door."

"Have you determined the exact number that should be on board when the operation begins?" General Gifford asked.

"Yes, sir, one hundred and two as things stand right now. That is subject to change if we lose anyone and don't have time to position a replacement."

"I think we should establish a deadline on that," the admiral said. "Offhand I would put it at minus twenty days. After that if any personnel are lost we won't replace them unless it's in an area so vital that we must."

"We have backups, sir, for every key slot, twenty-three all told." The major paused and looked around the table once more. "I have to report one snag—a bad one. Our operational plans are pretty well worked out, but as they stand now we'll have to sacrifice the crane operator. Maybe I'm not being tough enough, but I'd like to avoid that if I can. He'll have to be a damn good man and we don't have any to spare."

"Have you any preliminary thinking on that at all?" the circus performer asked.

The major nodded. "Yes, Walt. If there isn't any other way, I'm going to handle that part myself. That solves a lot of problems, including finding someone whom we can trust absolutely."

Admiral Haymarket was silent for a moment. "I have a thought," he said finally. "Let me develop it a little before we discuss it. Meanwhile I suggest that all of us apply ourselves to the screw problem, because at the moment that's the crux of the whole thing. At least it's a vital link."

"Amen," the major said. "If we can lick that one, we'll be a helluva lot closer to home than we are now."

"How about it, mama?" Moshe Glickman asked. "Do you think maybe we should tell him tonight already?"

Esther Glickman had been weighing the matter in her mind ever since the mail had been delivered. "I'm thinking that it would be a good idea," she answered. "But for you, you shut up and let me do it. And on your face no expression either until we know what he says." She turned to her other son. "And you, David, you'd better be there, but you're saying nothing—nothing at all. Understand?"

"Why not, mama? I can help."

"Best you can help by keeping quiet. After papa comes home and we have dinner, then we'll see." She picked up the official notice and read it over once again although she could have recited it by heart. "So maybe this is the best thing that ever happened to us." The last words stuck a little in her throat and she had difficulty giving them birth. She looked about her hurriedly, picked up a paper tissue, and wiped her eyes.

Moshe jumped up and went to her. "Don't cry, mama. Like you said, maybe nothing so good happened to us before."

David offered her a rumpled handkerchief. "Hell, mama, it's no sweat," he said. "If I can keep out of the damn Army we'll be fine."

Esther once more took command. "In the Army you'll be going," she retorted. "So here you followed that crazy man Orberg and when we needed you, where were you? In jail yet. Better you should have been in uniform; maybe there you could have helped."

"Mama, it's too late for that now," Moshe said. "When we get there, maybe we both join the Army; at least they'll have kosher food."

The door of the small Brooklyn apartment opened and Morris Glickman came in to greet his family. He kissed his wife and then asked almost casually, "Did it come today?"

Love welled up in Esther's throat and for a moment she lost the power of speech.

"Yes, papa," Moshe answered for her. "Today it came."

A little awkwardly Morris embraced his wife. It was not an easy thing to do, at least it was not as it had once been when she had been dark-eyed, long-haired, and slender and he had married her. He reached far enough around her now ample girth to make his presence felt and patted her gently. "Now now, mama," he said. "In a way the news is good. The waiting—the uncertainty, that's all over. I was tired of teaching anyway. The kids, they're worse every year. Now we can make plans."

"So what can we plan?" Esther asked miserably.

Her husband was equal to the challenge. "You know they need teachers badly in Israel. Here I don't think we have a future. Later, maybe, we can come back when things are better. Already I've talked to Mr. Farkas; when we can come back, my job will be waiting."

"Such a good man Mr. Farkas is. But will he be here to help us when we need it?"

Morris smiled and stepped back so that he could hold out his arms in confidence. "Of course! Didn't you know, he works as a partner with a gentile. A WASP yet, but a good man too; I trust him."

"Aw, quit your kidding," David interjected. "Who the hell knows if we're ever coming back. Or if we'll want to. Everybody seems to think that in a little while this'll all blow over." He flung himself down onto the davenport. "Crap, we're Jews and we've been taking it on the lam since Moses, so what do you expect to have happen now."

Esther was shocked. "David, such language! And in your father's presence. You should be ashamed!"

Morris Glickman rose above his son's outburst. "Gather around," he said. Obediently his wife and elder son drew up chairs close to his own when he sat down; after a few seconds David dragged in one of the dining chairs and reluctantly did as he had been bidden.

"It is time," Morris began, "that we should count our blessings. First, no matter what these people do to our country, in two weeks we can be out of here and out of their reach. We will be safe. How many Polish Jews didn't have that chance just before—excuse that I say the word—Hitler."

He leaned back and placed his fingertips together. "Second, for thousands of years other Jews have had to move when they had no place to go. Now we have Israel—we are entitled to live there and to become citizens if we want."

"And have to join the Army," David concluded.

His father looked at him; his features hardened and there was no love in his voice when he spoke. "David, for the first time I say it; I am ashamed of you. You are a coward. You would not fight for the United States of America where we belong, now you want to escape helping the one country where we will be made welcome and offered everything we need—the Jewish homeland."

"I'm no damned soldier," David said.

"No, a soldier you're not, but God willing where we're going they'll make you one. And a better man you'll be for it. My brother Herman died for this country; if we had had more Hermans in our Army, maybe we wouldn't have the trouble we've got now."

"O.K., he died—how did that help him?"

Morris ignored that. When they reached Israel it would be different; they would straighten David out. "I think," he said, "we ought to tell papa right away."

"Before dinner?" Esther asked.

"Yes—now. And we all go, otherwise he might not believe it."

"All right," David grumbled. "I know what you mean. I'll come."

Bravely Esther led the way down the narrow corridor to the back room. She tapped lightly on the closed door, then opened it a small fraction and looked inside. "Daddy, it's us," she announced.

As she entered the room old Ishmael Goldblatt looked up in concern. His expression deepened as the whole family trooped in, first Morris, his son-in-law, then the two boys, Moshe and David. He sat defensively, hunched in his rocking chair, a shawl draped across his shoulders for comfort, his gray hair straggling out from under his yarmulke like a tonsured priest. His glasses were perched halfway down on his nose in defiance of the optometrist's careful instructions because it suited his purpose better to wear them that way. As he stared at the assembling family, distrust deepened in his eyes: not of them, but of the thing, whatever it was, that had brought them to him in this manner. For he regarded every unknown thing, every unvouched-for person with a deep, ingrained, and perpetual suspicion.

"Daddy, we want to talk to you," Esther said. The words flowed from her in Yiddish with an easy grace; she was proud of her English, but her father had disdained to learn the new tongue—he had no need of it.

"What's wrong? What's wrong?" The old man's sunken eyes narrowed as he spoke and he thrust his head out as though to peer into the face of adversity.

There were only two other chairs in the sparsely furnished room. Esther sank into one of them while her husband, a little gingerly, eased into the other.

"Daddy, nothing is wrong," Esther assured. "We came to see you because this is a great day in our lives."

The old man turned his mind inward, but he could

think of nothing to celebrate and his face revealed his consternation.

"We've been saving our money," Esther continued. She took a fresh grip on herself as the searching eyes of her father probed into hers, trying to read out whatever she might be concealing from him. It was hard for her, but she continued with a smile on her face. "Morris has been doing well, and the boys have contributed too."

"So what do you want to spend it on?" Ishmael asked. His shoulders stiffened and he became as shrunken hard as a walnut shell.

Morris came to his wife's rescue. "Daddy," he said, "all of us, we have been having a dream. For this we have saved our money and for this we have worked."

"What kind of a dream? I don't like dreams, they're expensive."

"Expensive, yes," Morris continued, "but for what is money anyway? We want to move, daddy, and now we have enough so that we can."

The old man began to rock in very short arcs, as though to emphasize the manner in which his mind was working. "So why should we move?" he asked. "Here it isn't too good, but not too bad either. Morris, he has his work. To move to a better place just to live higher in society, it would be a throwaway—foolishness. We are happy here, we should stay here."

"Daddy, you don't understand," Esther said. Her voice became soft as though she were about to bestow a loving gift. "We aren't going to move just to another part of town. Brooklyn is Brooklyn. We're going to move—to *Israel!*"

At first the old man did not believe her. He did not believe anything until it had been proven to him, he accepted only the words of the threadbare Talmud which lay, as it almost always did, on his lap. "Israel?" He almost croaked out the word.

"Yes," Esther answered. "Yes!"

"Israel." The word seemed to stun him. He considered it, then sat silently, trying to think.

Morris knew him well. "Daddy," he said. "We have the reservations already. In two weeks we go. One day after we leave we will be in Jerusalem. Then, daddy, you can go to the Wailing Wall. All Jerusalem you can visit now. Our homeland."

Old Ishmael Goldblatt retreated within himself. As they watched him the arcs of his rocking began to lengthen and his bony thin hands loosened their tension on top of the book in his lap. At one time in his youth he had dreamed of helping to free the Holy Land and restore it to his people. He had never seen it with his own eyes, but it had been a vivid image in his mind for fifty years.

"Maybe they won't let us go," he said. The words seemed to form automatically on his lips.

Morris spread his hands palms up. "So why not?" he asked. "We've got the money, we can pay. I've spoken for the tickets already. A special flight; lots of Jewish people are moving to Israel because business has not been good lately. With them we go cheaper."

"Flight?" the old man questioned. "An airplane yet? No." He shook his head defiantly.

"Daddy," Esther said, "if you are wanting to go by boat, then we go by boat. But it costs a lot more; we'll have to wait and save more money."

Her father looked at her in suspicious disbelief. "The boat costs *more?*"

Esther nodded vigorously. "Yes, daddy, so many more meals they have to serve, so much longer they have to take care of you. And bedrooms for everybody yet."

He could not dispute that evidence, but for the moment he remained unconvinced. "We came on a boat," he said.

"Yes, daddy, and you were seasick most of the time, remember?"

"Besides," Morris added, "they don't have boats like that any more. Only very fancy ones for the rich, with lots of expensive servants."

"The meals on the airplane are all free," Moshe contributed. "You pay your fare and that's it. That's one reason the railroads went broke hauling passengers—too much for meals and too many tips."

At last the things they had been telling him began to penetrate into old Ishmael's consciousness. He sat up a little straighter and looked around the barren room in which he had lived for more than ten years. He saw its bleakness and the four walls which had shut him in for so long from an alien world he had refused to accept.

Then the first germ of a long dormant anticipation stirred deep within him. "Palestine," he said, addressing no one.

Morris nodded; he had read the symptoms. "Daddy, we're going home," he said.

Esther was a little startled; for the first time in her memory she saw a tear form in her father's eye; she rushed to embrace him so that they might share their joy together.

The Senate Office Building was curiously quiet. Technically Congress was still in session, but the President was not available to sign legislation, which would have been largely meaningless in any event. Some senators and congressmen made it a point to stay on the job, but they were largely standing by awaiting whatever future developments might come.

It was a little like walking through an elaborate play set, Hewlitt thought, as he went down the corridor toward Senator Fitzhugh's office. All of the fixtures of reality were there, but it was now nothing but an elaborate facade. Someday, perhaps, it would again be a center of genuine policy making, but that future time was not visible now.

Hewlitt was not happy about his errand, but he almost welcomed it as a change from the inaction which had been forced upon him. He had joined the underground to do something; now he was under strict injunction to look and listen, but to do no more until he was directed. This kind of passive role did not agree with him: it was too much like the casual life he had been living prior to the sudden outbreak of hostilities and their almost unbelievably swift result. He felt much more sure of himself now, and he wanted to put his powers to the test. The job which confronted him at the moment might be a measure of his diplomacy, but little more.

He found the door that he wanted, opened it, and discovered that the senator's receptionist was still on the job. "Are you Mr. Hewlitt?" she asked as he approached her desk.

"Yes, I am."

"Please sit down; the senator will be with you in a few minutes."

Hewlitt sat and looked through a newspaper; it was close to meaningless. Censorship had closed over all of the news media and what filtered through was almost entirely devoid of interest. The receptionist waited until he laid the thin paper aside and then offered a morsel for his consumption. "I don't know if you've heard," she said, "but the Brown hearings are off."

"I've heard."

"Seymour Brown was in here just a little while ago," the girl went on. "He told the senator that the Air Force simply didn't know how to fly the *Ramrod,* and that that was all that was wrong."

"I don't believe it," Hewlitt retorted. "In the first place, the Air Force can fly anything that can be flown. Secondly, if the airplane can't be handled by the average, properly qualified combat pilot, then it's the plane's fault, period."

"I think you're right about that," the girl agreed. She looked at her intercom where a light had just come on. "You may go in now," she said.

Senator Solomon Fitzhugh was almost exactly as Hewlitt had expected to find him; he was older-looking than his pictures suggested, but his familiar features were unmistakable. His manner was a bit weighty as he rose to shake hands; the government might have fallen, but Senator Fitzhugh clearly had decided not to join in the debacle. He was a United States senator and that fact had not just been impressed on his mind, it had been molded there.

"Sit down, sir," he invited, waving toward a chair. He used the word "sir" as a convenient tool with which to demonstrate his humility. It often greatly impressed casual visitors, particularly those from his home state, and he had learned its value. "Now tell me what I can do for you."

"I didn't come to ask anything of you, senator," Hewlitt said. "Mr. Zalinsky has directed me to call on you personally to discuss a matter which should not be committed to paper."

Fitzhugh nodded with understanding. "I take it that he would like to tender his regrets for his rudeness to me the other day. Please tell him that I consider the incident closed."

"The matter, senator, is considerably graver than that."

"I'm sorry. Suppose you go on."

"All right, sir. With your permission I'll come right to the point."

"One moment before you do: I don't quite understand your role here. Are you representing Mr. Zalinsky?"

"Not by any desire of mine, sir. As I believe I told you on the phone, I'm a government language expert on the White House staff. When Zalinsky moved in he tapped me because I'm fluent in his language and his English is somewhat limited."

"Is that why he declines to see anyone?"

"No, senator, that seems to be a policy with him."

"Thank you for the explanation. Please go on."

"I believe, sir, that not too long ago you wrote to the premier—"

Fitzhugh raised a hand and stopped him before he could continue. "Of course, I understand now. I did write a highly confidential letter two or three weeks ago and I've been very anxiously awaiting a reply. In fact I have a couple of bags packed in the event I might have to leave on short notice for overseas." His tone became a little more confidential. "You understand, of course, that if the President had been available . . ."

"Entirely, sir."

"It may be," Fitzhugh continued, "that the President, wherever he is, is already in communication with the premier. If you know this to be a fact, please tell me." He looked up, the question framed in his eyes.

"I'm sorry," Hewlitt answered. "I have no idea where the President is or what he is doing. In the past some traffic between the President and the premier did cross my desk, but now I'm entirely out of the picture."

Senator Fitzhugh laid his arms on his desk and leaned forward. The lines in his face seemed to deepen and his voice reflected his concern. "Since you have been in that position," he said, "you can be a great help to me now." He looked at Hewlitt, almost pleading with him. "If you could give me—just a résumé—of what went on just prior to the outbreak of the—the war. I have very urgent reasons for asking this of you."

Hewlitt shook his head. "I'm genuinely sorry, senator. You understand that I could not reveal that to anyone without the President's own authorization."

The senator played another card. "Please consider the present circumstances. You realize, of course, that our . . . opponents . . . have full and complete knowledge of what I'm asking. I don't want to have to aim in the dark."

"I do understand, senator, as you appreciate my position. May I tell you, sir, why I'm here?"

Fitzhugh sat back, disappointed, but undefeated. "Very well, Mr. Hewlitt, please continue."

"Senator, Mr. Zalinsky informed me just before I phoned you that your letter had been received and read. I profoundly regret to tell you this, sir, but it was not regarded with the gravity that it deserved. It is the premier's position right now that we have been defeated and are not in a position to negotiate concerning anything. According to Mr. Zalinsky, he has no present intention of meeting with you or continuing a contact in any way. This may change later, of course, but as of right now I have the most unwelcome task of advising you that the premier wishes you to discontinue all contact."

The senator sat like a man transfixed, his visitor forgotten. His lips moved unconsciously as they shaped words which were not to be spoken; his eyes focused on something an infinite distance away. He struggled to regain his composure. "I find this very hard to believe," he said.

"I well understand that, sir."

"How sure are you of your facts? I don't know you at all and I have never heard of you before."

"If I had any different facts to lay before you, senator, I would not have chosen these. My personal reputation doesn't enter into it."

Fitzhugh's voice acquired an edge. "You could be trying to take advantage of me. My position in regard to important public issues are well known and some of them are highly unpopular with the militarists. . . ."

That was a challenge Hewlitt refused to ignore. He was doing his best to be considerate of Fitzhugh, but personal abuse was beyond what he was willing to accept. He put a bite into his own voice to let the senator know precisely that. "Sir, if I must declare myself personally, I am in total disagreement with your announced position on the matter of the armed forces, but this has nothing whatever to do with the distasteful job before me now. Whether you have heard of me or not, the fact remains that I am not careless with the truth and in my position, which was one of high responsibility within certain limits until recently, the greatest accuracy was constantly required."

Fitzhugh spoke in a different tone. "If I offended you, I'm sorry. You must understand that I find your message incredible. The premier is my close personal friend."

Hewlitt held onto the advantage. "May I ask how often you have seen him, sir?"

"Only once, face to face, but we had a very clear and basic understanding . . ."

Hewlitt recrossed his legs and folded his hands in his lap; he was in the driver's seat now and knew that he would have to stay there. "Senator, I have some very specific information concerning your meeting with the premier; it comes directly through Mr. Zalinsky. I will leave it to you whether you wish to hear it or not."

"Yes, of course. I find no virtue in ignorance."

"On that point, sir, we are in complete agreement. You will have to accept my word that I did not invent this: Mr. Zalinsky told me very plainly that the premier saw you when you were in his country for only one reason. He wanted you to gain face from the meeting so that you would be reelected."

"I find that very farfetched."

It was a definite thrust in the old Fitzhugh manner; Hewlitt answered with one of his own. "It is exceedingly farfetched, sir, to find our country conquered and ourselves in the hands of victorious enemies. These people do not do things by the rational set of rules that we try to follow."

The toughness which had long characterized Fitzhugh on the Senate floor refused to let him yield. "Mr. Hewlitt, I will confide in you a little since I see that you are worthy of trust: the premier did not just grant me an audience for the sake of the news value, we had an extremely warm and very candid meeting of considerable duration. We share many views in common."

"I don't question that impression, senator; the premier is rather famous for his technique under such circumstances. Do you know what they call him in his own country?"

"No."

"Literally translated, 'the Actor.' "

Fitzhugh considered that and weighed it against the unpleasant realities he could no longer deny. When he had faced up to it, he looked at Hewlitt squarely and said, "In other words . . ."

"Man to man, sir, and American to American, you were had."

The senator drummed his fingertips slowly on his desk. "Did Mr. Zalinsky say that in so many words?"

"Substantially so, yes, sir." This time he felt that he had to add a bit more. "Let me say something on my own: I told you that I didn't agree with all of your policies, but at no time have I ever questioned your patriotism. It would be impossible to do so now. You've attempted something fine for all of us and, speaking as one individual, I profoundly appreciate it."

The senator had his thoughts elsewhere. "There is no possible doubt that Mr. Zalinsky has been instructed to advise me to attempt no more communications with his government."

"That is it, sir, precisely."

"You could not have misunderstood him."

"No, senator, I can guarantee that."

"How can you be sure?"

"Because of the precise words which he used."

"I would like to know what they were."

"I would prefer not to repeat them, senator, I have too much respect for you for that."

"Nevertheless, I want to know. I want to be absolutely certain in my mind."

"Very well, sir. Mr. Zalinsky said that if you didn't stop, it might be necessary to take your toys away from you."

"In those exact words."

"Yes, sir. I'm sorry."

A pause hung in the air, then the senator found his dignity. "Thank you for coming to see me, Mr. Hewlitt."

Hewlitt rose to his feet. "Thank you for receiving me, senator." That was not the moment to say anything more and he knew it. He shook hands formally and left. As he walked down the nearly empty corridor toward the exit, his relief at having the unpleasant interview behind him was overshadowed by a new opinion of Fitzhugh. Politically he still considered the senator a near disaster, but he had taken a tough one right on the chin and he had taken it like a man.

Walter Wagner was the finest athlete that his Pennsylvania high school had ever known. He was not particularly tall, but he had a phenomenal physique, extraordinary reflexes, and an agile brain. For three years he was a superb principal quarterback on the football team; he displayed an almost unerring ability to call the right play in a crucial situation and to scramble for yardage with dazzling changes of direction that kept the opposing linebackers in a state of sustained frustration. He was too short for basketball, but in the pole vault he took the state championship with a display of form that attracted the attention of the Olympic Committee. As his graduation neared, college athletic scouts descended en masse; he could have had a scholarship at almost any school he chose. Unfortunately he was not able to accept any of these offers; a critical situation at home complicated by a drawn-out final illness of his father forced him to abandon his plans for a higher education and go to work.

His first job after graduation was as a lifeguard. He had excelled at that, so much so that the manager of the pool where he worked had conceived the idea of featuring him in a diving exhibition every weekend as a means of attracting more patrons. After a few weeks he received an offer to join a water circus troupe in Atlantic City. The salary offered was not a great deal more than he was already making, but after the season closed, there was a possible tour of South America in the offing. That was tempting, because he had had a sustained interest in seeing the world for as long as he could remember.

Three weeks after he arrived in Atlantic City the featured high diver with the troupe was injured in an automobile accident, not seriously but badly enough so that he could not perform for at least two weeks. Walter Wagner had climbed his rigging on the day that the news had come in and had looked down at the tiny-appearing circle of water in the eight-foot-deep tank. Having watched the diver many times, he knew exactly how he let his body turn in the air and how he hit the water to avoid injury. Coming down the ladder to the twenty-foot level he had made a practice dive and found it easy. He dove several more times that same day from ever greater heights, but he was still far short of the tiny platform at the very top.

The manager of the troupe had warned him not to hurt himself; then with his conscience properly salved he waited and watched. It took three days for Walter Wagner to work his way up to the top, but he did not falter at any point along the way. Each time he knew that he was ready he went a little higher and tried it again; when he had mastered that step he moved up once more.

Three years after that the Great Cordova had become one of the standard and dependable attractions throughout much of the free world. He had added many features to his act to give it more color; he dove with lighted torches in either hand at night, he dove in a cape in the daytime which he discarded halfway down in his plunge. He had lighted rings installed on the side of his rigging and timed his revolving falls to pass through them with apparently almost no space to spare.

He had also discovered a new talent—a remarkable ear for languages. He learned with great speed and almost flawless accent. He found it fascinating, and delighted in learning the reactions of people around him by listening to their scraps of conversation.

One day he heard something that could have been meaningless, but on the other hand, perhaps not. He had stopped in at the American consulate that same afternoon where he was listened to with care. He left with the feeling that he might have made a fool of himself. Subsequent events established the fact that his call had been of some importance.

Two weeks after that he had visitors. The Central Intelligence Agency had done a fast and efficient job of checking his background, and the possibility that the information he had supplied had been deliberately planted had been considered and discarded. The visitors talked to him a little and thanked him for his cooperation. When they had done their homework a little more thoroughly they came back, this time with a proposition. They were well aware that a circus performer could travel almost anywhere that his bookings took him without arousing suspicion, and few people ever saw or took note of the face of a high diver.

He had handled relatively minor matters after that for

some time, the Agency arranging bookings for him as it became necessary. Then a big one had turned up and he had been assigned the job. The problem at hand concerned the United States Sixth Fleet in the Mediterranean. Before that one was over he had had a fight to the finish in a cul-de-sac in Port Said and had left a dead man behind him who would be sorely missed by an unfriendly foreign government. It had also brought him to the attention of the then commander of the Sixth Fleet, Vice-Admiral Barney Haymarket.

The fertile brain that he had displayed in high school had developed additional resourcefulness: at his request the Agency had located the high diver whom he had replaced in Atlantic City. Usually it was Walter Wagner who dove, but from time to time his invisible partner became the Great Cordova and thereby provided him with an unquestioned alibi. That had worked for almost two years before someone had finally stumbled onto the stunt. After that there had been other devices, but the cover had been exceptionally well maintained so that not more than a handful of men in Europe and Africa were aware that the Great Cordova was one of the CIA's most reliable operators. Since it had been a suspicious British agent who had unmasked the two-diver gambit, and since he had kept his discovery strictly within the home team, certain hostile forces had remained unenlightened despite the fact that the fearsome Colonel Rostovitch had devoted himself for weeks to trying to penetrate the identity of the man who had outwitted him in a particularly critical operation. He had been told only that his enemy was an Israeli agent, which was of no help to him because there were too many Jews and as it happened Walter Wagner was not one of them.

Knowing all of this, and in addition the highly restricted details of many other operations in which the Great Cordova had been concerned, Admiral Haymarket had tapped him very early in the game as one of the men he most wanted. From the outset Wagner had proved his value and the admiral had the utmost confidence in him. Therefore when the word reached him that Wagner had some ideas concerning Low Blow, the admiral was more than ready to hear them. All members of the First Team had access to him at all times, and when they came, he listened.

Wagner sat down in the admiral's office and asked, "How much have we got in photo coverage of the area where the *Magsaysay* is docked?"

"Plenty," the admiral answered. "We had this one cooked up quite a while ago and we did all that we could to prepare for it."

"In that case, I'd like to see the best detail shots you have of the immediate dock area, the sheds, and the access routes in particular. I might have an alternate idea that would spare the crane operator. We can't let Ted sacrifice himself, obviously, or anyone else if we can help it. I think that maybe we can."

They spent the next hour together going over the photographs that the admiral had assembled. They revealed every detail, even to the distances between certain of the buildings and the protective concrete-filled steel posts that had been installed to safeguard their corners where roadways passed by. After satisfying himself that it was still feasible, Wagner unveiled his plan; shoulder to shoulder with the admiral he went over certain of the photographs once more and sketched out an overlay.

"I think that it might work," the admiral said when they were through. For him that was a strong endorsement.

"Then in that case," Wagner said, "I have a small request to make of you."

"You want to handle it."

"That's right, and I want to go into the field because I'll have to be on the spot to pull it off. Ted Pappas will hate me for this, but I have the necessary experience and he doesn't—not in this area. And he can be too easily identified."

The admiral noted again the remarkable physique of the man beside him. "You aren't exactly invisible yourself," he commented.

"I've dealt with that before," Wagner answered dryly. "I'm your best bet and you know it."

The admiral could not deny that. "All right, Walt, it's yours. Frame up the whole thing, then let me see it. By the way, can you handle the screw problem? That's the real stinker, you know."

"I think so," Wagner said.

CHAPTER TEN

"I wish a report," Zalinsky said, "on your speaking with Senator Fitzhugh. You were successful?"

"I was successful," Hewlitt answered.

"He now has the understanding which was wished?"

"He does." He did not elaborate.

Zalinsky leaned back a little and surveyed Hewlitt with slightly closed eyes. "In what style did he behave?" he asked.

"On the whole, the senator took it very well; he knows how to control himself. It was a blow, of course, because he apparently had thought very highly of your premier."

"Aha, so now we are becoming clever." Zalinsky came up in his chair and leaned forward once more. "You are making the propaganda to me."

Hewlitt shook his head. "I stated a fact," he said, "and I answered your question. The senator was disillusioned."

"I do not know this word."

"It means that his eyes were opened, like waking up from a dream. Something he had believed in was shown to be no longer true."

Zalinsky worked his lips. "This I can accept," he said. "Is it now that you think he will go home?"

"I doubt it," Hewlitt answered him. "As far as he is concerned he is still a United States senator and on the job."

"Why not you told him also that is not true?"

"I didn't tell him that for two reasons. First, it was none of my business. Secondly, I don't believe it myself."

"You still think that you have a government, then?"

"Of course. And if you admit it, Mr. Zalinsky, so do you."

Zalinsky tightened and Hewlitt saw it, but he was unafraid. He knew the man better now; to cross him directly would be an invitation to disaster, but he liked to talk and discuss so long as things remained on that plane.

"Explain to me," Zalinsky said.

"All right. This is a very big and complicated country, very different from your own and run under a different system. Our people are different, our ways of doing things, even our recreations. You and your people would take years to learn the mechanism. It is like a vast machine that you have not built and have not been taught to operate. We have machines in this country that take months just to learn to run. You can't do it without the United States government; the whole thing would fall down around your ears."

Zalinsky fitted the tips of his fingers together. "You do not think that I have enough smartness, then."

"You would have to be at least a hundred thousand men to try it alone," Hewlitt said. "You don't have enough trained people to run your government and ours too. You have simply taken much more food on your plate than you are able to eat."

"You have given me to think," Zalinsky said. "Because it is the food that I must eat." He paused and glanced down at himself. "And already I am too fat."

"What did you do before you came here, Mr. Zalinsky?" Hewlitt asked. "I have read a great deal of your political material for many years and I never saw your name."

Zalinsky seemed to welcome the opportunity to reminisce for a moment. "I was first a factory manager," he said. "At a small factory where they made for women sweaters. It was not working well, there were not enough sweaters and they were of worse quality. So I was sent to see if I could fix."

"Did you?"

"First I investigated to find what was wrong—the equipment, the workers, or the materials. Also the designs, the planning, and the management. I found that something was wrong with the workers."

"Let me guess," Hewlitt interjected. "They were being given too much political indoctrination along with their jobs. It interfered with their production."

Zalinsky stared hard at him, not in animosity, but in frank curiosity. "Where you learn this?" he asked.

Hewlitt denied it with a shake of his head. "I didn't, I

just guessed. I know quite a bit about your country even though I've never been there."

"You have accuracy," Zalinsky admitted. "I stopped the lectures and made a closer watch of the machine operations. In a few weeks we had more and much better sweaters. I was told to start the lectures once more. To this I said that I would obey if they wished this more than sweaters. After that it was not furthermore a problem."

"Go on," Hewlitt invited.

"After a few months I am sent to one of our biggest steel mills. It will not work properly. This time I find that the machines are all mistaken—they are not in the right places. So I stop production and we move the machines with much work. For this I have terrible criticism, but in time the plant begins once more to work and we make steel. Before four months we have make more steel than if we had not made a stop."

"Mr. Zalinsky," Hewlitt said, "politics aside, the next time that you take over a plant, let me know. I'll buy some stock in it."

"So, you wish to exploit the workers!"

Hewlit refused to take the bait. "When you buy stock, Mr. Zalinsky, you're not exploiting the workers, you're betting on them."

Zalinsky's mood changed, he leaned forward and unconsciously dropped his voice to a lower tone. "I become aware that in politics you have talent," he said. "I give you warning—listen! Talk not out of this office, anywhere. Colonel Rostovitch, he is tougher than the steel I made. He is the planner that we are here. He listens, he knows. Himself he is now here and each day come more of his people. If he shoot you, I have no one to speak my own language."

"I'll be careful," Hewlitt promised. "Thank you for the warning."

He was thinking of Bob Landers as he walked out of the office; he was far from trusting Zalinsky, who was his immediate concern. The formidable Colonel Rostovitch could wait.

Marc Orberg leaned far back on the sybaritic davenport in his penthouse apartment, propped on his elbows, and ground his teeth in a combination of harsh frustration and mounting rage. His life, with which he had been so richly satisfied, was falling to pieces and he was unable to endure the humiliation.

He was not getting any publicity at all, and that was more essential to him than sex itself. The wild days of the Orberg decision against the draft were long past, so were the riots he had led against the police, the campus disorders, the bombings he had helped plan. He had accomplished all this, and now he was being ignored!

That was not the worst of the injustice that was being done to him. He had composed a new song that was a sure million-copy seller, as all of his songs were since he had become world famous, but the song had not sold a million copies because the bastards who were running things now had yanked it off the market because it was obscene. What the hell did they expect from him anyway, *Rebecca of Sunnybrook Farm?* It was a clever song, clever as hell; it could have been an even bigger hit than "Pigpen," the one the cops hated so much. But they had killed it just because it was about a naked woman who gets laid at the finish. Nat Friedman had warned him, but Nat was always warning him because he was a scared little runt and too cautious.

After that had happened he had decided to give a concert; he wanted to look again at an auditorium jammed with screaming, adoring faces; faces that loved him and hung on his every word, every gesture that he made. They would wait for him by the hundreds outside and there would be the business of the paper slips and a bunch of new girls to screw anytime he liked. Nat had booked the concert all right, after advising that they should lay low for a while. That had been like Nat, always timid, always afraid.

He had gotten all dressed up in his trademark costume, let them wait an extra twenty minutes for kicks, and then had come on stage, Marc Orberg in person, to look out at the vast emptiness before him with only a few hundred people gathered down front to hear him sing. They had made a fuss when he had appeared, of course, but the silent mockery of the thousands of empty seats in the big sports arena had been more than he could endure. They couldn't treat him like that; they had found that out when he had stalked off in a blinding rage.

Nat had calmed him down, had told him to go out and

sing so that they wouldn't have to give all of the money back, particularly on the performance bond that would run into real dough. Just to make Nat happy he had gone back on stage and had sung two songs; if more of them couldn't come, then that was all that they deserved. The applause hadn't been loud enough, the screams of delight hadn't been there, so he had walked out again, this time for good. He had performed; so no one got any money back and that was that. But it hadn't died there, because the humiliation of it had galled him every hour of every day afterward.

Not one damn girl had been there after the show, not a one to share his six-thousand-dollar bed and there wasn't another like it in the world.

He smashed a fist into the simulated fur upholstery as he realized once more that he hadn't been to bed with any kind of a female for days. He wanted a woman, even another of the timid little virgins out for the thrill of a lifetime, and getting it.

And when he had had Nat phone that clown Zalinsky in Washington, because it was high time that Marc Orberg was recognized and rewarded for what he had done, the self-centered fool had had the nerve to refuse to see him.

If he had had anything that he could have smashed, he would have seized it and beaten it against the wall.

Then a forgotten memory flashed into his brain. He had promised, long before any of the invaders had set foot on American soil, that he would be the first to welcome them. Since then, he knew, thousands of them had come and he hadn't met a one of them.

All right, it was something to do. He would make a big deal out of it somehow, and get some publicity. Pictures on the front page of him shaking hands with the commander, if there was one. All he had to do was to find the right time and place and then have Nat let the press know.

Going to meet a plane at an airport would be no good, flights had been coming in all the time for weeks.

Then he had an idea: there had been something in the papers about clearing a stretch of the Maryland east shore. Enemy amphibious forces were coming in and they were going to hit the beach in classic style. There would be a lot of action during the exercise, thousands of men and a major commander of one kind or another, and he, Marc Orberg, would welcome them! The news media would all be there and millions of Americans would hate the very idea of the unopposed enemy landing. He could ride into town in the commander's vehicle and shove it right down their throats.

He liked that, he liked it a lot. The idea grew and expanded in his mind until it gave birth to another. When that happened he found release at last from his blinding frustration and the acid anger that was consuming him. With his fame and prestige they would be damn glad to get him—as an active partner in the new government!

Hewlitt could hardly contain himself as Frank pulled his cab away from the West Entrance to the White House and entered the flow of home-going traffic. He sat silently, knowing that he had to, and waited to see if the enforced restraint of the past two days was to continue, but impatience burned within him.

"Did your girl friend put out yet?" Frank asked.

Relief flooded through Hewlitt. "If she doesn't pretty quick I'm going to get a new girl friend," he answered. "Have they had you wired?"

"I think so; I picked up some fellows following me and I didn't like the looks of it. Davy went over the car and found something. He didn't tell me the details. Anyhow, I think you're under investigation."

"How about yourself?"

Frank waited until he had emerged from closely packed traffic. "All right, I think. This morning the thing was gone from the car, so I'm thinkin' that it was sort of routine, general snooping around."

"Davy was sure?"

"You better believe it, and he's a good boy. I told you that."

"I believe it; right now I'm trusting my neck to him. Frank, I've got something: you were right about Captain Scott, I think I can prove it."

"Let's have it."

"When Bob Landers was shot Scott saw Zalinsky and got permission to bury the body—remember?"

"That's right."

"I didn't wake up to it until you slipped me that note in a fortune cookie, but normally Zalinsky doesn't see anybody; he turned down Fitzhugh and a lot of others who are pretty important. But Scott walked right in, and he's only a captain. And he got a concession on the first try. It doesn't add up."

"Now there you really got somethin', my boss will like that! He tol' me that Scott might be all right, but maybe not. I'll get this to him right away before anybody else can get trapped. Anything more?"

"Yes, Fitzhugh wrote Zalinsky's boss—the premier himself—and offered to negotiate as peacemaker for this country. I haven't seen the letter, but I don't need to. Zalinsky sent me to tell Fitzhugh to forget it and to pick up his marbles. The senator took it hard; he thought that he was going to emerge as the savior of the country."

"Not likely, not him."

"The Brown hearings are off, which isn't too surprising. Brown himself is claiming that the *Ramrod* was O.K. and that the Air Force didn't know how to fly it."

"Horseshit," Frank said. "Now listen, this is important—you ready?"

"Shoot."

"We're goin' to start movin', you included. I get the word that somethin' big is shaping up."

"I'm damn glad to hear it."

Frank stopped for a light and the conversation remained suspended until they were in motion once more. "I don't know anythin' about what it is, but it ought to be pretty good. Now this is orders: you tell Barbara that she's to move into Davy's house. An' she's to tell Mary to do the same thing. Just as soon as they can work it to make it look right."

"Frank, how can that look right? They're both pretty high-class government girls. They just wouldn't do that!"

"That'll be taken care of, you just pass on the orders. Remember that I tol' you we were going to make Davy's place into a real nice whorehouse. Not for real, of course, but it's goin' to look that way."

"I still can't buy it."

"You will, when you see how it works out. Has Cedric Culp been playing up to Mary like I said?"

"Yes, but not too much. He's married, remember."

"I know, but he could be playing around a little. It's been known to happen."

"Hell, yes."

"Now we're goin' to be showing some stag movies at the house tonight and you're to come, got it?"

"Yes."

"I'll pick you up about eight-thirty. You'll find out more after you get there."

As Hewlitt let himself into his apartment he reflected that the stag movies were a good gag—it would account for his presence in a questionable neighborhood and his associating with a cab driver if that fact ever came to light. And because of the prudishness of his own country, Zalinsky would believe it. Whether the invisible but deadly Colonel Rostovitch would was another question.

A few minutes after eight Hewlitt put on a turtle-necked sweater, a pair of dark slacks, and the most inconspicuous jacket that he owned. He exchanged the leather shoes he had worn all day for a softer suede pair with rubber soles and then slipped a few extra dollars into his wallet. He did not know what lay ahead for the evening, but he knew that he was not going to be wasting time watching stag films.

When he went outside at eight-twenty-five Frank was just pulling up. Hewlitt got in without making the mistake of looking around first.

As soon as they were under way Frank inquired about his girl friend and then provided some news. "You're goin' to meet my boss tonight. He was mighty pleased with that idea of yours about Scott. He wants to talk to you directly. He is a sharp boy; you'll find that out."

"Has he a code name?"

"Yes, it's Percival—not Percy; remember that."

"And you absolutely vouch for him."

"Hew, if he ain't straight, you can forget about the whole thing."

"Have you any idea what's on the program for tonight?"

"Not too much. I think it has to do with Scott, but I don't know for sure. Anyhow, there's more goin' on now and maybe Percival will have some things to tell you."

A half hour later, Frank pulled the cab into an unpaved driveway next to the house. A battered service truck parked at the end carried a legend for *Jones' TV Service.* Frank pulled up behind it and pointed toward a side door which badly needed painting. When they opened it to go inside, Hewlitt noticed that despite its weatherbeaten appearance it swung silently on its hinges.

There was a smaller group in the living room this time although the same volunteer bartender was on duty. "How about a drink?" Frank asked.

"I could go for a bourbon and water."

When Frank came back from the bar with two drinks Hewlitt looked around and asked, "Do you know who that Chinese fellow is?"

"You oughta know him," Frank answered. "He works in the restaurant where you ate with Scott."

Memory focused then and he recognized the quiet-mannered headwaiter. "I figured that you'd tumble to that," Frank continued, "when you got that fixed-up fortune cookie."

He hadn't tumbled and it bit into his confidence. "Is he your boss?" he asked.

"No, but he's a real good man. He thought up the fortune cookie trick and fixed the slip. And he got a good tape of your talk with Scott."

Hewlitt looked at him. "That place is bugged?"

Frank tasted his drink. "Sure, but this time we're doing it. Like I told you, this is no kid setup."

As he was speaking the bartender set up a small table and then loaded it with an eight-millimeter projector and five rolls of film. As someone else set up a screen he threaded the machine and adjusted the focus. "O.K., you guys?" he asked.

For answer the man nearest the door turned off the light switch. A hazy cone of light crossed the room from the projector to the screen and a not too clear image appeared. In what was obviously a motel room a man and a girl began to embrace while they were seated on a small davenport.

"All right, let's go," Frank said. He opened the rear door of the room and waited until Hewlitt had followed him into the narrow corridor. "Sorry you'll have to miss the show," he added, "but you know the plot anyway."

He led the way upstairs and then back to a rear room where he paused and knocked.

The man who opened the door was an even six feet tall, of narrow athletic build, and had on a suit which was trimly cut to his figure. He wore his hair in a near crew cut which suggested at once a military officer or a highly skilled technician accustomed to an active life. "Come in, gentlemen," he invited.

Frank performed the introduction. "This is Raleigh Hewlitt. Hew, this is Percival."

The man called Percival offered Hewlitt a hand that had steel in its fingers, then motioned toward two chairs which helped to fill what was essentially a sparse office. He sat down himself behind a simple desk with the manner of a man who knows precisely what he is about. Hewlitt estimated his age as between thirty-five and forty, but sensed at the same time that he could be wrong in either direction. Also he noted that there were no distinguishing characteristics in the man's features, they were normal and regular and that was all.

"Hew, I hope that you'll excuse me if I don't give you my name at this point," he said. "That isn't because of any lack of confidence in you; it's the way we have things set up."

"That's all right," Hewlitt answered.

"I've been authorized to give you some information," Percival continued. "I believe that Bob Landers told you that this organization was set up quite a while before we got into the late war; the President read the handwriting on the wall and prepared for what might happen. And did. You know which President I mean."

"Yes, sir."

Percival pulled out a drawer and stretched his legs across the top, tipping back in his chair as he did so. "Contrary to some press reports you might have seen, we had, and still have, a pretty competent intelligence organization going for us. Through it we got some very clear indications about what was coming, but the temper of the times—the public mood all across the country—made things difficult. The Orberg decision didn't help us, and there were other problems."

"Fitzhugh, for example."

"Exactly. He didn't consciously try to wreck things the

way that Orberg and Wattles did, among others, but he's been a damn nuisance."

"Do you want me to leave you two guys alone?" Frank interrupted.

Percival gave him a half gesture. "I'd rather you'd stay; some of this may concern you."

Frank nodded his compliance and lapsed back into silence.

"By the way," Percival said. "I understand that you had a meeting with Fitzhugh the other day."

"I did. He thought he was going to negotiate for us and save the country."

"A little late for that, as far as he's concerned." He laid his arms on the desk. "Getting back to cases, we've been keeping a file on you for some time, largely because of your language capability. We thought of using you to translate intercepted messages and other material that we might get our hands on. All of the reports that we have had on you have been good, particularly as regards your ability to keep your mouth shut."

"There isn't any choice about that," Hewlitt said.

Percival nodded his approval. "Glad that you see it that way. We had thought of pulling you into our headquarters, but as things have worked out, we want to leave you where you are for the time being. You seem to have established a certain rapport with Zalinsky that could be vitally important at the right time."

"That's all right with me," Hewlitt said once more, "but in a way, I'm disappointed. I'd like a little more action if that's possible."

Percival looked at him quite sharply for a moment, as though he were making a re-evaluation. "Before this is all over, I suspect that you'll get all the action you want. We have certain operations planned which you will know about quite soon."

Hewlitt leaned forward. "Where do I fit in?" he asked.

Percival rested his arms on the top of the desk and became thoroughly practical. "You know Captain Scott of the Air Force. We've had a tip-off that, for reasons unknown, he may be the person who betrayed Bob Landers—but it isn't definite. We've been watching him very closely. Frank here knows about that. When you came up with the fact that Zalinsky saw him on short notice, that was an important piece of information that we had missed. We want to move fast on this before he can do any more damage, *if* he is the person we want. I listened to the tape of your dinner conversation with him; there is no doubt that he was probing you for a possible entrance into the underground."

"He had me believing him," Hewlitt said.

"Remember—he may still be absolutely O.K."

"I hope that he is," Hewlitt admitted. "But if he is our man, then why did he blow the whistle on Bob Landers so fast? That couldn't help but hurt him in what he was trying to do."

Percival raised one forearm and pointed upward as though he were addressing a classroom. "Suppose it was the other way around. It is very possible that Bob got onto him. In that case, if Scott detected it, he would want to get rid of Bob posthaste in order to protect himself. And he could get cooperation from Zalinsky."

Hewlitt thought. "It's entirely possible, but very hard to believe. Scott seems to be so much a totally right kind of person. Also, what reason would he have to betray his country?"

Percival did not comment on that. "To get the answers to some of these questions, I had it in mind to use you—that is, if you want to come to the party. We can keep you pretty well covered and, if you're really interested, it would be a chance to get a little field experience. But there is a very real element of risk and in your case it could be accentuated—you can see why."

"What do you want me to do?" Hewlitt asked.

Percival studied him for a moment before he spoke. "We are up against a man who calls himself Colonel Rostovitch; he's a modern-day Beria who heads up the enemy secret police. That's a good old Balken term for any kind of a suppressive force. Rostovitch is a terror, and he's here now—ostensibly headquartered at what used to be their embassy. But he has other operating bases; one of them is a house something like this one which they have had for some time; we only got on to it a short while ago.

"If Scott is on the wrong side of the railroad tracks, we think that he will try to get in touch with you again. If he does, then you are to tell him that you have heard that there is an organization such as ours and imply—no more than that—that you might be able to put him in touch. This will be sticking your own neck out, of course. If he takes the bait, we believe that he will waste no time in going to that house to report. If he attempts to do that, then he will be dealt with."

"It sounds grim."

"It is; you were there when Bob Landers died."

"Then Scott . . ."

Percival nodded. "Yes."

"On the other hand," Hewlitt reasoned aloud, "if he is all right, then there is no harm done. We could probably use him."

"We considered that too."

Hewlitt thought of Bob Landers. "All right," he said, "I'm your man. When do you think that this will happen?"

Percival stood up. "If you're ready to go," he said, "we have it set up for tonight."

CHAPTER ELEVEN

The first thing that came into Hewlitt's mind after that was an all but forgotten incident of his boyhood. He had been complaining about a pain in one of his teeth; he was told that there was a cavity and it would have to be repaired. That would require an appointment with the dentist. After he had accepted all that, and was ready to prepare himself during the next few days for the ordeal that lay ahead, he had been told that the appointment was slightly less than a half hour away. He had had no chance for psychological adjustment before he had found himself seated in the chair. It was like that now.

"You see," Percival said, "if Scott is as dangerous as we believe he might be, we don't want him on the loose an hour longer than is necessary."

"I can understand that," Hewlitt replied. "You had me off balance for a moment, that's all. I think you'd better brief me."

"Obviously. Your part, actually, is quite simple, though not completely so. I understand that there is a bar you visit fairly frequently when you have been out for an evening."

Hewlitt was impressed that this detail of his private life was known, but he made a successful effort not to let it show. "That's right, it's only a block from my place. I stop there for a draft beer now and then; there's a piano player I like."

"Good. What I'd like you to do is to go there tonight when you leave here, just as you might ordinarily. Have a beer or two in your usual manner, but try to stay at least forty minutes if you can without being obvious about it."

"No problem," Hewlitt said.

"I can't give you any odds on this," Percival continued, "but we consider it possible that Captain Scott might drop in there. Have you ever seen him there before?"

"No, not to my knowledge. Of course I only really met him recently."

"Understood. If your movements are as well known to the other side as they are to us, with certain exceptions, then they will know about this habit of yours. *If* Scott should turn up, you can take it as pretty fair indication that he was sent."

"I'd certainly think so," Hewlitt agreed.

"In case he does, of course you will talk to him. Now listen carefully: if he stays off the subject of this organization, don't you bring it up in any way. Follow his lead. If he does show up, and does get onto that subject, then you understand what that means."

"Yes." Hewlitt had not moved in his chair for some minutes, he was almost afraid to do so now.

"Assuming that both of these things take place, then you are to tell Scott that you don't know if you can be of any help to him or not, but you will ask around discreetly. I don't want you to commit yourself; no good agent ever does that except in an extreme emergency."

"I understand."

"Now, if possible we want Scott, again assuming that he is our man, to go to the enemy's house to report. He wouldn't dare to use the telephone. So you are to tell him, in confidence, that you have heard a wild rumor that because of the amount of enemy traffic that is passing through the Baltimore Bay Tunnel, an effort is going to be made very soon to blow it up. Treat this very carefully, act like you don't believe it yourself." For a moment Percival relented and a half quirk touched the corners of his mouth. "Don't, incidentally," he added, "because there's no truth to it at all."

He became totally serious once more. "The hardest part of your assignment will be to make him believe that you just picked this up, that you believe it to be a wild rumor, but that it just *might* be true. In our right minds we would never do anything like that, but they don't credit us with too much sense in that way. Whatever you do, don't overdo it—don't repeat the story, for instance, to be sure that he got it. Then break it up and part as warm friends. Put yourself in that frame of mind—if you don't, there's a good chance that he might read you out and that would blow the whole thing. Keep it in the forefront of your consciousness that he is your close and trusted friend, your comrade in arms. Believe it, and you'll convince him."

Hewlitt drew in a deep breath. "And then what?" he asked.

"Go home in your usual way. Shortly thereafter your phone will ring and someone will ask for Roger Samuels, who has a telephone number closely similar to yours, by the way. If Scott did not show, simply tell the caller that he has the wrong number and hang up immediately. If Scott did show, but if the conversation did not go as I have outlined here, stay on the line. Your caller will apologize for disturbing you. Say, 'That's quite all right,' and then hang up."

"Hang up immediately if Scott did not show," Hewlitt repeated. "If he did, but if the conversation remained neutral, wait for an apology and then say, 'That's quite all right.' "

"Correct; with your memory you won't have any trouble. Now if Scott did show, and if you planted the story as directed and feel confident that he bought it, in answer to the apology you are to say, 'That's quite all right. You didn't disturb me.' In that event, wait ten minutes and then go out the back door of your building, turn right, and walk toward the corner. There's an all-night store there in case anyone notices you going that way. There will be a cab parked near to the corner. Get in and tell the driver to take you to the Hot Shoppe just across the bridge on the Virginia side. If he does, eat something and then go home. If he doesn't, then go where he takes you."

Hewlitt had all but forgotten that Frank was still present; he turned and looked up, but received a negative shake of the head in reply. "You and me shouldn't be seen together too much except for the regular times," Frank said.

Hewlitt turned back to Percival. "Then what?" he asked.

Percival stood up. "You'll be told. Just follow instructions and don't attempt to improvise. That's all."

From downstairs there came a small stir of noise indicating that the show was either over or in an intermission period. Once more Hewlitt shook hands with Percival and then followed Frank out the door. He felt a certain confidence that he could carry off the role that had been assigned to him, because he instinctively liked Phil Scott anyway.

Frank dropped him off in front of the bar and then wished him good night. As the cab retreated down the street he stood on the pavement for a moment as though he was deciding whether or not to go inside, then, holding himself at a casual emotional level as far as he was able, he opened the door and stepped through.

His first thought was to look around carefully to see if Scott was already there, but before he had finished closing the door behind him he realized the mistake that would be. Instead he headed toward the rear of the narrow room so that if he was to have a visitor, the resulting conversation could be held in relative privacy. He looked straight ahead and avoided even glancing at the bar patrons. He rubbed his chin as he walked, and then massaged the muscles in his throat. It was the gesture of a man who has just engaged in an activity he would rather not publicize, a selfconscious covering up of inner embarrassment.

He had almost reached the piano bar when he felt his arm touched; he turned and there was Scott, dressed in casual sports attire which suited him well. "Buy you a drink, Hew?" he offered.

For a moment Hewlitt looked slightly startled. It was perfectly genuine; he had not expected a possible contact to be made so soon. Then he shook hands. "Let's go in back if you don't mind," he suggested. "I feel like sitting down quietly."

The small rear lounge was largely empty. A corner table invited them with a frosted glass candle holder glowing softly in the semi-darkness. As Hewlitt sat down he admired the easy way that Scott put down his own drink and drew up a chair. "On the town, Hew?" the captain asked.

Hewlitt shook his head. "I dropped in at a friend's house for a little while, that's all."

Scott signaled to the cocktail waitress. "I was supposed to play bridge tonight, but the fourth didn't show up. Do you play, Hew?"

The question remained unanswered while the girl came over and took the order for a drink for Hewlitt and a fresh one for Scott. When she had retreated in a swirl of miniskirt and black pantihose, Hewlitt picked up the conversation. "Sometimes, Phil; it depends. Not much lately."

For a full half hour the conversation remained sterile: the casual comments of two men concerned with matters of much more moment than the things they had chosen to talk about. Hewlitt did not have to remember the role assigned to him; the more he sat in Scott's company the more he found himself establishing empathy with the man. Although his presence there was almost a total betrayal, he forced that thought out of his mind and considered only that they had met casually. Then he began to hope, almost to pray, that their meeting had been exactly as Scott had indicated that it was, a completely accidental encounter. He liked Scott, he wanted him to be cleared of suspicion. In the underground he could be damn valuable and he had the guts to do things—he had already proven that.

"Hew," Scott said, "I was wondering: do you expect this thing to last forever?"

Hewlitt glanced around automatically to be sure that they were not being overhead. "Nothing ever does," he answered cautiously. "But I have a feeling that we have a lot worse ahead of us before it all ends, one way or another."

Scott nodded over his drink. "You're right, you've got to be. But, Hew, it doesn't make sense." He stopped and visibly put down the anger which was trying to edge his voice. "Look, we've got a helluva big and powerful country here, two hundred million of us live in it, and I don't care what the box score says, nobody can take over an establishment like that and make it stick."

"They had colonialism in Southeast Asia for two hundred years," Hewlitt said. "The people there had nothing to start with, but eventually the European powers had to get out. The Dutch out of Java, the French out of Indo-China, the British out of Burma."

"True, but in some of those places the commies came in —they backed Ho in Indo-China, for example. Nobody that I know of is going to back us; we got ourselves into this corner and we're going to have to get ourselves out."

Hewlitt toyed with his glass. "You're in the Air Force," he said. "You tell me how."

"There's too many of us; some of the people who believed what Fitzhugh told them know better now; even Wattles has lost his black following."

"The Air Force is great—the best," Hewlitt told him, "but what are you going to fly—*Ramrods*?"

Scott leaned closer and looked down at his glass for a moment.

"Hew, look at it this way: there are a lot of them here, but they're still outnumbered something like ten thousand to one or better. That's just a guess, of course. With all their planes that our brilliant Mr. McNamara thought were obsolete, and their missiles, and their navy, and their garrison troops, they still don't have enough to keep us in tow, not if we choose to do something about it."

Hewlitt carefully made no answer; he did not want to commit himself that soon.

"At the moment the Air Force is down, but it isn't out. We still have some resources left."

Hewlitt looked up at that. "Can you make them count?"

This time Scott remained silent for several seconds, then he said, "Damn right."

"That's good to hear."

"Consider what happened, Hew," Scott continued. "When they pointed the loaded gun at us, and we were stuck with the *Ramrod* as our principal air superiority system, the President made that speech about saving human life and plain gave in. Well, the armed forces aren't in being to say that a war that's forced on us is too risky and then bow out. But the President is the commander in chief—or he was. He put out the order to lay down our weapons and it was a court-martial offense not to do so—we are the instrument of national policy. The whole damn Sixth Fleet had to put into port in the Med without firing a shot, because the order was final and absolute. Even the nuc subs had to turn themselves in."

"There wasn't much choice about that part," Hewlitt said. "The terms weren't published, but they knew exactly how many we had and they laid down the law: if every one of them wasn't in port and surrendered within fifteen days, then the ICBM's would be let loose."

Scott dropped his voice to a confidential level even lower than it had been before. "I heard that two of them were scuttled by their skippers just the same."

"Four," Hewlitt corrected. "They made port as ordered, then opened the sea cocks or whatever they do and scuttled right at the docks. As soon as the salt water hit them they were so much expensive junk."

"Hurrah for the Navy," Scott said. "Let's have one more for them."

"For the Navy, yes," Hewlitt agreed.

He caught the girl's eye and indicated another round. Neither man said anything until the drinks had been served, then when the pianist began to play "Ebb Tide" Scott used the sound of the music to cover his voice.

"Hew, I think that there's something going already. In a lot of different places. I told you that we're not through yet, and you can bank on that. The Navy will have a few tricks up its sleeve, too. I'm darned sorry that Haymarket was killed, he was one guy they never buffaloed. He told Fitzhugh to cut his throat—remember?"

"Of course."

"Well, there are other guys as good or pretty near as good. I wouldn't tell you this if I didn't trust you, but I'm working on a few contacts now."

"If I can help you, let me know," Hewlitt said. He did not have enough time to consider that before he had the words out, but he decided that it was about the only thing he could have said. It had committed him, but not too deeply, and it had been a natural reaction.

"Maybe you can," Scott said slowly. "It could be. If you hear of anything . . ." He shook his head. "I'd better not," he concluded.

"As you like," Hewlitt replied. His orders had been to follow Scott's lead and not to improvise.

"Hell," Scott said, "I don't know why I'm playing chintzy with you. In your job you had to have every clearance that there is."

Hewlitt said nothing.

"You're in a pretty sensitive spot right now. You know what's going on as much as anyone. Well, there's an opposition shaping up; Bob Landers was part of it until he got caught in a million-to-one fluke—he left a note in a drop and one of their surveillance people shooting for something else entirely just happened to catch a frame of him doing it. It wouldn't happen again in ten thousand years."

"God, what a break!" Hewlitt said, barely voicing the words.

"I worked for him, I think you know that." Scott looked around for a moment as a couple got up to leave; he waited until they were out of the lounge. "If you find out who replaces him, don't tell me—but pass the word that I'd like to know, will you?"

Hewlitt nodded. "Of course, if you want me to. But considering that I work directly for Zalinsky, I'll be poison—you know that."

"Maybe yes, maybe no."

It was the time, Hewlitt knew, to make his move. Exactly as he had been told. "Thanks for the confidence, Phil. I don't know what I can do, but I'll try. I hear some things occasionally." He hunched himself over the table so that his voice would have minimum range. The piano player started a Marc Orberg tune, but switched after a few bars and picked up the verse of "Black Moonlight" instead. "Do you want to know a wild one? There's a lot of enemy traffic on U.S. 1, mostly from Andrews going north. They've all but closed the Baltimore Bay Tunnel to civilian traffic."

"I've heard that."

"Well, they may not be using it much longer."

Scott lifted his eyebrows. "So?"

"That's what I heard. I don't see how anyone could do it, not and get away with it, but somebody thought of it, anyway."

Scott shook his head. "It wouldn't be a smart thing to do; we need the tunnel more than they do, but I still wish them luck. Cheers."

The phone rang in Hewlitt's apartment less than five minutes after he had closed the door behind him. He picked it up and was surprised to hear an inviting female voice on the line. "Hello, Rog."

"I think you have the wrong number," Hewlitt responded. It was definitely not Barbara, and he was almost certain it was not Mary either.

"Isn't this Mr. Samuels?"

"I'm sorry."

"Oh, excuse me. I know it's late."

"That's quite all right. You didn't disturb me."

Hewlitt did not allow himself to think what the words might mean. Instead he carefully looked at his watch and waited until precisely ten minutes had passed, then he went out quietly through the rear exit, made his way to the street, and started walking toward the corner. He held himself carefully, well aware that he was literally taking the first steps in a new direction for his life. Steps which could conceivably also bring it to a sudden end. He was not afraid; if that was the way that things were slated to go, so be it. He was out of the groove, and he felt it almost physically with every part of his being.

He heard the sound of a car behind him, but he did not turn to look. He was aware that it was slowing down, but his intelligence quickly told him that so far he had said and done nothing since leaving Davy Jones' house that could be challenged. He had a valid excuse for being where he was in the event he was to be questioned.

The car went past, slowed up, and stopped three hundred feet ahead, close to the curb. It was a battered black taxi, an anonymous member of the Washington fleet. Hewlitt did not hurry; when he was opposite the cab he hesitated for a moment as though he were making up his mind. Then he walked over, bent down, and spoke to the driver. "Are you free?"

"Where do you want to go?"

He could not see the man in the shadows; he was a Caucasian of fairly small stature, but that was all that was visible. "The Hot Shoppe on the Virginia side."

"O.K., hop in."

As the taxi pulled away, Hewlitt realized that he had no real idea where he was going or what would be expected of him. He had two things in his mind: his recent conversation with Scott and the fact that the cab had appeared at the appointed place exactly on time.

The cab passed what would have been a logical turning point for the Fourteenth Street Bridge and headed instead toward a somewhat rundown residential area. Hewlitt sat back and relaxed; if he were questioned now he would claim that he had been deep in his own thoughts and had not even noticed where the cab was going.

He rode on for another twelve minutes, then the driver interrupted his thoughts. "I'm gonna drop you beside a house, understand? Don't go in, go down the side to the rear yard. You'll meet someone there."

Before Hewlitt could answer he felt the pull of the brakes as the car swung close to the curb. He got out and remembered to hand the driver a bill from his wallet. Without comment he turned his back, glanced at the unpromising structure before him, and then went as he had been directed. Uncertainty returned to him for a moment when he found that the backyard was almost totally shrouded in darkness. At first he could not see whether anyone was there to meet him or not. Then he was aware of a man before him whose face he could not see. He heard the words, "Come with me, please," and followed as directed. Behind his guide he went through a gate in a board fence, crossed another yard, and went into the back door of what appeared to be a totally dark house.

For the second time that evening he followed someone up a set of back stairs, then down a side corridor to the front room. Not a light showed anywhere, but enough illumination came in through the large front-facing window to allow him to pick out three more figures who were gathered silently in the darkness. One of them stepped forward and allowed what light there was to outline his features for a moment; Hewlitt recognized Percival.

"We received your message," he said softly. "Are you absolutely sure of your information?"

"Totally," Hewlitt answered.

"Then come over here."

Set back from the window there was a stubby telescope on a tripod; the instrument itself appeared to have an unusually large aperture for its short length. "Take a look," Percival invited.

When Hewlitt bent over slightly to peer into the eyepiece he was startled to find that he was apparently viewing his objective in close to broad daylight. "If you don't know it, it's a sniperscope," he heard Percival saying. "It has a light amplifying system."

"I've heard about them," Hewlitt said. "They really work."

"The Viet Cong found that out. Now, do you see the steps of the house in the lower left of the image?"

"Yes."

"That's the entrance to the enemy's safe house that I told you about. We've been watching their people for some time and they invariably come from the direction that you're watching. Can you see clearly?"

"Quite."

"Then stay right where you are. Don't touch anything else in the room. Keep your eye glued to that telescope. If you see someone coming, observe him closely. If you can make a positive identification of Scott, tell me. Don't hesitate, but be sure. Got that?"

"Yes."

"One more thing. If you identify Scott absolutely, and if he turns into that house, we will take action. Never mind the equipment; that will be taken care of. Your job will be to go out as you came in as quickly as you can and still be careful. Someone will be with you, follow his instructions. That's all."

Hewlitt did not answer; he felt no need. He fixed his eye to the scope as he had been directed.

At the end of the first half hour he began to feel cramped. He turned his neck the other way and used his left eye to maintain his vigil. During his momentary shift of position he glanced around the room and saw that the other figures were clearer now. One of them, almost motionless like himself, held the butt end of a rifle which was resting on a tripod.

For a moment he felt a strong revulsion; he did not want to give the word that would cause a man to be killed. A man with whom he had shared drinks a short time ago. Then he fixed his mind on the unforgettable picture of Bob Landers' body lying on the South Lawn, and remembered something Scott had told him in the bar. This wasn't child's play and he knew he had to face up to that fact.

"Target."

The word came from the man with the rifle who was also looking through a telescopic finder. Hewlitt looked and saw the figure coming into his field of view: first his feet, then his trouser legs, his torso, and finally the face of Captain Philip Scott. He looked very carefully for three additional seconds, but there was no mistake; he was wearing the same clothes he had had on in the bar. "It's Scott," he said, just loudly enough to be heard.

"You are certain?" This from Percival.

"Certain."

He did not want to look, but he could not escape from the eyepiece. He saw Phil Scott walk the few remaining paces to the front of the building, watched as he turned, and followed him as he started to mount the steps. Then he heard an angry, muffled spit bite the air in the room.

He saw Phil Scott appear to hesitate, raise his arm as though to shield his eyes from the absent sun, and then falter. He slumped downward, tumbling backward from where he had stood, until his body lay sprawled flat where he had paused moments before.

"Let's go," Percival said.

Shaken, Hewlitt went out the door, hurried along the corridor, and ran down the steps. The others were directly behind him. Once he was outside in the air his mood abruptly changed, he was the hunted one now and his mind was totally set on escape. When he reached the backyard of the opposite house he heard the single word, "Wait."

Although his mind urged him to flee, he did as he was told. Others came behind him, carrying things he could not see even though his night vision was now effective. Then he made out the outlines of a car that was parked there; he noticed that when the doors were opened no lights went on automatically. "In the front," he was directed.

He was barely seated when the vehicle started. It moved down the narrow space between two adjacent houses and entered the all but deserted street. No other traffic was visible for some distance either way. Hewlitt found that he was wedged between the driver and Percival.

They were off the streets again within five minutes; the driver turned into a dark, unguarded parking garage which was normally used only during the daylight hours and the very early evening. Behind the first spiral ramp other vehicles were waiting, including the cab that Hewlitt had ridden in earlier.

The three other men, all of them carrying equipment, left the car without a wasted motion and moments later were on their way separately, driving out by different exits. Percival lingered for just a moment to speak to Hewlitt. "Are you all right?" he asked.

"Yes, I'll make out all right. My first experience, of course."

"I know—and it isn't easy. But he *was* guilty."

Hewlitt nodded. "I know that. In the bar tonight, he made a bad slip."

"Tell me."

They were already alone except for the waiting driver who was not close enough to hear. Percival was obviously anxious to go, but he wanted the question answered first.

"He told me how Bob Landers was discovered. He said that he was accidentally photographed leaving a note in a drop. True or false, he couldn't possibly know that, unless . . ."

"Of course not. Good work. Go home."

"Yes, sir."

He went quickly to the waiting cab and was relieved when he felt the vehicle moving under him. Twenty minutes later he let himself in his back door, undressed, and prepared for bed. But he had no thought of sleep; the image of what he had seen, the silent unreality of it all, kept repeating itself, over and over, in his mind. He could not banish it or forget that he had given the signal that had destroyed a man's life.

It was hell, because he had been an intelligent man, a capable one, with fifty more years of life ahead of him.

He turned the lights as low as he could, then mixed himself a stiff drink. He sat down on the edge of his bed, glass in hand, and waited for the alcohol to release the bonds that were tied so tightly around his brain.

CHAPTER TWELVE

Colonel Gregor Rostovitch was in a sustained rage that not even the passage of the long hours of the night had been able to mitigate. His frustration was rekindled every time that he allowed himself to think once more of the setback that had been thrust upon him, and the added fact that he had an enemy who had not yet been totally liquidated.

Ever since his late teens he had been accustomed to giving the orders and having them obeyed. Blinding ambition had been the beacon of his life—that and his intense hatred of the Jews. He was a man of violence; both his hands were heavily scarred from having been smashed into men's faces and his body bore the marks of two unsuccessful attempts at assassination. By the time he had reached the rank of colonel in his nation's army he had a reputation so fearsome that he had chosen to remain known by that title.

When he had been appointed head of the secret police he had made results his one objective; the methods of obtaining them were evaluated by him from a practical standpoint and no other. Scott, the American, had been a good case in point. He had first appeared in a certain vital location in Europe at a time when the plans for the overthrow of the United States were well advanced. Not even the premier knew as much about them as did Colonel Rostovitch, who was himself their principal author. There were certain things, the colonel had decided, that the premier would be better off not knowing. The premier had continued with his playacting while the colonel had done the hard core work. One minor piece of information which he desired and did not have was known to Lieutenant Scott; he therefore set out to get it.

Scott had been probed to find out where his weakness lay. It lay in immaturity and the earnest desire to love someone and to be loved in return. That called for a woman of singular talents, of which the colonel had a number available. He made a shrewd choice and then waited for the inevitable results; every man had his price, despite the fact that he might not know it himself.

Scott had been completely determined to be loyal to his country and to his military obligations, but he had been broken down with ruthless efficiency. Misleading information had been fed to him and then what had appeared to be supporting evidence. Convinced that his superiors had already openly discussed certain information which had been entrusted to them, and by then almost blindly in love with the highly skilled and extraordinarily lovely young woman who had been assigned to the job, he had unknowingly yielded to the expert questioning which had been concealed in her apparently idle, devoted conversation.

Just before the matter was to have been concluded, the lieutenant had been promoted and assigned to an even more sensitive area. The colonel had changed the instructions immediately and ordered him kept on the string. During the next few months he had been so carefully manipulated that he had gradually become truly convinced that the best hope for humanity, including that segment of it in his own country, lay in overcoming the aggressive lust and ruthless demand for profits that motivated the capitalistic system. His reward for this eventual conversion had been a physical and emotional ecstasy beyond anything he had conceived of as possible.

When it had been at its apex it had been snatched from him by the inhuman action of a high military superior, or so he had been made to believe. Rage had destroyed his reason and he had crossed over the line. He had been kept there by a firm promise—that the girl around whom the earth and all of the other planets now revolved would in one way or another be found and restored to him.

Scott had rationalized, as many other men had done before him, that he was fighting for the woman who was to be his wife and for the right to live with her in a finer and better world. On his own he had done his utmost, looking for her whenever and wherever he could, but he had been many thousands of miles removed from the Hong Kong dance hall which had been the scene of her next assignment.

The colonel was furious because Scott, whose unexpected position right in the White House had already been highly useful, had been shot dead literally on his own doorstep. One of his secret operating bases would now have to be abandoned; but that was nothing compared to the intolerable fact that his enemy had scored a decisive, if small, victory over him. Not since he had lost the most ruthless and efficient agent he had ever had in an alley in Port Said had he known a similar frustration. Scott had represented a heavy investment, and a successful one. Furthermore, he had been bearing some kind of important information or he would never have risked coming to the place he had at that hour of the night.

Also extremely aggravating to the colonel was the lack of any clue to the identity of the person or persons who had scored on him. His people had located the place from which the shot had come, but a thorough shakedown of the premises a few minutes after Scott had died had turned up nothing.

His instructions, which had been relayed to Scott, had been merely to probe the translator Hewlitt for a possible lead into the underground. The fact that he had come down to report in person clearly indicated that Scott had discovered something of real importance. In that deduction the colonel was correct; his agent had discovered that Raleigh Hewlitt, who worked in Zalinsky's own immediate proximity, was himself a member of the underground organization and had tried to feed him a preposterous story during the tête-a-tête in the bar. That piece of information had died with the man who had detected it—as it had been intended to do. The cock and bull story about the Baltimore Bay Tunnel would never have brought him to the house at any such hour, but the knowledge that Zalinsky was being directly observed by an underground agent would. Scott had been, for the most part, highly intelligent as well as sensitive, and it had been his undoing.

Certain facts revealed by Scott's death caused the colonel to do some hard thinking. First, the shot had been fired by an expert marksman, not by an amateur, and with sophisticated equipment. Casual assassins do not have sniperscopes available. Secondly, it had taken some competent work to uncover the carefully concealed intelligence center and it had been done so well that the colonel had had no inkling that his private location had been blown until the news had been delivered by the cadaver on his doorstep. Thirdly, and most significant of all, he had been challenged. Challenged by a totally invisible adversary who obviously knew what he was doing.

The colonel smashed one mauled fist against the top of his desk: he would answer that challenge and he would answer it in language that would bring his opposition to its knees in short order! He had plenty of people and more were coming; he would stop the general surveillance and similar activities in order to direct all of his resources squarely against whatever underground there was that had flung this defiance into his face. Every person on his staff had been hand-picked and then toughened to be a totally relentless, utterly effective weapon. They had done little so far in the United States except for those who had been operating in the theater for some time; now they would do a great deal. A very great deal.

The colonel slammed his other fist down. It was total war and in that heartless game he was the deadliest player there was. At that moment he dedicated himself to total success and nothing else. He knew that he was to be the next premier of his country, but his ambition did not stop at that. The biggest obstacle was all but out of the way now—one more victory over what had to be a puny opponent and then . . .

He blocked the rest of it out of his mind. He did not want to dwell on it—he had other things to do first.

At her berth in the San Pedro harbor the fishing vessel *Dolly* was being prepared for sea. She had a new crew and a new skipper this time, which was not unusual. She was, if anything, too large for her job, and as a result the cost of operating her had discouraged several previous owners. In addition, her speed was a knot or two less than it would have been if her lines had been a little more skillfully laid out. She was sturdy, there was no denying that, and she could withstand the roughest weather she was likely ever to see, but her efficiency as a working vessel was a few notches lower than most of the other craft engaged in the same line of activity.

It did not take the experienced Japanese-American fishermen who were berthed next to her very long to size up the man who proposed to take her to sea this time. He was experienced around the waterfront, that was clear; he had a fair knowledge of commercial fishing operations, and he was obviously determined to do his best. If he did very well, and if luck was with him and his crew, it was quite possible that he might have a profitable first voyage. But it was quite clear that he had never been at sea before in command of a vessel such as the *Dolly;* it was a new venture for him—possibly his effort to establish himself independently so that he could be his own boss henceforth. He was a nice guy and the crew of the neighboring vessel wished him good luck.

In all probability the *Dolly* would be out for some time. It was possible that she could hit a run of fish and be back in port again in a matter of days, but it was also unlikely. Wisely her new captain was provisioning her well; in that he showed evidence of some sound experience, since well-fed men work much better at sea and it is extremely costly to have to put into port for resupply if the luck runs bad or the weather turns foul for extended periods of time.

Whoever the new owners of the *Dolly* were, they had proper consideration for their vessel and her crew; for once a chief engineer had an ample supply of spare parts to stock and enough money to spend to make all necessary and advisable repairs. The men who were to go to sea on her obviously appreciated the fact that the port work was being well done. It was also clear to the old hands nearby that they were being well paid, because many of them were young and seemed capable; crewmen like that could have their pick of the available jobs, and the *Dolly,* while sound and well built, was no particular prize on which to be sailing. That was their business, however, and no one interfered. It could be a cooperative venture with a good bonus available if all went well.

When the time came, the *Dolly* cast off and moved through the harbor at the prescribed five knots with more dignity than she had displayed for some time. She went past the breakwater as a Japanese freighter was coming in and an hour later was no longer visible. The last pleasure boat to sight her saw her headed off in a northwesterly direction.

When she was completely by herself at sea, her captain summoned his first mate to the bridge. "Have you been over her thoroughly?" he asked.

"Yes, sir, every inch. We've checked and double-checked. Also our final security report was go. One item: Lieutenant Hanson speaks fluent Japanese."

"I know that."

"Of course, sir. What I was going to say was, he tuned in on the crew next to us while we were being discussed; they did notice the nature of our personnel, but attributed it to the fact that we are paying well. From the way they spoke Lieutenant Hanson doubts very much that they will talk about the matter with anyone."

"Good. It appears then that everything is A.O.K. Set up the radio watches and break out the long-range radar. You know what else to do."

"Ay, ay, sir."

The captain reached out and laid his hand on his mate's arm. "One thing more before you go, Jimmy. Things may look tough, and they are, but the Navy is at sea."

A grin broke out on the mate's face. "Right you are, sir! As of this moment I'm peculiarly happy. Think of all the guys left back on the beach."

"I am. You are now the best executive officer at sea with the United States Navy and I expect you to live up to it."

The lieutenant was a young man and full of vitality. "Let me know if you have any complaints, sir."

As the dusk fell on the *Dolly* she kept on her steady course toward the fishing grounds south of the Aleutians. In the wheelhouse standard navigational methods were keeping her on course; the chart was in plain view. Deep in her hold, in a location almost impossible for any ordinary inspection to find, a highly sophisticated inertial platform was in operation. There was also much other equipment which had come on board in a series of disguises—obtained, packaged, and delivered under the personal direction of Stanley Cumberland. It had been stockpiled very carefully, and very secretly, weeks before the disaster to the country had struck. Admiral Haymarket had selected most of it himself with its eventual purpose clearly in mind. He had also made a personal selection of the crew that was to use and maintain it; when Lieutenant James Morton, Jr., of the United States Navy had been described as the best executive officer at sea, his qualifications for that distinction had not rested solely on the fact that he happened to be the only one. He was gifted with enormous resourcefulness and was something of a mechanical genius. In addition to that he was a damn fine sailor, which was what the admiral had looked for first.

A great deal was resting on the *Dolly* now, on every member of her crew, and particularly on her captain. In his selection the admiral had gone the limit. He had had more or less the pick of the entire Navy, barring a few men who had already been selected for even more important duties and responsibilities. The man he had chosen knew the very grave risk that faced him and every member of his crew, and he had welcomed it.

Hopefully, the *Dolly* was about to write a few fresh paragraphs in naval history.

When Raleigh Hewlitt seated himself at his desk on the morning after he had witnessed the shooting of Philip Scott, he felt himself a different person. He was not happy that he had seen a man die, but there were other considerations, one of them being some millions of other Americans who were also people of value and whose lives and futures had been betrayed by the man who had paid with his life for what he had done.

His manner was a little firmer than it had been; he felt a certain increase of confidence. He had helped to make possible a counter-thrust against the enemies who were now occupying his country. Mr. Zalinsky would have given a good deal, he knew, to share the information that was locked in his brain.

Then Zalinsky rang. Hewlitt went into the Oval Office with his usual paper and pencils to see what it was this time.

Zalinsky motioned him toward a chair without looking up. Hewlitt sat down and relaxed—he felt that he had earned the right to do that now. The administrator affixed his signature to a document before him and then gave him his attention. "I extend to you my deepest regrets," he said.

Hewlitt looked properly surprised. "Concerning what?" he asked.

"Captain Scott."

Hewlitt lifted himself slightly out of his chair and then sank back down again. "What's happened to him?"

Zalinsky gave him the X-ray eye treatment. "You do not know?"

"No—please tell me."

"He is dead."

Hewlitt sat in silence for a moment, his head down. Then he blinked his eyes and pressed his teeth together before he spoke.

"You shot him." He made it both a question and an accusation.

Zalinsky shook his head. "No, I did not shoot him. Somebody did, but for yet I myself do not know who is responsible."

"But I saw him," Hewlitt protested. "It was just last night . . ."

"In this city you have much crime upon the streets," Zalinsky said, "and I have not had time to adjust it yet. He was out late and encountered death."

Hewlitt wondered how much of that Zalinsky believed, then knew that he did not believe it at all. "Captain Scott was a fine officer," he said, as though he were still stunned and thinking aloud. "What have they done with his body?"

"I am uncertain; I have not been told. It is now time to pass to another matter, have you preparation?"

"Yes, go ahead." He swallowed hard and gave just enough indication of trying to get himself under control.

"Our premier has given a new order which all must obey, I myself also." He stopped and waited, possibly measuring Hewlitt's reaction and he surveyed him with solid appraisal.

"What is the order?" Hewlitt asked, knowing that he was expected to do so.

"Each person who is sent on occupation duty it is now required to explain at least one person our system and its goodness. Therefore is doubled the truthfulness. Then once again, and continuing."

"It sounds like a chain letter," Hewlitt said.

"I am unacquainted."

Hewlitt saw no need to explain all the details. "It's something that doesn't work."

Zalinsky hardened. "This will work," he announced. "Always what we do works—it must. Failure is not allowed. I myself personally must make intelligent one person, for this I have selected you."

"Mr. Zalinsky," Hewlitt said, "don't try."

The administrator shook his head. "I agree, it is a waste of time when I have so muchness to do. But it is required. We begin at once. Make me a question."

Hewlitt leaned back and crossed his legs. "All right, since you put it that way. Explain to me why you are banning the Jews from public office. What do you hope to accomplish?"

Zalinsky put his fingertips together in the manner of a teacher. "I must ask from you a favor; we speak my language, yes?"

"Certainly."

"It is a great relief for me," Zalinsky admitted, at once more at ease. "I have promised myself that I will speak nothing but English, but it is a very difficult and sometimes irrational method of communication."

"Agreed." Hewlitt noted that it was like talking to a different man. Zalinsky's very personality seemed to change.

"Now as to your question: in the first place, so far all that we have done is to uproot some of these people and require them to find other work. In this process we have admittedly caused some of them inconvenience and probably some financial loss as well. Do you condemn this?"

"Of course I do," Hewlitt answered. "It is inhuman, and that is the exact word, to single out a group of people and then treat them this way solely because of their religion and racial background. And by doing this, you will cause millions of Americans who aren't Jewish to hate you for it."

"You consider this un-American?"

"We went to war against Hitler."

"Yes, but it was thrust upon you—you kept more or less out of things until after Pearl Harbor. And you didn't fight Hitler because of what he was doing to the Jews."

Hewlitt was forced to backtrack. "You are right, but we deplored his genocide and did our utmost to stop it."

"But would you not, under special circumstances, do what we are doing to the Jews now?"

"Never. Mr. Zalinsky, this is, or was, a free country. Perhaps you do not understand what that means."

Zalinsky leaned forward and pointed a finger at him. "But you did; you forced people to register because of their race, then you threw them into concentration camps and kept them there for years." Zalinsky paused for a moment, and then continued. "You forced them to dispose of their possessions for pennies, and solely because of their ethnic background you imprisoned them, your own citizens who had done nothing to deserve it, under armed guard."

Then Hewlitt remembered. It had happened, just as Zalinsky had described it, and there was no way to refute it.

"In World War II your General DeWitt forced every one of your citizens who was of Japanese ancestry to register, then he shipped them all off like cattle. They had no choice. It is also a fact of history that you may not know that even then not one of these people ever helped your enemies."

"That is true, Mr. Zalinsky, and it was wrong," Hewlitt admitted. "It happened because after the surprise attack on Pearl Harbor, the Japanese in this country, I should say the Japanese-Americans, were totally mistrusted."

Zalinsky dismissed that with a wave of his arm. "Then in that case why didn't you imprison the Germans and the Italians too? It would have been the logical thing to do."

Aware that he was at a disadvantage, Hewlitt said nothing.

"Returning now to the Jews," Zalinsky went on. "They have had two thousand years in which to accommodate themselves to the rest of humanity and what have they done? Some have become like other people, yes, but most of them have demanded to remain Jews above all else. They demand to be accepted equally in every way, then also demand that they have the right to remain forever different. It is impossible. Do you believe that they are the one and only chosen people of your God?"

"No," Hewlitt said, "but if they want to believe that, that's their business."

Zalinsky put his elbows on the desk that properly belonged to the President of the United States, and leaned forward. "For again two thousand years the Jews have cried that they had no homeland, and insisted upon their Jewishness. Now they have one—all right, let them go there and be as Jewish as they like. They stay here only to make money . . ."

"No," Hewlitt interrupted, "I cannot agree with that. They are Americans, *this* is their homeland. And why don't you allow your own Jews to go to Israel if they wish?"

Zalinsky deliberately stopped for a few seconds to let the fact sink home that he had been interrupted. "The fact that we discuss this, it is proof of the problem. If the Jews were able to integrate with other people, then you would not have in your language any such word as anti-Semitism. It exists because in twenty centuries these people have insisted in keeping themselves apart. Now we are assisting them to do just that."

Something in Zalinsky's tone warned Hewlitt that the atmosphere was changing. He had been a little too bold, and a sudden chill was developing rapidly. "I see," he said, and was careful to sound like a dutiful student.

Zalinsky studied him for a moment, then accepted his apparent change in attitude. "We will talk more later," he said stiffly. He hesitated and then added, "You will go."

It was from a totally unexpected source that the colonel got the first break in his campaign. It came from Midwest America, where the true nature of what had happened to the country was just beginning to be understood. In that section, far from either of the great oceans which formerly had guarded the nation's shores, a steady belief had prevailed that the whole thing was some kind of a political mishmash which would be straightened out eventually at the conference table. As the days passed and concrete evidence of the disaster failed to appear, an illusion arose that the United States was simply too large and too powerful to be taken over by anybody. Then the enemy began to arrive. When a police chief was forcefully ejected from his office, and when the mayor of a major city was summarily barred from the building that had been his headquarters, the reality began to sink in. And a certain small-time police informer who also gathered information for anyone who would pay decided that the coming of the new bosses could very well mean an additional source of revenue.

Colonel Rostovitch did not as yet have too many men to spare for distribution around the country, but with more arriving each day on a basis of strict priority he made a first deployment. His instructions were explicit and basic: ferret out any kind of underground activity, organized or otherwise, and deal with it summarily. Originally his plan had been far different, but the matter of the Jews could come later. He had lost a round, and in the power-conscious world in which he lived a fast and effective counter was imperative. No one had ever crossed swords with Gregor Rostovitch without paying heavily for the privilege, and that record was not about to be broken.

In a good-sized city, west of the Mississippi but east of the Rockies, a little man known only as Archie spent almost the whole of his waking time wandering about, usually in a mild state of alcoholic fog, living an apparently hand-to-mouth existence. What food he was seen buying came from the half-price bakery outlets that sold day-old merchandise and from the bargain bins in the markets where the dented and disfigured cans were dumped at marked-down rates. He was so patently impotent and unqualified for any sort of gainful employment that he became the tolerated invisible man—like Father Brown's postman so commonplace that no one took any real notice of him.

All or much of this was window dressing, as were the threadbare clothes that he wore and the servile manner that he exhibited whenever anyone amused himself by buying him a drink or standing him a hot dog smothered in hot mustard and raw onions. While not visibly a man of property in the usual sense, Archie was not nearly as close to the extremes of mere existence as he appeared. He was a collector of information, a beachcomber who gathered his findings on the fringes of society and then sorted them out, carefully evaluating who might buy what. It was remarkable that he had been able to continue for so long without having been exposed for what he was, but he had been endowed with a near genius for footwork of the kind that skillfully avoids trouble of any kind whenever it appears in the offing. Several times he had arranged to be clapped into jail during periods when he was most anxious not to be found at his usual haunts; this had provided him with unshakable alibis as well as the proper respectability of a minor police record.

One of his steady clients was the police department—not everyone within that organization, but one or two individuals who had demonstrated over a period of time that they could be both close-mouthed and liberal in the cash they handed out. This arrangement had worked out well on both sides because of Archie's sometimes remarkable ability to appear to sink into the woodwork or to maintain a façade of simple stupidity so effectively that he was hardly regarded as a human being. Those who knew Archie, or saw him around, had put him down long since as rum dumb with the ability to go to the men's room on his own about the limit of his capability.

Some of Archie's clients did not even know who he was. They were aware only that if they inserted a certain ad in the classified section, they would receive a telephone call. By phone they made their wants known and agreed upon a price. Later, if all went well, they would be called again and the details of the transfer of funds and information would be arranged. Archie did not have a social security number and the Bureau of Internal Revenue took no notice of him. Somewhere, in some forgotten corner of the nation, there was probably a record of his birth which had not been consulted since the day that it had been filed. His police record, by very special private arrangement, did not exist at all since most of his arrests had been matters of mutual convenience. Where he kept his money only Archie knew, but it was suspected in one or two quarters that the amount might be quite substantial. As indeed it was.

Fortunately not handicapped by any feelings of sensitivity or requirements of conscience, Archie decided very promptly that the men who had come to his city from abroad would be just as anxious for his help as any of his other clients, and they should not be adverse to making the necessary payments. The way to obtaining their trade was simple: find out something that they would like to know and then open negotiations. It might even be necessary to give one or two tidbits away, but that investment could be recovered later by adding a suitable surcharge on to some more important item.

One of Archie's outstanding talents was an almost unerring ability to evaluate properly the worth of his stock in trade; he seldom made a mistake. But the invaders from overseas represented something new entirely and he had had no experience with similar customers to draw on. It was therefore all but impossible for him to appraise the amount of interest that would be aroused by the simple and not very spectacular fact that out at the university a small group of students was meeting secretly and probing for possible ways of frustrating the occupying forces.

Students were not very important. And Archie's common sense told him that their efforts, after all of the mighty military forces had been rendered impotent, were meaningless. More important and significant sabotage efforts, which were quite likely to come later when the general citizenry finally woke up to what they were up against, might well bring in some good fees. He decided, therefore, that in this instance it would be politic to give away a free sample. For this he resorted to his old ally, the telephone.

He had read the paper and knew whom to ask for. When he had the man himself on the line he indicated that he had some "valuable information" and used a well-tested formula to introduce his method of operation. He was very coldly received until he stated what it was that he had to tell. The reaction to that was positive, so much so that any idea of giving it away swiftly left Archie's mind. He arranged terms for a modest amount, which was his come-on technique that had worked out so well in the past, and then at once delivered his merchandise. He hung up the phone with a welcome sense of well-being; he had already made the transition to the new management and he was probably the first businessman in the city to do so.

Most ordinary citizens were totally unaware of the long-range listening devices which were capable of picking up a conversation held in normal tones in the middle of a deserted football field. Highly directional microphones, sound mirrors, and similar equipment, some of it artfully miniaturized, had been developed through two or three generations of design without ever receiving very much publicity. The eight undergraduate students at the university, who were meeting under the leadership of Miss Sally Bloom, might have known that such things existed, but they had never expected to encounter any of them. They were, therefore, totally unprepared when a force of eleven very tough, uniformed men broke in on them. Under the direction of one other foreigner, this one in civilian clothes, they were literally yanked out of their meeting room and hurried outside behind the building.

There was a brief, very rough, interrogation. "Who is the leader here?" the civilian demanded in guttural, heavily accented English.

Sally bravely raised her hand. "I am," she answered. "Why does it concern you?"

The man in charge did not bother to answer her question. "You are plotting against us," he declared instead. "You will tell me at once who directs you—everything. Otherwise . . ." He stopped to let his words be understood.

"We are a college drama group," Sally said, looking her accuser in the eye. "We have been working on the outlines of a new play. One that will be about what has been happening to the country."

The civilian took two steps forward and smashed his open hand across her face. As a brief spurt of blood appeared at the corner of her mouth he drew his arm across her body until his hand was behind his ear, then he whipped it out and hit her again, backhand. For just a moment he kept his attention on her; he did not see the look of desperate determination on the face of the slightly built young man who was at her right. He almost missed the young man's lunge toward him; he was too late to block effectively the untrained fist that was aimed at his jaw. As the student tried to bring his left into his middle, he raised his knee; with his two hands he rammed the youth's face hard against the solid bone of the kneecap and then, as he fell, kicked him viciously in the groin.

He seized the Bloom girl by the arm and expertly twisted it up sharply behind her back. As he did, the men under his command formed a quick cordon around the six other students, who still did not quite realize what was going on. "Who directs you? Talk!" the leader said, and then sharply increased the pressure on the thin arm he had trapped.

Sally Bloom could not help a tight, short scream of pain, but she said nothing. For three full minutes, the longest and most fearful of her life, she endured the questions, the blows on her body, the exquisite agony in the socket of her arm. Slowly the young man who had tried to help her got back onto his feet, still doubled over with the intense agony in his groin, a fearful burning that he did not think that he would be able to endure for another hundred seconds.

Unexpectedly the leader unlocked Sally's twisted arm and with it threw her to the ground. "You!" he said, pointing to one of the six who remained. "Come here."

Thrust forward by one of the uniformed men, the student complied. The man in charge wasted no time in subtleties; he ripped the young man's shirt open, took out a cigarette lighter, and directed how his victim was to be held. Locked on each side by a toughened man far stronger than himself, the youth was helpless. The man before him lit the cigarette lighter and then held it close under the student's armpit.

Pain was immediate and overwhelming. In a few seconds he could smell the odor of his own burning flesh and he wanted desperately to vomit.

"Tell me," the inquisitor demanded, "who directs you?"

The blinding pain took total possession of the student, his muscles turned to jelly and his whole body became a caldron of consuming fire. His mind lost all will except to stop the terrible agony; it had no strength for anything else. "I don't know," he screamed. "Only she knows." He could endure no more; the sudden shock, the things he had witnessed, his own brief but unendurable ordeal conquered him; and he went limp.

At a distance, terrified students and a few older adults were beginning to gather, but no one dared to venture closer than several hundred feet from the scene of the sudden, unexpected inquisition.

"Stand them up!" the leader directed in his own language. His command was quickly obeyed; the little group of students was lined up in a row, except for the Bloom girl, who lay where she had been thrown. The young man who had tried to attack the leader stood where he was shoved, still bent over, his hands unabashedly holding on to his cruelly injured groin through his clothing.

The man in the plain, ill-fitting business suit pulled the girl to her feet. "Tell me," he demanded. "Tell me and save their lives!"

"I don't know," she sobbed. "I don't know. He calls me by telephone. . . ." She was incapable of more.

The man who held her marched her forward two paces and flung her with the others. Then he barked a command in his own language.

There was a thick, ugly sound as eleven holsters were opened and the guns they contained were drawn. The only other female student in the little group began to scream; the soldier who had hold of her slapped her hard into silence. For a moment she was still, then, her eyes wild, she let out another terrified burst of sound.

One of the male students, larger and more muscular than the rest, made a sudden quick motion and broke the hold by which he was held. In a supreme burst of effort he sprinted for the corner of the building and momentary safety; the man who had been holding him laid his weapon across the elbow of his left arm, took aim, and fired. The blast of the gun reverberated in the air; the athlete jerked suddenly upright, reached out to claw at the air, and then fell forward. He lay inert and soundless where he fell.

The leader waved his arm toward the others. The screaming girl was silenced first; a bullet in her brain ended her final shriek in mid-spasm. The student next to her fell to his knees and lifted his clasped hands in supplication. He was next to die; three quick shots in his chest cut him down.

A hoarse burst of screaming, this time from a masculine throat, pointed the next victim. The man behind him reversed his gun in his hand, then holding it by the barrel he smashed it down with vicious force onto the skull of his victim. Almost a full inch of the handgrip disappeared into the cranium with the sound of suddenly breaking ice.

A very young student, wide-eyed with horror, was frozen into immobility. Only his lips moved as he said, "Mother!" Then his staring eyes became empty as a sudden black hole in his forehead marked the end of his life.

The next of the young men stood still, speaking words of hope for a better life to come. ". . . Thy kingdom come; Thy will be done, on earth as it is in . . ." The angry, violent bark of a gun ended his prayer; his body slumped very quietly to the ground.

The leader seized the blouse of Sally Bloom and in one powerful jerk ripped it from her body. Her slender torso was revealed, milky white and crossed by a small brassiere which proved that the breasts underneath were minimal. "Are you a Jew?" the man demanded.

If they were to be her last words, they were brave ones. "Yes, I am a Jew," she declared. "God bless America!"

"No!!" The sudden outcry came from the young man who had tried to defend her. Forgetting the still frightful pain in his groin, he threw himself in front of her, offering her the protection of his own body.

The leader in the business suit produced his own gun from a concealed holster, then motioned that the student was to be moved aside. The youth's arms were seized; he was forcefully pulled away and then turned around so that his horror-stricken eyes could witness the sight as the bullets fired in rapid succession tore the frail brassiere away, and hear the sound of the shots blasted back from the wall of the building.

In the terrible moment that followed he knew that all of the others were dead and that he himself would die within the next few seconds. He turned, faced the man he had at least struck with his fist, and said, "Pray to God, because you're next."

He did not feel the bullets that bit into him, only the first one that was deliberately pumped into his abdomen where it would hurt the worst. Somewhere within his expiring body he found the strength to endure it all and to face death unafraid.

So died Gary Fitzhugh, only son of Senator Solomon Fitzhugh, as his now vacant physical being collapsed to the ground next to the silent shell of the girl he had loved.

CHAPTER THIRTEEN

Like the slow fingers of winter feeling their way across the country in late October, the deepening effect of the defeat began to grip every part of the nation. The heavy transatlantic air traffic had changed pattern until some ten thousand of the enemy were being ferried westward each day. Not many other travelers booked the available flights; the United States had been stripped of its tourist appeal, and few Americans were in the mood for pleasure travel in Europe. Grim foreboding overshadowed the whole country as the realization sank home that the worst was not over and that still more difficult and dangerous times lay ahead.

During the original days of the occupation the orders had been to continue all of the normal functions of the government until further notice. As a result policemen and firemen still manned their posts, the courts sat and handed down decisions, and the postal service continued very much as before. They functioned, however, in a shadow world in which the will of the enemy was in absolute control and tightening its grip with each passing day.

As the fall approached the New York Philharmonic Symphony Orchestra announced the cancellation of its season. No reason was given; the bare statement was allowed to stand without amplification. There were reports that no conductor of stature could be found to assume responsibility for the orchestra, so many of the leading maestros being Jewish, and more accurate ones that the orchestra was having difficulties filling all of its chairs. Estimates of the Jewish makeup of the orchestra varied between fifty and ninety per cent, but whatever the true figure might be, there was little doubt in the world's greatest Jewish city that the enemy was directly responsible.

For the first time since the President had announced the nation's surrender, "in order that human life may be saved and we may be spared the horror of nuclear conflict," there was real and genuine concern about the future. No longer was there a general trust that something would be worked out through diplomatic channels; now there was no hope ahead and the total, conscienceless takeover by the enemy emerged from a projected picture on a movie screen to a living, brutal, three-dimensional reality.

Although the normal means of national communication were under tight censorship and control, a changing attitude became visible throughout the whole country. Without fanfare or announcement, Marc Orberg recordings quietly disappeared from the market. Where it had once been impossible to walk through Times Square without hearing his voice projected at the passersby from at least a half dozen record stores, now there was no indication that he had ever appeared on the scene. The blow-up posters of him, life size and larger, were no longer to be found. A single Village shop, owned by a heteroclite young man tightly shrouded in his own ideas, displayed a window streamer that read: WANT ORBERG RECORDS? WE GOT 'EM. The banner had been up only two days when the store was broken into at night by persons unknown and the stock was badly vandalized. Less than two weeks after that unpublicized event no Orberg songs could be found on the market, performed by himself or anyone else. None were played on the air.

In the Negro areas of many of the major cities the common sign FREE WATTLES became much less conspicuous. Negro Americans ranging from the affluent to those on welfare gradually shifted the focus of their interest from their own problems to those of the nation as a whole. Militants who had prophesied that the coming of the enemy would mean a new stature and dignity for the black man were faced with a reality that did not conform to their predictions. In sharp contrast the rural areas, particularly in the Midwest, were hard hit by the abrupt ending of the farm programs which had been in operation for many years. Price supports and many other government aids to agriculture were terminated without notice, and with the termination went a hard warning that no excuses would be excepted in lieu of full production.

Not much more than three months after the President's

capitulation there were more than a million of the enemy within the continental United States; one for every two hundred Americans. The long-held private lands in Hawaii, which had been controlled with great determination by the five pioneer families, were taken over, but none of the acreage was made available to the land-hungry residents who had long hoped to have the monopoly broken.

Many announcements were made; rules were laid down and enforcement became arbitrary. There was no avenue of appeal, no recourse except obedience—immediate and complete. Of all of the pronouncements made, the one which caused the greatest stir concerned the change of language. As soon as enough teachers could be brought over, the American public was told, instruction would begin immediately in the enemy's language. Five years would be allowed for the transition; after that all use of the English language would cease except for authorized scholastic programs and necessary research projects. All newspapers, magazines, books, and other means of printed communication would have to be changed over. No one, regardless of age, would be excused from studying the new required language. "It must be now remembered," the official announcement had said, "that currently and henceforth we own the United States by right of conquest. It will soon cease to exist as a separate nation."

An additional problem appeared, this one without any announcement whatever, when it was discovered that the supply of major household appliances was rapidly diminishing. Increasingly urgent calls from wholesalers to their sources of supply revealed that almost all of the available production was being shipped overseas. The cost was paid and no more, but production was ordered kept at a maximum level. One of the largest national manufacturers finally got a statement from the controlling enemy office: it said tersely that there was a greater need for comforts in the victorious nation which had sacrificed so much in order to make military triumph possible. America had too much already, and the situation could be expected to last for some years.

The weeks of the occupation progressed without any sign that complete surrender had left any resource out of the enemy's hands. There was not a family which did not feel the pressure, or inwardly cringe under the steady progression of pieces of bad news, one after the other, without any mitigation or evidence of even a ray of hope. The massacre of the college students was known everywhere, and in many areas hopeful little groups who had planned to establish an opposition framework realized the hopelessness of their position. There were millions who cursed the men in Washington who had allowed this to come about; a prime target of this invective was Senator Solomon Fitzhugh, the renowned dove who more than any other single individual had cut the ground out from under the armed forces and sapped the morale of the entire country. A famous sentence was quoted uncounted times in bitter hindsight; it became the password of those who hoped that someday they could do something. It appeared on handbills printed and distributed under the noses of the occupying forces by men who knew that capture meant immediate certain death. Long forgotten in the wave of isolationism brought on by the unpopular Vietnam war, it came back too late to help in the existing crisis. It became instead a bitter reminder to be recalled again if freedom ever returned, that eternal vigilance is the price of liberty.

The sun had been in the sky for only an hour or so when a nondescript car turned off the highway in western Colorado and headed up a dirt road toward the open country. The two hunters it carried had little to say to each other as the car went up one grade and down another; instead they kept a careful watch looking for evidences of wildlife and for any signs of movement in their range of vision. After they had driven a quarter hour over the steadily narrowing road, they saw on their left the boarded-up entrance to an old mine shaft. Someone had taken the trouble to string a few strands of used barbed wire around the barricade to prevent stray cattle from falling to their deaths down the abandoned opening. A badly weather-beaten sign warned any human passersby that the site was dangerous. The hunter who was driving took careful note of the old mine, but said nothing; he continued on up the road until it terminated, for all practical purposes, a half mile farther on. There he pulled the car off into the brush and set the parking brake.

The security personnel who guarded the underground headquarters of Thomas Jefferson had had the car under observation almost from the time that it had left the highway. As the vehicle had passed the concealed entrance the occupants had been photographed by precision automatic equipment utilizing a classified film which yielded ultrasharp images almost totally devoid of grain. As the two hunters, rifles in hand, began to walk back down the road toward the old mine shaft, their progress was followed. At the same time other sensitive equipment in nearby concealed locations swept the area to determine if any other persons were within visual or audible range. The findings were negative.

When the first of the hunters reached the barbed wire at the head of the shaft, he laid his left hand on one strand and took hold of another, three feet from it, with his right. Almost at once he felt a slight tingle of electricity, the invisible acknowledgment that he had passed surveillance and that the surrounding area was clear. A half minute later there was no sign of the hunters; the old car that they had been driving was all but invisible in the brush where it had been left.

Lieutenant Colonel Henry Pritchard, the search and rescue pilot, received them in his office and immediately offered coffee. His manner was cordial but preoccupied; all of the members of the First Team were under heavy strain as the action date for Low Blow drew closer. It was necessary to provide for every contingency well in advance, because everything had to go on the first try. If it did not, for any reason whatsoever, the whole Thomas Jefferson operation would be dealt a body blow. The possibility of an oversight, no matter how slight, haunted everyone concerned and kept them rechecking and re-rechecking until the tension became almost intolerable.

"How do things look?" the colonel asked. "I haven't been out of this hole in months."

The hunter who had been the passenger in the car answered him. He was dark and not as tall as his companion, but he knew that the question had been directed more or less at him. "It isn't good. You have all of the factual news, but the invisible part, the sagging of the national will to resist, is bad. The people are frightened."

The colonel nodded. "The slaughter of the college students was a bad one. It upset some of our fringe people pretty much and we had to drop quite a few."

"How did you manage that?" the first hunter asked. He was blond and heavy, the weather-beaten man of the western outdoors in appearance—a helicopter pilot by profession.

"We put out the word that despite our best efforts, we had to face the fact that the situation was hopeless. We added that we believed that some of the other free countries of the world would eventually come to our rescue and that there was some hope that the government that had overrun us was due to collapse. Our higher-up people were all solid, of course."

"Did they buy it?"

"I think so: I just gave you the bare bones of it; Ed Higbee prepared the story and when he got through I was ready to believe it myself."

"I miss his column," the smaller man said. "I used to read him whenever I had the chance. I hope that he'll go back to it someday."

"He may," the colonel answered, "but he has another idea. When this is all over, he wants to run for the Senate. If it all works out, that might put him up against Fitzhugh; he's from the same state."

"Then he's in," the blond man cut in. "Fitzhugh couldn't get elected constable today—if we had elections."

A small light went on on the panel of the colonel's intercom. He noted it immediately and got to his feet. "Dave," he said to the helicopter pilot, "you can wait here if you'd like; no offense, but you know the rules. Commander, if you'll follow me, the admiral is ready to see you."

Admiral Haymarket, too, showed the strain that he was under. He motioned his visitors to chairs and personally drew three cups of coffee without asking first if they were wanted. When he had seated himself behind his desk once more, he could have been on the bridge of his flagship steaming at flank speed into the battle of Midway.

"Commander," he began, "at the price of the added risk I wanted to bring you here so that we could talk face to face before this thing kicks off. When it does, you will probably be, without exaggeration, in one of the most vital command situations in the history of the United States Navy."

"I'm well aware of that, sir," the commander answered. "Completely aware."

The admiral tried his coffee and then continued. "I'm not going to go into details as to how we decided on you for this mission and we assumed only one thing—that you would volunteer."

The commander chose his words with great care. "Right now, sir, there are quite a few people, especially in light of recent events, who would question my right to call myself a hundred per cent American. I wonder, sir, if you can conceive what it means to me to have this chance to prove them wrong."

The admiral tilted back in his chair for a moment, then sat upright again. "Commander, I think that I can. I know that I'm a WASP, a White Anglo-Saxon Protestant, but I've served with too many good men of other persuasions not to be aware."

"Another thing, sir," the commander continued, "I don't know what guardian angel worked overtime to help get me picked for this assignment, but speaking purely as a man, it's worth my entire life to me to have it. I'll give you the very best that I've got to offer."

The admiral tapped a folder on his desk. "Judging by your service record, commander, that's all we'll need. I chose you for this because you're one of the very best that the Navy has, and you were available. All I can say is that I'm damn glad you weren't at sea and tied up the way that so many of our people are now. God willing you will be at sea shortly; I'd give everything I have to go with you."

"As of now, sir, with your permission your name will be posted on the crew list. You will be the only member on TAD elsewhere."

"Commander, you do that. And just one more thing: if I don't see you again before you leave here . . ." The admiral stood up. "Good luck."

"Thank you, sir. We try to make our own luck, along with our drinking water."

"You will." The admiral shook hands. "Go on to your briefings and use that brain of yours. If you see anything you don't like, let us know immediately. We've got other submariners here, but none of us pretends to know it all."

"Thank you, sir."

When the commander had gone the admiral sat down again and stared at the wall in front of him. Then he turned to look at the small framed portrait of another naval officer that stood on his side table. For several seconds he studied the features of his son and then slowly shook his head. "You're awfully damn good," he said softly. "But I couldn't risk it. I picked the best that we've got—now may God help him."

The warden of the federal penitentiary at Leavenworth had known for some time that he would be replaced. He therefore had all of his records in order, all of his routine work fully current, and everything within the institution that he controlled in the best condition that the circumstances permitted. When he received a phone call which informed him somewhat bruskly that his successor would be there the following day to take over, he leaned back in his chair, considered the situation carefully, and decided that he was ready. He had been planning to retire for some time anyway.

His successor, who arrived alone, was shown into his office shortly after nine o'clock the next morning and afforded him a considerable surprise: he had not been expecting a woman. Because she was an enemy of his country, the warden made her welcome with formal courtesy, wondering as he did so how in the hell she proposed to head up an institution which contained several hundred of the most incorrigible male criminals that the nation had produced. However, that was now her problem.

The new warden sat down and stated her purpose in quite good, if accented, English. "I have arrived to become the head of this prison," she announced.

The warden waved his arm through the air to suggest the whole of the installation. "Very well; if you have any official documents to establish that fact, I will then formally turn over control to you."

"It is correct that you should ask that," the woman answered. "I have such documents and I show them to you gladly if you can read my language."

The warden shook his head. "I'll have to take you on

faith, then. I had been notified that someone was coming, but to be truthful I was not expecting a lady."

His successor surprised him by smiling; as she did so she seemed to be, for the moment, a quite agreeable person.

"I understand; you were not told. Nevertheless, I am a penologist. I have been running a women's prison, but I was for this one selected because I have the English."

"You certainly do. I will take as much time as you would like to show you around and acquaint you with all of our facilities."

"You are very kind—I did not expect this. You may call me Marinka; it is much easier to say than my last name, which it is very difficult for you to pronounce."

"As you wish, Marinka. My assistant, who is thoroughly acquainted with our entire operation, will be staying on, that is if you wish him to do so."

"Of course."

"Good. Then perhaps you would like to begin by sitting here."

Marinka raised her hand. "Please no, I am comfortable here. I have read of your prison and I know already most of the major facts. One question I must ask: do you have any inmates now who are special problems or troublesome?"

The warden considered that for a moment. "No, not really. All of our inmates, or the great majority of them certainly, are hard cases, but we have them well controlled. We have Wattles here, as I expect you know. He has been one of our problems, but I presume you will be releasing him shortly."

"His term—it is almost up?"

"No, but you know who Wattles is, don't you?"

"Please to help me."

"He is, or was, our most aggressive black militant. He is due in for quite a while yet, but you might recall that he has been one of the prime forces in supporting—your cause."

"What was his offense?" Marinka asked.

"Almost everything in the book, actually. He has done several murders—also arson, sexual offenses, armed robbery, and a number of instances of inciting to riot, desecrating the flag—which is a rather serious offense over here, by the way—and quite a few lesser violations. He is in for mayhem; his victim was a federal judge."

"I am instructed," Marinka said slowly, "to operate this prison as I myself best see fit. This includes the privilege of granting parole which I know that you do not have. But I see no reason to turn loose such a man as that."

It was hard for the warden, because he did not want to like her and he was doing so in spite of himself. "Your people at home may want him out," he suggested. "He was quite effective in helping to tear down the power of our government for a while."

Marinka fumbled in her handbag for a cigarette and waved off the offer of a light. "I understand all that," she answered. "Now that you remind my memory I recall him and what he did. He is a troublemaker; he would give us as much difficulty as he did you." She drew on her cigarette and took time in letting the smoke out of her lungs. "I should stop this, I know—but my work, it is nervous exhausting. The Wattles man: I translate for you a phrase that has been used in our history. We will let him rot."

When Zalinsky rang for him, Hewlitt went into the Oval Room and waited.

"You will call former Senator Fitzhugh, I wish to see him," Zalinsky said.

Hewlitt bent down to make a note, concealing his surprise by the action.

When he offered no comment, Zalinsky dismissed him. "You will go."

As soon as he was back in his own office Hewlitt picked up the phone and put in a call to Senator Fitzhugh's office. He stayed on the line and had the secretary within a matter of seconds. "May I speak to the senator," he asked. "This is Raleigh Hewlitt at the White House."

The girl's voice lacked its usual smoothness. "I'm very sorry, Mr. Hewlitt, but Senator Fitzhugh isn't taking any calls at all." She hesitated. "You've heard, haven't you?"

"Yes, I've heard." It was totally inadequate, but he could not think of anything else to say. He forced himself to be a little more businesslike. "You may remember that a short while ago Senator Fitzhugh was quite anxious to have an appointment with Mr. Zalinsky."

"I remember that."

"I just left Mr. Zalinsky's office. He instructed me to get in touch with the senator and tell him that he would like to see him."

The girl's voice became tighter over the phone. "Mr. Hewlitt, knowing how he is feeling right now, if you could spare him that I'd appreciate it more than I can tell you. He's taking it terribly hard. And Mr. Zalinsky being who he is, and representing . . ." She stopped and let it hang there.

Hewlitt knew that he had to counter that even though he did not want to. "Please believe me. I feel very deeply for the senator and I don't want to disturb him. I am concerned that if he doesn't respond within a reasonable time, they might take some kind of action. There's a policy, you know, not to allow us to go against their wishes in any way. It's very strict."

There was a pause on the line. "I'll speak to him, Mr. Hewlitt, as soon as I feel that I can and see what I can do. He's literally ill, and you might tell Mr. Zalinsky that. Would you let me have your home number."

That painful and awkward conversation had only been over for a minute or two before the phone rang. Hewlitt picked it up and acknowledged.

"Hello." He recognized Barbara's voice.

"Hello back."

In contrast to Senator Fitzhugh's secretary she seemed almost cheerful. "Mary and I are going to have a little housewarming tonight. Nothing very big, but we thought you might like to come."

"What time?"

"Whenever you like after eight-thirty. Suit yourself."

"I'll see you, then," Hewlitt said. "Can I bring anything?"

"No, it's on us tonight. That isn't a pun, by the way."

"I didn't think so." He hung up with an unresolved question in his mind; it could have been the simple invitation that it seemed, or it could have been the signal that something new was stirring.

On the way home he asked Frank for a fill-in. "There's been a little reorganizin' for one thing," the driver told him. "I'm being given something new. I'm not so sure, but I think maybe you might be seeing Percival tonight."

"Will you be there?"

"Can't say—it depends on what he says."

"Has anything gone wrong?"

"Nothing like that, at least I don't think so."

After Frank had dropped him off Hewlitt reviewed the setup once more in his mind; when he had finished he was still far from satisfied. It was difficult to come up with a believable reason why two higher-level government girls would choose to move into an old house that was in an essentially Negro neighborhood. The fact that the whole city of Washington was now more than half Negro did not help very much. Frank had said something a while back about establishing a whorehouse, but he had not regarded that remark very seriously.

Shortly after nine he caught a cruising cab and took it to within a block and a half of his destination. He paid the driver and then walked the remaining distance to Davy Jones' residence and place of business. He could not keep from looking to see whether he was being observed. He was jumpy, he recognized that fact and made a conscious effort to recover his mental equilibrium.

Mary Mulligan opened the door to him and motioned him inside. "Barbara will be down in a minute," she said and then excused herself. He walked into the living room and found Davy Jones there. The place had been spruced up quite a bit since his last visit; the makeshift bar had been replaced with a quite acceptable new one complete with stools. The floor had been freshly carpeted. Much of the furniture was also new; it was not of high quality, but it was a major improvement on the pieces which it had replaced. The walls, which had been a somewhat questionable white, had been redone in a light blue which went well with the darker-toned carpeting. New drapes hung at the windows; Hewlitt noticed that they were of heavy material and lined; furthermore they had been hung so that they overlapped instead of meeting in the usual butt joint.

"Evening, Mr. Hewlitt, how do things look to you?" Davy asked.

"Very nice—quite an improvement."

"Some friends of mine helped me with the payments. If we're going to have young ladies living here, the place has to be classed up a little to make it suitable."

"I'm with you," Hewlitt agreed. "Are you going into the roominghouse business?"

Davy looked at him for a moment. "You could put it that way if you want to. It's a little idea that I had and some of my friends liked it."

"I see." He didn't exactly, but a few things were beginning to take shape for him. "Are there going to be any other guests here tonight?"

Davy nodded. "He's upstairs—just got here a few minutes ago. He's a busy fellow. And some others are coming to the party too."

Hewlitt raised his right hand behind his ear and looked the question at his host. The tall Negro shook his head. "Checked it a few minutes ago; everything's O.K. Long-range microphones can't penetrate into here, and nobody's tried yet to install any equipment. They probably will now, for a time, although there's been a lot less of that going on lately—I don't know why."

Barbara came into the room wearing a green cocktail-length dress that set off her figure to striking advantage. "Hello, Hew," she said. "How do I look—suitable for a high-class brothel?"

"Based on hearsay evidence only," Hewlitt answered her, "I'd say you're perfect. I'm ready to become the first customer."

"When the time comes we'll see. Right now, believe it or not, officially I'm a virgin—and it's all your fault. Davy, fix me a drink, will you?"

In response, Davy went behind the bar and from there surveyed Barbara with careful appraisal. "Damn it all," he said, "why did you have to get yourself born white?"

"We all have our problems," she answered him.

The doorbell rang; Davy went and ushered in Cedric Culp, the White House press secretary. Despite the nature of his job he was inclined to be somewhat quiet and seldom had a great deal to say that was not of an official nature. He was a short, stocky man, but he had played football in college and had a reputation as an athlete. During the winter months he was gone many weekends up to the ski slopes.

"Evening, Hew," he said. He shook hands with Davy

Jones and greeted Barbara with a frank admiration of her appearance. "The best in the house," he said.

"Mary is supposed to be your girl friend—remember."

Culp turned serious. "I will. Only it's hard sometimes; Marion may hear some gossip."

The doorbell rang once more. Davy answered it and admitted two of the secret service men normally assigned to the White House detail. Barbara motioned them to sit down. "This is all that are coming," she told Davy. "I thought it best not to have us all here together the first time."

"Good idea," Culp agreed.

When the newcomers had settled down Barbara informally took the floor. "Tonight we're due for a briefing from one of the higher placed people in our organization. His code name is Percival; that's all I can tell you, except that I'll know how to recognize him. Hew, you've met him, haven't you?"

Hewlitt nodded. "Yes, the man I've been working for introduced me." He stopped when he heard a sound behind him, turned, and saw Percival coming into the room.

There was no need for introductions. Percival took one of the bar stools and swung around to face the group. He looked at Barbara for a moment and then asked, "Are you satisfied as to my identity?"

"Yes," Barbara answered. "And now that I've seen you, I know who you are."

"Do I have your confidence?"

"Absolutely." She spoke the word without emphasis, but with full meaning.

Percival looked around. "The rest of you, except for Hew and Davy, will have to take me on faith." He surveyed the group once more. "I know each of you well by reputation, so from my standpoint, at least, we aren't meeting for the first time. I know what you have been doing over the past several weeks and I know too that each of you has been implicitly following the instructions that were passed on to you."

"That wasn't much," one of the secret service men said.

"It was a great deal," Percival corrected him. "You've collectively provided us with more valuable information than you may realize. It's helped us. So much so that we're moving this unit closer to the center of our operation. I'll be working with you directly as well as through Barbara's contact and Davy here."

"Something's moving, then," Culp said.

"Something is. You may not know this, but we have a large and highly competent organization. And we're not powerless. This is all totally secret information; don't discuss it, even here. Now, because of the importance of your location, and the level of talent that you represent, I've been instructed to tell you that there is a central nucleus that's running this outfit. We call it the First Team, and you'd better believe that they are. They're all men of extraordinary capacity and they aren't working in the dark. They're on the job continuously and they have resources—more than you might imagine. You can thank God for that."

"That's what I wanted to hear," the other secret service man said.

Percival stopped while Davy put a drink in his hand; he sampled it and then spoke his thanks. "Now about this house," he went on. "It's protected in a good many ways. It has certain features which make it all but impossible to bug without our knowing it immediately. Some useful equipment is stored here. And if it becomes necessary, we have a way of getting you out; not a sure one, but it's a good bet and a lot better than nothing."

He tried his drink once more and then set the glass down carefully. "Now for the cover for this place. Insofar as the enemy is concerned, and probably the neighbors as well, it's going to be a private brothel, of which there are a considerable number in this city. We arranged to have both of these young ladies evicted from their quarters. They did a suitable amount of apartment hunting before they came here on Hew's suggestion—that is if anybody ever asks. We're moving two more of our girls in here; both of them are totally reliable. Hew, you spoke to one of them on the phone, if you remember. So you see the setup."

"We come here to see our girls," Culp said.

"Right, and sometimes spend the night, as anyone would expect. All four of the girls have agreed to this, so their reputations go out the window."

"That's not a consideration," Barbara said.

"Will we be told when to come?" Hewlitt asked.

"Yes, and also you can come on your own for purely social reasons if you'd like. Davy will front as the owner and very tolerant landlord."

"There really are places like this," Mary said.

"Lots," Percival answered her, "so feel easy in your mind. It's a very good cover for the men coming here. One or two more points that are important: first, if anything happens to me, my replacement, man or woman, will be Rodney. Secondly, when you come in, never say a compromising word until you have looked at the bar first. If these is a bottle standing on it, any kind of a bottle, that will be the danger signal—even if someone is sitting there with it. Pay no attention to what he or she might say about it being all right. If you use the bar, never set the bottle on the top unless you mean it as a definite warning."

He lowered his head for a moment or two; when he looked up his face was possibly a shade more serious than it had been before. "I'll tell you this," he said. "The work you're doing, the risks you're taking, aren't for nothing. You'll know soon enough. When it breaks, some of you may have a lot more to do—you'll be informed. Stay with it."

Hewlitt looked at Barbara wondering how all of this sat with her. She looked back at him evenly—clear-eyed and unafraid. At that moment he had a vague stirring, a first realization that perhaps he was falling in love with her. As a woman she was totally desirable, but much more even than that she had an inner strength, an intelligence, that set her way apart from the rest. She could pull her own share and more. She was a helluva girl.

"Any questions?" Percival asked.

"You made it all very clear," Mary answered him. "We'll do the best we can."

There was general agreement, unspoken but indicated just the same.

Barbara was the cell leader, and she summed it up for them all. "God bless this whorehouse," she said.

Marc Orberg was impatient and restless. His trip had begun badly when he had discovered that first-class seats had been discontinued by the airplanes and he had been compelled to ride in a seat much too narrow to suit his sense of luxury. Furthermore, the people who had taken places next to him had talked in whispers and then gone to the back of the aircraft to sit by themselves. No one had asked him for his autograph on the whole trip.

To hell with them! They would hear about him again soon enough; in the new role he was about to assume they would be coming to him in droves, begging and pleading for favors. And if there were any good-looking chicks among them, they knew what they could do if they wanted him to help them.

At the beach he was disappointed in the press turnout for the landing. The fact that he would appear in person had not been adequately announced, although Nat had sent out all of the usual notices. However the hour was still early, he had seen to that so that no misguided publicity seekers would be there ahead of him to get in his way. To be sure that he would be recognized by everyone on sight, those who were landing and those who had come to witness the spectacle, he had put on his trademark clothing: the laced shirt, the tight trousers, the high-topped shoes. There was only one Marc Orberg—there could be only one because no one else had his combination of looks, talent, and solid cast-iron guts. He was afraid of nothing and nobody; he had proven that when he had busted the whole damn United States Government with the Orberg decision against the draft.

He walked a few steps up and down. There was no son-of-a-bitch in the whole Goddamned world who could stand up to him. He had never been to Sweden, but he knew that they adored him there because his parents had been Swedish and because no one had ever punished the establishment the way that he had. They liked that kind of thing in Sweden. He tossed his head back and looked up into the sky. He let his imagination take over for a short while and visualized himself, still youthful and full of the vigor that made him great, standing before the Royal Academy and receiving the Nobel Prize—the youngest man ever to be so honored.

He broke the chain of that daydream and came back to the present; the limited number of people who had come to see the show were looking seaward and pointing. He looked himself and saw in the clearing visibility that the ships were there, closer than he had expected them to be. The operation would be under way on the beach well within the hour; from the looks of the flotilla the place where he had stationed himself was close to ideal. He sat down to rest himself for a few minutes and to think about the speech of greeting he was going to make. From his vantage point he surveyed the beach and saw that there were now press photographers on hand; actually one good one connected with the wire services was all that he needed, two or three made it sure. He spotted at least half a dozen, so that part of the operation was well in hand.

He lay down on the sand, chewing on a straw that he had plucked, and looked into the sky. Once more he felt the total satisfaction of knowing that he would not be willing to trade places with any man in the world—he had everything that money could buy and he was going to have a great deal more. There were light cumulus clouds floating overhead, he amused himself by studying them and picking out the fanciful shapes that suggested themselves to him.

He was aware that there were more spectators gathering—some of them, most of them in fact, would have come to see him. If he showed himself he would be mobbed and would have to scrawl signatures on a wild assortment of pieces of paper, including matchbook covers. He was happy where he was, the peace of the seashore was affecting him and he was enjoying it as an interlude, a moment of calm in his striking and extraordinary life.

He lifted his head enough to see what was happening on the water. The ships were close in now and the first of them were putting landing craft into the water. It was too early for him to appear. The first boat, that would be larger than the others, would be the one he wanted; it would contain a commander of sorts; he would tip off the press and then make his speech of welcome officially to him. That would infuriate about a hundred million Americans at the least and every one of them would be reminded again that Marc Orberg was king and there wasn't a damn thing they could do about it.

It was some forty minutes later when he spotted the landing craft he was looking for. It was, as he had anticipated, larger than the others and there would be vehicles on board which a commander would use. It would be landing a little way up the beach, which was fine; the more people who saw him running to meet it the better. That was what he wanted them to do; once again he had outsmarted the whole pack and they would find it out, as they always did, just a little too late. The announcement had been made, of course, but one of the secrets of his success was that he always produced more than anyone expected. He wouldn't disappoint them this time.

It was essential that he time the thing exactly right. He rose from his semi-hiding place; then began to run down the beach at an easy lope which showed off the play of his muscles under his tight clothing and gave everyone a good chance to recognize him. The distance was a bit more than he had realized, or else the exertion of running in the sand pulled on him more than he had expected, so that when he reached the scene where the vehicles were rolling ashore he was slightly out of breath. He stood there, letting his chest rise and fall, watching the stolid-faced men who were coming up onto the beach, rifles in their hands, puppets engaged in mock warfare against an enemy which did not exist—on the beach or anywhere else in the world anymore. They were the conquerors, nameless numbers on a military roster who knew only how to do what they had been told.

One of them, a minor noncommissioned officer of some sort, waved him aside. Marc laughed at him; the man did not know who he was, of course, and that excused him.

He spotted the commander without difficulty. He could not read the ranks on the uniforms, but the way in which the man conducted himself revealed him at once as the person in charge. The precision with which the door of his vehicle was snapped open and held for him indicated his importance. It was an absurd little panel hardly a foot high which made it slightly easier to mount into the otherwise open military-type car, but it was enough to symbolize his authority. As the commander came up the beach with properly impressive strides, Marc fell in beside him and with his breath still a little short asked, "Do you understand English?"

The commander glanced at him for just a moment and then answered his question by saying, "Go away."

That was all that Marc needed. "I'm here to welcome

you," he half shouted. Out of the corner of his eye he had detected a press photographer aiming at him and he wanted to be sure that he was heard.

"No," the commander said, and strode on.

"I'm Marc Orberg," he announced, his breath coming a a bit harder as he sought to keep up with the man who had not been running for the last few minutes. "Marc Orberg!"

The commander ignored him.

That was impossible; Nat, the damn fool, should have told them to expect him, he should have arranged to have the commander briefed in advance. With the man he was trying to greet ignoring him he was running the risk of being made ridiculous in front of the press and all of the spectators. He knew immediately that he could not recoup by waiting for the next important-appearing person; his initial failure would be reported gleefully from coast to coast. The muttonhead in the stiff uniform would have to be made to listen.

Marc spurted forward, then turned and faced the man squarely as he came on. Then he held out his hand, a gesture that could not be ignored. If the jerk didn't understand enough English it really didn't matter. There were three photographers now; they seemed to have come up out of the sand.

"Welcome to America!" Marc recited. "For decades this country has suffered under the lecherous greed of the capitalists. You have come . . ."

The commander thrust out his arm and brushed him aside. Then he mounted stiffly into his vehicle.

Full-blown rage took hold of Orberg. He had worked and suffered for these people, he had paved the way for them more than any man who had ever lived and this was his thanks, the gratitude due him! As the vehicle began to move slowly in the sand he ran alongside. "You have come to make us free of the . . ."

The commander was ignoring him, making him totally ridiculous before the whole world. "Listen to me, you goddamned pig," he shouted, "I'm MARC ORBERG and . . ."

The commander leaned sharply forward and barked a command to an aide sitting in the right front seat. The man responded at once; Marc saw him as he jerked out a pistol, saw the vicious weapon abruptly pointed at his own abdomen, and heard the blast of the shot.

A stab of sudden pain almost paralyzed him; with frightful speed it grew and became unbearable. His knees failed him; the soft sand suddenly became a morass. His lungs pounded in unfelt pain because of the burning horror in his belly; he pitched forward and for an instant felt the hard thump of the sand against his face.

The pain engulfed him; the agony became so frightful that his mind refused to do anything but focus on it in total desperation. He did not even know his own name anymore —only the all-consuming fire of incarnate hell that was raging in his body. He tried to kick his legs to mitigate the agony, but he could not tell if they had responded or not. Then, consumingly, he wanted to die; desperately he wanted death to terminate the intolerable pain he could not endure for another second. He tried to cry out to his god, but he had none to answer him.

Then he knew that he had been picked up. It came through to him that he was being carried, then the pain became the whole universe, consuming him alive. When he was thrown down, the hard contact with the ground went unfelt, for in the last moments before the two uniformed bearers cast him aside, consciousness left him and he entered into a world of total darkness.

CHAPTER FOURTEEN

In common with a great many other American industrial installations, the Hunters Point Naval Shipyard in San Francisco Bay was having considerable difficulty in maintaining a satisfactory work force. The occupying authorities who were in direct control of the facility had issued stern edicts against either quitting or slowing down on the job, but the normal attrition which affects every large employee group kept the size of the payroll steadily shrinking while the usual inflow of new applicants dropped almost to zero. Despite the reduction in personnel, during working hours the shipyard presented its usual picture of apparent total confusion continuously sustained at a high level. In the submarine drydocks the modification work which had been under way at the time of the Defeat continued under close control by the enemy for the eventual benefit of his own fleet. And at berth eight, near to the end of the North Pier, the U.S.S. *Ramon Magsaysay* remained tied up under intensive twenty-four-hour guard.

The presence of the *Magsaysay* at Hunters Point was a departure from the normal procedure. She had been en route from Bremerton, where she had loaded her missiles, to the Pacific Missile Range for her test firing when her captain had received urgent and classified orders to proceed to Mare Island. The *Magsaysay* had been within three hours' running time of the Golden Gate when the word had come through that Mare Island, the normal habitat of the nuclear submarines, was already loaded to capacity and to put in at Hunters Point instead. She had still been there, undergoing modifications to some of her conventional systems, when the President had made his announcement.

The enemy had known all about the *Magsaysay* and had lost no time in seizing her when they had taken over the yard. It was quickly decided that the work in progress would be continued under strict supervision, but that no chances would be taken of allowing any false heroics. She was too deadly a weapon for that. All of her stores were removed, along with as much vital equipment as could be passed up through the thirty-inch hatches that were the largest openings in her pressure hull. While this work was still in progress a former U.S. Army 105-mm mobile fieldpiece was moved to the end of the pier and installed there, where it could keep a watchful and lethal eye on the *Magsaysay* and all that went on around her. The powerful gun was manned twenty-four hours a day by a succession of crews that were brought in and out by special vehicles in order to prevent any contact whatever with either the military or the civilian personnel of the shipyard. A white ring fifty feet in radius was painted around the fieldpiece; posted signs warned that anyone stepping within the ring, accidentally or otherwise, would be shot immediately by a member of the gun crew on duty. Near the brow which led from the pier to the deck of the *Magsaysay* a radiation detector kept a continuous watch over the shutdown power plant deep within the hull. Under the water the nearly twenty-foot diameter propeller of the *Magsaysay* was reportedly chained to the piling.

The growing shortage of personnel had not interfered materially with the progress of the work going on within the *Magsaysay*'s hull. Most of the essential modifications had been completed and the estimates posted in the commander's office indicated that she would be ready for takeover in approximately three weeks' time. Most of the manpower loss was reflected in the support services; the massive dumpsters were for the most part completely filled with scrap a good part of the time, supplies were late in arriving, and the general housekeeping of the big yard slipped to a level that the American commander would not have tolerated for a day. A growing number of armed enemy guards patrolled the whole area and saw to it that the level of activity at least appeared to remain at a high level.

The flow of message traffic between Hunters Point, Treasure Island, Alameda, and Mare Island was heavy and continuous, but despite the level of his responsibility, the still acting commander scanned most of it personally. He was a square-built man with some remaining grizzled hair and a perpetual expression of harassed concern. That expression did not alter to the slightest degree when, in the midst of hundreds of communications, he found an unavailability report on a piece of welding equipment. He glanced at the clock, disposed of a number of additional messages, and then turned his attention to the personnel sheets. After studying them for a short while, he sent off a signal to Mare Island urgently requesting an additional crane operator.

As a result of that near demand a new man showed up for work the following morning. The enemy had a look at him before he was allowed on base and concluded that he would fit into the pattern of what was being done at the yard. He had an exceptional physique, the obvious result of much manual labor, and spoke with a fairly heavy mid-European accent which was approved; not being a native-born citizen he would probably be less averse to working for a foreign power and doing what he was told. As soon as the man was cleared and given his work permit, he was assigned to the huge high crane which provided the heavy lift capability required on the North Pier. After a brief period of instruction on the equipment he was allowed to carry on alone; the results were satisfactory and his presence on base was thereafter taken for granted. The commander never saw him and once he had made the work assignment, never displayed the slightest interest in his presence. He carried a heavy load and obviously had no time for such individual matters.

Few others saw the man either; he rode high up at the base of the boom in a control shed which provided him with shelter as well as an excellent view of all of the surrounding area. It was a considerable climb up there from the ground and it required a cool head to make it. The crane operator had few visitors.

All of this was watched with the closest attention by Admiral Haymarket at his headquarters and by the other members of the First Team who remained with him. It was difficult for the admiral, because the greatest operation of his career lay immediately ahead and for the first time he would be unable either to witness or to participate in the action. By his own dictum it was out of the question and he accepted that fact.

If anything were to happen to him for any reason, General Gifford was fully qualified to step in and take his place, but the general already carried a very heavy responsibility functioning as executive officer and would be extremely difficult to replace.

Next in the chain of command was Colonel Prichard. In addition to a full slate of line responsibilities, he was one of the primary idea men, one of the brilliant brains who examined every possibility that suggested itself and hundreds more that did not.

Major Pappas handled operations and did so with close to total efficiency. He could not be spared from that job where his computer-type intellect carried literally thousands of details without forgetting even one. Without him in that job, the whole organization would suffer severely.

Ed Higbee was a total specialist in his own field—the manipulation of words. He was also a phenomenally resourceful planner and idea man, but his prime value lay in the documents which he had already drawn up, the propaganda he had designed, and all of the other political weaponry he had devised. His role in the whole Thomas Jefferson effort was about to become much more significant and he had to be held in readiness.

Stanley Cumberland was the mechanical genius who could devise almost anything imaginable or lay his hands on someone who could. The coordination of all supply and special equipment came under him and he delivered with apparently unhurried infallibility. He could not be replaced.

Where field operations were concerned Walter Wagner was the best of them all, a fact that was fully recognized. Because his experience and technical capability were so valuable, the admiral had had no intention of letting him participate personally in Low Blow. He had held to that decision until Wagner figuratively had laid an ace on his desk. The admiral couldn't refute it: it was the high card and it was valid. He had therefore yielded and Wagner had left the underground facility to carry out his mission. There was high risk involved, but once he had gone, Barney Haymarket was eternally grateful that the best possible man was on the scene and calling the signals. The planning had been superb and when the time came, if anyone alive could, Walter Wagner would pull it off.

The day that he left Major Pappas retired to his quarters and was by himself for some time.

On the morning of Operation Day the major got up at five, breakfasted, and then sat down to go over the fourteen alternate emergency plans he had prepared for perhaps the fiftieth time. He examined them once more minutely, for it was not too late to spot a flaw, a single item that would not fit ideally into position, and switch to another operational technique. It was an additional factor of safety, plus which it diverted his mind from the fact that the Marine Corps in the person of himself was not taking a direct part in the action. He was interrupted before he had finished and went at once to the operational room. He took his place at the table, surveyed the empty chair where Walter Wagner normally sat, and then banished every thought from his mind but the effort at hand.

The data available were sketchy, but the bits and pieces were firm. The special clothing was reported ready and waiting. The weather forecast was favorable. The critical personnel were all in good health, positioned, and ready. Most important of all, there was no evidence whatever that there had been any leak. That was not conclusive, as the enemy could be playing his own game, but every person who had an assignment had sworn that he would report at once the slightest lapse on his own part or the observed error of anyone else. The final security check had shown everything apparently airtight.

The clock on the wall silently measured the intervals of time, its large-sweep second hand continuously maintaining its slow unbroken pace, as though to remind everyone present that the passing moment would never return and that the time of deadline was coming unrelentingly closer.

Then the most important message of all came in. It was in the form of a code which supplied no details, only a single bare fact. The commander of the Hunters Point Naval Shipyard reported that all was ready.

The admiral drummed his fingertips on the tabletop, waited, and watched the message board.

Two more dispatches came in, code messages concerning minor details which were nonetheless encouraging—they were both positive.

Then at last the one that he was waiting for came, and in letters that spelled it out in the clear: MARE ISLAND—READY.

They all looked at the admiral, the members of the First Team and the others who stood back against the wall of the room. The admiral did not see them; his mind was totally occupied. In three seconds he made his decision.

"Go," he said.

Lunch provided a respite for Hewlitt; as he ate alone he found himself once more thinking of Zalinsky and apprais-ing his attitudes. He and all of his people were intellectual vultures who kept circling, waiting for someone to make a slip or a mistake—then they would exploit it to the limit. They had kept the free world forces on the defensive for years by that sort of tactics, by charging and attacking—by pointing the finger of accusation and never giving anyone the opportunity to criticize them. It had worked, it had worked well enough that the people of the United States did not know where their President was and a man who had no business there whatsoever occupied the White House—which was only a little worse than the thing that had hap-pened to the same structure during the War of 1812.

When he returned to his office he called the operator and received the message that Senator Fitzhugh had been trying to reach him. He returned the call and had the senator's secretary on the line after a few seconds.

"Mr. Hewlitt," she said, "Senator Fitzhugh would like to talk with you. To be perfectly truthful I don't know what it's about, but he suggested that if you are free this evening, perhaps you and he could have dinner together."

Hewlitt realized at once that he could not and should not refuse this invitation.

"I would be very glad to dine with the senator," he re-sponded. "When and where?"

"Senator Fitzhugh said only that he would like as quiet a place as possible, one where he would not be too widely recognized. Perhaps you might have something in mind."

Hewlitt did, but he knew better than to specify it over the phone. "Why doesn't the senator come to my apartment if he would like to do that? I would be happy to offer him some pre-dinner refreshment and then we can go on from there."

"At what time, Mr. Hewlitt?"

"Say seven."

"Fine, I'll notify the senator. Are you still at the same place in Georgetown?"

"Yes, I am."

"Seven, then, unless I call you to the contrary."

Once more Hewlitt found himself with thinking to do. He did not know what the senator wanted with him, but he could guess in several different directions. Mentally he stacked them up in his mind and then tried to work out a plan to deal with each of them.

He picked up the telephone and dialed the number of the safe house. Davy answered promptly, "Jones' TV service."

"This is Mr. Hewlitt," he said.

"Yes, sir, what can I do for you?"

"My TV went out on me last night—sound but no picture. It's intermittent; sometimes it's fine, then it goes out again."

"I understand, sir. I'll go out there right now if there's someone to let me in."

"I don't believe that there is now. How about five-thirty?"

"That's fine, sir, I'll be there."

As he hung up Hewlitt thought that that had been a nice bit about the fault being intermittent: if anyone went in to check and the set performed normally, it would still not disprove that the call for service had been genuine.

When Hewlitt arrived home he found Davy waiting for him in the hallway. He admitted him and then gave him substantially the same account that he had over the phone of the supposed trouble with his set. Davy knelt down before it, turned it around and took off the back. Then he opened his kit of tools and extracted a compact piece of equipment which Hewlitt had never seen before. It was a professional product and something about it suggested at once that it was classified.

It was self-contained, at least it carried its own power supply and required no external source. "The set looks all right at the moment, Mr. Hewlitt," Davy said. "If you don't mind, I'll wait a little while and see if the picture will go out for us."

"I'd appreciate it if you would, and it probably will," Hewlitt answered. The two men understood each other perfectly as they played out the game for the benefit of any possible eavesdropper.

"May I use the bathroom?" Davy asked.

"Yes, of course."

With the instrument in his hand Davy walked toward the rear of the apartment. He went into the bathroom, closed the door, and after a suitable interval flushed the toilet. As he came back he walked carefully around the walls, holding a thin wire antenna in his left hand.

"The picture is flickering a little," Hewlitt said.

"Yes, sir, I see it."

That meant that the search for listening devices was not completed.

Fifteen minutes later it was. "You're clean, Hew," Davy said. "Unless they've developed something new and revolutionary very recently. Let me check if anyone else has been in here."

He made a careful inspection of the inside of both of the doors that gave access to the apartment; he opened each of them slightly, and checked the surfaces of the tumbler latches. When he had finished he came back to the living room. "Tentatively, I doubt if anyone has been in here who wasn't invited," he said. "They could have a duplicate key and may have used that, but they probably wouldn't go to that much trouble when there's no need."

"You're sure that it's all right?" Hewlitt asked to be certain.

"I'm betting my neck on it." He indicated the piece of equipment he had used. "You don't know that, of course, but it's highly sophisticated and almost impossible to fool. Also it's entirely passive and gives no evidence that it's being used. We've been trying to fool it ourselves ever since we've had it to see how it will stand up and we haven't been able to get past it once."

"That's very reassuring," Hewlitt said. "Let me make you a drink."

"Rain-check, please. Anything of interest?"

"Frank knows. I'm expecting Fitzhugh, at his request. If I can, I'll steer him to the Chinese restaurant."

"Excellent, we'll get a tape of whatever it is. The place is safe, by the way, we keep a constant check."

Davy replaced the back on the TV, but not before he had installed a new part in the picture circuit. "Just in case someone gets curious," he said. "Remember that I didn't guarantee that your phone isn't tapped; that's another matter entirely."

"Right. I understand."

Before he left Davy made out a receipt on his service pad for a cash payment covering the call and the new part. Then he shook hands and let himself out while Hewlitt put the false receipt on an accumulation of other papers. When he was alone once more he evaluated the inspection that had been made and decided that it had been dependable; that piece of interesting equipment and the way in which it had been used somehow inspired his confidence. So, for that matter, did Davy himself; the more he saw of the man, the more he was convinced that he knew what he was doing. And if there was a part in his television set that could be responsible for an intermittent picture, that would be the one that had been replaced. It would all check out if anyone was interested enough to look.

Senator Fitzhugh arrived at ten after seven. Hewlitt was a little surprised to note for the first time how large a man he was. So often that was true of successful politicians; many people seemed to feel that a physically big man would be able to represent them more effectively and somehow the votes he would cast would be more authoritative. It wasn't true, of course: Harry Truman was a good case in point. On the other side of the fence, Hitler had been a small man too.

In Hewlitt's modest apartment the impressive, white-haired senator seemed slightly out of place. He settled himself into a chair and accepted a drink as anyone else might have done, but he kept looking about the room as though he were expecting something to happen or someone else to appear. Hewlitt, his own glass in his hand, sat down reasonably close to his distinguished visitor. He did not presume intimacy, but he offered himself as a companion if the senator wanted it that way. He had asked for this meeting, so presumably he had something to say.

After a few seconds of silence it became evident that Senator Fitzhugh was ill-at-ease. He continued to look about; it struck Hewlitt that he might be unconscioiusly hoping that some interruption would occur and he would not have to unburden himself of whatever was on his mind.

Finally he decided to speak. "Mr. Hewlitt," he said, "I have come here to see you more or less as an act of desperation."

"How may I help you, sir?" Hewlitt asked.

Again the senator fell silent, apparently sorting out his thoughts one at a time. "I am concerned that in some manner we might be overheard," he said finally.

Hewlitt remembered the desirability of having any significant conversation taped. In a way it would be a betrayal of the senator's confidence, but presumably anything Fitzhugh had to say to him should be reported if it was of value.

"I have no reason to believe that these rooms have been wired," he said, "but considering what we both know, I'm being exceptionally cautious. Your secretary told me that you would like to eat in some out-of-the-way place where we could have some privacy."

"That's correct—yes," Fitzhugh answered.

"Quite close to here there is a small, very quiet Chinese restaurant I go to sometimes. The food is quite a bit better than average, and they have a number of booths where it is possible to sit unobserved."

"Chinese food is not my especial favorite," the senator said, "but at the present time I don't care very much what I eat and the place you suggest sounds suitable. Let's go there."

Hewlitt had a second thought: he was satisfied in his own mind that they were not being overheard and it might be that in a more public place Fitzhugh would be totally reluctant to talk at all. "Is there anything I can do for you before we leave?" he asked.

Senator Fitzhugh shut his eyes and let his head sag; he made no attempt to disguise the pain that crossed his features or the tightness that came after that. For a moment Hewlitt wondered if he was ill, then he saw the senator's body shake under the effect of a silent, unheard sob. When he looked up again his eyes were wet, and his mouth betrayed his anguish. "Not unless you can tell me how to get back my son," he said.

He remained that way, silent and still, for three of the longest minutes that Hewlitt had ever known. The senator was a widower, and his son had apparently been the only person close to him for some time. Hewlitt swallowed and then sat as still as he was able, respecting the man's grief. He knew, he had been told, that Gary Fitzhugh had died a hero and someday he would be honored for it, but that did not breathe back life into his body or restore those who had perished with him.

At last the senator regained control of himself. "Let's go and eat," he said.

At the restaurant they were received by the unemotional headwaiter who welcomed them and guided them to the same back booth where Hewlitt had sat with Phil Scott. If the headwaiter had recognized Senator Fitzhugh, he gave no indication. "Enjoy your dinner, gentlemen," he said when they were seated, handed them menus and then withdrew.

The business of ordering food and having the first of it served occupied a few minutes. During that interval the senator said very little; his thoughts were elsewhere and he barely escaped being rude. He ate his soup with apparent relish since he put it down quickly, then waited once again until the several dishes that comprised the main course had been put on the table. He helped himself to sweet and sour pork, added a few pieces of the pineapple, and then at last seemed to have brought his thoughts back closer to home.

"Mr. Hewlitt," he began, "I am turning to you for one reason and one reason only; you have demonstrated to me that you can be relied upon to maintain secrecy. I don't know you very well, but I have little choice left to me."

Hewlitt pitched his voice properly low. "Senator, my one dedication at the present time is to my country. That may sound old-fashioned to you, but I am in dead earnest about it."

Fitzhugh nodded his approval, then helped himself to a second of the serving dishes. He blinked for a moment and then said, "My son died for that."

"I know, sir," Hewlitt answered. "He was an American hero, worthy to stand beside Nathan Hale. Some day before long he very well may."

"Mr. Hewlitt," the senator said, "you once told me to my face that you totally disagreed with me and the policies I have followed for many years. I also remember another man who advised me to cut my throat; the worst insult I have ever received during my years in public office. He is dead now, but if he were not I would be willing to tell him that—in the light of recent events—I could forgive him that rudeness."

Clearly the senator did not expect any comment, and Hewlitt kept still.

"In Mr. Brown we have an example of what I call a militarist; a man who was, and I presume still is, dedicated to forcing the nation to up its defense budget to buy all kinds of equipment of doubtful value, or no value whatever. I cannot call him a patriot; he is a moneymaker and that is apparently all that he lives for."

"I have to agree with that," Hewlitt said.

"Mr. Hewlitt, as you already know, much of my recent activity in the Senate, I mean during the past few years, has been predicated in part on certain very firm and solemn assurances I was given in apparent total sincerity while I was abroad. There were also many other considerations which I don't wish to go into now. All that I am saying is: my position was firmly founded on principles in which I believed and to a major degree still do. Do you understand what I mean?"

"I believe so." Hewlitt took his time in drinking some tea. "Let me state a point, senator: no one likes war—no rational person. It's an unmitigated horror. The only reason that any nation gets itself involved in war, if it is not an aggressor, is because the alternative to armed conflict is even less acceptable. We're getting some of that now."

Senator Fitzhugh drained his own teacup, refilled it, and emptied it again. "Which brings us to the matter I wished to discuss with you. You will not repeat any of this?"

Hewlitt shook his head. "Not without your permission. You recognize the possibility that we may be being overheard."

"I know, I have been listened to in my own office. But I will accept that risk. Mr. Hewlitt, my son was a member of an organization dedicated to the recapturing of the United States, to setting it free. At least that was his belief. All of the others who died with him had the same objective. Apparently Miss Bloom, with whom he was keeping company, organized the group. How that little segment of innocent students"—he fought for his composure—"how any of them came to believe that they could accomplish anything with their pitiful resources I can't imagine, but it was for this that they died."

Hewlitt felt for him, more than he had realized. "You have my complete sympathy," he said. "I never met your son, and that was my loss."

Senator Fitzhugh inclined his head in acknowledgment, then he went on. "I want to ask something of you. It may not be possible—if so I will understand. For some time you have been in the White House and very close to certain important and highly secret matters. I'm not asking you now to betray any of the trust placed in you; I recognize that that is impossible. However, in view of your past and present work, I consider it barely possible that if such an underground organization did exist, you might know of it."

"That's very nebulous, sir," Hewlitt warned.

"I recognize that, I just said so, but there is that chance. Here is what I'm asking of you: I want to know if there is such a thing or not. If I could feel that Gary . . . died for something real, something that does actually exist, perhaps I might be able to bear his loss just a little better. At least I pray to God so."

Hewlitt thought. He could say nothing, he knew that, but he had to respond in some way. Then he saw what he could do.

"Senator, right now I'm doing what I have to; I don't like it but I have no real choice. Where I am, it is conceivable that I may hear of something, as you said."

The senator was listening intently.

"If that happens, I'd like to have your permission to disclose whatever part of this conversation is necessary. You can see why: without it I could end up in the middle, not able to say anything either way."

Senator Fitzhugh pondered that and saw the logic of it. "You want me to place it entirely in your hands," he said.

"Yes, sir, otherwise I'd be powerless to do anything."

Fitzhugh paused, then picked up his cup and drank a little more tea. "I have no choice," he said, "but it isn't very much of a risk. I have nothing to live for now anyway."

CHAPTER FIFTEEN

As Summers, the workman, made his way down the length of the North Pier at Hunters Point Naval Shipyard, he carried his box of tools in his right hand. Even as acutely as the enemy personnel watched everything that went on with unrelenting attention, none of them noted the fact that this particular technician had previously always carried his work box the other way. He walked the full length of the pier unchallenged and did not shift his toolbox over until he had to reach inside his work clothes for the pass that would admit him to the closed-off work area which surrounded the *Ramon Magsaysay*. By the time that he had done that, he had already notified all of those who were directly concerned and who had been able to see him that the decision was *Go*.

After completing the formalities and allowing himself to be searched for possible concealed weapons or materiel, he opened his toolbox for the customary examination. It was looked at closely as it always was, but nothing was amiss. All this done, he was allowed to cross the short brow onto the deck of the *Magsaysay* and then down an open hatch into her interior.

In the kit of tools that had passed inspection there was a steel measuring tape which had been substituted for the one he normally had. In appearance and weight it was an exact duplicate; if anyone were to attempt to use it, the tape would unreel a good five feet before it began to bind as though something was jammed in the internal mechanism. It was a beautiful piece of equipment that had been created by Stanley Cumberland. It was also somewhat dangerous. It carried the highest priority; Walter Wagner had brought it with him when he had come to the Coast.

For the twenty-three other members of Operation Low Blow who were employed inside the hull of the submarine it was a very long morning. No tension could be evident in the air; the enemy inspector on board roamed about constantly and was at everyone's elbow several times during the first few hours. There were others on board too who had no knowledge of Low Blow or any suspicion that it existed. Two of the key personnel knew about the steel measuring tape; Major Pappas left nothing to chance and there was a remote possibility that something might happen to Summers. If that occurred, they would carry on for him.

Everyone, even including the enemy security inspector, came up at noon to eat on the pier. No foodstuffs were allowed on board the *Magsaysay* or any other ship undergoing work at the yard; that had been the rule long before the enemy had first set foot on American soil. Just before the lunch break was over, the enormous traveling crane which served the North Pier came slowly up, bringing a large electrical unit of some kind for the surface ship tied up at berth seven. When the load had been set down the boom of the crane rose a little higher in the air before the overhead monster moved back in the direction from which it had come. Summers saw it and so did the others who understood; everything was in order and the word was still go.

The apparent chaos of activity characteristic of a major shipyard in operation resumed very shortly after that; the men assigned to the *Magsaysay* returned to their jobs under the ever watchful eyes of the guards at the brow and the gun crew a hundred feet away. When they were back inside the ship once more, the security inspector haunted them constantly, watching almost every move that they made. He spoke no English and none of the men working under his scrutiny could determine how much he did or did not know about the intricate mechanisms of the nuclear submarine.

On his left wrist Summers wore an inexpensive watch which nevertheless kept excellent time. He looked at it occasionally as most men do who work by the hour, and kept at his task. At six minutes after three in the afternoon he took the steel tape out of his kit of tools and made a short measurement. That done, he put the tape in the pocket of his work clothes and completed the adjustment he was making. Then he began to walk toward the rear of the ship.

When he was not far from the reactor compartment he

glanced at one of the men working there who gave him in return an almost invisible nod: the inspector was not in the immediate area. As soon as Summers had passed him, the workman picked up a length of pipe and began to maneuver it up the passageway. It was a simple action, but it formed an effective block that would guarantee Summers at least a few seconds of needed privacy.

Summers moved quickly, but with careful precision. He stepped into a preselected niche and took out the measuring tape. He pulled up on the pin which when depressed activated the rewind mechanism and turned it to the left. The two halves of the tape container fell apart, revealing a small capsule in the center. Summers dropped the capsule carefully into the palm of his left hand and then put the steel tape away. Up to that point he had consumed only eight seconds.

The capsule was made of two sleeve sections; using both hands he pushed them together until he heard a slight sound from the inside of the tiny container. Then he placed it with great care behind a run of exposed piping where it was out of sight and securely wedged into position. His job done, he turned and waited until the passageway was clear. A minute and a half later he was back at his work station, his face impassive as he appeared to concentrate entirely on the job before him. Less than three minutes later the enemy security inspector was looking over his shoulder; he gave the man a cursory glance and then continued with what he was doing. He knew without looking again at his watch that he had just over an hour and a quarter to wait.

Master Chief Petty Officer Anson Summers was a man accustomed to responsibility. He held the highest security clearances necessary to his job and had served with distinction in the United States Navy ever since he had enlisted shortly after graduating from high school. He had seen combat action many times. He had served under Sharp, Burke, Johnson, Moorer, and Haymarket, and had known all of them personally. He was a complete professional in his job as well as a family man with five children. Until he had been selected for his latest assignment, the proudest moment in his life had been seeing his eldest son graduate from the Naval Academy.

To all of this he added one more unexpected ingredient—

a remarkable natural ability as an actor. That had been discovered on an occasion when some new shellbacks were being initiated and Chief Summers, as King Neptune, had turned in a notable performance. A Marine officer on board, Lieutenant Pappas, had remembered that and stored it away in what later proved to be an encyclopedic memory. For a Navy man of Summers' dedication to play the part of a not too gifted workman over a period of weeks had been a severe test, but he had carried it off brilliantly.

The hour that lay immediately before him was the hardest of his career. If for any reason the capsule did not work it would be his fault; he accepted that without question. He had done exactly as directed, but there had been no way to check, no procedure to make certain. He kept on at his work, but the minutes crawled by and it was all that he could do to contain himself and maintain an indifferent exterior.

Precisely at four-thirty, almost to the second, Operation Low Blow entered its second phase.

The evidence of a radiation leak initially appeared on an indicator inside the hull on the working bridge. The man who saw it first gave a convincing performance himself as he stared for a frozen second or two and then hit the alarm. The enemy inspector heard it and jerked a small instrument out of his clothing; it began to sputter like an endless chain of miniature firecrackers. Forgetting himself, he shouted an order in his own language.

He did not need to be understood, every man on board knew the meaning of the still-sounding alarm; they literally ran for the hatches and went up the ladders one after the other with frenzied speed, the inspector among them. By the time that the first of them had reached the deck of the submarine, the radiation detector on the dock had already responded and was climbing rapidly toward the danger zone.

Overhead in the crane housing Walter Wagner had been waiting with the icy nerves of the experienced professional agent; he was at this moment uncommitted himself, but he had been greatly concerned for the success of Summers' mission. He knew that if it had been properly placed the capsule would work; Stanley Cumberland had guaranteed that. When, right on the minute of the projected time, men began pouring out of the submarine far below he felt a surge of elation; he reached to one of the controls of his great machine and watched the boom move in response slightly to the left.

From the window of his home close to the shipyard a ham radio operator observed the movement through binoculars which he had been patiently holding before his eyes for almost an hour. Moments later he was on the air calling CQ. He was heard at once by sensitive equipment which had been monitoring his frequency, and a waiting signal was relayed immediately to the underground complex that was the headquarters of Thomas Jefferson. The message board in the conference room came alive with letters which quickly spelled out: THE ISOTOPE HAS BEEN DROPPED.

As soon as he had read that, Admiral Haymarket slumped back in his chair. He and as many others as had been able to obtain permission to come in had been waiting for that word, almost all of them aware that for the past several hours the whole operation had narrowed down to one man. The saving factor had been the knowledge that the man in question was almost totally reliable and because of a particular talent was not likely to give himself away.

General Carlton Gifford clasped his hands on the table before him and murmured, "Thank God." He did not care who heard him.

Lieutenant Colonel Henry Prichard looked at Ed Higbee, the journalist. "Now if they'll only buy it," he said.

Higbee nodded his head with the confidence of the totally competent propagandist. "They will," he answered.

Stanley Cumberland puffed at a cigar and said nothing. As usual his face was a mask, but the admiral knew that he had to be feeling the satisfaction of the developer of something that had worked precisely right.

Only Major Pappas did not take a moment to relax. He carefully laid aside three of the alternate plan sheets before him—they would no longer be required. He would have given anything to have been in Walter Wagner's shoes at that moment, but it had had to be Wagner and he knew it; if the decision had been his to make he would have called it the same way. The mission was what counted—the mission and nothing else.

Cumberland spoke to the admiral. "Good man you've got there."

Haymarket agreed. "That kind is the backbone of the Navy. Real pros, every one of them."

"Let's have some coffee," Higbee suggested. It was a good idea because they would all be there for some time. A very long night lay ahead.

Far out in northern Pacific waters the fishing vessel *Dolly* plowed ahead slowly on her course. Already her hold had begun to fill with her catch, but by all visible signs her luck had up to that point not been too good, which was consistent with the relative inexperience of her crew and of the new captain who had taken her over.

In the small communication room the executive officer of the U.S.S. *Dolly* listened intently to a news broadcast from the States. It was as sterile and controlled as all such broadcasts had been for the past several weeks, but Lieutenant James Morton was not unduly concerned about that. When the sports part of the newscast came he leaned forward pressing his palms against the tabletop that held the equipment. Almost three thousand miles away the announcer supplied the principal game scores and then turned to the results of local interest. On the last item he fluffed, then he corrected himself and reversed the figures he had just given.

Lieutenant Morton could not help letting out a short yelp of joy; then he contained himself and hurried toward the impromptu wardroom. When he arrived there his face told the story before he could speak. "Sir," he said addressing the captain, "Low Blow is under way. The isotope has been successfully dropped."

The skipper looked at him. "Morton, you look ill. Do you feel all right?"

Morton straightened up. "Sir, I feel just fine."

Lieutenant Hanson, the Japanese language officer, corrected him. "No you don't, you look terrible. Come to think of it, I don't feel very well myself."

"The whole crew looks sick to me," the captain continued. "I wish that we had a medical officer on board. But since we don't, I am going to prescribe medicinal spirits all around."

"I didn't want to mention it, sir," Morton redeemed himself, "but I *have* been feeling faint lately."

"In that case we are within Navy regulations; we can't afford any general illness now."

"Absolutely not, sir," Hanson agreed. "I'll break out the prescription immediately."

All hell broke loose within the shipyard in a matter of minutes. By the hundreds the workmen dropped their tools and fled toward the gates. The enemy who were present knew that this exodus could not be stopped and were not at all sure that it should be. Of all of the people in the yard, the commander seemed for the moment to be the only one who knew immediately and correctly what to do; as soon as the report was confirmed, which was within a matter of seconds, he seized the direct-line phone to Mare Island and demanded the commander there on emergency priority. The startled operator responded and cut into a conversation that was in progress.

"Ed," he barked as soon as the line was clear, "*Bent Spear!* We've got a radiation leak from the *Magsaysay*."

The Mare Island commander reacted at once. "How bad?"

"Don't know yet, but the Geigers are going mad; we're evacuating."

"I'll get the nukes to you as fast as humanly possible. Hang on."

He hung up long enough to issue urgent orders; two minutes later he was back on the line. "Any change?"

"No new reports. I'll give you anything I get as fast as it comes in."

"Right. I'm after helicopters. A land party will depart ASAP. Ten minutes at the outside. Motorcycle escort. Clear for choppers if I can get any. Set up the gate clearances."

"Wilco. How many are coming?"

"Eighty to one hundred."

"Right." The Hunters Point commander hung up. He had barely done so when his enemy overseer demanded his attention.

"What is nukes?" the man asked.

"Nuclear specialists; no one else can handle this stuff."

"They must be examined and searched; it will take hours."

The commander lost his temper. "God damn you, man, this place can be blown sky-high together with half of San Francisco in the next ten minutes! That includes you and me. Don't you know what a nuclear pile can do!?"

"Yes, but . . ."

"Take your 'buts' and shove them right up your ass. If those nukes don't get this under control, they'll find your balls hanging on a cherry tree somewhere in the state of Oregon. Now get the hell out of my way!"

To talk like that to an occupying officer meant immediate execution, that had been made clear. Because the commander had forgotten that vital fact in his excitement and worry, the overseer read his concern as genuine; he also had no desire to meet a sudden nuclear death himself. "They can do nothing," he declared.

The commander answered, "Maybe that's right, if it is we're dead men right now. But if anyone can handle it they can and you can thank God that they're willing to try."

"They have their orders."

"Monkey face, there's something you don't know. In this country we don't order men to kill themselves. Those men are all volunteers and you'd better believe it. They're the best technicians on nuclear material in the world and they don't know what fear is."

He had no more time for the overseer; he picked up two more phones and began to issue urgent orders. When he had a brief moment of respite he made one more call—this one to his home. "Honey," he said to his wife, "listen! Don't ask questions. Grab the kids and get the hell out of here. Go south down the peninsula as fast as you can and keep on going as long as you have gas. Fifty miles anyway. Don't stop for anything." He banged the phone down.

The Mare Island line rang. He scooped it up and uttered a scant syllable in acknowledgment. "We'll be ready," he said after he had listened for a moment. "Who's the officer in charge?"

As soon as he had a reply to that he spoke once more. "The dock is being cleared; will you need the crane?"

Once more he listened. "All right, I'll keep him on. You'll get everything we've got. For God's sake keep this off the news broadcasts if you can!" He hung up.

"What is required?" the overseer asked. For the first time

since the commander had met him he gave signs of being reasonable.

The commander ticked the items off on his fingers. "Call your gate people and tell them that emergency personnel are coming in under police escort from Mare Island. You've already screened them all up there, so for Christ's sake get them on board fast. Two, get all unnecessary people off the base—the regular work crews. Keep all of our own security personnel. Keep the fire crews, the crane operator on Pier Nine, and the *Magsaysay* work force; the nukes may want to question them about what happened."

The overseer nodded. "This is wise. The protection gun crew, they must stay too."

"That's up to you, but they'll be in serious danger."

"They are our soldiers; they expect that."

"One more thing: if you can keep the personnel on the job, keep the cafeteria open—I don't know how long this will take."

"They will stay—they will not be allowed to leave."

A phone rang. The report was terse: radiation levels close to the *Magsaysay* were still climbing; the external danger point was coming closer. The commander swept up the Mare Island phone and relayed the news. In return he was told that the nukes were on their way out of the yard by surface transportation; no helicopters had been available on short notice.

The commander dropped the phone onto its cradle and for a moment panted for breath.

"Do you know what you called me?" the overseer asked.

The commander looked at him dully. "No—what was it?"

"Monkey face."

The commander passed a shaking hand across his square, worried face. "Sorry—you've been decent enough, I guess."

"I will give orders," the overseer said and reached for the on-base telephone.

The commander began, under his voice, to pray. His brow was wet and his respiration was faster than normal. At that moment he had nothing more to do. He could not understand the orders that the overseer gave in his own language, but they were obviously several in number. When the man had finished he looked and asked, "Any trouble?"

"We will help all we can."

The commander was not sure whether he meant that or not, but he nodded his head in affirmation. He drew breath to speak and then said nothing at all.

The shipyard had emptied rapidly; the news of what had happened could not be kept quiet, and a nuclear explosion was predicted at any moment. Literally in frenzy the men fought to get out the gates and as far away as possible. Use of the few available telephone lines was forbidden; they were blocked off to keep the traffic moving as rapidly as possible.

The rush was over and the base had quieted to a hush when the sound of police sirens could be heard coming from the direction of the Bayshore Freeway. Red lights came into view, then three large buses in convoy traveling as fast as the city surface streets would permit.

The head sentry on duty saw the familiar Navy-blue color of the vehicles and waved them through with an urgent sweep of his arm. The sooner the men in them were on the job, the better his chances would be to survive and live to see his wife again.

A base vehicle, provided by the commander, was waiting just inside the gate. It turned its own red lights on and swung in ahead of the motorcycle escort leading the way toward the North Pier. In three minutes' time the buses were within sight of the *Magsaysay* and under the watchful eyes of reenforced enemy security personnel who hoped that the radiation level was not yet high enough to endanger them.

Two hundred feet short of the end of the pier the buses pulled up and the men inside them began to pour out. In the first beginnings of twilight they looked like invaders from some hostile planet; the heavy decontamination suits that they wore transformed them into anonymous, unrecognizable creatures who were superficially human, but who clearly lived on another plane.

Awaiting them was an enemy officer who stepped forward and demanded, "Who is leader?"

Before he got an answer the first of the suited nuclear specialists, a piece of electronic gear in his hand, strode across the brow and swung himself down the hatch into the submarine's pressure hull.

The commander appeared on the scene, shadowed by his

overseer. "What's the problem?" he asked of the enemy officer.

The man turned to him. "I am Kepinsky, nuclear expert. I check everything."

"Get a suit, then," the commander answered.

"I inspect all equipment."

"Go right ahead."

The efficiency with which the nukes went to work was obvious to the enemy personnel; it answered any questions as to whether or not they were the experts they were supposed to be. On the pier a short conference was held between the enemy security head and the three enemy personnel who had come down from Mare Island, one on each bus. The commander could hear them, but he could not understand a word. When the brief huddle broke up, he noted that those concerned seemed to have been satisfied, at least about something.

Kepinsky took his place at the end of the brow and examined each piece of gear briefly for a few seconds. One he held out and put aside, refusing to permit it on board until it was opened up before him and he could see the interior. "I know this not," he said.

"New; classified," the man said who was carrying it.

"All right."

Floodlights came on the pier, lights which had been installed by the enemy to allow inspection at any hour. The crew manning the 105-mm fieldpiece was relieved and replaced by three fresh men, who put on their helmets and took up their position as though nothing whatever had happened.

More equipment arrived; a group of trucks under escort came heavily out onto the pier. One of them, a huge flatbed vehicle with multiple wheels on its rear axle, carried a large piece of electronic gear which appeared to weigh three or four tons. The crane was summoned; on instruction the operator picked it up gently and set it down close to the end of the brow. Kepinsky looked it over for a full minute and then said, "You may use it."

Other gear was placed by hand until the end of the pier was comfortably filled with equipment, barring only the forbidden circle painted around the rapid-fire field gun. Everyone seemed to know about that and kept clear.

After some minutes one man came up out of the submarine, motioned to Kepinsky, and then joined the commander. As soon as the enemy nuclear expert was with them he reported, "There's a leak in the reactor, it seems to be expanding slowly. She's freshly fueled, which doesn't help. Radiation level inside the hull is well above toleration limits, so keep everybody out who isn't suited and doesn't know what he's doing."

"How long to fix it?" the commander asked.

"If we're lucky, several hours. It could be days. Keep the area clear of all unnecessary personnel, for God's sake; if it ruptures, then anything can happen."

"Have you enough men?"

"I think so. It's too early to be sure but there's only room for so many, of course. We work in short shifts to keep the exposure down." He turned to Kepinsky. "I know you probably want to go on board, but right now it's hell down there. Of course you can do what you want."

Kepinsky once more read the radiation detector which was standing a few feet away and for the moment appeared to be satisfied. "I see everything," he instructed. "You tell me everything."

"All right."

In the underground headquarters of Thomas Jefferson the message board had been busy. Plates of food had been placed on the table, but they had been generally ignored. The conference room was filled to near capacity by the many men who had worked for so long on Operation Low Blow and who were almost desperately anxious for every bit of incoming news.

When the word came through that the nukes from Mare Island had been admitted to the base without delay of any kind, General Gifford allowed himself the luxury of a smile. That end of things had been his particular responsibility; he also happened to be a lodge brother of the yard commander who obviously had done a completely convincing job. The enemy personnel were almost fanatic in their suspicion of everyone and everything; faking out such men called for much more than ordinary talent and total effort.

The admiral very much wanted to know if word of the events at Hunters Point had been passed to Colonel Rostovitch. That relentless, ruthless, and eternally questioning man might well see through the whole thing in a flash and if he did, that would be the end of everything. Rostovitch was too intricate a plotter himself not to recognize the signs, and he had a fearsome reputation in counterintelligence. The admiral had considered the idea of trying to get to Rostovitch to insure that he would be fully engaged at the time of Low Blow, but none of the assembled intellects comprising the First Team, or their almost equally bright back-up personnel, had been able to suggest anything that had a reasonable hope of working. Also there was the strong possibility that the colonel would read out any attempts at himself, as he had done many times before, and would be immediately alerted. The admiral had wisely decided to leave Rostovitch alone for the time being. He could be dealt with later on.

Major Pappas laid aside two more contingency plans which would no longer be needed. So far the show was right on the road, but that was no guarantee that it would remain that way. Too many very tricky gambits lay immediately ahead.

CHAPTER SIXTEEN

The first darkness of the new night saw no visible letup in the intensive work that was being done in and around the inert, silent submarine. The eerie, white-suited figures from Mare Island contrasted starkly with the dead black hull of the *Magsaysay* which lay in the water with only the sail and the top of her deck visible. On the dock the radiation detector still indicated a level close to the danger point; the men of the regular work crew who had been detained were gathered on the opposite side of the pier, keeping out of the way.

The commander was there also, nervously pacing up and down from time to time, then stopping to ponder some additional problem. It was not all acting; he had good cause to worry and he knew it. During the next several hours the effects of surprise would all wear off and in the coldly realistic small hours of the night it would be a different ball game. Furthermore, there was a great deal to be done yet and every bit of it would be difficult and dangerous. All the enemy had to do was to bring in a qualified crew of nuclear experts and it would all be over. They could appropriate the decontamination suits and have a look for themselves. If that occurred, everyone concerned would be lined up on the dock and shot right there.

Inside the hull of the *Magsaysay* a great deal was going on. In the forward part of the ship, which had been screened off from the live radiation, three men who had stripped down to their skivvies were carefully getting into wet suits which were part of the submarine's standard equipment. They helped each other to strap on SCUBA gear and then went through a series of careful checks, particularly on the rebreathers. As they were finishing another man came into the compartment. He still had on his decontamination suit, but he had taken off his headpiece and was holding it under his arm. He was a little less than normal height, slightly dark in complexion, and of slender build.

The nearest of the divers nodded to him. "Ready, captain," he said.

"Good. The pre-launch check is set in eight minutes. The best of luck, Hank."

"Thank you, sir, we'll do our best."

There was no more time to spend in conversation; the captain refitted his headgear and went back through the hatch. Down the passageway he was met by a colleague who was waiting for him.

"So far, so good," the man said. "The light-up crew is ready and standing by."

"The emergency isotope?"

"Positioned and ready."

"Carry on. Keep me informed about the situation on the pier—that's the uncertain element."

"Ay, sir."

Slightly more than six minutes later Morrison, the man who had been doing the talking for the Mare Island team, came across the brow, removed his headgear, and went up to speak to the commander. Kepinsky joined them to hear what was being said.

"All right, I can give you the preliminary word," he reported. "We have a leak, and a potentially very dangerous one, in the pile. We haven't got it pinpointed yet, but we know the general area and we've started to get in there."

"How dangerous is it?" the commander asked.

"Bad enough. We're working in very short shifts, but we're protected and the crew knows what it's doing."

The commander did not like the use of the word "crew," it was too suggestive of the truth, but his lined face gave no clue to that fact. "How about the day men?" he asked. "We're still keeping them here."

"Why don't you send them up to get something to eat; by the time that they get back we'll know whether we're going to need them or not," Morrison suggested.

"Good idea. Anything else?"

"We may need a lot of wash water; if you can rig some hose lines that would be a help. Also, since we're going to be here all night at least, could you have some food sent down. We can't leave the job and there may be contamination."

"Show me what is happen," Kepinsky interrupted.

"I need something to draw on."

The commander went to his car and produced a block of paper. He supplied a pencil from his pocket and then walked over to where the day crew men were still waiting at the opposite side of the pier. "You guys go and eat," he said. "We may need you, we don't know yet. Tell them at the cafeteria that I said it's on the house."

The men got up and started down the pier. The commander looked about and saw that the number of enemy guards had been somewhat decreased; a half dozen were still in evidence as well as the omnipresent gun crew, but there was no evidence that they were more than casually interested in what was going on. They stood and waited, and would continue to do so until they were given orders to the contrary.

Apparently Kepinsky was satisfied with the explanation he was given; he even looked a trifle worried when he rejoined the commander. "It is ungood," he said.

"I don't like it, either, but I have confidence in our boys," the commander responded. Wearily he raised his arms and rubbed his fingers through his hair.

Morrison recrossed the brow and went down the rear hatch. As he did so the radiation detector suddenly showed a gain and a red light mounted on the dial went on. It remained that way for several seconds and then subsided. Kepinsky moved back a few feet but stayed where he could keep a careful watch over the instrument. He had had experience once with a leak in a nuclear pile in his own country and the results had been disastrous. There was, however, no way that he could leave; he remained because he had to, and waited.

The fresh spurt of radiation produced a noticeable reaction from the guards who remained on the pier. Apparently they were not sure what was happening, but it was obvious that they were suddenly afraid. One by one they drew back as far from the submarine as they dared. They could not leave their posts and they knew it, but self-protection was uppermost in their minds.

None of them heard the slight noise which came from the opposite side of the ship when the lead diver, his face and hands blackened, opened the sail door as quietly as he could and looked out carefully into the night. The South Pier was sufficiently far away to give him a measure of protection. With practiced care he slipped through the opening, crossed the few feet of curved decking, and slid all but silently into the water.

Five seconds later the second man followed. In addition to his SCUBA gear he had a sack of tools. He too slid into the water so expertly that there was a minimum of noise or movement to betray him. The two men below the surface swam carefully, one behind the other, toward the stern. When they reached the propeller they waited until the third member of the team joined them, then with the aid of a carefully shielded faint light they tried to measure the extent of the task before them.

The propeller itself was formidable: it was more than nineteen feet in diameter and dwarfed the men who hovered near it appraising the substantial chain which had been woven around it and the rudder post a half dozen times. One end reached over in a lazy underwater arc to the base of the pier.

The lead diver followed it quietly and invisibly until he saw how it had been secured. He did not touch it; instead, using a tiny light of his own, he studied it carefully until he saw two thin electrical wires which had been fastened with insulating staples to the back of the post to which the chain was attached.

He maneuvered into the limited space behind the post and with his diver's knife removed three of the staples. One at a time he very carefully scraped the wires completely around for a distance of four inches. When he was entirely satisfied with his work he used the limited amount of available play to wind them tightly together. He was careful not to put too much strain on the joint until he was absolutely sure that he had a secure electrical connection. Then he swam back to see how his two companions were doing.

The job of putting the chain around the propeller had been crudely accomplished, probably because the men who had done it did not expect that any inspection would be made of their work. It had simply been wound around the propeller blades and the rudder post enough to insure the fact that the drive system was immobilized until it was removed. Silently the underwater trio conferred by signs. The head diver held up two fingers; each of his companions showed three. He accepted their verdict; he swam to the side of the submarine and with the aid of his light looked at his underwater watch. He waited ninety seconds, then at the exact five minute interval he tapped very gently against the pressure hull.

He was answered almost at once by four evenly spaced knocks which could have been someone at work in another part of the ship. A full minute of silence passed; sixty measured seconds to break the continuity in case anyone had taken note of the audible signals. Then the diver tapped twice, waited, then tapped three more times.

A single knock acknowledged the message; as soon as he had heard it the diver swam away.

Inside the hull the crewman who had been listening went forward to find the captain as rapidly as he was able. "Sir," he reported, "I've got the word from the Seals. The screw is fouled, but they estimate that they can clear it within three hours."

Although he already knew the time to the minute the captain consulted his watch once more, then turned to his exec who was close by. "We'll gamble on that—we've got to. Pass the word to the light-up crew to get started and to make the best time that they can." He knew that the job would take close to six hours, and that it was an extremely critical operation which could not be hurried beyond a certain point.

The men in the reactor compartment were anxiously awaiting that order. The three who were assigned to this important duty knew that from the moment they were authorized to start, time would be vial and that none of it could be wasted. The dropped isotope would mask the increased radiation level; the cooling water was another matter, but there was a cover for that—at least so they had been informed. Their job was to get the pile going and to ignore everything else.

On the dock Kepinsky was having second thoughts. He knew the acute danger that a mishap in the nuclear pile represented, but to remain on the pier without making a personal inspection could be interpreted as negligence. He had been rationalizing, he realized that, and danger or no danger, he would have to go below. If some eighty Americans could brave the peril no excuse would be accepted for failure on his part to make a personal inspection and determine what was going on. He spoke to the commander. "I wish a suit," he said. "At once I myself going to see."

The burly man who ran the shipyard looked at him and shook his head. "All right, it's your neck. I'll get someone." He walked to the end of the brow and shouted.

It took a moment or two before he was heard, then Morrison came up on deck. The commander motioned him to come onto the dock and then waited until the man had removed his head covering. "Mr. Kepinsky has decided to make a personal inspection of the interior of the hull," he said. "He wants a suit and would like to go on board as soon as he can."

"We don't have any spares," Morrison answered. "I'll have to get one of my men up and they can change here on the dock." He went back on board and disappeared down the hatch once more. He returned within a minute followed by another man, then came across the short brow with enough evidence of speed to keep Kepinsky satisfied. Without being instructed the man in the decontamination suit began to remove the protective clothing; he was obviously unhappy, but carried on because he had no choice.

It was some minutes before Kepinsky was ready to enter the hull. In that interval of time a considerable change had taken place within the submarine. The three suits worn by the diving team had been carefully hidden and the team had been warned by an emergency signal. The slight sounds coming from the extreme rear of the ship ceased almost at once. The isotope which Chief Summers had placed had already been moved to a suitable and difficult-of-access position in the reactor compartment where it continued to pour out its raw radiation, no less deadly because it was invisible and unheard. Within two minutes all superficial evidence of light-up had been removed and even to an expert eye the environment of an authentic emergency was close to complete. If the unwelcome visitor brought any kind of a Geiger counter or other instrument with him, it would give all of the properly misleading answers.

It took Kepinsky considerably longer than he wished to get into the somewhat complicated decontamination suit that he had borrowed. He was helped, but the assistance seemed to do nothing to speed him on his way. As he struggled to encase himself properly he cursed the weakness within himself that had kept him standing on the dock for so long when, as he knew now, he should have been inside the submarine making a firsthand inspection of everything. His stomach knotted when he realized that the only report he could give as of that moment would be based on what he had heard and what he had been told by the Americans. The only tangible thing he had seen himself was the reading on the radiation detector on the dock. When he was fully ready he went across the brow behind the supervisor and climbed down inside the hull.

He was almost relieved to discover that every one of the men on board was hard at work doing all of the things he knew to be necessary. Because of his suit he could not be recognized, but he was unaware of the red flashlight signals that had been given just prior to his coming on board.

He spent almost thirty minutes examining everything and was satisfied, first that this was a real and authentic nuclear mishap and second that he could so report on the basis of close personal inspection. His own position was now far more secure, and with that knowledge relief flooded through him. He still could not explain his delay in seeing things for himself, but with the data he had now he was confident that he could conjure some kind of a realistic excuse that would sound valid.

He was tapped on the shoulder by Morrison, who then indicated the dial of his watch. A radiation counter close to the reactor compartment was going like mad, which was adequate warning. It had to be genuine because the independent instrument on the pier, which was known to be untampered with, had been telling the same story. Kepinsky turned his back on the hard-working men crowded into the available space and made his way up the ladders with no regrets. Later on, at an appropriate time, he would go inside again.

Not until he was well out of his protective clothing did the real work inside the submarine resume. The waiting divers were signaled, the light-up crew went back to work, and the cooling pumps were started. On the dock the day-shift men came back as a group, escorted by two guards, obviously both tired and unhappy. When the decontamination suit had been returned to its proper owner and the man had gone about getting into it once more, Morrison joined the yard commander for a brief conference with both Kepinsky and the commander's overseer tuned in.

"I think we can let most of the day-shift men go home," he said. "I'd like to keep a few on hand for extra work if that can be managed, particularly plumbers if there are any."

"How about relieving them and calling some fresh men on the job?" the commander suggested.

"You might have trouble getting anyone to come in; the word will be out now all over town. One suggestion: the men are used to this ship. Up in the forward end, shielded from the radiation, there are some bunks which they could use. Then when we need them we can wake them up."

The commander appeared to consider that. "Why not," he said finally, "if we can depend on them to stay out of the way until they're needed."

"They will, I can guarantee that—if they value their skins."

"How many do you think you'll need?"

Morrison glanced over at the waiting men. "Half of them would be enough."

The commander walked over to where the day-shift workers were gathered. "Some of you can go home now," he said, "the rest of you we'll keep on for a while longer. You're all getting overtime, so take it easy."

There was a brief murmur from the men, but the assurance of the extra pay was obviously what they wanted to hear. Quickly the commander sorted them into two groups, then he dismissed the first contingent and saw them start down the pier—anxious now to get away. "We've made some arrangements for the rest of you," he announced. "We've got the radiation shielded off from the forepart of the ship. There are plenty of crew bunks down there that you can use. So you might as well sack out, and if we need you we'll wake you up."

"I don't think we'd like that," Summers said. "It's too dangerous."

The commander bristled. "Listen, you, in case you haven't heard, things aren't the way that they used to be. We're all taking orders now whether we like it or not. Personally I don't like it, but there isn't a damn thing I can do about it. Right now the job is to protect our own men and the people that live close around this base."

"We still get paid?" Summers pressed.

"Yes, you get paid—overtime rates even while you're in the sack."

"All right." Resignedly Summers got to his feet.

Slowly the others followed suit. Morrison, bulky in his decontamination clothing, led them on board and escorted them down the front hatch well forward of where the critical work was being done. Kepinsky carefully counted them; there were twenty-three. They could do no harm where they were going because he personally had seen the thorough precautions that had been taken to seal off the front end of the submarine.

A Jeep driven by an enemy security agent came slowly down the pier and stopped beside Kepinsky. "A report is wanted," the agent said in his own language.

"I just came up from the submarine a few moments ago," Kepinsky answered. "I made a personal inspection in detail. It is presently very hazardous down there."

"Is there any question?"

Kepinsky shook his head emphatically. "None at all; our own equipment was the first to detect the leak. They are working to repair it very efficiently; they have no desire to have a disaster in their own community. If they fail they will all die and so will many others all around here."

"You are taking a chance, are you not?"

"Yes, but it is my duty. You can read the meter for yourself."

The security man was satisfied. As he turned his vehicle around he reflected on the fact that it was his good fortune that he was not a nuclear expert. If Kepinsky lived through it the rot might still be buried deep in the marrow of his bones and there was a good chance that he would never sire any more children. He left the area at a steady pace and was grateful that the security headquarters lay on the other side of a low hill.

With the day crew no longer in evidence, the night settled down to stillness and waiting. A truck arrived from the cafeteria and set up a chow line of sorts to feed the men who were working inside the ship. When the word was passed they came up in small groups, ate hastily, and then went back below again. They showed the strain of their work on their faces and Kepinsky did not envy them. He kept no count of the number that ate, but it would not have helped him if he had because he did not know the exact number of men who were working down inside the pressure hull. He therefore was unaware that one man chose not to show himself. This man's features were somewhat distinctive and his smaller build was in contrast to some of the others'. Because there was a slight element of risk, he chose to go hungry.

The commander had left together with his omnipresent shadow, the overseer, who followed him even when he went to the latrine. A small handful of guards remained on duty, but they were relaxing as much as they dared. The depressive effect of the inert night was thick in the air. A small truck came with a relief gun crew which took over the heavy fieldpiece on the extreme end of the pier, exercised it briefly, and then settled in to maintain watch for the next several hours.

On the side of the hull of the submarine two light taps followed after a pause by a third drew a prompt reaction from the man who was stationed to listen for that signal. He reported at once to the exec. "Sir, the Seals report ready to come aboard." He did not elaborate; to do so would have been unnecessary. The word was passed to the con and to the captain that Seal recovery was under way.

From the starboard sail door a thin line was tossed into the water. When the man who had thrown it felt a pull on the other end he carefully scanned the visible area and saw no evidence of any observers. He gave a quick tug and then watched as a man in SCUBA gear appeared almost silently out of the water. When he was safely inside the procedure was repeated. The lead diver was the last to come up, his flippers also leaving froglike marks on the otherwise dry decking.

At almost the same moment a crew of two men came up from the rear hatch, activated a hose, and began to wash down the above-water part of the decking. Kepinsky silently approved of that; decontamination washing had been going on off and on since shortly after the men from Mare Island had arrived. Three minutes later there was no sign whatever that anyone had made use of the sail door or left footprints of any kind.

Inside the con the lead diver was making his report. "The screw is clear; the chain that was fouling it was equipped with an electrical circuit, but I shorted it out. Before we came back on board we made a full inspection of the hull to the best of our ability. Everything looked all right."

"That's fine, Hank," the captain said. "You know the importance of what you did. When you've changed and your hair is dry, you'll find some chow up on the pier."

"We can use that, sir. How's everything else coming?"

"So far, on schedule. But we don't know what they may do at any time."

"Is the diversion all set?"

"Yes, but I don't want to use it except as a last resort; it's too risky for the personnel involved. Pass the word I said 'well done.' "

"Ay, ay, sir."

Some twenty minutes later Kepinsky decided that it was time for him to make another inspection. Once more he had to go through the business of getting into a decontamination suit; by the time he was ready to go below the necessary preparations for his visit had been made. The light-up was well advanced, but as much as possible had been done to mask that fact; Kepinsky would have to be alert indeed to detect what was actually going on. If he did, then he would have to meet with an incapacitating accident almost at once—a dangerous procedure, but under the given circumstances there would be no choice.

Fortunately that drastic procedure did not prove necessary; the enemy nuclear specialist spent only sixteen minutes below this time, and it was his extreme good fortune to meet the chief of the night security force just as he was returning to the pier. At first the security chief did not recognize Kepinsky, but when he pulled off his headpiece and came up to him, it was proof positive that he had been diligently on the job. The security man had a brief visit with him and then left rather quickly, particularly since Kepinsky had said something about stray radiation sticking to his garments. The security chief confirmed the report of his man who had been down on the dock previously that Kepinsky was letting nothing get by him and that the nuclear trouble was very real. He was also convinced that the men at work were doing their utmost best to prevent a catastrophe and that they would in all probability succeed. He fervently hoped so, because he had only recently arrived in this new land where there were so many highly attractive girls, and as yet he had not had an opportunity to go to bed with even one of them.

The few security personnel stationed on the pier were relieved and replaced; a few more men from the submarine came up and ate. After that the food was taken away and the night was still. Kepinsky was grateful that it was not colder; as it was he felt a decided chill and knew that it would be much worse before morning. He had not dressed for this sort of thing and his native pride would not allow him to borrow anything other than the essential decontamination suit from the subjugated personnel.

But he did not go away. He remained stubbornly on duty because he had not been relieved and no one had told him that his job was finished.

Below decks his continuing presence forced a firm decision. "If he shows again," Morrison said, "we'll have to pull the emergency isotope to chase him out of here, and that will make things a lot harder all around. If we can't do that, then we have no other choice than to take him out of the picture."

The exec agreed. "I can't see it any other way—in fact I'd save the isotope for a last-resort stand. He's the enemy and I know it, although he's individually a decent enough guy."

"When it hits the fan they'll shoot him anyway, so it doesn't make much difference."

"True." The exec looked again at his watch and made a decision. "Things are getting too close now for us to play any more games. If he wants to come down, do everything that you can to discourage him short of giving the show away. If he won't be persuaded, then we'll simply have to take the only way out."

Morrison agreed. "I'll set it up. We have a plan ready."

"It's in your hands."

At three-thirty in the morning the night security chief decided to have another look, not because he wanted to, but because he knew that he might be criticized if he didn't. He took a Jeep and went back to the pier where Kepinsky was still visible in the near darkness. The floodlight had been turned off shortly after midnight in accordance with the usual procedure since the graveyard shift had been shut down. The few security guards were silent and still, on duty but not within earshot. "Any changes?" he asked.

Kepinsky shook his head. "It is a long slow process; I know this. They are very skillful men. Very privately I tell you that in some respects they are ahead of us."

"It is best that you not say that publicly."

"I have no such intention," Kepinsky agreed. "I tell you because you are entitled to know everything."

The security man was properly flattered. "I shall say nothing. You have been down again?"

"Yes," Kepinsky lied. The guards could disprove him, but he knew they would not be questioned.

"You are a brave man," the security chief said, and drove away. Like many others he placed a higher value on the lives of his own people than he did on those who had been subjugated.

After the chief was once more out of sight, Kepinsky, for lack of anything better to do, looked up into the sky. Overhead the massive bulk of the heavy lift crane obscured many of the stars. In the east, across the waters of the bay, the first very faint hints of lightening were beginning to show. It was probably the false dawn, he thought, but when the real one came he would receive credit for having been continuously on the job throughout the night. He was not a warlike man; he had chosen to become a scientist and had expected to work only in his own homeland. Now he was standing on a shipyard pier many thousands of miles from the home that he loved and from his small family that had seen him off with tear-streaked faces. He thought about them and wondered if they would enjoy life in this new land.

He was colder now and he wanted very much to go to bed. He crossed the pier to the north side and seeking the even darker shadow of one of the crane's legs he urinated into the water. He felt much better after he had finished; he had not been aware of the pressure that had been building inside his bladder; it was like that sometimes when his mind was fully occupied elsewhere. He looked toward the east once more and saw that the sky was perceptibly lighter —it was later in the decaying night than he had thought. He looked again at the submarine, then at the radiation level indicator. For the first time the reading had changed; it was encouragingly lower. The Americans, he had to admit, were good. They had worked the whole nuclear thing out in the first place; Russia had gotten it through Fuchs, MacLean, the Rosenbergs, and the others who had fed them the secrets and saved them years of laborious research. After that France had come into the picture, England, and the People's Republic of China. The Chinese had botched it; there were strong rumors of nuclear disasters at their testing grounds. How the Americans had ever been conquered was something that he did not understand. The word "subversion" was often used, but that sort of thing was out of his ken. He had at first hoped that he might see America one day as a visiting scientist, but that was not the way it had worked out.

He was cold and it was sure to be much warmer inside the submarine. And the decontamination suits were warm too. Plus which it was undoubtedly his duty to take one more look; the meter indicated that things were coming under control and he could confirm it when he was asked. He went to the brow and called to a man who was on the deck.

Morrison, when he appeared, did his best to dissuade him, but Kepinsky knew what would be expected of him; despite the consideration he was being shown he felt he had to insist. Once more a man was called on deck to give him his suit and once more he went though all of the motions of being properly encased in the radiation protection.

He went down the hatch feeling a little better; the chill was already disappearing from his body and he was in an environment that appealed to him even though the circumstances were far from agreeable. Obviously the Americans were doing well; when he saw the results himself he wondered if it would be within his dignity as a member of the occupying forces to commend them on their work. Someday all men would have to get along together, and that would be accomplished only through millions of relatively small personal contacts. He would see.

He went to the power compartment with no suspicions whatever. He began to look about him and then he realized something; the reactor pile was working—it had to be. That meant only one thing, and in a startling, upheaving moment of revelation he saw the whole truth. He stood stock-still and used his brain; then he turned and raised both of his enclosed arms in front of him, placing his palms together in an unmistakable gesture. He walked quickly out of the compartment and went forward. He made no attempt to go up the hatch when he passed the ladder, but he held his arms up in a gesture of surrender.

When he had gone as far as he was able he pulled off his headpiece and faced the several men who had followed him. The man immediately behind him took off his own headgear and revealed a strange face, hard-set and determined. "You are escaping," Kepinsky said.

"Yes, we are." It was the exec, although Kepinsky did not know that.

"Please, who is in charge?"

"I will do."

Kepinsky gathered all of the courage he could muster. "Please take me. If stay, I am shoot." He stopped. He wanted greatly to put his case more eloquently, but his knowledge of English was largely only a reading skill for technical material.

The executive officer hesitated for a bare moment. In that interval Kepinsky remembered a phrase he had read. "Political asylum," he said.

Another man pushed by and came forward. Kepinsky reacted when he saw him, for despite his smaller stature he realized who he was.

"He knows, captain," the exec explained. "He's asking for political asylum—he wants to come with us."

"Political asylum?"

"Yes, sir. We had every intention of taking action, but he raised his arms . . ."

"I understand."

"I help," Kepinsky pleaded. "Will work."

Morrison ventured to speak. "He's been decent enough, sir, just doing his job."

The captain wasted no more time. "Asylum granted. The first misstep of any kind—dispose of him."

Kepinsky's face burst out in sweat. Morrison pushed him by the arm into a tiny cabin and quickly posted a guard; there wasn't time for anything else.

The captain had already left to return to the con. He glanced at his watch, then dismissed the matter of the unwanted guest from his mind—Morrison was highly responsible and would take care of it.

The quartermaster spoke. "Eleven minutes."

The captain heard but did not answer; his mind was totally on his ship and the job immediately ahead. The long night was all but past and the near impossible had been accomplished; the screw had been cleared, the pile had been lit, and power was ready. All of this had been done directly under the eyes of the enemy by a group of icy-nerved, exceptionally resourceful men. Navy men. Then in a moment of strict fairness he conceded that the Air Force was good when it had anything to fly, the Army too, and of course the Marine Corps. That mental obligation discharged, he turned back completely to the mission at hand. "Final check," he ordered.

The departments reported quickly; the crew was in command of the ship even though she was still tied to the dock and under the barrel of a rapid-fire field gun that could pierce her hull with a single round. The responses were all affirmative; the *Magsaysay* was ready. The captain looked once more at his watch, then folded his arms and stood still in the middle of the con. All he could do now was wait.

Colonel Gregor Rostovitch had had a very large evening and night. He had not had a woman for some time and the need for one had been growing on him. He had had no time for any niceties or any desire to be subtle; he had given orders that he was to be provided with a qualified female, and he had expected results. Then he had returned in savage mood to his self-assigned task of ferreting out the American underground organization. It was not going well. The usual devices were not bringing in the leads; no convenient informers had appeared since the incident in the Midwest, and that had concerned only an impotent group of college students. The colonel wanted and demanded more action; he maneuvered an increasingly large number of agents into every critical area that he could pinpoint and read their reports with total attention, but the solid results were not there. Whoever his opponent was, whoever was playing the game from the other side of the board, was no amateur and the fact that no evidence of activity had appeared above the surface meant nothing. Something had to be going on; the colonel knew that, and he was determined to find out what it was. When he did he would smash it: smash it so hard that no one else would dare to challenge the new authority that had been clamped onto the United States of America.

The one satisfaction the colonel had was the relentless progress of the Jewish segregation program. His hatred of those people was complete, and where Hitler had failed, he would succeed. Hitler had been a maniac, a madman who despite his incompetence had very nearly succeeded. If men like Rommel had been allowed to run things, professionals who knew their work, it would have been different: Churchill would have danced at the end of a hangman's rope, England would have been swept into Fortress Europe, and iron discipline would have broken the back of resistance.

Discipline! The lack of it had destroyed the United States, the command of it would very shortly raise Gregor Rostovitch to the peak of his country's hierarchy, and after that . . . He dropped it because he had thought it out many times before to its conclusion and he knew what was to come. He knew his own strength, his relentless toughness, and the power of his intelligence. He knew accurately that he was vastly superior to the Austrian paperhanger and that he would not and could not be stopped. The military power behind him was absolute, and the man did not live who would dare to get in his way. Except for some subversives in the occupied United States, and they would be exterminated!

The woman who was delivered to him was in her early thirties, attractive enough to be interesting, and willing if she knew what was good for her. After five minutes in her company he sensed that she too knew her business and was ready to deliver the merchandise. That mollified him to a degree: his physical appetites were as strong and driving as his political thirsts and he had no compunctions about gratifying either.

He took the woman to his quarters and in a preliminary tryout found her as competent as he had expected. On the strength of that he had a good dinner sent up for both of them and after that plenty of side delicacies and top-quality liquors. He got very little actual sleep that night and he desired none; his animal instincts were at their peak and the woman gave him great satisfaction. When at last he ceased, because the alcohol he had taken into his system would no longer be denied, he sank into a kind of stupor and remained that way until early morning. Then he roused himself, shaved, dressed, and was ready to do battle.

He was in his office well before nine, going through the reports which had accumulated on his desk, searching every one of them for the vital piece of information he needed. He was two-thirds of the way finished with this task when he read again with incredulity the words before him and then slammed his clenched fist hard against the desk top. If he felt any pain he was unaware of it. "Fools!" he screamed aloud. "Fools!"

Disbelief racked him: somehow, in some manner, his people in charge of a West Coast shipyard where a fully armed, nuclear-powered, ballistic missile submarine was berthed had allowed more than eighty unidentified Americans to board the potent ship at one time and to occupy it throughout an entire night. The colonel was in a frenzy; his rage boiled like liquid oxygen as he grabbed for the telephone. All of his persistent questions about what had been going on behind the façade of nothingness were answered; the Americans were preying on the gross stupidity of his people.

He got on the line with blazing fury and demanded an instant connection to San Francisco.

At precisely minus six minutes the commander of the yard, who had caught a brief catnap in his office, arrived with his overseer in his vehicle and climbed out in the thinning darkness. He first read the meter to determine the radiation level and then called to a man who was patiently hosing down the deck. In response a message was passed to the supervisor on board the submarine, and moments later Morrison came across the brow. As the three men met, a slow-moving, flatbed truck appeared rumbling its way down the pier. It had aboard one of the massive dumpsters used in the yard, a steel open-topped container used to collect scrap and waste material. Laboriously the truck turned around and backed into position somewhere near to the submarine's stern.

"We've got things under control now," Morrison reported. "Another four hours and we'll be able to shut down."

The commander wiped his sleeve across his brow. "We'll be safe, then?"

"That's right; no problem. We've called the day workmen onto the job. Some of them have responded, the rest want to go home."

"God damn them!" the commander exploded. "They're working for me; let me handle this. Mind if I go on board?"

"Be my guest."

In visibly mounting rage the commander strode rapidly across the brow and clambered down the front hatchway. The overseer started to follow, but Morrison held up his hand. "He'll be right back," he promised.

Less than a half minute after the commander had disappeared the first of the day crewmen began to come up. Stiff-jointed and still shaking off the effects of sleep, they came across the brow and waited on the pier for directions. They sat on convenient bollards, one or two of them yawning and rubbing the upper part of their legs, the others contenting themselves by staring across the water. They were men who had slept in their clothes and who had no desire to be up to witness the first light of the day.

Far above them the overhead crane came alive. The sling slowly descended from the end of the boom as the whole upper assembly began to rotate to the left. The maneuver was neatly done; the cables hung in almost perfect position to be hooked onto the pier dumpster. Since it was almost half the size of a boxcar the truck driver beckoned for help; two of the day workmen responded and gave a hand in fitting the hooks into the four corner shackles. When the brief job was done the driver stepped back and signaled to the operator far overhead.

In response the cable came tight and the dumpster with its load lifted off the concrete. Again the whole massive upper structure of the high crane began to turn to the left, the dumpster hanging at the end of a hundred feet of extended cable. The turning motion increased slightly, then stopped abruptly. Because of the long cable, the dumpster continued in motion, arcing forward lazily over the water off the north side of the pier.

Then the crane mechanism began to rotate in the opposite direction, and with gradually increasing speed. The dumpster resisted the change in direction, but as the angle of the cable increased, its inertia was overcome and it began to swing back. Its momentum built up rapidly; someone shouted, but the boom continued to turn and at the same time to come down a few degrees in angle.

The dumpster swept across the pier just above the concrete with inexorable power directly toward the heavy mobile field gun mounted at the end. Its speed was not too great, but its sheer mass was overpowering. The gun crew had less than five seconds of actual warning; one man jumped successfully flat onto his face—then a violent terrible crash of steel against steel tore the still air. Despite its tons of weight, the gun and its carriage were driven by the impact over the edge of the dock; there was a second's pause, then a massive splash as it disappeared into the water.

At that precise moment action erupted among the men on the pier. The workmen who had been resting against the bollards grabbed the lines which held the submarine and threw them over; the truck driver raced for the brow. On top of the sail two men suddenly appeared holding automatic weapons in their hands. One of them fired a short warning burst over the heads of the startled enemy guards, then he leveled his weapon in an unmistakable command. The man toward whom he aimed threw up his arms; he had no chance otherwise and he knew it. Quickly his colleagues understood and did the same. They stood frozen as the few workmen on the dock ran one after the other back across the brow onto the deck. Then, very slowly, the long black shape of the U.S.S. *Ramon Magsaysay* began to creep forward.

The brow began to turn, lost its support, and fell clumsily down between the pier and the moving submarine. On the deck some of the workmen were rapidly pulling in the lines while those not needed lost no time in getting down the hatchways.

On the middle of the pier one man who was being left behind came abruptly to life; suddenly he lunged forward and started sprinting toward the ship with desperate speed. When he reached the edge of the concrete he jumped with all the strength he had, hurling himself toward the sharply curved, smooth deck of the submarine. A workman saw him coming, braced himself as best he could, and grabbed him as he landed. He had no idea who the jumper was, but the man's face was a mask of fright. The workman had not a moment for anything but his assigned duty on the lines; he grabbed them up again and jerked his head toward the hatchway.

In the enemy security office the direct-line telephone rang. The chief picked it up, listened for a few seconds, then paled in sudden alarm. He jumped to his feet, yelled out an order, spoke rapidly into the phone, and then dashed out of his office. With urgent gestures he assembled his total force on hand, then he got behind the wheel of a vehicle as fast as he could and turned the key with shaking fingers.

At the bottom of the hatch ladder the commander of the shipyard confronted his overseer, who had just jumped for his life. "Keep out of my way!" he roared, and cursed the luck that had allowed the man to come on board. Then he thrust his head through the hatch to check on what was happening.

On the bridge atop the sail more men appeared. A coolly efficient Officer of the Deck was already directing the still very slow forward progress of the submarine. There had been no opportunity to warp away from the dock, and moving this close to the edge of the pier was dangerous. The bow was already past the end, which relieved the pressure somewhat; once the stern could be swung a safe distance away from the piling the acute hazard would be over.

The captain stood silently on the bridge, watching everything that was going on. The phone talker who was also there was young but determined; he relayed the orders crisply and showed no signs of fear.

What was left of the dumpster still dangled from the great high boom which stretched well out over the water.

"Left five degrees," the OD directed.

"Left five degrees," the talker repeated and passed the order below. Seconds later the stern began to show movement away from the pier.

Then the captain looked up. Very high overhead the figure of the crane operator was visible out on the catwalk which ran the length of the boom. He was bent low and moving forward as fast as he safely could. He continued on, right to the end, and then stopped with nothing but dizzying height and a vast emptiness before him and looked down fearlessly at the submarine far below. Carefully he judged the rate of her progress; when the turn was well begun he raised his arms to shoulder height, held them out, and slowly leaned forward into the open void.

For several fractions of a second he seemed to hang there at an angle over empty space, then he began to fall. Gradually at first, then with increasing speed, he dropped, his body rotating slowly in the air as he held it straight, his arms now at his sides. He plunged downward at mounting speed for a long three seconds like a hurtling meteorite, and then hit the water. He went straight in, feet first, and disappeared. Seven seconds later his head came up less than fifty feet from the port side of the submarine, which was moving a little faster now as it turned into the channel.

A crewman who had been waiting safely behind the sail stepped forward and threw a light line expertly behind him. As the ship moved forward the diver caught it and held on while some mechanism he could not see pulled him in. As he felt the hull with his feet he heard the shouts of men from the pier behind him; a bullet plowed the water beside him.

He was on the deck in another three seconds and running in a zigzag pattern the few steps to the sail. He found sanctuary behind it where the crewman who had thrown him the line was holding open the door. As he stepped inside he noted that all of the top hatches were already closed and secured.

On the bridge the OD said, "Seventy turns." The scattered shooting at the submarine had stopped; she was pointed at 355 degrees now and the Oakland Bay Bridge was visible in the first light some four and a half miles ahead.

The speed of the ship began to increase until there was a visible bow wave beginning to build.

"All ahead full."

"All ahead full, sir," the talker repeated and relayed it below. In the now almost unearthly quiet well before sunrise the whole desperate venture seemed to be suddenly almost a peaceful cruise. The captain, with binoculars, was carefully studying the shoreline on the port side. The enemy knew now and had known for some minutes, and they could be expected to be taking some action. What that action might be he did not know but he was gravely concerned. Although the tide was in and just beginning to ebb, he knew that he could not depend on more than fifty feet of water depth, and *Magsaysay* drew almost thirty-seven feet on the surface.

He felt a sense of comfort in the increasing speed. The ship was accelerating now as fast as she could without causing excess cavitation, but he still had a fourteen-minute run to reach the Bay Bridge at the rate they were going. The bow wave built up slowly, giving testimony to faster progress through the water.

"All ahead flank," the OD said.

"All ahead flank." The order went below for maximum speed. Once that order was given nothing more could be done to hurry the ship's progress; hopefully the very early hour would catch some of the enemy forces literally asleep. A mile out from shore the *Magsaysay* passed the Army Street terminal; she was moving better now and her forward speed provided a light breeze on the bridge. The OD felt it gratefully and nodded to the captain, who smiled a little tensely. By the grace of God there was no visible traffic ahead likely to get in the way. There was plenty of water, but a big freighter maneuvering in could have forced an alteration of course which would be expensive in time, and every minute was increasingly precious.

"Steer three four seven."

"Three four seven."

In the calm water of the bay the submarine rode so smoothly as to seem almost still. When the speed at last reached and passed twenty knots, the OD could almost sense the captain's reaction, although he gave no outward indication. There was nothing more that could be done now that was not being done, running on the surface toward the open water of the Pacific. There was a little comfort in the fact that full surface speed had not yet been attained, the ship was still accelerating; the bow wave was still building up.

"I know the temptation to save an extra five minutes," the captain said, "but don't let her get within small-arms range of the shore. Two thousand yards minimum except where we can't help it."

"Yes, captain, will do."

Magsaysay was making twenty-one and a half knots and still gaining slightly. She could go much faster submerged, but that would not help her now. Ahead the Oakland Bay Bridge was visibly much closer than it had been.

"Steer three three zero," the OD directed.

"Three three zero, sir." The phone talker retained his calm and passed the order crisply. He was a good young professional and the captain took note of it. Because of the extraordinary circumstances, he knew very few of the crew members who were serving under him, but that would be rectified.

Twenty-two and a half knots showed—that was about the best that she could do, although her full performance spectrum had not yet been determined; she was the first of her class and she incorporated a number of refinements that had not yet been fully explored. In the east the sky was very bright now and there were beginning hints of the sunrise to follow.

Four minutes later *Magsaysay* began to pass under the Oakland Bay Bridge.

"Steer three one zero."

"Three one zero, sir."

The OD checked a bearing on the Alcatraz water tank.

"They could be laying for us at North Point," the captain reminded.

"Yes, sir, I'm keeping Blossom Rock on the port side."

The mile-and-three-quarter run to the rock took an agonizing five minutes; during most of the time the captain kept a careful watch on the sky, looking for planes. The OD was tense now; the element of surprise had been dissipated and all hell would be breaking out wherever in the area the enemy had forces in being. The fearful firepower that *Mag-*

saysay represented was well known, and every possible means that could be employed on short notice to stop her would be totally committed.

One more landmark: the Blossom Rock was passed. "Steer two six nine."

"Two six nine, sir."

With unruffled dignity *Magsaysay* slowly turned until she was aimed straight toward the Golden Gate, three and a half miles ahead. Ten precious minutes would be needed to reach it. After that the land area would be left behind, but beyond the gate there lay eleven and a half miles more of shallow water and Four Fathom Bank that would force the submarine to use the ship channel until at last she reached hundred-foot-deep water and minimum diving depth. Meanwhile she was moving on the surface in clear and gaining daylight, a broad wake marking her exact position.

CHAPTER SEVENTEEN

When Operation Low Blow had been in its final planning stages, Admiral Haymarket had sketched out the primary areas of major concern and determined in his own mind whom he would assign to be responsible for each of them. For all of the coordinating and operation at Hunters Point —Walter Wagner. Ted Pappas had wanted that assignment desperately, but he could not match Wagner's field experience or his exceptional ability to dive unhesitatingly and safely more than a hundred feet from a crane boom into the water. There had not been any other acceptable method of recovering the crane operator available and therefore he had had to concede.

The mechanical and supply details went of course to Stanley Cumberland. Pappas, with his near genius for detailed planning and organization, was given the job of making everything fit and preparing a full set of alternate plans to meet every visible contingency.

Ed Higbee was committed to the second phase of the master plan, to be activated if the first part succeeded. There his almost uncanny knowledge of psychology, propaganda, news distribution, and negotiation would be of prime value. That left one more vastly important job and two extraordinarily capable men to handle it—the protection of the *Magsaysay* from the moment that her lines were cast off until she was safely hidden under the vast waters of the open Pacific. General Carlton Gifford had accepted the assignment with dedication and relish; it was right up his alley. His first action had been to request the help of Lieutenant Colonel Henry Prichard, the search and rescue specialist who was celebrated for a cast-iron nerve and the ability to handle himself even during extreme emergencies. More than forty men marked for death had been saved by him and not one of them had ever seen him display the least recognition of fear.

Together the two Air Force men had gone to work systematically to produce a miracle, and the magnitude of the task did not dismay them. They had begun by carrying on a highly selective recruiting program concentrated on the West Coast. They had found people in the armed forces, in law-enforcement agencies, and in such civilian organizations as Mensa and the Masonic Lodge. The Japanese-American Citizens League provided help and a few were chosen through the Knights of Columbus. Ham radio operators were very carefully culled over and a handful were selected. Lastly, a few men were picked from the ranks of the Teamsters Union. When the job had been completed the necessary backup force numbered almost five hundred men and a few women. Of all of these very few knew what they were to do or why, but they were all highly qualified in one way or another and every one of them had a proven ability to keep his or her mouth shut.

The next step had been the organization of this work force into a cell system so that any possible leak could be stopped within a local area involving, at the maximum, ten people. Certain outstanding individuals were chosen for supervisory duty, and they in turn came under the direction of full-time field personnel who reported directly to the headquarters of Thomas Jefferson.

In the meantime, detailed operational plans had already been drawn up. It was recognized from the start that a high degree of flexibility would have to be incorporated into every phase of the effort since a large number of unpredictable variables could not be eliminated. But variables or not, the job had to be done and Gifford was determined that it would be.

With the aid of the personnel selected, a close day-to-day watch was kept over the enemy throughout the San Francisco region. Every piece of equipment that was taken over was noted and recorded. The people concerned were evaluated and in some cases probed for weaknesses. Whatever the enemy did, wherever he established a force of any kind, he was watched and the information gained was passed on to the operations room. Colonel Prichard was in charge of that. Laid out on a huge table he had a detailed presentation of the San Francisco Bay area and all of its military facilities. Everything that the enemy did was noted and marked on it. The board was kept up to date on an hour-by-hour basis and manned around the clock.

As S (for sailing) day grew closer, the operational orders were prepared and passed to the waiting people in the field. Most of them still did not know what was to take place, but they did know that a major move was to be made and that they would be part of it. Every enemy post or installation that could in any way interfere with the safe departure of the *Magsaysay* from Hunters Point was kept under surveillance and a specific team was appointed to deal with it. To minimize risk and protect secrecy to the utmost, General Gifford confined most of the scheduled efforts to apparently simple, nonspectacular procedures which in many cases could be interpreted as accidents or simple bad luck—unless someone took the time to put them all together into a single pattern. But that could not be done until after the event, and then it would be too late.

Forty-eight hours before S time the operational personnel were deployed. In certain parts of San Francisco and its environs, repair and construction crews showed up to work on street installations. In each case they had the proper blueprints and work orders; their legitimacy was established. They closed off some roadways—as they apparently had to—and began to dig trenches in the usual manner. These activities were widely scattered, and when they were viewed against the background of all of the other street work going on at the same time, no visible pattern was apparent.

At Beale Air Force Base three teams moved in and positioned themselves well before they were due to go into action. At various other military installations where the enemy was present and had any combat capability, other personnel already on the job were backed up and reenforced. All of this was made easier because the enemy was still relatively new in the area, not yet deployed in any major strength, and convinced that the fervent desire of the United States for peace at any cost was adequate insurance against any uprisings.

At Hamilton Air Force Base three enemy fighter pilots who had been assigned to put on a show of force should that ever become necessary regularly dined at the only local facility where their patronage appeared to be welcome. They liked American food and the good liquor that could be had to go along with it. The only thing missing was suitable female company, but that had proved to be very hard to come by in the United States under the circumstances.

On the evening before S day they ate as usual, but the occasion was marked by the fact that three American girls were seated unescorted not too far away. After some discussion the pilots tried an approach. It was not successful, but on the other hand it did not appear to be a flat rejection. After a little more talk, they decided to try again. This time they had better luck.

All that was being done was known in general terms to the captain of the *Magsaysay;* each place where something might go wrong was known to him also, and he was at least forewarned. The most critical area was the possibility of air attack; surprise would help a great deal in forestalling any effective land-based action against the submarine, but even traveling at flank speed she would lie exposed for over an hour on the surface, and in that time an air attack against her could be mounted and carried out. Against such an action she would be helpless; the water she would be in would not allow her to maneuver and she carried no antiaircraft defense whatever. The Bay area was surrounded by military installations where the enemy was in possession. Almost from the moment that she had slipped her moorings the thought of air attack had been foremost in the captain's mind; once Blossom Rock had been cleared and the Golden Gate lay ahead, he knew that the time of greatest peril was at hand.

In his Washington headquarters Colonel Rostovitch had been informed within minutes of his own emergency phone call that in some totally unexplained manner the *Magsaysay* had been seized and was attempting to put out to sea. With furious energy he began to mount a counterattack. He was not too familiar with the geography of the Bay region, but he knew in general terms that the fugitive submarine would have to negotiate some inland waters before she would be able to reach the Pacific, and that was where she would have to be caught.

He summoned subordinates, who came with all haste and the knowledge that something drastic had occurred. Rostovitch whipped them into action with a few words, then he stormed into his communications room so that not a moment would be lost in finding out what was going on. As the reports began to come in, minor disasters seemed to accumulate. In San Francisco three seized U.S. Army tanks were being kept more or less on the alert to deal with any possible mob uprisings, but only one of them was able to respond to the call to action; the crews of the other two could not be readily located in the predawn on the West Coast. When the one available tank had started out, it had encountered unexpected road construction which had forced a maddening delay.

At Hamilton Air Force Base all three of the posted fighter pilots were discovered to have been out on an extended party with some girls they had met the night before. They seemed unable to rouse themselves and reportedly acted like men who were in a trance. At McClellan the single fighter plane available and armed was discovered to have nearly empty tanks. When an effort was made to refuel it, the main gas tank cap stuck and, when force was applied, it broke loose from its fitting. It was a very minor thing, but the plane could not get off the ground.

At Beale, of the two available interceptors, one had a damaged wingtip as the result of a careless truck driver's backing into it the day before; the other had a routine flat tire. The supply depot was secured, so a tire had to be removed from the damaged aircraft and switched with the flat. Two airplanes had to be jacked up to accomplish the change, and only one set of the proper-sized jacks could be located on short notice.

At Mather Air Force Base no suitable aircraft of any kind were available. At Travis, the great transpacific terminal of the Military Airlift Command, a plumbing rupture had allowed several hundred gallons of injection water to get into the main fuel lines. Before this was discovered several aircraft had been loaded with the contaminated mixture; they could not be flown until their tanks had been completely drained and the fuel systems cleaned out.

Alameda Naval Air Station had a few transports on the field, but not a single combat aircraft capable of an attack.

And so it went: Moffett, Castle, and all of the other air facilities within a realistic range reported trouble of one kind or another. Before the third such report had been received, Rostovitch knew that a thorough campaign had been staged without his being forewarned. His fury raged to the point where he seemed on the verge of apoplexy, but he could do nothing. He did not know how long it would take the submarine to reach a safe haven in the Pacific, but he sensed without being told that he would not be able to muster anything from anywhere in time. He seized a phone once more and ordered a maximum, unceasing effort to find and capture the saboteurs. He ordered the American commander of the Hunters Point Shipyard seized and held in maximum security for his personal interrogation. The man who had been assigned to guard and watch over him was to be treated likewise. All of the American agents, when captured, were to be executed publicly at once.

Then he thought hard. There had to be some way to locate and destroy the *Magsaysay* while she was still close in, some system of detection that would reveal her position. Offhand he did not know of any, but that was not his field. Information was what he needed; once more he jerked up a telephone and hurled an order into the mouthpiece.

The OD on the bridge looked straight up at the mighty structure of the Golden Gate Bridge. "They might take some potshots at us from up there, sir," he said.

"Pretty difficult," the captain answered. "If anything does start, you and the talker get below on the double."

"With your permission, sir, negative."

"That goes for me, too, sir," the talker said.

The captain raised his binoculars toward the bridge, then once more searched the sky. He was acutely aware of a low fogbank that lay not too far ahead; that was one prayer answered, although any enemy fighters that managed to get airborne might be equipped with sophisticated modern radars. Mercifully, traffic was not proving to be a problem; since the United States had fallen, waterborne commerce to and from her shores had dropped off to a considerable degree. The radar reports from below indicated that the ship channel was, as of then, free and clear.

Six minutes later the first of the fog began to dilute the stark brightness of the sky. The *Magsaysay* continued on at flank speed, racing now for the deep water where she could find sanctuary. The first real motion of the Pacific caused the submarine to begin to roll, but the knowledge of what that signified negated any sense of discomfort. A thin all-over haze surrounded her as she continued southwestward toward the ship channel. Then, visibly, it became more dense and the sky was erased in a dull whiteness. The ship was alone now, just as though she were on some voyage in space, plowing ahead at her best surface speed, dipping and rolling under the force of the moving water, making steady progress past the shoals that lay astride the harbor entrance.

Eleven minutes later she entered the ship channel. It was a critical time, since for the next three miles there would be no doubt where she was and if the outer exit were to be blocked in any way, she would be trapped. Ten additional, slow, agonizing minutes passed in the fog-clouded atmosphere.

The captain said nothing, he was keeping his attention on the fathometer and the increasing depth of water underneath his ship's keel. The water was a little rougher now and the *Magsaysay* was rolling fairly heavily. The depth was eighty-four feet.

"Dave," the captain broke his silence, "prepare to take her down."

"Ay, sir."

The necessary orders were passed below into an atmosphere that was already completely professional. The men of the crew, those who had come aboard in decontamination suits and those who had been masquerading as day workmen, had almost all managed to change into the standard poopie suits worn by Navy submariners at sea. Many of the men had worn them under their decontamination gear; the rest had drawn theirs from the stock on board. The dropped isotope had been expertly recovered from its hiding place and put back into a safe container. The prediving preparations were gone about smoothly and precisely, the crew for the first time looking the part of a hand-picked, coordinated team.

A depth of ninety feet registered as *Magsaysay* turned

twenty degrees to starboard and took up a heading of two seven zero—due west. On the bridge a message came up from below and the phone talker passed it on to the OD. "Ready to dive, sir."

"Thank you."

The fog hung on, shrouding the submarine visually, but not from the prying eyes of radar. The captain remained as quietly composed as he had seemed from the first moment that he had taken his place on the bridge, but the OD was well aware of all of the things that must be unreeling themselves in his brain. It was so close now, but it was not yet a sure thing. Once under the water the speed could be increased more than ten knots, and much more sophisticated equipment would be required to pinpoint the ship's position. Eventually it would be all but impossible and then, at last, Operation Low Blow would be an accomplished fact.

"One hundred and three feet, sir," the OD said, "and deepening."

"All right, Dave, take her down. Make your depth fifty feet. Five degree down bubble."

"Ay, sir."

The phone talker left the bridge first, then the OD, and finally the captain. After he had passed through, the hatch was closed and secured.

Steadily, and without haste, the bow of *Magsaysay* began to sink lower; the wave changed in contour and crept closer to the base of the sail. Presently the sail itself began breaking the oncoming water; it continued to do so as the flat missile area behind it came awash and then the visible part of the stern. The sail alone was above the water after that, sinking steadily and flooding as it did so. It began to move forward at a slightly faster rate, gradually disappearing until only the top remained. Water came onto the bridge deck, conquered it, and then took possession of the rest of the structure until only the shaft of the periscope remained visible, churning up a tiny wake behind it. Then it too disappeared and the surface of the water returned to a solid pattern of waves and swells untouched by any man-made creation.

Admiral Barney Haymarket sat all but motionless, a cup of coffee set before him, watching the message board and the face of the clock beside it. The last message to be received was still displayed: *Magsaysay* had been seen to disappear into the fogbank which lay a short distance off the coastline. Some transport aircraft had been observed, but nothing of a combat type had been spotted.

The clock continued to measure off the minutes, an emotionless indicator which supplied data but could not interpret them.

Major Pappas spoke from halfway down the table. "She should be out of the channel now."

They all knew that, but it helped somewhat to put it into words. Then it fell silent again, the clock now the center of all attention unless the message board chose to come alive once more.

At the end of almost twenty minutes more of waiting the admiral picked up his coffee cup and tasted the now lukewarm brew. It was taken as a signal; in response a little stir of movement began in the room.

The message board flashed: BEALE OK. That meant that the operational personnel who had been assigned there by Colonel Prichard had made it safely back to their base and were considered out of immediate danger. Better news still was the fact that no other message concerning the submarine itself had come in. When another ten minutes had been measured off and no more signals had been received, the admiral got to his feet. "Gentlemen," he said, "I believe they pulled it off."

That broke the tension which had lasted for so long. There were other hazards still ahead, but the most difficult part of the operation appeared to have been concluded satisfactorily. As the admiral turned toward his office he caught the eye of General Gifford and motioned. The general arose and followed him; among the rest only Major Pappas remained where he was, waiting for a possible final confirmation. If anything went wrong at the last minute and the submarine could not dive, he had one more remaining emergency plan to deal with the situation.

In the confines of his office the admiral sat down and faced his second in command. "What do you think?" he asked.

The general took his time about lighting a cigar. "We're not out of the woods yet, but we can start breathing again.

As I see it, it will take them a minimum of twenty-four hours to muster and position any kind of an ASW force and by then they'll have an eight-hundred-mile radius to attempt to search."

"It's possible that they could find her."

"Possible, yes, Barney, but they don't know how. Their technology simply isn't up to it, I'm confident of that. And if they get very very smart about the resupply operation, it still won't do them very much good unless we have terrible luck. And as you know, we're protected against that."

The admiral shook his head as though to clear his brain. "I'm going to sack out for a little while, Carl, and I think that you should too. Pass the word that I'm to be notified immediately if anything concrete comes in."

"Will do. Where do we go from here?"

Admiral Haymarket pressed the base of his palms hard against his skull just above his ears and moved them back and forth. "Let me get six hours' sleep," he said. "After that we'll eat and then start in on the next phase."

In the quiet of his very modest study the Reverend Mr. Jones addressed himself to the packet of mail which had just been handed to him. He sorted out the junk literature, set aside two or three bills which would have to be attended to, and then explored the rest. On the very bottom of the pile there was an airmail letter with an Israeli stamp. He opened the letter carefully because there was a twelve-year-old girl in his congregation who collected stamps, unfolded it, and began to read:

Dear Rev. Jones:

Although we had planned on settling in England for a while, we have now arrived in Israel, where we have received a cordial welcome if somewhat spartan accommodations. The vast influx from America, as well as many others who are arriving daily from Europe in fear of a pogrom there, has crowded this small country almost to the bursting point. Hazel, Molly and I are living in a tent dormitory with something more than a hundred others. We have been given army-type cots which are necessarily placed as close together as practical in long rows. We take our meals in a chow line which is the most suitable method under the existing circumstances.

As far as doing anything to establish ourselves is concerned, that is entirely out of the picture at the present time. We are refugees pure and simple and all that I have been able to do so far is to work in the labor crews that maintain the camp and add to it whenever we have the materials with which to work. More people are pouring in every day and we count ourselves lucky to have the places that we do in the tent community.

I do not think that we shall ever forget your kindness to us during one of the darkest hours of our lives. The fact that someone cared, someone not of our own people, was tremendously heartening. I must confess that I have never felt too strongly attached to Christians (in the literal sense of the word), largely because of my bringing up; I was always taught that being a Jew was far superior to anything else. You and your family have awakened me to how limited this viewpoint is, surely the brotherhood of man transcends all narrowness and divisions of attitude because of creed. You have demonstrated this and I have learned from it.

Perhaps I should not speak of this, but I and all of the others who benefited from your thoughtful generosity prior to our departure from our homeland, know that you received a grievous insult from one of us who is of orthodox persuasion. I never admired a man more than I did you at that moment; I witnessed the whole thing and it was all that I could do to restrain myself from taking physical action against the man who was so unspeakably inconsiderate. The person in question was persona non grata *among us from that moment forward. We were all together for some time and the contempt with which he was treated, had you witnessed it, would have told you how deeply all of us felt for you who had ministered to us. He has already made himself highly unpopular here and I cannot predict a very bright future for him.*

If we are ever so lucky as to return to our homeland, I hope that we may become friends. You are indeed a man of God and may His peace be with you always.

Most sincerely,
Jack Bornstein

The Reverend Mr. Jones reread the letter very carefully. Then he bowed his head. He prayed for the Bornsteins and for all others like them. He gave thanks also for the Great Commandment that had taught him what to do . . . "that you shall love one another as I have loved you."

When he had given thanks also for the blessing of his ministry and the grace that had been given to him, he arose once more, picked up the letter, and then opened the door.

"Doris," he called to his wife. "Could you come here for a moment? I've got something to show you."

Hewlitt could not define it, but he felt that a change in the atmosphere of the White House had developed during the noon hour. He sensed it almost as soon as he returned to his desk. Major Barlov stopped by and asked him some questions, none of them significant but all of them probing for something that was not disclosed. He saw Zalinsky only briefly; the administrator was as loaded with work as always, but he kept looking at Hewlitt as though he expected to read a sign in his features that was not there. By the time he was ready to leave for the day he knew definitely that something was up, but he had no clue as to what it might be.

Frank was not able to help. The burly cab driver listened to Hewlitt's report, but he could offer no information. "Percival will know, you can bet on that," he said. "He hasn't been around as much lately; somethin's been keeping him busy. He's about due back."

When he was inside of his apartment and alone, Hewlitt lay down on his back, stared at the ceiling, and tried to fit the pieces together. The underground cell to which he belonged had been meeting for some time and had passed along a quantity of essentially trivial information, but there had been no real action. He had resigned himself to weeks, and probably months of this sort of thing with the eventual hope that it would all mean something in the end, but with the determination also that he would keep on with the job as long as he was asked to serve.

He got himself something to eat, then sat down to work on the notes he was keeping on the day-to-day activity in the White House. It was a perfectly innocent document which contained nothing that he was not supposed to know and presumably could discuss with anyone he chose. If the country were ever freed, then his notes, properly amplified, could be the foundation for a book he might eventually write.

When the phone rang he answered it without enthusiasm; his mind was on other things. His mood changed abruptly when he heard Barbara's voice. "I'm lonesome," she said. That was all.

"We'll have to do something about that," he responded, and was aware that it sounded trite.

"It might take a while."

"Time well spent." That was a little better.

He put away his manuscript in his desk, where it was there to find if anyone took the trouble, put a few things into a small case, and set out to answer the summons. When he arrived at the safe house Davy Jones let him in with a smile. "Percival's back," he announced as soon as Hewlitt was safely inside. "He wants to see you. Barbara's here, and the rest of the girls."

"Barbara phoned me."

"Of course, I'm stupid—sorry. You fixed to stay all night?"

Hewlitt nodded. He, Cedric Culp, and the two secret service men who belonged to the cell stayed over often enough to give credence to the façade that the house was a private brothel. They were seldom there together, although three of them had a sleeping arrangement on the second floor. One of the secret service men had moved in with the girl called Nancy, but that had been by their mutual consent. What they did was their business, and the rest of the little group did not interfere.

Barbara appeared and kissed him casually. A few moments later Percival joined them and occupied one of the bar stools. Hewlitt sat beside him; Davy served up the drinks as though this was the beginning of a festive evening. He had a certain style about him, Hewlitt noted, that suggested a devil-may-care attitude. People could be acquainted with Davy Jones for a long time and not really know him. It could be an expert defense that he had developed because he was a Negro, or merely a reflection of his own complex personality. Whichever way it was, Hewlitt liked Davy a great deal and had learned to trust him.

Mary Mulligan joined with the two other girls who now lived in the house: Nancy who had originally been of the First Lady's staff, and Melanie, who was the interesting and highly attractive offspring of an American father and a Korean mother. She was quite slender and had a liquid grace that appealed to many men. There was nothing about her manner that revealed the exceptional intelligence she possessed. She spoke perfect French effortlessly and had a conversational knowledge of three additional languages.

The new bar was large enough to accommodate them all; when Davy had supplied refreshments to everyone, Hewlitt began. "I don't know if any of the rest of you encountered this," he said, "but when I got back from lunch this afternoon, there was a decided change in the atmosphere. I can't prove it by anything specific, but I felt it all around me. Barlov asked me a lot of questions and Zalinsky wasn't himself at all."

"Did anyone else get a similar reaction?" Percival asked.

"Very definitely," Barbara said. "In fact I was talking about it to Mary—she picked it up too. We were going to tell you about it. What's it all about?"

Percival consulted his drink before replying. "All of us have been waiting a long time for something tangible, some really effective action against the enemy. We've got it now. It happened this morning in San Francisco."

"Give, man, give," Davy said.

"All right. Just before dawn a United States Navy crew took possession of a newly commissioned, fully armed, fleet ballistic missile nuclear submarine and took her out to sea right under the noses of the enemy."

"Good God!" Hewlitt said. "How did they ever do it?"

"We've been working on it for weeks—longer, in fact. There's a remote chance that they might still mount a successful attack against her—she's still pretty close in—but I doubt it very much. That's about the size of it. She's the newest and the best that we've got and she's under the direct control of the First Team; in fact one member is on board her right now."

"What's going to happen?" Melanie asked.

Percival went back to his drink. "Nothing for the immediate present; the submarine just escaped this morning. In two or three weeks a lot could happen. Remember: a missile-firing submarine, one that packs as many warheads as this one does, is principally a deterrent."

"Do it or else," Davy said.

Percival nodded at him. "That's about it. In case you girls didn't know, one modern FBM like this one packs more firepower inside her hull than has been released in all of the wars in the world's history. That includes World War II and the two nuclear explosions in Japan."

"One thing," Mary interjected. "This opens the bag as far as our organization is concerned. They know now that we exist and that we have a considerable capability."

"They do," Percival agreed. "You can count on one thing: they're going to throw everything they have into finding and destroying that submarine, because she's our big gun now."

Nancy, who had remained silent up to that point, spoke in her slightly reedy voice. "But she can't stay at sea forever; she'll have to put in to port for food and supplies. So if anything's going to happen, it can't wait too long."

Percival agreed with her. "That's true."

"In other words," Hewlitt said, "it could all be over in another ninety days—one way or the other."

Percival handed his empty glass to Davy. "Yes, the chips are going to be down from here on in. It may get pretty rough, but we're prepared for that, too."

It was after twelve before Hewlitt turned in. There had been much discussion until they had stopped to hear the eleven o'clock news. Not a word was said about the submarine or anything else that could be associated with it. Hewlitt was used to that—he had heard many newscasts which took no notice of the major story of the day because it had not been made public and perhaps never would be. The tight control of all the news media was one of the things he resented most about the enemy occupation; withholding classified information was one thing, but total news management was another. When the news was over the girls went upstairs, Davy left on an errand of his own, and Hewlitt found himself alone with Percival.

"When this is all over, I'd like to know who you really are," he said. "That is, if you'll be able to tell me."

"I think so," Percival said. "I won't break the cell system now for reasons that you fully understand; part of your own protection comes from the fact that we know that we're playing for keeps and we don't take any chances that we can possibly avoid."

"I fully understand that."

"Good, because there's something I want to discuss with you. Would you like to get a little closer to the First Team in this operation?"

"I'd like that very much."

"At an increased risk?"

"That's part of the game, isn't it?"

"Yes," Percival agreed, "it is. There's another thing: after what we've just done to them, they're going to try twice as hard to ferret us out now. There's a man named Rostovitch . . ."

"I know," Hewlitt interrupted without thinking, "I've heard about him. He's supposed to be a very hard case."

"He is, and I have that directly from a man who faced him once. He won't show any mercy of any kind; if he gets you that's it and we won't be able to help you—at least you won't be able to count on it."

"What are my orders?" Hewlitt asked.

"For the moment—none. We're going to play this a little differently; you'll know in time what to do. Settle for that. Are you still willing?"

"Yes, I think so."

"Good, I'll pass your decision on up. At least one member of the First Team knows all about you; he'll be handling this personally."

"I hope I'm to meet him."

"Very possibly you will."

"By the way," Hewlitt said, "who is Amy Thornbush?"

"I don't know—why?"

"The first time I met Zalinsky he said to me, 'You know Amy Thornbush.' It was a statement not a question. I don't know any Amy Thornbush and I wondered if you did."

Percival took out a small notebook and a pen. "I'll look into that; there isn't any Percival either, if you follow me."

"I do, and I hadn't thought of that."

"You have a good memory."

"I've had some training—self-administered."

"That could come in very handy. From now on your conduct, particularly as regards this house, is to remain unchanged, but you are out of the White House cell; you'll report directly to me and not to anyone else—all right?"

"Yes, of course. Do you mean by that that I'm not to confide in Frank anymore?"

"Not at all: in fact if you need to see me in a hurry he has certain contacts that can help you. But you're going to play a new role and I don't want you to be going through intermediaries. If all goes well, you may be in at the most interesting part."

"I'd like that."

"Good. Go to bed."

Hewlitt did not know when Percival left the house, and he did not concern himself with it. He went up to the small room that he used for his overnight visits, undressed, washed his face and hands in one of the two available bathrooms, and turned in. The bed was not as comfortable as it might have been, but as it had before, it would do.

He had no recollection of anything before he went to sleep. The next thing that he knew was that he was being vigorously shaken and that a flashlight was burning in the room. Then he heard Davy's voice cutting through to his sleep-charged brain. "Hew, hurry! Into Barbara's room—now. *We're being raided!*"

As he came to, Davy literally yanked him to his feet and pushed him into the corridor. Barbara's room was opposite; without ceremony Davy opened the door and shoved him inside. Hewlitt turned quickly to ask a fast question but he had no chance; the tall Negro was whipping the sheets off his bed and destroying the signs of recent occupancy.

"Hew, hurry!" He heard Barbara's voice come out of the semi-darkness, then he saw her sitting up in the double bed. With a quick sweep of her arm she gestured. When he stayed at the safe house he slept in his shorts; he had them on now and nothing else. Barbara apparently wore nothing at all; he had a stabbing glance toward her and saw a magnificent pair of breasts, then her urgent voice caught him once more. "Strip," she urged. "Get into bed, fast!"

He had been in bed with women before, but for a fraction of a moment he hesitated. He was fully awake now, but this was not just a girl—this was Barbara which made things different. Then he heard a sound from her, it was not a spoken word but an almost animal gasp of desperation. After that it took him only four seconds to get out of his shorts, fling them into a chair, and run the three or four steps to the side of her bed. As he did so he heard sudden noises downstairs, sounds of abrupt forceful entry.

He had been slow to waken, it had cost several seconds, but he made up for it now. As Barbara held the covers up for him he sprang into her bed. "Hold me," she commanded. He put his arms around her and pressed her naked body to his own. He did not have time to react to the feel of her; within seconds the corridor outside was suddenly full of men.

The door to the bedroom was jerked open and the beam of a powerful light cut through the darkness. It found the bed and held steady, blindingly, on the two heads that were close together. Hewlitt raised himself on one elbow and, in a voice he managed to make sound startled, called out, "What the hell!"

Two men came in, one holding the light. Unceremoniously the other jerked back the covers and surveyed the two naked bodies pressed together. He hesitated for several seconds, drinking in as much of Barbara's body as was visible. Then with one hand he pushed her shoulder, turning her onto her back.

The man studied the body revealed before him, then tossed the covers back into position. For a few seconds the other swept the light around the room, then they were gone.

"God damn them!" Hewlitt raged. "I'll kill every one of them!"

It was for their benefit, of course, if they heard him, and Barbara knew that; she pressed an arm across his chest commanding him to remain in bed. Hewlitt thought and realized that that would be the natural thing to do; charging naked through the corridors in pursuit of armed men would be idiotic and no sane person would do it, no matter how furious he might be.

They heard a scream from Mary's room, but it was one of fright and not terror. "Stay here," Barbara whispered in his ear. "She's all right. I know."

He could do little else; his clothes, apart from his shorts, had been left in the other room and in a few seconds Davy had probably taken them away. There was the sound of a man going downstairs and more tramping in the corridor, but the bedroom door remained shut.

"What if any more of them come in here to look at you?" Hewlitt asked her softly.

"Let them," she answered. It was not tight-lipped, simply practical—the only possible solution to an acutely dangerous situation.

Hewlitt thought next of Davy and wondered if he needed help. He half-started to rise when once more Barbara held him down. "Don't," she said. "You can't do anything."

Tense as he was, he knew that she was right. How any girl could keep her cool in the midst of an enemy raid with an unexpected man in her bed he did not know, but Barbara managed it. He took comfort in the realization that he had heard no sounds of violence, no scuffling, no cries of distress or pain. Mary had made no further outcry; the whole noise level seemed to be dropping. Then he heard at least two men going downstairs, which could mean that for the moment at least they were alone.

Then he felt Barbara's finger across his lips. At that moment he remembered a story he had read as a boy—about someone who was pretending sleep in a flophouse that was being raided. He had heard the intruders depart in just the same way, but he had lain perfectly still for a full half hour, breathing steadily as though he had been in deep slumber. Then, finally, he had heard the man who had been waiting patiently and noiselessly just outside his door at last give up his vigil and walk away.

Presently he became embarrassingly aware of the girl beside him. He had often thought how rewarding it would be to be in bed with Barbara, but it had not been a casual thing with him. Now, out of necessity, Barbara was beside him: warm, close, and naked as a girl in bed should always be. His nerves were still far from composed, but with the first respite from the raid that had just taken place, he could no longer ignore the circumstances.

His thoughts were interrupted by more noise from downstairs and the sound of angry voices. He recognized Davy's baritone in the jumble of heated talk. There were additional sounds from outside and then at last the coming of a blessed quiet. Five full, tension-locked minutes passed, then there was a soft tap on the door. "Yes?" Hewlitt responded.

The door opened just enough to allow Davy to slide in. "Our guests have gone," he said. "Sorry if you were inconvenienced."

"Say that you were and I'll bite your ear off," Barbara whispered.

Davy heard her, but he made no comment. "We were warned just in time," he said. "They didn't find anything. Hew, I'll get your clothes back to you as soon as I can."

"No rush," Barbara said. "He isn't going anywhere."

Hewlitt heard her, but his mind was preoccupied. "How about it?" he asked. "Has this house had it? They know where we are now."

"They've known all the time," Davy answered. "We wanted them to. Tonight they came for a look and found just what they were expecting. There's a lot of stuff hidden here, but they didn't come close to any of it."

"How about Percival?"

"He's all right, he left some time ago. Now get some sleep if you can." He went out and closed the door behind him.

When they were alone once more, Hewlitt discovered that Barbara was shaking a very little as she lay beside him. For a moment he wondered if it was because of him, then he felt her arm tighten around him. "I was scared," she confessed in a whisper.

"So was I," Hewlitt said softly. "I still am a little."

It was awkwardly silent then; he felt that he should say something, but he was not sure what. "This may not be just the time and place to mention it," he managed, "but, well, corny as it may sound, I *am* falling in love with you."

She tilted her head up toward him and there was a slight movement of her body against his own. "Thank you. When you're in bed with a naked lady, it's quite appropriate to tell her that you find her nice."

She turned sideways until she was facing him, her breasts pressed firmly against his chest. Although the only light was what came in from the streets, he could see her very clearly. Her hair was billowed about her face; at that particular moment her normal attractiveness was enormously amplified as though some undiscovered alchemy had transformed her into the most beautiful and desirable woman who had ever been born.

He banished from his mind the thoughts that had been shuttlecocking back and forth about the raid, the inspection of her body that he had witnessed, and the almost violently abrupt manner in which they had been thrown together.

He kissed her, reasonably gently at first, but when he knew that she was fully and freely, even joyfully responsive, he let himself give way to a mounting passion. She was a woman who knew how to give of herself, and to receive back all that she gave—and more. He was immensely grateful, because this was the way he wanted it to be—the way he had dreamed it would be.

He ran his hand down the smooth subtle curvature of her back, his fingertips relaying the magic feel of her skin. She made a very small noise and his blood pounded harder because of it. He held his hand against the soft contour of her buttocks and then pressed her hard to him in the beginning moments of realization.

CHAPTER EIGHTEEN

More than one thousand miles northwest of San Francisco, four hundred and twenty-five feet below the surface of the Pacific Ocean, the captain of the U.S.S. *Ramon Magsaysay* sat in his small office, in full command of his ship, his crew, and himself. Seated before him was one of the two enemy representatives who were on board his command, the one who had literally jumped for his life at the last minute when the submarine had been slipping her moorings at Hunters Point. Standing in the doorway, by invitation, was the commander of the shipyard whose overseer the uninvited guest had been.

"What is your name?" the captain asked.

The man responded with a cascade of syllables that was all but incomprehensible. It appeared to start out with Klem, but that was all that could be understood.

"All right," the captain said. "I can't pronounce that and I'm sure my men can't either. We'll call you Clem. Why did you come on board?"

"Because it was not my wish to die. While I watch I see nothing, but you do everything. For this I am shooted immediate fast. This is undesirable, so when I understand, I jump."

"I see. Suppose we had been stopped by your people before we got away?"

"Then I say I jump to prevent you."

The captain looked at the commander. "He's candid, anyway."

"I can't honestly blame him too much," the shipyard man said. "In his position I think that I would have done the same thing. He didn't have much choice."

"Nor do we. All right, Clem, I will grant you political asylum on board this ship for the time being. We can't give you anything to eat, you understand that. Every man in this crew was forewarned that there would be no way to get any supplies on board and that we would all have to go without rations for at least three days."

"That fool everyone," the ex-overseer volunteered. "Nothing to eat, cannot go."

"Well, we did manage to smuggle some packets of soup mix on board under some of the decontamination suits, but that's all we've got. No coffee, just drinking water that we make."

"Thank you for my life. I am glad I am live to feel that pain of hunger. I am patient."

"That's fine, Clem. Understand that if you make the slightest attempt to interfere with the operation of this ship, you will be treated at once as an enemy spy." He looked up at the shipyard commander. "Suppose you take over responsibility for the POW's," he said. "I'm badly understaffed as it is, and I don't have any men to spare."

"I'd be glad to."

"Good. We'll cover for you while you're in the sack. Ask Mr. Wagner to come in, will you?"

Even in a poopie suit Walter Wagner could not conceal his remarkable physical development. The captain invited him in and gestured toward a chair. "One of the privileges of being in command," he said, "is that I was on the bridge and saw you come off that crane. How high were you when you dove?"

"About a hundred and four feet," Wagner answered. "It looks spectacular, but it isn't difficult when you're used to it."

"It would scare me witless."

"The only thing that disturbs me is that I had to blow my cover. Now everyone in the business knows that this country has an agent who is a high diver. Up until now I could go almost anywhere as a circus or carnival performer and no one ever questioned it."

"I don't know what the future holds," the captain said, "but if this cruise is successful, you might be able to retire and do whatever you'd like."

Wagner shook his head slowly. "I'd like to believe that, but just about the time that things quiet down all around something pops up somewhere. It always has."

The captain nodded unhappily. "I wish you weren't right,

but I know that you are. Essentially we're in the same business. Anyhow, we're all naturally very proud that we have a First Team member on board. I'd like to pass the word on that if you don't mind."

"All right, but keep it low-key. Major Pappas wanted this assignment very badly, but there was no way to get him off the crane except to come down the ladders, and that would have been out of the question. I could get off and into the water in something like five seceonds, so that settled it in my favor."

"Have you had some soup?"

"Not yet; I stuffed myself before I came on board, so I'm in good shape."

"Good enough. You have the run of the ship and, while I'm in command, if you have any directives they'll be followed."

Wagner got to his feet. "I'll leave all that to the admiral; you'll be hearing from him."

The captain stood up as well. "We already have. We didn't transmit, but our orders stand unchanged."

"Thank you, captain."

"You're more than welcome, sir."

Colonel Gregor Rostovitch was in a mood of intense concentration. Spread out on the top of his desk was a series of charts and maps to which he was giving his undivided attention. The *Magsaysay* had gotten away and due to the fact that he had been inadequately staffed and poorly served, no one so far had been made to suffer for it. Accepting the fact that the submarine was loose in the Pacific, the colonel was now intent on tracking her down. One thing was greatly in his favor: by all report she had no provisions on board and she would have to put in somewhere very promptly for supplies. Canada was the likeliest choice, but there was an important treaty with Canada which the northern dominion, probably for the sake of its own hide, was adhering to scrupulously. Any services rendered to the *Magsaysay* would be interpreted as an act of war, and Canada would be brought under the gun just as the United States had been. Air patrols were out searching for any supply vessels, but on the surface of the Pacific that was an almost hopeless task. However! The colonel did not know the exact range of the fugitive submarine's missiles, but he was acutely aware that if she could make her way into the Atlantic, that would put almost the whole of his country within her easy reach. Sixteen rounds of ballistic missiles, each one equipped with multiple, directable nuclear warheads, represented fearful firepower that could wipe whole nations off the map, and from underneath the ocean; she did not even need to surface in order to fire.

Bitter as the pill was, he accepted the fact that the men on board were actually an integrated submarine crew that had been assembled right under the noses of his thickheaded people. The whole thing had been carried off superbly well, which told him that it had been a professional operation all the way. That confirmed the fact that somewhere within the United States there was an organization which had just handed him the greatest defeat of his career. The underground was not an allusion, and it was not made up of weakling college students. Very well! The counter was first to find and sink the submarine. That done, he would requisition more men, have them sent over, and set up a system of terror that would destroy the underground and force the total, absolute and final surrender of the United States, not so much to his country as to himself.

There were only three rational ways that the *Ramon Magsaysay* could get into the Atlantic: through the Panama Canal, which was obviously impossible, around Cape Horn, or under the Arctic ice cap. The southern route would be safer and she had almost unlimited fuel—enough to take her completely around the world four times at the equator. Against it were the time required and the need to restock her larders. South America was liberally supplied with his own agents who could make any stop down there ill-advised.

Her obvious choice was to transit the ice cap; once she was safely up in the Beaufort Sea there would be no stopping her, but to get there she would have to pass through the Bering Strait. There was no alternative, and in the narrow confines of those strategic waters she would be at a great disadvantage. To stop her some very important people would have to issue orders, but that was no problem. Gregor Rostovitch usually got what he wanted.

The colonel's immediate furious rage began to ebb away. Replacing it was the total intensity of the skilled tactician beginning the careful planning of the placement of his forces.

Senator Solomon Fitzhugh was unable to shake off the deep depression that had taken hold of him; it seemed to him that everyway he turned, everything he attempted to do, reminded him of his son. For the first time he was alone in the world, there was no other human being who truly cared about him. His national image as a statesman was tarnished to the point where his sincere and deeply held convictions inspired only hatred. And the fact that his only child had been savagely murdered was unknown to the public or that he had died, even if mistakenly, for his country. He was denied even that.

In the venerable old mansion in which he lived Senator Fitzhugh kept one servant, a man who had been with him for many years to look after his various needs. Beyond that he lived by himself and, despite his former prominence in the Senate, he had received few invitations since the nation had fallen and the number of visitors who came to see him had dwindled until he found himself alone a great deal of the time. And the more he was by himself, the more acutely it came to him that at a time when he should have been in his prime, his life was closing in around him, as though he was sliding down the inside of some gigantic funnel.

He was surprised, therefore, when he heard his doorbell ring at a few minutes after eight in the evening. He was expecting no one, and even the diversion of the mystery story he was attempting to read had not revived his sunken mood. Presently his man came into the room. "There is a lady to see you, senator," he said.

"Who?"

"Mrs. Robert Smith."

"I don't believe that I know her; what does she want?"

"I couldn't say, sir, but she did indicate that you would wish to see her and that it might be to your advantage to do so."

"I see. What sort of a person is she?"

"Very much of a lady, sir, I would say."

"In that case show her in."

The woman who came into the room was of uncertain age;

the senator guessed at forty, but she could have been somewhat less or perhaps quite a bit more. Her grooming was subdued but perfectly executed. The suit that she wore had the simplicity that bespoke both taste and quality. She was decidedly attractive; the senator was reminded of Greer Garson when he had first seen her in *Goodbye, Mr. Chips.* He rose to his feet.

"Good evening, Mrs. Smith," he welcomed her, "please sit down. What may I offer you?"

"Thank you, senator, it isn't necessary to trouble yourself."

"No trouble at all, what is your preference?"

"Suppose we talk first."

"As you wish, Mrs. Smith."

When they were alone she began the conversation. "First of all, senator, I must apologize to you for coming at this hour without an appointment. There were well-considered reasons why I could not make one."

"Are you selling something, Mrs. Smith?"

"No, I am not."

The senator was at a loss; he could think of no reason why this woman had come to see him. Her refinement was obvious, but he was nevertheless slightly disturbed.

"Today, senator, I believe some workmen were on your property."

"Yes, there were some people from the electric company. This is an old house and they were concerned about the wiring." He paused. "Mrs. Smith, I don't want to sound old-fashioned in this day and age, but I don't want to expose you to the risk that your visit to my home might be misinterpreted."

"I most sincerely hope that it is," she answered him. "If anyone is sufficiently interested, I would much prefer him to have that belief; it would probably satisfy him."

That was not the answer the senator had expected. "You mean—the occupying forces?"

"Senator, the men who were in your home today were not here to examine the wiring; they were a security detail. Their real purpose was to make sure that no listening devices had been installed."

"In preparation for your visit?"

"Yes."

The senator stirred himself. "Mrs. Smith, are you sure that you wouldn't care for some refreshment?"

"Tea, then, if it's convenient."

The senator left the room long enough to place the order. When he returned he was cautious and serious. "Now, Mrs. Smith, please tell me what I can do for you."

"Very well, senator, I shall. It has come to me through roundabout channels that following the tragic death of your son you wanted to know if there was such a thing as an American underground, and if Gary had belonged to it."

"Yes," Fitzhugh said, "that's correct."

"From this point forward our conversation must be totally confidential. I am aware of your sworn obligation to protect the national security."

"You may absolutely rely on it, madam."

"I am doing so, senator. The answer to your question is that there is an active and powerful American underground. It is very well organized and equipped. It was established some time ago under the previous administration when the President foresaw the possibility of what has since taken place."

"But I knew nothing of this!"

Mrs. Smith leaned back in her comfortable chair and carefully crossed her legs without display. "At that time, senator, some careful steps were taken to see that you did not hear of it. It was kept secret from all but a very few people who were directly concerned."

"But they did not hesitate to recruit my son," he said bitterly.

Mrs. Smith looked at him. "I understand your distress, senator, and I sincerely sympathize with it. Gary did become a member, because for some time he had been going with Sally Bloom and she was a very patriotic young woman."

"But what could a group of undergraduate students hope to do?"

"Principally, senator, they were to serve as a listening post; institutions of higher learning have been under attack for some time."

Fitzhugh passed a hand across his face. "Yes, I know that." He thought some more and then framed a question. "Mrs. Smith, I take it that you are acquainted with Mr. Hewlitt?"

She shook her head. "I've never met him, senator, and I'm certain that he's not aware that I exist."

"I see, I thought perhaps . . ."

"Mr. Hewlitt is extremely cautious and discreet, senator, but I am aware that you had a conversation with him a short while ago and my call on you this evening is related to that."

"I am reassured."

"Senator, I have some news if you care to hear it."

"By all means."

"One of the reasons why I am being so candid with you in telling you about the underground is because our enemies have already found out."

Senator Fitzhugh leaned forward. "You mean that they are now in a position to destroy it?"

Mrs. Smith smiled. "No, senator, on the contrary—they know only for sure that it exists. I believe that at one time you opposed the construction of the *Ramon Magsaysay* and the series that was to follow her."

The memory came back. "It was an extremely provocative appropriation at the time—that was my position."

"Your position, senator, is quite well known. I don't wish to be cruel, but I am forced to say that I consider the death of those eight students very provocative also."

Despite himself sweat broke out on the brow of Senator Fitzhugh. He was a proud man and the tenets to which he had clung for so long refused to loosen their grip on him. "I was defeated," he said, "they built the submarine anyway."

Mrs. Smith was about to speak when the door opened and the senator's man brought in the tea. He served them and then withdrew. Not until he had been gone several seconds did the conversation resume; then it was Mrs. Smith who spoke.

"Senator, yesterday, very early in the morning, the underground succeeded in putting a fully qualified Navy crew on board that ship, getting her away from the enemy, out of the Golden Gate, and into the Pacific. The submarine is out there now, fully armed, and under American control."

The senator jerked forward. "Good God!" he said. "This is terrible. To provoke them like that, at a time like this—it's a disaster."

His guest's manner hardened. "Senator, you seem to be constantly concerned with what our enemies think of us. I could name the man who is directing their entire campaign, and I can assure you that he is not to be appeased. He is a ruthless murderer; it was on his direct orders that your son Gary was slaughtered, and all of those who died with him. Are you still trying to win his goodwill?"

Fitzhugh felt literally ill. "No," he said, "of course not."

"The man of whom I speak respects force and nothing else. I could tell you a great deal about him. He is a sadist, a torturer, and a man of insane ambition and vanity. He is already in a position of great power and is using it ruthlessly to increase it still more. He is here now."

"In this city?"

"Yes. Furthermore, the Actor is having some increasing troubles that even his very fancy footwork may not be able to overcome. If he is overthrown, and there is a steady history to support that, this man will become the new premier."

The senator looked searchingly at his guest. "The submarine?"

"It is barely possible, Senator Fitzhugh, that with this potent a weapon at our disposal we may be able to fight fire with fire. *Magsaysay* carries more than one hundred and fifty nuclear warheads, and she can deliver them to practically any target in the world. That the enemy can understand. Because they understand it, they have no desire whatever to be on the receiving end."

"It's possible, then, that we might be able to bargain."

"Not bargain, senator, dictate. They have more firepower than we do, but if they can't find and destroy that submarine, their goose will be cooked and they know it. She can fire at will and they have no knowledge of who is controlling her. If they do find out, it makes no difference; her captain is one of the finest the Navy has and he already has his orders."

The senator gave up. "It's nuclear war, then."

Mrs. Smith took her time to drink her tea. "No, senator, not necessarily. You yourself might help to prevent that."

"Are you a member of the underground, Mrs. Smith?"

"Yes, I am."

"Your name, then, isn't Mrs. Smith."

"No, senator, it is not."

"You seem very well informed. Tell me, are genuinely responsible people in charge of all this? Please reassure me if you can."

"Senator, we call them the First Team, and for good reason. The are the best that this country has, better by far than either of us."

"Would I know any of them?"

"I'm sorry, senator, apart from the quality and ability its members represent, I can give you no information whatsoever concerning the First Team. Now I have a question for you: if you found yourself in a position where you could support and help your country in this struggle, as a representative of our legally constituted government, would you be willing?"

"Why do you ask me?"

"To obtain an answer." She returned to her teacup, her poise unruffled.

Solomon Fitzhugh let his head sag as he understood what was being asked of him. The old stubbornness returned and then, once more, the image of his son.

He looked up. "I will try," he said.

"Thank you, senator."

As she rose to her feet Fitzhugh got up also. He looked at her and appraised her once more. "Since I am now committed," he added, "is it proper for me to ask you who you are?"

She studied him for a moment or two. "It would be much better if you did not," she answered, "but since I have asked something of you, I will give you something in return. You understand that I am trusting you with my life."

He thought of the submarine and the fearful authority that it represented. "I will protect it with my own," he promised.

"Very well, Senator Fitzhugh, I accept that. I am Sally Bloom's mother."

CHAPTER NINETEEN

In the budding first light of the very early morning the U.S.S. *Dolly* was moving forward slowly in a gentle sea. She was in far northern waters, a long way from her home port, her holds partially filled with the catch of her past many days. Her luck had been only fair, which made it very clear why she had sought out fresh grounds if anyone was curious.

The water was an iron gray, devoid of color and seemingly without an end to its vastness. The *Dolly* rolled slightly under a leaden overcast sky, a cumbersome and unsophisticated vessel built for prosaic work and unendowed with glory. On this morning, despite her plodding nature, there was a fresh trimness aboard her; her entire crew was up and briskly about. On the bridge her navigator was keeping his chart minutely up to date. He had made his last celestial observations some hours before, then the overcast had forced him to continue on with dead reckoning and LORAN. Despite the almost limitless expanse of water that surrounded him in every direction, he was holding the ship to very close tolerances with the maximum accuracy that his available resources would permit. On the fantail the Officer of the Deck held his binoculars before his eyes; standing to his left a signalman was ready, his two flags in his hands.

Overhead, on top of the mast, the radar antenna revolved relentlessly, sweeping both the surface of the ocean and the sky above it with unbroken diligence. On the bridge the captain and his executive officer were both on hand. The captain too was maintining a lookout while Lieutenant Jimmy Morton, all business at this critical time, kept a close watch over the ship's chronometer and the navigator's chart directly below it. Lieutenant Hanson stood by, waiting as was everyone else with everything for which he was responsible in readiness. The *Dolly* rolled steadily, making only five knots at reduced speed.

"Minus ten minutes," Lieutenant Morton reported.

The captain heard, but gave no acknowledgment as he continued to study the sea around him. Every few moments he glanced at the radarscope; once he was uncertain and looked inquiringly at the operator.

"No contact, sir," the man responded without taking his attention off the face of the tube for more than a second or two.

The ship's cook arrived on the bridge with fresh coffee and a plate of rolls. Morton accepted a cup automatically and sipped from it as he watched the navigator plot a minute change in the ship's position. The near scalding brew that he drank black awakened his throat lining, then he could feel it enter his stomach. He set the cup in its rack, looked once more at the chronometer and waited a few seconds more. "Minus five minutes, sir."

"Pass the word," the captain directed.

Lieutenant Hanson heard him and responded. "Minus five minutes," he called down to the deck. The signalman standing close to the stern shrugged his shoulders to loosen the muscles in his arms. His feet were carefully planted to absorb the rolling of the ship, his attention kept fixed on the surface of the water.

The *Dolly* plodded on, quartering the gentle wind that was moving the water. Everything else aboard her seemed still, only the steady turning of the radar antenna gave a definite sign of life. The officer of the deck removed his binoculars for a moment to wipe his eyes with his sleeve; then resumed his watch.

"Three minutes, sir." Morton reported to the captain.

"Position?"

"Within five hundred yards, sir," the navigator answered. He did not qualify it; the captain knew that his celestial work had been forestalled by the overcast.

"Carry on."

"Ay, sir."

The sweep second hand of the chronometer began another measured circuit of the dial.

"Contact!" the officer of the deck shouted without removing the glasses from his eyes.

The signalman leaned forward and strained his vision; it took him several seconds until, far back in the path of the wake, he was able to make out what could have been the tip of a periscope.

"Identify," the OD ordered.

The signalman snapped his arms up and crossed his flags above his head. Then, rapidly and precisely, he wigwagged out the letters L-O-W-B-L-O-W.

Three seconds later through his binoculars the OD began to read out the first of a series of irregular flashes of light that appeared close to the top of the periscope tube. When he had finished he turned and carefully avoiding dramatics called forward. Lieutenant Hanson relayed the message to the captain. "Sir, the OD reports confirmation, it's *Magsaysay.*"

"Radar?" the captain asked.

"Negative, sir."

"Keep your eyes on that tube."

"Yes, sir."

"Mr. Hanson, advise *Magsaysay* that the radar shows all clear."

"Ay, sir." The word was passed and the signalman spelled out the message. Presently the reply came back. "*Magsaysay* will surface, sir, and come alongside."

The captain of the *Dolly* received that decision with gratitude, it would make things a little easier, although he had been prepared to go either way. He checked first that his ship was maintaining course and speed, reaffirmed the radar finding, and then allowed himself the luxury of watching aft for a few moments.

In the wake of the fishing vessel the tube of the periscope grew taller. Then there was a break in the pattern of the water and a black object could be seen slowly appearing. It grew higher until numbers appeared and it could be identified as the sail of a submarine. As the captain of the *Dolly* watched, the black object continued to emerge from beneath the water like a process sequence in a science fiction movie. Then the water broke well forward of the sail as the main hull began to appear; nearly four hundred and forty feet long, the *Magsaysay* contrasted almost violently with the unimaginative but sturdy *Dolly.*

As she began to close the distance between herself and

the *Dolly,* the *Magsaysay* sliced through the water as though the minor swell did not exist. Presently men appeared on her bridge, men who in no way suggested that they had had no food for more than three days. They looked crisp and professional in the poopie suits which had been developed for comfort during long submerged cruises.

As the *Dolly* held her heading with all of the precision of which she was capable, the *Magsaysay* gradually overtook her on the starboard side until the bow of the submarine almost reached amidships of the fishing vessel. Because of the very low profile of the nuclear ship there was no venturi effect to draw the two of them together, but the maneuvering was delicate nonetheless. On the *Dolly* the crew was rapidly uncovering the hatches; the derrick operator readied his equipment.

On the curved, black, wet deck of the submarine a forward hatch came open. Three men came out rapidly and positioned themselves around the opening. One of them threw a light line expertly across the *Dolly;* it was retrieved and a telephone cable was pulled across the short distance that separated the two ships.

From the galley of the *Dolly* the cook appeared carrying a large kettle. He was followed by three other crewmen, all heavily burdened with containers of food. As soon as the telephone connection had been made, the captain of the *Dolly* spoke to his opposite number. "Congratulations, sir, we're glad to see you. We didn't know until we saw you that you'd made it. We have hot chow, and plenty of it, ready and waiting."

"Outstanding, send it over. We only verified your position a short while ago."

The captain of the *Dolly* spoke to his exec. "Start the stuff moving, Jimmy."

"Ay, sir." Lieutenant James Morton had been waiting for this moment from the first time that he had set foot onto his ship and he needed no urging. He called to Hanson on the deck; moments later the derrick went into action. There was no way to rig a high line between the two ships plus which the movement of the water kept them both rocking gently, but the derrick operator was up to the challenge. As soon as the prepared food had been set down on a waiting pallet he picked it up and swung it expertly across the narrow strip of water and onto the deck of the submarine. It was a tricky business, but he had a very long boom; the longest in fact that the outfitters of the *Dolly* had dared to install. In addition, it had a telescoping feature which gave it an additional, normally invisible twenty-four feet. The fishing vessel, despite its size and bulk, heeled over considerably as the transfer was made, but that had been calculated in advance too.

"Do you need some extra hands?" *Magsaysay* asked.

"Negative, we're in good shape. Enjoy your chow."

"We'll start feeding right now; keep the stuff coming."

The pallet lifted off the deck of the *Dolly* once more, this time carrying supplies which had been specially packaged to fit through the thirty-inch-in-diameter hatchway, which was the largest opening in the pressure hull of the submarine. As fast as the pallet was unloaded, more prepared loads were brought up onto the deck of the *Dolly* from the holds below. Had it been necessary, the whole operation could have been done while the *Magsaysay* was well under the surface, but it would have been more difficult and the hot meal which had been prepared would have had to have been put into waterproof containers. Overhead the steadily revolving radar antenna kept watch over the surrounding sea and the air. Very low-flying aircraft could have defeated it and surprised the operation, but that was a calculated risk which had been accepted as too unlikely to be a genuine hazard.

In two hours' time the *Dolly* had been emptied of all of the carefully prepared materiel which had been brought on board her in a dozen different disguises. Food, medical equipment, critical spares—all were transferred and passed below by relays of men on *Magsaysay*. As the process was nearing its finish, the captain of the submarine used the phone link once more. "Is there anything we can do for you?" he asked.

"Negative, sir, we're in good shape."

"I have a problem; we have two political refugees on board. They came with us uninvited at the last moment."

"I understand, sir."

"Considering what we have ahead of us, I'd rather not have them on board. On the other hand, I don't want to wish them onto you either; you don't have the facilities."

"We'll take them, sir—no problem. Send them over. What is their attitude?"

"Satisfactory, I'd say, particularly now that their bellies are full. But if you're found with them, it could be the end. That's the problem."

"I think we can handle that, sir. We have some well-concealed compartments if we need to use them."

"If you're willing, it would be a big help to us."

"No sweat; we're glad to do it."

On its last trip the pallet brought back Kepinsky and the man called Clem. After that final greetings were exchanged and the two Navy ships wished each other well. The phone line was cast off and *Magsaysay* began to drift slowly away from he rsupply ship. As soon as there was enough water between them the submarine began slowly to add speed; the slight wave at her bow increased as she pulled ahead. Then the wave began to creep backward as the bow dipped downward. The men of the *Dolly* watched as the powerful warship gradually disappeared under the surface. When the sea once more showed no sign of her presence, the captain of the *Dolly* spoke a silent prayer. That done he turned to Lieutenant Morton. "Carry on, Jimmy."

"Ay, sir."

As the sun reached its zenith *Dolly* was busy fishing, heading as she did so in a southwesterly direction. In another three days she would be in safer waters where she could more easily play her new role of a Japanese fishing ship headed back to her home islands. Lieutenant Hanson, the Japanese language officer, moved his bunk into the radio shack where he would be on hand to handle any unexpected message traffic. All that the *Dolly* and her crew asked for then was the mercy of God and, if possible, another day and a half free of observation.

To Erskine Wattles the injustices which had been heaped upon him and his people were compounded by his own long detention after the nation's new masters had taken over. Every inmate of Leavenworth knew that there was a new warden from overseas and that she was a woman, but the routine of the prison continued almost unchanged. As the days made their dreary pilgrimage, one after the other, he waited—with fuming impatience and, at last, with a burning sense that something had gone radically wrong. He was a dynamic leader of the new movement; the movement had triumphed but his reward, the fame and the power that were now rightfully his, had been much too long in coming.

Then, at long last, two men arrived at his cell with the information that the warden wanted to see him. He stepped forward eagerly, his head suddenly high; he discarded the prison shuffle and tried to begin to walk with the swagger he had cultivated long before.

When he reached the warden's office he was put into a chair well back from the woman who studied him from behind her desk. As she did so he judged her, deciding in his mind what disposition he would make of her once he was outside.

She spoke to him, in English. "You are loudly asking to see me. What is it that you want?"

Wattles had little time to waste on her. "I want to get out of this Goddamned stinkin' hole," he almost shouted. "Do you know who I am?"

"I know very well who you are." She surveyed him dispassionately, as though he were a laboratory animal she was observing. "You are a murderer, a rapist, an arsonist, and you have made mayhem upon a federal judge in his court."

"Goddamned right I did!"

"Your sentence is not up. When it is, I will decide whether to let you go or not."

He started to rise out of his chair, but he was thrust back down again by one of the two guards who stood watch over him. He looked again at the woman behind the desk; she was not too old and she was good looking. Instantly his mind froze on his plan of vengeance: she would pay with her body. He would have her held down by the same two apes who were beside him now, then he would climb on her and stick it in so far and so hard she would feel it in the back of her throat.

His common sense told him that he would get nowhere abusing her now—he would have to play it cool. "You know why you're here?" he asked. "Me, that's why. You ask the bosses where you come from."

In answer the woman picked up a folder from her desk, opened it, and studied the contents once more. It was for his benefit; she knew what it contained in fullest detail. "I am aware," she said when she had finished, "you are criminal—nothing more. Your politics, it makes no difference. You are a bad, dangerous man."

She was going to say more, but he would not let her. Raising both fists, he slammed them onto the arms of the chair. "Your boss will kill you," he yelled.

Calmly she shook her head. "To me this prison was given to run," she said. "It is to me to decide what to do. I tell you now that I alone am in charge; it is how we do things. You have made much trouble screaming in the night that you must be let out quickly. I send for you to tell you that it will not happen. You do not love us, you do not love me. You love only yourself."

Wattles turned livid despite his dark skin.

"You have yet eight years to serve. You have this time to learn that you are nothing, that we do not desire you. If you do not learn, we will keep you longer. As long as we wish. If you more trouble make, I will put you in solitary. That is all."

Back in his cell Erskine Wattles sat on the edge of his hard bunk and cursed the name of the God who had betrayed him.

On Unimak Island in the Aleutians the operator of a secret electronics communications facility listened carefully to WWV and once again checked the accuracy of his chronometer against the time tick broadcast. It was precisely on. That verified, he turned his attention to a specialized receiver that was crystal-controlled and to the backup unit which was its exact duplicate and which operated from an entirely separate power circuit. Both pieces of equipment had built-in checkout circuits which continuously monitored their performance; both read out that their parent circuitry was working perfectly.

At minus ten minutes the operator started the tape recorders, sensitive instruments that could detect and preserve the faintest sounds captured by the receivers. The highly directional antennae were properly positioned and tuned; everything was in readiness. Then, carefully and methodically, the operator checked everything once more. He knew the importance of what he was doing and he was taking no chances. Even he did not know that at another site, of which he was not aware, similar precautions were being taken for the same purpose; Colonel Prichard was not a man to leave anything to chance.

Precisely on the second that it was expected a very short, unreadable three-second transmission was received. It came and went so quickly it was almost like the winking of a flashbulb without the brilliance to announce its presence. To hear it, anyone for whom it was not intended would have had to have had the necessary underwater antennae properly tuned and precisely aimed; the chances of that happening by accident were mathematically almost invisible.

As soon as the message had been recorded the operator on Unimak relayed it on by secret circuit; it was received and transcribed in the underground headquarters of Thomas Jefferson very shortly thereafter. The news that it conveyed gave Admiral Barney Haymarket the greatest emotional lift he had known since the first indefinite messages had been received from San Francisco which indicated that the *Magsaysay* had probably made good her initial escape. All that he had had to go on at that point had been the likelihood that he had a ship at sea, but within vulnerable range of the enemy, unprovisioned, and with a highly hazardous at-sea supply operation setup which would depend to a large degree on luck—sea conditions and the lack of enemy interference. He had gambled with those odds because it was the best that he had been able to do, but he had not liked it and it had worried him out of two consecutive nights' sleep.

The message he had in hand now was enough to make him call together all of his immediate associates who were available. Major Pappas had been asleep; the distinctions between night and day in the underground facility had been erased and the clock had become the sole arbiter of time. It had taken the major almost four minutes to rouse himself, get out of bed, dress, and report to the coffee bar where the admiral and the rest of the members of the First Team, with the exception of Walter Wagner, awaited him. He apologized for his late appearance.

"As far as I am aware, Ted," the admiral said, "that's the first time that you've been in the sack for the past three days. Now here's the word." He looked around at the small group on which he relied so much. "We have a report from *Magsaysay*."

He stopped long enough to let his team understand the full meaning of his words. "She rendezvoused with the *Dolly* and resupplied successfully. There was no interference, and she reports no ill effects; all hands are well."

"Three to one she unloaded her refugee passengers," General Gifford said.

"I'd go stronger than that," the admiral answered. "I'm sure of it. Anyhow, she is presently on her way north and at least she is in better trim than she was."

"Have they had a chance to check out the armament?" Ed Higbee asked.

"No definite word on that, but I'm certain she wouldn't have reported all well unless . . ."

"Of course; sorry." Higbee resorted to his coffee cup; he didn't often make mistakes like that. "It's good to know that Walter's all right."

"No reason he shouldn't be," Prichard said. "He told me when I asked him that he's done a hundred and twenty-five feet and apparently it didn't bother him a bit."

Stanley Cumberland shook his head. "Specialized ability, I never cease to marvel at it. You find it all over the place and there's no real explanation. Training and practice, of course, but I wanted to be a violinist and after three years I gave it up as hopeless. It's got to be born in you."

Major Pappas did not comment on that; he contented himself with drinking his coffee.

"Anyhow, gentlemen," the admiral continued, "the only question now is, do we start phase two immediately, or wait until *Magsaysay* is over the next hurdle?"

"I say we go," Higbee said. "Every hour of delay now gives them more time to absorb and think. Let's keep the pressure on."

"He's right," Colonel Prichard agreed. He did not waste words.

"Those opposed?"

There was no response to that.

The admiral had a little more of his coffee. "All right, Ed," he said to Higbee. "It's your ball now, yours and Ted's. Let's see some action."

Higbee rubbed his hands together. He was entitled to; he had waited a long time. "You will," he promised.

Hewlitt noted the change of atmosphere once more as he answered the summons to the Oval Office. Usually Zalinsky continued with whatever he was doing and paid him no attention until it pleased him to do so; this time the administrator watched him as he came in and kept his eyes on him while he seated himself and waited.

After a pause of a few seconds Zalinsky spoke. "Today we will converse in my language; I do not desire to practice English."

Hewlitt responded with an idiom which in essence meant, "That's fine with me."

"You have heard about the submarine?"

That called for an instant decision, and Hewlitt made it. "Rumors," he said.

Zalinsky shook his head. "I do not understand you Americans. First, when you have everything, you refuse to fight back. Then, when you have nothing, you take desperate chances that cannot succeed."

"We took a desperate chance in 1776," Hewlitt said.

Zalinsky waved a hand. "A good slogan, I grant you, but what happened that far back is no precedent for today—you know that."

While he was speaking Hewlitt saw the way out of a dilemma. "Let us talk about the submarine for a moment," he said. "I have heard rumors, as I said, but they confiict. What happened?"

"Tell me first what you have heard."

"One of our nuclear submarines is at sea manned by a Navy crew. She escaped in full daylight from the Bremerton Navy Yard. She is supposed to be fully armed with missiles."

"That is all?"

"That's enough, I would think."

Zalinsky remained silent for a few seconds more. "I will give you some very good advice," he said. "Stay out of this." Hewlitt looked at him. "How can I help it?" he asked. "I have nothing whatever to do with the Navy."

Zalinsky returned his look. "It is good that you sleep with your girl friend; I approve of this. It is normal and healthy. But the house where you stay: there is a visitor sometimes who is part of your underground. This we know, and who he is. You understand?"

Hewlitt did not dare to reply. Instead he said, "I hope to marry her."

Zalinsky nodded. "A good choice, I think—and very wise of you to try her out first. And she you, of course. In my country this attitude would not be approved, so you see I am becoming a little bit Americanized."

"Congratulations," Hewlitt said. "Thank you for your advice. Will there be anything else?"

"Only one thing—I am not feeling too well, find for me please a good doctor. Especially one I can trust—you understand."

"Fully."

"Thank you very much." It was the first time that Zalinsky had been that courteous in either language. It could have been automatic, but Hewlitt thought otherwise. If the submarine never fired a round, at least she had proved something and the lesson could not be ignored. By Zalinsky or anyone else. The notorious Colonel Rostovitch had something new to think about, and catching a submarine at sea would not be an easy matter. Not if the crew knew what it was doing, and he was willing to bet, on the basis of performance already proven, that it did. He wondered if the rumor he had heard, and had not repeated, was true—that the captain was a Jew. Not that it made any difference, but it might make things more interesting.

As he climbed into Frank's cab to ride home after work, his mood had changed somewhat. Zalinsky's words about knowing the identity of an underground agent who came to the safe house from time to time came back to him and gave him cause for worry. Not for himself; he had progressed beyond that point, but Percival was a valuable man as all men were valuable, and his loss would be acute. As soon as they were out in traffic and sufficiently by themselves Hewlitt asked for and got the all-clear signal to talk. "I want to get word to Percival," he said. "It's urgent."

"All right," Frank said. "They're giving me a rest right now. The idea is that when a guy's been busy for a while they rest him just in case anyone's tailin' him. It throws them off. But I can get word to Percival. You wanna talk to him?"

"Better just give him the message. Zalinsky told me today that he knows an underground agent is calling at the house. He knows this and who he is."

Frank digested that quickly. "If he told you that, then he had a reason. I'll get it to Percival right away, but if he was plannin' somethin', he wouldn't let the cat out of the bag like that."

"I wondered about that," Hewlitt said. "You tell him, but cover your tracks—they may be watching to see how I communicate."

"Right. I'll be careful. We've got a way and it's pretty foolproof. *Holy hell!*"

Hewlitt did not understand until he saw a sedan that had cut in front of the cab with scant inches to spare. Frank hit the brake and turned hard toward the curb to avoid a collision; the sedan led him, forcing him over. Within moments both cars were stopped; in the seconds that it took, Hewlitt understood that they were being intercepted, that he was undoubtedly the reason, and that Percival was not the only person whose disguise had been penetrated.

He felt a desire to panic, but he thrust it down. He had been living under tension for so long now he had his reflexes conditioned and his mind schooled. When he saw two men jump quickly from the sedan he knew that they were after him. Frank saw them too and quickly raised his hands in a gesture of surrender—exactly what he should have done, Hewlitt thought. There was no need to blow Frank in this operation.

When one of the men yanked the rear door open on his side Hewlitt knew Frank was out of it. He looked up into a cold, emotionless face that told him nothing. "Out," he was directed.

As Hewlitt complied, the man showed him a gun and motioned to the sedan. Hewlitt walked to the car and climbed in as though it was his personal choice to do so. As soon as he was safely inside, the man jumped in beside him and the car took off with a burst of speed that left black rubber on the pavement behind it. At the first intersection the sedan turned right with screaming tires; Hewlitt was forced against the second of his captors. Then, unexpectedly, the man spoke. "Take it easy," he said. "Percival sent us."

It could be true or it could not. The man spoke in perfect American English, plus which he had volunteered the information and knew the code name. Against it was the fact that Percival was probably already blown, and there was nothing in the rule book that said the enemy always had to talk with an accent. There were plenty of good agents who were letter and accent perfect in languages other than their own. So Hewlitt sat back and waited as calmly as he could for whatever was to happen next.

The car swung into traffic and slowed down, inconspicuous once more in the mass of vehicles. Unless some witness had been quick enough to catch the license number and had reported it very promptly, there was almost no chance of effective pursuit. Furthermore, the police department was now under enemy control and was operating far below its usual level of efficiency.

As the minutes passed the car worked its way toward the Maryland border. That reminded Hewlitt of his meeting with Barbara in an unoccupied house; the first time that they had been together alone. He thought about her, wondering what she would do if she were in his position. The same thing that he was doing, he decided. His thoughts were interrupted when the car turned into the driveway of a private house. The man on his right got out, opened the side door of the building, and motioned Hewlitt inside.

It was clearly a better-class residence; the furnishings were of very good quality and the paintings which decorated the walls were original oils. That in itself was reassuring; the premises denied the thought of violence and spoke only of good manners and cultured people. When they reached the living room he was motioned to a chair; there was no hostility in it, but there was authority just the same. Hewlitt sat down and attempted to compose himself, he was certain that he had been brought here to meet someone, but if it was a member of the underground, there would have been no need for the peremptory manner in which he had been kidnapped. He confirmed his first impression when the three men who had brought him sat down too and waited. Then a woman came into the room.

Hewlitt stood up automatically. She walked up to him and held out her hand. "Mr. Hewlitt, I believe," she said. "I am Mrs. Smith, do please sit down." Hewlitt sat, and noted that the other men in the room had stood up too.

"Gentlemen," Mrs. Smith added, "I think that Mr. Hewlitt and I would like to be alone, if you don't mind."

That was the first thing that was really reassuring. Hewlitt did not suffer from the illusion that all comely women were automatically desirable people—even if they acted that way. But if she was willing to be alone with him when she had more than adequate protection available, it could be taken as a good sign. The three men who had brought him went out as Mrs. Smith walked to a corner bar. "A drink, Mr. Hewlitt?" she invited.

"Perhaps later."

"Very discreet of you," she said and resumed her seat. "Mr. Hewlitt, your invitation here was very abrupt for a definite reason; we had to establish the fact that you did not come of your own free will. You will see why presently."

She paused in case he had anything to say, but he chose to wait.

"To put your mind at ease, let me assure you that I know all about you and I have had very complimentary reports concerning your work from Percival."

"I see."

"Do you recall his telling you one evening a short while ago that if he were ever to be replaced a person answering to a certain code name would take over?"

Hewlitt opened his mouth to say yes, and then realized that it would be an open confession. "Please continue," he said instead.

Mrs. Smith nodded. "You are indeed very careful and I fully approve of it. Let me assure you that Percival is perfectly all right, but I have come into the picture for a very good reason. I work for the First Team, Mr. Hewlitt. I am Rodney."

He recalled the code name at once; the fact that it was a woman who bore it was surprising, but no more than that. Percival had specifically mentioned that the code name could be applied to either a man or a woman.

"How do you do," Hewlitt said.

If she noted his careful restraint, she did not comment. "Mr. Hewlitt, the last time you talked to Percival he asked you if you were willing to take a more active role closer to the center of our operation and you accepted. After he cautioned you that it would involve a considerably increased risk he asked you again if you were still willing and your exact words to him, I believe, were 'I think so.' Is that correct?"

He had to believe her then. There were only three possibilities: the obvious one, that she was genuine; the second, that in some way Percival had been captured and made to talk; or that the safe house had been bugged. If either of the last two was the case, everything had gone to hell in a rocket anyway and he might as well speak freely.

"That is quite correct," he said. "Are you a member of the First Team, Mrs. Smith?"

She shook her head. "No, Mr. Hewlitt, I am not, but I work directly for them."

"You have my admiration," Hewlitt said.

"Thank you. Now let me get down to cases; you are at this moment a very vital element in our planning because of your position and your exceptional ability to talk with our enemies in their own tongue. Also your integrity and judgment are both highly rated; in the opinion of some of our key people you have come a long way since the night that you identified Philip Scott—who was, incidentally, the person who betrayed Bob Landers; we know that definitely now."

"What do you want me to do?" Hewlitt asked.

"Mr. Hewlitt, you already know about the escape of the nuclear submarine *Ramon Magsaysay* from Hunters Point. I am prepared to give you quite a bit more information about this operation. For example: she has successfully rendezvoused with a large cache of supplies that was positioned some time ago. She is now fully provisioned and equipped for a long voyage. She has fuel enough to steam more than a hundred thousand miles, and the crew manning her is made up entirely of hand-picked volunteers who are prepared to remain at sea almost indefinitely."

"This is most interesting."

"It most certainly is. This submarine is armed with sixteen *Poseidon* missiles of the latest type. It is commonly understood that each of these missiles is equipped with six separate nuclear warheads, all of which can be targeted and directed separately. A more accurate figure is ten. And she has other combat resources. The amount of firepower that she represents is so great that literally no nation on earth could stand up under it, and there is no nation that is not within her range. She is a fearful weapon."

"All this being true," Hewlitt said, "the enemy must be mustering every resource he has to find and sink her."

"Of course, but with their present capabilities they probably cannot; they don't have the technology. We have very accurate and up-to-date reports on what they can and cannot accomplish."

"They may try hostages, then. I have heard a great deal about a Colonel Rostovitch; he is supposed to be totally ruthless."

Mrs. Smith nodded. "He is, that is unquestionably right. But if he tries that, *Magsaysay* will fire at his homeland. I dislike to refer to it, but two nuclear explosions of very low yield compared to what *Magsaysay* can deliver brought Japan to her knees when she was prepared to fight fanatically to the very end."

Hewlitt had a question. "Mrs. Smith, I take it that the submarine is operating under the orders of the First Team, is that right?"

She nodded.

"Not the Navy."

"No."

"And the Navy men operating her are agreeable to this."

"Entirely so; at the moment I would say that the First Team *is* the Navy—among other things."

"This understood, Mrs. Smith, why am I here?"

"If you are willing, to be the go-between, the bridge between our organization and the enemy. It is quite a sensitive assignment; you cannot afford to make any mistakes."

Hewlitt remembered something. "Mrs. Smith, when I talked to Zalinsky today he told me that he knows the name and identity of one of our key people who occasionally visits Davy Jones' place. That could only be Percival."

"If he told you that, then there is little cause for concern—he was probing. As a matter of fact, Percival has an excellent alibi for tonight if he should need it."

"I think he should be warned, though."

"He will be, naturally. Now, if you don't mind, I have arranged for you to remain in this house at least overnight —it may be longer depending on certain other events. I'm sure that you will be quite comfortable. These premises are considered very secure."

Hewlitt looked at her again. "Am I likely to miss work tomorrow?"

Mrs. Smith got up. "At the moment that is quite possible. If so, it will probably be to our and your advantage."

"As long as they know that I've been kidnapped I presume it will be all right."

"Oh, they know—we saw to that." She walked toward the bar. "Before I go on, would you care for a drink now?"

"I think it would be a very good idea," Hewlitt said.

CHAPTER TWENTY

Deep down in the quiet dark waters of the northernmost Bering Sea the U.S.S. *Ramon Magsaysay* moved forward at reduced speed. For several hours an invisible but persistent tension had been slowly building throughout the whole ship; there was not a man on board who had not felt it in the air. At sixty-five degrees north latitude the speed had been cut for the sake of greater quiet. All of the ship's acute sensing devices were operating, but there was no sweep of radar, no pinging of sonar. All detection was passive. To the best of her ability she was hiding, for immediately before her was the narrow passage of the Bering Strait.

Inside the submarine only the navigator's chart and the readouts from the inertial platform and other positioning devices gave any visible clues to her position. On the con, the nerve center from which the ship was controlled and operated, the captain stood waiting, listening to every report given and reading the faces of the instruments that supplied continuous vital data. All contact with the outside world was indirect and appeared largely in the form of numbers. Human senses as such had little to go on; there was nothing to see apart from the largely unchanging interior of the submarine, no way physically to sense the climatic cold of northern Alaska or to draw even one lungful of the Arctic air. The Seward Peninsula lay off to the right, but it was a textbook fact only—detached and remote. Yet the knowledge that it was there gave rise to the awareness of danger, and Walter Wagner, who was on the con by special permission of the captain, could feel it like a living thing.

He knew, as did every other man on board, that the enemy would be waiting for them with everything that he had been able to muster and position in the time available.

And *Magsaysay* was strictly on her own; if anything happened to her there would be no escaping into the frigid water, where human survival time would be a matter of brief minutes. And if the ship sustained damage and could not maneuver, there would be no rescue party to recover the men trapped inside her hull.

The captain interrupted his thoughts. "We may have a break here, Walt. It's been abnormally çold even for this region this fall, and there is at least some ice in the strait. If it's thick enough, it may impede surface traffic."

"That would complicate things for aircraft too, I imagine," Wagner said.

"True. Against us is the fact that they know our speed and when to expect us. Any attack subs that they've been able to get into position will be faster and more maneuverable than we are—they don't have missile bays to contend with."

"Will they be nukes?"

The captain shook his head. "Impossible to say: it depends on their deployment just before we broke loose—what they had available that they could get here ahead of us. Perhaps nothing."

Wagner did not allow himself to fix on that hope for a moment; it was wishful thinking and little else. The enemy was noted for his tenacity of purpose, he would be up there somewhere if all he had was rowboats.

"And we can't use SUBROC when there's an ice cover," Wagner noted.

"Right. I'm keeping them in the tubes because in open water they give us a major advantage."

A crewman arrived with fresh coffee. With the brew there was a plate of freshly baked sweet rolls; the captain bit into one mechanically while he kept his attention focused on the readouts that surrounded him. In his own compartment the navigator was silently at work, continuously updating the position of the ship from the inertial platform data.

Wagner did not have to ask when contact with a possible enemy force would be made; the tight, controlled atmosphere within the submarine answered that question before it could be born. The men went about their work quietly, waiting for the sensing devices to give warning as the ship moved steadily and silently forward. Each minute that passed brought the crucial strait a quarter of a mile closer, and also the Arctic Circle, beyond which the *Magsaysay* would be once more in open water and free of its narrow constrictions.

He reached for a sweet roll; his hand was still in the air when over the one M.C. intercom a single word broke the quiet. *"Contact."*

The exec was closest and he responded. "What is it?"

"Submarine, sir," sonar responded. "She's echo-ranging."

"Range and bearing?"

"Not yet, sir, too far away."

The captain took the one M.C. "This is the captain speaking. We have a submarine contact at maximum range. All hands man battle stations." He turned to the exec. "Rig for silent running. Depth three hundred; get in as close to shore as you can."

"Ay, sir."

With that single terse response the whole atmosphere changed; Wagner saw and felt it. The watchful waiting was over; the hopes of getting through unchallenged had gone. The ship was in a combat situation now and swiftly preparing for action. From the elevated platform of the con he saw men hurrying to their appointed stations—*Magsaysay* was preparing for action.

He looked at the captain, and saw that he remained very much as he had been—quiet, in unquestioned command, and unshaken. His ship and his crew were his immediate prime concern, but the whole immediate future welfare of his country was on his shoulders also. If *Magsaysay* did not get through, then Operation Low Blow with all of its intensive planning, effort, and dedication was over.

"Can I help?" he asked.

"Chief Summers is in charge of damage control; if he needs help you could make a hand there."

"Gladly. Shall I go now?"

"You might as well wait here for the present."

Reports began to come in quickly: the torpedoes were readied; the ship was headed toward the shallower water where she might more easily escape detection. The exec called sonar on the M.C. "Anything more?" he asked.

"She's still some distance away, sir, and echo-ranging at random intervals. I haven't got her pinpointed yet."

The captain nodded but said nothing; at fifteen knots his ship moved forward, a powerful steel phantom in the water, but not one designed primarily for underwater combat. In all probability her opponent was.

The almost intense quiet inside the submarine continued. As minute passed minute she inched steadily closer to the strait itself—and that was progress she had to make if she was eventually to reach the Beaufort Sea and the relative freedom of the vast, ice-coated Arctic waters.

It was fiercely real, every moment of it, yet it was surrounded with the aura of an illusion. For all that was actually visible the ship could have been maneuvering somewhere off the coast of Australia.

In the sonar room the operator listened with his eyes closed, intent on capturing any sound that would convey a scrap of additional information about the unseen submarine somewhere out in the waters just south of the strait. His trained ears discounted the ocean noises that came through, the evidence of the restless sea that surrounded the ship and through which she was moving. He heard another ping, faint but definite; he concentrated on the sound he had just heard and decided that it had been a minute fraction louder. The enemy was drawing closer.

The *Magsaysay* was moving nearer to the Seward Peninsula and the Cape of the Prince of Wales that marked its extremity; that meant that the hostile had to be somewhere in the semicircle between one hundred and eighty and three hundred and sixty degrees. A bearing slightly to the right of true north was also a possibility; that would put it directly in the strait itself where maneuvering room would be at a minimum. There, if she was an attack type, which was almost certain, and a nuke to boot, it would be a tough go.

Another ping came through the operator's headset, and immediately after that a second one, loud and clear. The sonarman responded almost instantly; he drew a quick breath and reported. "He has contact." The silent stealth of the *Magsaysay* had been penetrated; her position was known.

The captain had been expecting that, moment by moment, and he was prepared. "All stop," he ordered.

Two or three seconds later the screw went dead in the

water. The submarine coasted forward gently, then, as her control surfaces began to lose effect, she began to drift downward. The depth gauge began a slow climb, an emotionless mechanical indication that the ship was settling toward the bottom. Within the hull there was an intense quiet, an awareness that the battle had been joined and that the odds for the moment were in favor of the enemy.

Sonar reported again over the M.C. "Torpedo in the water."

The captain did not speak or move; he waited silently for the next report.

It came within a few inert, suspenseful seconds. "Two units in the water, bearing three ten degrees, bearing drift slightly right."

The meager information gave the attack party its first opportunity for action; the data were quickly set up in the fire control system. That done, the urgency of waiting returned.

Sonar came on again. "First unit drawing rapidly to the right." In the forward end of the ship Chief Summers listened and knew that that would be a miss. Out of two shots one almost certainly would have to be a miss; it was the other one which counted now.

"Second unit zero bearing rate, coming straight in."

That was what Summers had feared; the incoming shot was aimed right down *Magsaysay*'s throat. The captain feared it, too, because he could do nothing in the few seconds that remained. He had one hope and all that he could do to help it was to pray. Underneath him his ship continued to sink slowly toward the bottom.

Then the silence inside the hull was broken from the outside; from bare audibility an insistent whine grew rapidly, ballooning in intensity with terrifying urgency. Summers and his shipmates had all faced death before; they faced it now a second away.

The deadly noise swept the length of the ship as it skimmed overhead, faded, and was gone.

"Active sonar," the captain directed; after a few seconds he gave another order. "All back full."

The unexpected command was obeyed immediately without question; within seconds the power being applied could be felt throughout the length of the hull. As the propeller cavitated the sonar pings went out; the inertia of the ship was great and the backward acceleration was very slow.

"Contact," sonar reported. "Range four eight hundred yards, bearing three zero eight."

"All stop," the captain ordered.

Wagner could not follow his logic; he had expected some kind of evasive action and the reverse maneuver had him baffled. But he trusted the captain implicitly; if he had ordered full astern, there was a reason behind it.

"Range four eight hundred yards, bearing three one zero." As rapidly as the information was supplied it was fed into the fire control system.

"All ahead full."

"All ahead full," the phone talker repeated. At that moment Walter Wagner understood one thing: that the captain was stirring up the water behind the ship, doing so deliberately. He deducted correctly that this was to confuse the enemy sonar briefly and to make it harder to read the ship's position accurately.

"Resume course."

"Ay, sir."

No mean schemer himself, Wagner understood that one almost immediately: the enemy would expect evasive action since in all probability he was already reloaded and ready to fire again. At that game *Magsaysay* would be at a serious disadvantage, but by resuming her course she might be doing the one thing he would not expect. In addition there was the advantage that the ship was under way in the direction she most wanted to go.

"Range four six hundred yards, bearing three one three."

"Shoot one."

"Ay, sir. *Shoot one.*"

"Shoot two."

"*Shoot two.*"

"All stop."

"All stop, sir."

Once more the submarine fell silent except for the torpedo room forward, where fresh rounds were being loaded into the tubes. The men doing that knew that a countershot was a near certainty, but they had no time to dwell on it. While two fresh torpedoes were being moved into position the ship began to settle once more; she had limited forward speed to dissipate this time and the control surfaces lost their effectiveness very quickly. On the con the exec watched the face of a clock, keeping track of the parade of the seconds.

Sonar reported once more. "Torpedoes departing, range three five hundred yards."

"Passive sonar," the captain said.

"Passive sonar, sir."

Silently the ship drifted deeper into the water; the depth gauge needle moved very slowly, sterile of any emotion, performing its mechanical function as it had been designed to do.

"Hit!"

The captain remained motionless, waiting for the added word he was expecting. It came almost at once. "Incoming torpedoes, two units." It made no difference then if the reported hit was valid or not; the enemy submarine had put two shots into the water and regardless of what had happened to the launching vehicle, they were independently on their way.

"One unit bearing left."

That was good news, but the shots were sure to be spread—automatically, one would have to miss.

A knot of steel-clad seconds was measured off by the clock.

"Number two unit bearing slightly right."

The tension did not ease. In those tight moments Walter Wagner wondered if the enemy commander had directed his shots that way anticipating evasive action and if *Magsaysay*'s captain had outwitted him by maintaining a straight course very briefly instead.

"First unit passed." That was the expected news. Silence became rigid in the submarine as the second sound-seeking torpedo, which could be equipped with a proximity fuse and possibly a magnetic anomaly detection system, grew louder in the sonar.

The sound of the torpedo propeller could be heard as it passed by, slightly above and only a little to the right.

"All ahead full."

"All ahead full."

Once more *Magsaysay* began very slowly to gain headway in the water, her control surfaces gradually taking hold and aligning her on course. On the con the captain began to walk back and forth. Being careful to keep out of the way, Wagner studied him and was relieved to discover that he was human after all. For there was a fine mist of perspiration on the captain's forehead, not from fear, but from the weight of responsibility that was his and that he had to bear.

The exec went to the M.C. "Sonar, do you have anything?"

"Negative, sir. Do you wish me to go active?"

The exec looked at the captain, who shook his head.

"How good was the hit?" the exec asked.

"Definite, sir, I'll swear to it."

"Carry on."

"Ay, sir."

It was silent again after that. For the first time since he had been on board the submarine, Walter Wagner felt closed in. Claustrophobia did not disturb him, but he wanted almost desperately to see what was going on; he felt like a blind man who must depend on his ears alone to tell him what is happening. There was a multitude of possibilities: the submarine that had attacked them might be playing possum; the hit could have been fatal or, as far as he knew, minor. There might be many other potential attackers in position, and *Magsaysay* was not an attack-type submarine—she carried only a very limited torpedo load. In fact she had a mixed load which included some SUBROC missiles, highly useful in certain situations, but cutting down her available torpedoes still more. And there was the element of battle luck with which he was all too familiar: in any kind of conflict situation luck could have a lot to do with it—such as setting a well-aimed torpedo slightly too shallow. The breaks of the game worked according to the law of averages. The breaks had all been good so far; a bad one was due any time.

Gradually *Magsaysay* began to pick up speed, overcoming her inertia and the strong tendency of the propeller to cavitate in the water. When a full half hour had passed and there was no sign of any further activity Wagner assumed that they were somewhere in the Bering Strait, but the frustrating inability to see anything but the inside of the submarine denied him the sharp sense of reality. Minute by minute, as the ship moved onward, he gave thanks that another half mile had been covered; had he been running things from the enemy's side he would have had some surprises prepared; the waters could have been mined by aircraft.

"Why don't you go and get some chow?" the captain asked him.

That was as polite a dismissal as he had ever heard. "Good idea," he answered and climbed down from the con onto the main deck. In the wardroom he discovered that he had been hungry without knowing it. By common consent no one had referred to food when the ship had been running without any provisions; now that there was plenty once more he still seemed to feel the discomfort of those days before the *Dolly* had been found ready and waiting.

After he had finished his meal he wandered to the small stateroom which had been assigned to him and the commander of the Hunters Point shipyard. He found his colleague there trying to pass the time with a book on submarine operations and tactics. He put it down gladly when Wagner appeared and welcomed the opportunity to talk.

They were still so engaged when *Magsaysay* first pushed her nose into the beginning waters of the Chukchi Sea. Fifty-eight minutes later, intently at work at his station, the navigator reached with his dividers once more and plotted her position one half nautical mile north of the Arctic Circle. Now there were only vast waters ahead and the shrouding cover of the great ice cap.

Feodor Zalinsky was thoroughly worried because it was already midmorning and his interpreter had not yet reported for work. He had been informed, of course, that the man Hewlitt had been seen being kidnapped on the street, but that was not what caused him concern. He was particularly afraid that Rostovitch had him.

If that were the case, then that meant that the position and authority he presently held were being challenged. Previously, not even Colonel Rostovitch would have dared to interfere with members of his personal staff without at least advising him first. But if Rostovitch did not have Hewlitt, then who did? Zalinsky could not answer that question and it haunted him.

He picked up a phone. "Get me Colonel Rostovitch," he said.

As soon as the connection was made he was on the firmer ground of his own language. The conversation was brief; the colonel, who was in his usual biting mood, denied any knowledge whatsoever of Hewlitt's whereabouts. This in itself was bad news, since the chances were better than ninety per cent that he was lying. Zalinsky hung up and then considered carefully what he ought to do next. Rostovitch technically reported to him as the head of the occupying authority, but in real fact the ferociously ambitious colonel headed his own organization and reported back directly to the premier himself.

Zalinsky was most concerned over his own position and its protection. The question before him was a simple one: had Rostovitch picked up his interpreter and if so why? Hewlitt himself was a minor pawn in this kind of a power play and what happened to him was incidental. At the same time he had recognized a certain ability in the man and even Rostovitch might find him troublesome for a short while.

He was still pondering the matter when the silence of the Oval Office was broken by a brief tap on the door. Before he could respond it was swung open and he was startled to see Hewlitt himself standing there. The surprise of his arrival was compounded by his appearance: he was unshaven and his hair appeared to have been given little or no attention. His clothes looked as if he had slept in them and his tie was crumpled and limp.

"I am glad to see you," Zalinsky said in his own language. "Are you all right?"

Hewlitt came into the room, almost an incongruous figure in the vaulted dignity of the White House office. "Yes, I'm all right," he answered. "Please excuse my appearance; I came here in a hurry because it was urgent."

"Evidently."

Hewlitt stood before him, disheveled but nonetheless fully in control of himself. "Mr. Zalinsky," he said, "you'd better stop whatever you're doing and listen to me; I have something very important to tell you."

Senator Solomon Fitzhugh stepped through the doorway into the VIP suite and displayed his membership card to the young lady at the desk. "Good morning, senator," she greeted him. "Nice to have you with us again. Your flight will be departing on time for a wonder."

"I believe you have my ticket," Fitzhugh said.

"Yes, right here, sir." She produced it. "You should have a nice flight; the weather's good all the way and it's quite pleasant in Chicago this morning."

"Thank you."

"You aren't leaving us are you, sir?"

He did not like the question, but he answered it courteously. "For a little while. Congress isn't meeting at the moment and I'm allowing myself a short vacation. I have a small place in Upper Michigan where I can get some rest."

The girl handed him his ticket. "Have a good time, senator, if that's the thing to say right now. Anyhow, good luck."

"Thank you," he acknowledged.

A little more than an hour later he was airborne and headed westward from Washington. He sat alone, paying no attention whatever to the attractive woman two rows behind him, who was apparently totally concerned with her own affairs.

At Chicago he was transferred to the Butler ramp where he boarded a twin-engined private aircraft which bore no markings other than its registration number. His departure was quite private, so there was no notice taken by the general public when the lady who had been on the airliner boarded also. Two planes took off shortly after that, one of them headed for Upper Michigan, the other pointed toward Colorado. Both had high-altitude capability and were soon out of sight of all but the air traffic controllers, who had a great many pips to watch on their radarscopes.

"It is fantastic," Zalinsky said. "Furthermore, it is very difficult for me to believe even a word of it."

Hewlitt had expected that. "That is up to you," he continued in Zalinsky's language, "but it happened just as I have reported it to you and I haven't added a thing. There is no need to."

Zalinsky spread his hands. "But it is impossible; when you had everything, an immense military establishment, vast resources of nuclear weapons, milllions of men under arms, you were defeated almost by default. Now you have almost nothing and now it is that you choose to put up a fight. Against impossible odds." He shook his head.

"We've been over this ground before," Hewlitt retorted. "As for the truth of what I have been telling you, you know that the submarine left San Francisco; practically everyone in the country does by now. And if you check, you will probably find that one attack-type submarine is missing from your navy.

Zalinsky dropped into a brown study, his face heavily furrowed, his chin on his chest as he slumped back in his chair. He thought for some moments before he spoke again. "Let us say that it is all true—everything you have told me. You are then risking everything on one single submarine, a ship that can be found and sunk by the most powerful navy in the world."

"Perhaps—but you haven't done it yet."

"Suppose that I believe that you were selected to be the messenger because you know me and can speak my language. I would like to believe it for your sake, but I do not. You are a member of this underground; it is not logical that they would trust you otherwise."

"You can believe that if you want to, but I told you that we trust people more than you do; we are not as suspicious."

"Colonel Rostovitch would not believe it, not for a moment."

"I'm not talking to the colonel, I'm speaking to his superior—in position and I believe in intelligence also."

Zalinsky stretched as he had a habit of doing. "It is not necessary that you flatter me if I am indeed as intelligent as you claim. What is now proposed?"

"That we continue as before while you communicate with the premier and inform him of the facts. Presumably he will want to make a decision."

"That is all?"

"Substantially, yes. Except as I explained to you. No more people are to be shot."

"It is blackmail."

Hewlitt nodded. "That is part of the system. You will recall those words."

Zalinsky seemed quite suddenly to be very tired. He did not look well, and Hewlitt recalled his previous request for a doctor.

"I will tell you something," Zalinsky said. "Never before in your life have you been as close to death as you are at this moment."

"Every soldier must accept the risks of his profession."

"But you are not a soldier. I have trusted you and you have betrayed me."

"That is not true, Mr. Zalinsky," Hewlitt answered. "I did not ask for this role—it was thrust upon me. You told me once that you did not expect loyalty and would not believe it if it were offered to you. I remind you of the terms: that this conversation is confidential between you and me, this is to give you reasonable time to consult your government and make such arrangements as you would like. You are the first and only one to know what you know now."

Zalinsky thought some more. "Rostovitch will kill you."

Hewlitt leaned forward and once again successfully ignored the gnawing tension which had grippped him from the moment he had come into the office. "Mr. Zalinsky, the people whom I talked to were not joking—they meant what they said. If anything happens to me, whether it's Colonel Rostovitch or anyone else, that will be taken as a sign that the terms are not accepted. In that event the order will be given to the *Magsaysay* to fire. You know what that means! And if anything does take me out of the picture, then you will have to deal with someone else—the First Team will see to that."

Zalinsky bestirred himself and some of the old fire came back into him; he leaned forward and quite suddenly was as cold-eyed and hard as Hewlitt had ever seen him. "And you claim that you do not know who the First Team is?"

Hewlitt shook his head, wishing that his stomach would remain still for just a moment. Then he forced his voice to remain level. "They didn't tell me that, and you know yourself that they wouldn't. I don't know who they are, how many, or where—but I do know now that they exist."

Zalinsky looked hard and long at him, appraisal and

suspicion amalgamized into a hard alloy. "There are other things you do not know," he said suddenly. He paused and the words sank into Hewlitt; he waited then for the sentence of death to be pronounced against him. "This submarine, we know all about it. About the high diver who has been one of your CIA agents for a long time. And the captain—he is a Jew."

For a moment the tension relaxed; Hewlitt shook his head. "No," he said.

Zalinsky thrust a hard cold look clean through him. "How do you know?"

"It came out in our conversation."

Zalinsky banged a fist on top of the President's desk. "He *is* a Jew, I was told so. We know."

Hewlitt watched him intently, knowing that for that moment he held a higher card. "He couldn't be, Mr. Zalinsky."

A fierce light sprang into Zalinsky's eyes. "Do you know who he is?"

"Yes."

"What is his name?"

"Nakamura. Commander Ishiro Nakamura."

As Zalinsky slowly sagged back into his chair Hewlitt stood up. He had had about all that he could endure and he had to make good his escape. But he held himself successfully in check so that his voice was his own when he turned at the door.

"By the way, Mr. Zalinsky," he said, "I haven't forgotten your request for a doctor. I'll do the very best that I can, but there may be a problem—so many of the very good ones have been forced out of the hospitals recently. Now if you don't mind, I'd like to go home and clean up."

Zalinsky raised an arm and waved him away.

CHAPTER TWENTY-ONE

By the time that the first snowflakes were beginning to drift down into the gorges which separated the peaks of the Rockies one from another, the grip of economic depression had closed over the whole of the United States of America. The stock market was again operating, but it was a world of illusions and shadows; the substance of business growth and development was gone. Makeshifts and substitutes once more became a forced reality; good merchandise of almost any kind was increasingly hard to find. And skilled services normally available at short notice were spoken of more and more in the past tense. The whole pattern of living underwent a substantial change in outlook: people no longer planned for the future, they planned for the day immediately ahead and hoped to live it out in peace. Following that, if all went well, they would try to prepare for the next.

The rumor of the escaped submarine spread rapidly, peaked, and then gradually died away for lack of any kind of nourishment. There had been rumors also that England, France, Germany, and the Republic of China had formed a common front to bring about the liberation of the United States with a number of other powers, great and small, offering to contribute their share. Japan was reputed to be holding to a cautiously neutral position; the Pope had called for a withdrawal of the occupying forces and offered his good offices to bring about a peaceful settlement of all remaining outstanding problems. Israel also declared for the United States, but she was so desperately overwhelmed by mass migration from the United States that all of her resources were strained to absorb the influx and meet the continuing challenge of the militant Arab states at the same time.

Throughout most of the United States the feeling was

common that the severe hold that the enemy had clamped onto the country would have to be relaxed; the shock of defeat and the near terror of the early occupation were past and gone, and the time was judged ripe for the occupying forces to ease their grip and start talking about the eventual day when national sovereignty would again become a reality. But as day succeeded day there was no evidence whatever that this was to take place at any time in the visible future. The enemy if anything was even more in evidence and he intruded himself into almost every facet of American life.

As the edge of winter began to be felt and the skies grew leaden overhead, the U.S.S. *Ramon Magsaysay* touched secretly at Wainwright, Alaska. Although the enemy was in substantial possession of the continental United States, the vastness of Alaska and its remoteness from most of the commercial and industrial activity of the nation had spared it from the same intensity of occupation and supervision. It had been possible, therefore, for two massive propeller-driven C-124 Globemasters to cross the vast open tundra of the Arctic on apparently routine missions and to set down at Wainwright on the eighty-six-hundred-foot runway unchallenged. There had not been a single representative of the enemy there, or any agent to report to him what was going on, when, under cover of a thick, steady snowstorm, the multidecked airlifters had been unloaded and the cargo had been transferred to lighters. By morning the supplies that the aircraft had brought in were gone; the planes themselves departed shortly thereafter despite the continuing snowfall, heading for Point Barrow and other stops along the northern supply route. Two passengers were carried out of Wainwright, men who were indistinguishable in their heavy parkas and cold weather clothing from the crew members who had come in.

Four days later the commander of the Hunters Point Shipyard reached the sanctuary that had been prepared in advance for him in Canada. As a presumed rescuee from the Yukon Territory he attracted little notice and, despite the presence of agents in the area, there was no notice of his arrival or any intimation as to his identity.

Walter Wagner returned almost quietly to the underground headquarters of Thomas Jefferson. As soon as he had showered and changed he sat down with his colleagues and filled them in completely on the operation. For the first time full details were available; in the extensive debriefing, which took some time, Wagner brought them all up to date to the moment when he had ridden back toward Wainwright in a lighter, the snow shrouding even the ice-choked sea, and the nuclear submarine already invisible behind him. When he had finished, Admiral Haymarket spoke for them all. "Walt, I don't need to tell you what your part in all this meant, but at the same time you know as well as I do that it was a team effort—here, at Hunters Point, at Mare Island, and at all of the places where we held them up and kept their aircraft on the ground."

"Right, sir," Wagner answered. "One other thing: I had a good chance to observe the crew. I never saw a better bunch of pros in my life. You can depend on them all the way, no matter what happens. The boys on the *Dolly* were just as good. Any word from them, by the way?"

The admiral nodded. "They went into this thing knowing that they were expendable and that we couldn't let them abandon their ship in the middle of the northern Pacific without giving too much of the show away. I've had a report; they're close in to Japan now and the arrangements for their reception are in good order."

"At a time like this," Major Pappas said, "it's nice to have friends."

"Anytime," Stanley Cumberland commented.

The admiral grew grimmer for a moment. "As soon as we knew that *Magsaysay* had it made through the Bering Strait and that the show was definitely on the road, we put the interpreter, Hewitt, in. So far it looks as though the estimates we had on him were accurate; we got a feedback which indicates very strongly that he did deliver the goods —apparently he shook up Zalinsky quite thoroughly."

"Since we pretty much had to choose one from one," General Gifford said, "it looks as if we lucked out."

"As long as Zalinsky himself stays in the saddle Hewlitt should be effective," Colonel Prichard commented. "Against Rostovitch it would probably be a different matter."

"Things are getting into my area now," Higbee said, "and I'm working on that."

"Great, Ed," Prichard answered, "but remember that

this man, no matter how willing and courageous he may be, is an amateur and he'd be up against the roughest pro in the business. Ted or Walt could handle him, but even they'd have to push to do it. Propaganda won't erase that."

"Propaganda wasn't what I had in mind. He'll need some help and I plan to see that he gets it."

"Anyway, gentlemen," the admiral said, "we've given them three weeks. By the end of that time . . ." He did not need to finish the sentence. Every man there knew that at that moment *Magsaysay* was already under the ice cap and, barring incredibly bad luck, before the ultimatum would expire she would be far to the east, close to Atlantic waters and within missile-firing range of the enemy's homeland.

Despite a slight chill that tinged the air, Hewlitt was comfortable as he drove south from Alexandria, with Barbara close beside him. He kept the car going at an even speed; neither said anything—they were sharing a common mood.

At last Barbara spoke. "When we get back, are you going to stay at the house tonight?"

He looked at her for a moment. "I'd like to."

She drummed her fingertips gently against the upholstery. "More and more I find myself thinking in terms of time. How much of it we may have left."

Hewlitt drew breath. "I know, I feel it all around me. Every time I see Zalinsky. Sometimes he looks at me as though he was asking for something, other times he ignores the fact that I'm alive."

Barbara looked out of the window for an interval despite the fact that there was little to see. "Hew, you know, don't you, that he's got some pretty deep troubles of his own?"

He glanced at her. "Internal or external?"

"External. I debated telling you this, but I think you should know—it may help in dealing with him. The Actor's in serious trouble. More than that, their whole government is."

He considered that as he drove, keeping his eyes on the road. "Not just another power play?" he asked.

Barbara shook her head. "No—it's more than that. All Europe knows about the submarine of course—everybody does. But it isn't that. When they tried to take us over they simply bit off too much. Now they've got China applying pressure from the east and a lot of other powers nibbling at their flanks. And they don't have any friends to speak of."

Hewlitt eased the car around a curve. "They're pretty elastic. And they have a habit of landing on their feet."

Barbara didn't want to argue the point. "All right, maybe they will. Meanwhile there's us."

Hewlitt looked at the road. "I've been thinking about that," he said. "Right now I'm in a pretty risky position. I can't complain; I asked for it. This may sound funny to you, but I've never been particularly concerned about myself in all this; maybe I'm being fatalistic—I don't know. The only thing that's been on my mind recently is the thought that if I don't come out of it, I won't have you around anymore."

"I've thought of that too," Barbara said.

The restaurant they were headed for appeared too soon, it was there and it could not be ignored. Hewlitt pulled into the parking lot and let the topic die as he turned off the ignition. One thing had been settled anyway: he would be back with Barbara again that night and, the way things stood, he had minimum difficulty adjusting himself to the situation. She was his girl now and that was good enough for him. And it was good enough for her, too, which was the important thing. "Ready?" he asked.

"Yes," she answered and warmed him with a soft smile.

As Frank drove them both to work the following morning Hewlitt once more counted off the days that remained before the ultimatum that the First Team had issued would expire and Zalinsky would be expected to give his answer. He could respond at any time, or he might ignore the whole thing. If he did that, then what would come next was still uncertain. One thing was clear: simply giving up was about as far from Zalinsky's normal behavior pattern as it was possible to get. Something else would have to happen first.

When he had cleared through the White House guards and had been searched as always, he settled himself at his desk to await whatever was to come. Zalinsky knew that he was a member of the underground, that was sure, but it was a minor consideration. He hadn't done too much so far in that role; perhaps he was destined to make up for lost time.

He phoned Cedric Culp on some routine matters, went through the mail that had been sorted out for his personal attention, and checked the appointment pad. He presumed that Zalinsky was inside, as he invariably was, even though there were no stiffly written notes or directives left for him to heed and obey. He had to give Zalinsky one thing: the man worked from dawn to dusk and sometimes later than that. He was probably a good manager and administrator; his problem was that he was trying to be the President of the United States without any help or willing cooperation from the subjects of his directives. And in a strange country, and through the medium of what was to him a difficult foreign language.

If he had been born an American, Hewlitt thought, and had been raised that way, he could have been a major success in industry: president, perhaps, of some leading corporation. The vision of Bob Landers' execution would not go away, but against it stood the certainty that Bob at least had been saved from Rostovitch and shipment back across the Atlantic to face torture and whatever else might have awaited him there.

When the summons to the Oval Office came it was not the usual minimum sound of the buzzer; the crispness was replaced by a too-long pressure on the button—a variation that put Hewlitt on his guard immediately. His first thought was that someone else was in the President's office, but he did not wait to speculate on it; he picked up a pad and pencils and went inside.

Zalinsky was sitting as usual in the President's chair, but his body was slumped across the desk. His arms were stretched out until they almost reached the farther edge and they were in motion, working like the oversized antennae of some probing insect. He was uttering no sounds, but his body was fighting to find some position which would bring relief from an invisible inner agony. Hewlitt dropped the things he was carrying onto the top of the desk and bending over Zalinsky spoke to him in his own language. "Are you in pain?"

"Yes." The single word was tight and strained, forced out by a man holding himself under severe restraint. Hewlitt scooped up a phone. "Medical, quick." Seconds later he had his connection. "This is Hewlitt in the Oval Office. Mr. Zalinsky has been taken acutely ill; send up the doctor immediately." He hung up and turning once more to Zalinsky began to help him off with his coat.

The phone rang. He picked it up and spoke his name. "The doctor isn't here, Mr. Hewlitt," he was told. "The nurse is on her way."

"That may not be enough; get an ambulance as fast as you can."

"Yes, sir, right away."

It was a struggle to get Zalinsky out of his coat; his body was solid and surprisingly heavy. The man himself tried to help, but he was in pain and at the point where he barely had control of his body. Hewlitt managed to free him, using main strength at one point to pull the collar down from his shoulders. As he was finishing the hasty operation the door to the office swung open and two people came in; the middle-aged nurse Hewlitt had seen before and Major Barlov, the head of White House security under the new administration. Hewlitt spoke to him without ceremony. "Help me," he ordered. "I want to lay him out on the floor."

The major cut him with one quick suspicious glance, then he called out through the door. That done he came quickly to give Hewlitt a hand; between them they lifted Zalinsky out of his chair and stretched him on his back in the middle of the carpet. As the nurse bent over, Hewlitt loosened Zalinsky's tie and took off his heavy shoes.

The nurse was on her knees, a tray of limited medical supplies beside her. Zalinsky, fully conscious, ignored her; he closed his arms across his abdomen and began to roll in short jerks from side to side.

"I'm not sure, but I think he could be passing a gallstone," the nurse said. "That's terribly painful. About the only thing we can do is to take him to the hospital or else put him into a tub of very hot water. That gives relief sometimes."

Hewlitt wiped an arm across his forehead. "I've called an ambulance. Where the hell is the doctor?"

"He's down at the clinic, Mr. Hewlitt; he's helping out because of the doctor shortage. We haven't needed him here for a long time, not since . . ."

"Well, we need him now! Did you send for him?"

"No, I didn't know it was this bad. I brought antiacids—things like that."

Minutes later one of the enemy guards appeared at the door and spoke rapidly to Barlov. "Two ambulance men are here, shall we search them?"

Barlov beckoned with his arm. "No, there is not time; bring them in at once."

Hewlitt listened, then spoke to the man on the floor. "Can you hear me, Mr. Zalinsky?"

"Yes." The same word again, the same filter of severe pain.

"Hang on; the ambulance is here. We'll have you at the hospital very soon."

Zalinsky held his eyes tightly shut and said nothing. Hewlitt helped as the two medical attendants lifted Zalinsky onto their folding cart and began to wheel him out of the office. "You stay," Barlov directed.

"No," Hewlitt answered him. "He may need an interpreter—and I can describe his symptoms."

"I will come too."

"All right."

They were in the corridor by that time. The ambulance attendants were efficient; within three minutes Zalinsky had been loaded through the back into their vehicle and transferred to the built-in bed. Hewlitt sat down on a jump seat with Barlov beside him. "Walter Reed as fast as you can," he ordered.

The ambulance took off with the voice of the siren climbing and the red lights on top flashing their message of urgency. In the right front seat one of the attendants picked up a microphone and radioed ahead. On the narrow bed Zalinsky continued to thresh his body, twisting and turning in a strange, unreal silence as though his fierce pride would not allow him to utter a sound for fear that he might cry out. "Can you help him?" Hewlitt asked the attendant in back.

The man shook his head. "Not without a doctor's order, unless it's to save his life. We'll be there pretty quick; he'll be all right after that."

Sixteen minutes later the ambulance turned sharply into the grounds of the Army medical facility. White-coated personnel were waiting outside despite the chill temperature; as the ambulance pulled up they rapidly removed the patient and wheeled him inside into a receiving room. There, waiting, was an obviously senior physician who had all his preparation made. "What medication has he been given?" he asked as Zalinsky was expertly transferred to the receiving table.

"Nothing," Hewlitt answered. "I came into his office about a half hour ago and found him doubled up in pain. He hasn't said anything, but it seems to be abdominal—the nurse guessed that he might be passing a gallstone."

The doctor turned to his patient and began an examination. It took him less than a minute, then he picked up a syringe. "That or possibly a kidney stone," he said as he loaded the needle. "I'm giving him some Demerol—that will give him relief."

"I must know what it is," Barlov said. He had come in the room unobserved.

"It's the right thing," Hewlitt answered him. The doctor gave him a grateful glance as he rolled Zalinsky over, pulled down the band of his trousers, and exposed the proper quadrant of his buttocks. Zalinsky winced slightly as the needle went home, but he still made no sound. When the injection had been completed and Zalinsky was once more lying on his back Hewlitt spoke to him. "This is Walter Reed Hospital," he said. "It is one of the best medical facilities in the country. The shot you have been given will ease your pain quickly. Do you need anything?"

"Remain," Zalinsky said.

Hewlitt did, Barlov beside him, and waited. Presently he could discern a lessening of the tension in Zalinsky's body. Gradually, almost visibly, the pain ebbed out of him. The lines in his face relaxed and the almost fierce grip that he had been holding on himself quietly evaporated. As it did the physician unbuttoned Zalinsky's shirt and began to probe his upper abdomen. Then he released his trousers and continued testing with his fingers. When he had finished he turned to two of the white-coated attendants who had met the ambulance on arrival. "Take him in and get him ready for surgery," he ordered. Then he turned to Hewlitt and spoke to him, ignoring Barlov.

"I believe that your nurse was right," he said. "We can

make some quick tests, but all the indications are that he is passing a gallstone. In his general condition I believe that his gallbladder should come out, but I won't give a final opinion until the tests are run."

"How serious is it?" Hewlitt asked. "And do you know who he is?"

The doctor nodded. "I know. Not too serious, I'd say; we do them here every day. He's heavily overweight, but that is a complication we've met before."

Major Barlov stepped forward. "I am not doctor," he said. "Our doctors are the best, but we have not one of our own here."

"I believe that you can place your confidence in us," the physician said. His voice was dry and factual, indicating that he had dealt with the enemy before.

Barlov continued with the same disregard of personal feelings that had characterized him since his arrival at the White House. "It is necessary that the one and best surgeon be assigned," he said. "The best and the best only."

The Army doctor spread his fingers and pressed his palms against the tabletop on which his patient lay. "A very good man will attend to your countryman," he said. "I may even do it myself. As for the very best, you can't have him. Ordinarily he would be assigned without question, but he isn't available. The best man we had here was Colonel Newman, who is a noted specialist in abdominal surgery. He can't help you now because you forced him out of the service. Colonel Newman," he added coldly, "is Jewish."

Senator Solomon Fitzhugh sat alone on the glassed-in porch of the mountain cabin which had been his temporary home for the past several days. Away from the familiar environment of Washington, and separated from the things he knew and understood, he had spent much of his time in thinking. It was precisely for that purpose that Ed Higbee had arranged the sojourn for him. He had also made a very careful choice of the caretaker-cook who kept things in order and provided excellent meals. The two men had talked, of course, but Fitzhugh specifically avoided inviting any opinions. If he was going to do the thing that had been asked of him, then it would be in his own good time and out of his own personal conviction. He had no intention of allowing himself to be shoved into anything by anybody.

He was expecting "Mrs. Smith" and had prepared himself, mentally and physically, to receive her.

Despite the fact that she had been surprisingly candid with him, she still represented a considerable mystery to him. That she was a woman of rare intelligence and breeding he did not question; she was quality clear through, and no actress, no matter how gifted, could ever have portrayed such a role without possessing the same qualifications herself. He remembered Greer Garson again and thought that the comparison was apt. But for one thing, he did not even know her correct name—she had admitted at their first meeting that the "Mrs. Smith" was an alias. He was still far from satisfied that she did not intend to use him, well beyond the point which he had already agreed to.

But there was one fact that he could not deny: assuming that she had spoken the truth, her daughter had been gunned down in the same massacre that had robbed him of his son. A daughter who very probably had recruited Gary to her cause and had thus directly caused his terrible and cruel death.

He did not hear the car arriving; he was quite unaware that anyone else was within miles when the caretaker came to the door of the porch and said, "Mrs. Smith is here."

Solomon Fitzhugh rose to his feet in time to greet his visitor.

"I do hope that you have been comfortable, senator," she said.

"Yes, quite," he responded. "Would it be proper to inquire to whom this facility belongs?"

She caught the word "facility" and correctly diagnosed its meaning. "It is privately owned, senator; it belongs to a retired industrialist who uses it as a retreat when he wants to get away from everything and enjoy peace and quiet."

"Am I to assume, then, that he is aware of the fact that I am using his property?"

The smile she gave him melted the stiffness that had

been shaping his words. "You are his particularly invited guest; he inquired concerning your welfare this morning."

"Is he a member, too, of your underground?"

"He is a very fine man you will hold in high regard if you have the opportunity to meet him. Senator, I have something for you." She produced a large plain manila envelope and removed some typewritten sheets from it. "This is the text of the address we are asking you to deliver. We are fully aware that in the past you usually wrote your own and had them polished up afterwards; this one has been written for you, principally because it contains a good deal of information that you would have no way of knowing. I will ask you to accept my assurance that it is entirely true and correct—there is nothing misleading or otherwise improper."

"I presume that I am permitted to edit and correct this as I best see fit."

Mrs. Smith firmly shook her head. "No, senator, we request that you deliver it exactly as written. If there are any questions that you would like to ask, I will be glad to answer them for you if I am able."

Fitzhugh took the manuscript and then laid it on a small table beside his chair without looking at it. "Mrs. Smith—I am continuing to call you that although I presume that your proper name is Mrs. Bloom—I have the distinct feeling that I am being used."

It was quiet for a few moments, then Mrs. Smith spoke again. "Senator Fitzhugh, I believe it is time you understood certain basic things: the situation our country is in, the circumstances that got us into it, and what some of us are trying to do about it. So far all this seems to have eluded you.

"Certainly war in any form is a terrible and completely irrational means of settling disputes between nations or any other political bodies. And unfortunately weaponry has been advanced to the point where we are in a position to exterminate ourselves if we aren't very careful. The approximately one hundred men on board the *Ramon Magsaysay* have the power, self-contained within themselves, to wipe several whole nations completely off the face of the globe."

"But dammit, woman, that's what I've been saying all

along!" He paused. "I'm sorry if I spoke intemperately; please excuse me."

Mrs. Smith dismissed it with a wave of her hand. "I am fully aware of what you have been saying, senator, and I am glad that you agree with me so far. Now we come to a salient point which, among other things, accounts for the fact that we have met and that you are sitting where you are at this moment. It is this: no rational nation fortunate enough to have responsible leaders ever chooses to go to war except for one reason—because the alternative to it is even more unacceptable than the horrors of the conflict itself. After Pearl Harbor was attacked, the United States was faced with a clear choice—either engage in war or submit to the rule and dictation of the militant fanatics who were in control of Japan at that time. In short, surrender.

"Now, any party to a war action can presumably bring it to a close at any time by submitting to the will of the enemy. But can you visualize what it would have been if World War II had been won by Germany and Japan? In the case of the Japanese we were at that time a hated foreign race, and to a considerable degree we had brought that upon ourselves. Their treatment of us, had the regime then in power won their victory, is something I doubt that either of us can imagine accurately. But it would not have been pleasant."

"Mrs. Smith, I don't think . . ."

She silenced him by raising her hand. "Now you can ask yourself if nonresistance is so precious to you that you would be willing to permit our enemies to continue as they have been doing, to continue the massacre of people and to exterminate freedom as we know it from the map of our country."

Fitzhugh leaned forward and tapped the tips of his fingers against his knee. "But, Mrs. Smith, you forget that your daughter and my son would be alive and well today if they had not engaged in underground activities! There was no need for them to be involved, but they were—and eight young people died. I'm not altogether satisfied that it wasn't to a considerable degree your fault."

Mrs. Smith rose to her feet. Her voice did not change and the expression on her features remained composed. "Senator, I credited you with holding your convictions honestly and believing in what you said and did. I am now forced to alter my opinion; you suffer from one of the worst faults that can beset a human being. You are pigheaded, senator, anxious only to expound your own viewpoint and unwilling to give a hearing to any other. I believe that you were once advised to cut your throat. I am impressed with the wisdom of that proposal." Mrs. Smith rose and walked out of the room.

The senator got to his feet, his body tense with anger as she left. When he was once more alone he sat for some time in thought. Then he picked up the speech that had been left with him and began to read. He turned the pages very slowly at first, then a little more rapidly as he began to get into the text. When he had finished it all he put it down again.

He leaned back, shut his eyes, and took refuge for a moment in the remembrance of his son. It was almost as if Gary had been able to return to him once again for a few brief moments. He saw no images, he only felt the illusion of a presence. And then, when his tortured brain could think of nothing else to do, he tried to ask his son what he should do.

He received no answer, of course, but in his pain he had succeeded in conjuring up the shadow of something that once had been, and was well remembered. And he knew what Gary would have done. What he had done. It was not humanity, then, it was not the United States of America, it was not even the people of the state that had so narrowly returned him to his seat in the Senate. It was Gary, his boy, his son, his hope for posterity and thereby a measure of immortality that could not be realized now. He had blamed Mrs. Smith in what he had conceived of as a burst of righteous anger. Now, in the cold reality of what he had read, he knew that he could no longer avoid and deny the truth. In the bitter dawn of his enlightenment he knew at last that at least in small part he also had himself to blame.

When Raleigh Hewlitt arrived for work the following morning his first action was to ask Major Barlov if there was any news concerning Zalinsky.

"Yes," the major told him in his own language. "Mr.

Zalinsky underwent surgery during the night. His gallbladder was removed. The operation was successful and he is resting as comfortably as could be expected this morning."

"Good," Hewlitt said.

Major Barlov appeared ready to say something else to him, but apparently changed his mind and walked away. Hewlitt considered it briefly and then dismissed it from his mind. The White House grapevine was still highly efficient, and whatever was going on, if anything was, he would hear of shortly.

There was one matter that occupied his mind and which he knew that he should think out to its conclusion. With Zalinsky in the hospital, and probably under the effect of sedation, the ultimatum that had been handed down to him by the First Team could well be thrown off schedule. Through Frank he would have to get word of what had happened to Percival; the illness of the administrator might very well be something that was being kept secret for the time being. As soon as the fact was known, if it was not already, he probably would receive revised instructions. He was still turning this situation over in his own mind when, to his surprise, the buzzer which summoned him to the Oval Office sounded once briefly. He picked up a pad and pencils, opened the door, and went inside.

Seated behind the desk was a man whose hair was cropped close to his skull, revealing a white scar running above one ear. He was a considerably bigger person than Zalinsky and, although he had a substantial frame, there was no evidence of fat. He wore his clothes better than Zalinsky did, although the material and cut were of the same indifferent quality. All this Hewlitt saw, but his attention was captured and held by the man's face. It was venomous; severe in the way that the skin was stretched across the bones, and viciously cruel. The eyes of that face burned into him and Hewlitt felt that they saw clear through into his soul.

"Good morning, Colonel Rostovitch," he said. That was a minute victory, since the man did not have to tell him who he was.

Rostovitch looked at him for a full half minute without saying a word. Hewlitt waited until the scrutiny was half over, then he calmly sat down. He knew that the first moment he showed fear or allowed himself to be put on the defensive he would be destroyed. He was on a shaky raft, but it was afloat and he intended to keep it that way.

The voice of Rostovitch bit through the air like a living thing. "I did not tell you to sit down."

Hewlitt fought down the temptation to yield; if he stood up again he would be a defeated man and he knew it. "I always sit down when I come in here," he answered. "Mr. Zalinsky prefers it that way."

Rostovitch ignored that as too trivial to notice. "You are an agent; as soon as I finish with you, you will be taken out and shot."

Hewlitt lifted his shoulders and let them fall. He believed it, knew that it was true, but refused to give the man before him the least satisfaction. That gave him the courage he needed.

"If you do," he said, "it will finish you. The Actor is in a rapidly weakening position—you know that, because you are going to be his successor. That is, if things stay as they are right now. But if you take me out, then you will be personally face-to-face with the man who has beaten you twice already and has the firepower to do it again."

He saw the dangerous reddening of anger flush the face of the man behind the President's desk, but he was on a course from which he could not deviate one moment. He kept the initiative because it was his only lifeline. "I was put in the position of being his spokesman—his and the people who surround him. I don't know any of them or even who they are."

"I do!" Rostovitch shot at him.

Hewlitt paid no attention. "I didn't ask for this assignment, but now that I've got it I have no choice but to carry it out. I was elected because I speak your language; at the moment I'm a messenger and nothing more. If you want to do something about that submarine, you can send any messages you like through me. I'll deliver them exactly as you give them as soon as they contact me—whenever and wherever they do."

"You have been sleeping with Amy Thornbush."

Amy Thornbush, that name again!

In a flash he saw a gamble, a huge one, but if it paid off it might mean a reprieve—it could be the key to one more chance. Up to that moment he had been icy cool because in his mind was the unshaped thought that he was already a dead man: Rostovitch had promised to shoot him and there was no doubt that he would. Therefore it made little difference what he said. But Amy Thornbush might bring him back to life—if he guessed right.

"Yes," he answered. It took him hardly a second to get that out. *"And so have you."*

Rostovitch stared at him. "Maybe," he said. Intensity burned out from him until it was like a consuming fire. "Meanwhile I give you a message; *deliver it!*"

"As soon as I can. What is it?"

"We have devices of which you do not dream. We have used them. Inform them that their submarine, the one named for the Filipino traitor and that has the high diver on board, was found and sunk by us early this morning!"

CHAPTER TWENTY-TWO

Admiral Haymarket was still in bed when the first word of Zalinsky's illness reached the headquarters of Thomas Jefferson. Major Pappas received the message on behalf of the First Team; as soon as he had read it he made an immediate decision that despite the strain the admiral had been under he should be awakened and advised at once. The unexpected event would obviously throw the entire timetable off and was bound to have a material effect on the very careful plans which Ed Higbee had drawn up for the next phase of Operation Low Blow.

His long years in the service had taught Haymarket how to wake up from a sound sleep and be alert enough to make a major decision within a few seconds after that. He had carried a great load of responsibility for many years and because of that he had been forced to condition himself to being on duty twenty-four hours of every day. It took the admiral little time, therefore, after he was given the news, to digest it and then to call an emergency meeting of his staff to be held in thirty minutes' time. That done he got out of bed, allowed himself the luxury of a full shower, shaved, dressed, and made his way to the boardroom where a breakfast to his liking was awaiting him at his place at the head of the table.

Major Pappas was already there. Stanley Cumberland came in, his usual long, lean composed self, and sat down with the general air of a man who listens to a problem and then routinely disposes of it. Walter Wagner and Colonel Prichard arrived together, closely followed by General Gifford with a thick folio under his arm. The last to come in was Ed Higbee, who took his place silently and prepared to listen with the ears of a trained reporter before he would have anything to say. Backing them up there were others of the support framework who also headquartered at the underground complex. Dr. Heise, who had prepared the supposed corpse of Admiral Haymarket, was present, as was the helicopter pilot who passed so well as a hunting guide.

The admiral was handed two more messages which he read before he convened the meeting. "Gentlemen," he began, "up to now things have been running so smoothly I have been waiting for the other shoe to drop—something had to go haywire somewhere. Well, it has." Then he told the news and filled them in with the details he had just learned.

"What are his chances of survival?" Colonel Prichard asked.

"Dr. Heise?"

The white-haired physician answered without hesitation. "Barring complications of which I am not aware, very good. He is very much overweight, but in this situation that shouldn't be too material. There is an element of risk, if he has surgery, but I would assess it at less than ten per cent at this juncture."

"But he will be out of circulation for a while."

"Yes, admiral, for the next week count him out of everything. After that he will still be recuperating, but he will be able to make some decisions—if he is still in a position to."

"Precisely." The admiral looked around the table. "All of the intelligence that we have been getting indicates that Rostovitch has been closing in on him; if I know that man he will lose no time whatever in taking over in Zalinsky's place. As of right now, I would guess that Feodor Zalinsky has a damn sight better chance of recovering his health than his job."

General Gifford responded. "I'll support that fully, especially in view of the information flow we've been getting from the White House. Zalinsky isn't hacking it, no one man could, and this is undoubtedly his out. The question now is: how can we exploit this to our advantage?" He looked at Ed Higbee for an answer.

Higbee took his time. "As of this moment that will be hard to do—finding an advantage, I mean. I believe it would be a safe assumption to go on the basis that the ball has passed to Rostovitch as of right now. I've been over this with Ted Pappas and we have a plan ready; it was drafted to meet the unlikely event that Zalinsky was assassinated, clobbered in traffic, or otherwise taken out of the picture. That is just what has happened now. You tell them, Ted."

Major Pappas was as inhumanly efficient as always. "Assuming that Colonel Rostovitch is in the driver's seat, then the whole formula of attack must be changed to fit his known characteristics and personality. First, we must have confirmation; I don't see much room for doubt, but I don't want to shoot in the dark."

"I agree with that completely," the admiral said.

"Thank you, sir. To continue: as soon as we are certain that Rostovitch has taken over the show we will immediately tighten the security around our White House people; depending on the exact circumstances, we may want to take some of them out of there. When that has been done, then I propose that we mount Operation Counterweight at once. It will be rough and we may lose some people, but it will send the colonel a message in language he can understand."

"Can we do Counterweight?" the admiral asked. "Does the situation still permit?"

"Yes, sir, as of two days ago it does and there is a very high probability that there has been no change. The operational team can be positioned very rapidly. They have been keeping current on any developments and they have reported none."

"They are fully prepared as to exact targets?"

"Chapter and verse."

"Go ahead, Ted."

"Sir, if I could be excused for a moment, I'd like to get my file on this. I don't want to trust to memory." As he turned in his chair a member of his staff handed him the wanted folder.

Pappas opened it and wasted no time on unnecessary comments. "To handle Rostovitch we will have to bear down. In the case of Zalinsky, the potential that the *Magsaysay* represents was judged to be enough. With Rostovitch it is a different matter; he will know immediately that if we succeed he will have had it and he will therefore gamble with everything that he's got and go the limit."

"She may have to fire, then."

"I would be prepared for that, sir; it may be the only

means we have of putting enough pressure on him to make him yield. He takes to defeat very unkindly; Walt can tell you about that."

Walter Wagner nodded his head in agreement.

The major continued, as coldly factual as before. "Now as to the White House: we have two units operating on the inside, each entirely independent and neither aware of the other. They report through different channels, and if one is blown the other has a good chance of remaining intact."

"Is Mark aware of all this?" General Gifford asked.

"Yes, sir, he is. You know the level of confidence we have in him and there was no question of his need to know. He is in the field and will direct any operations that we may have to stage."

"I have some ideas on that," the admiral interjected, "but go ahead."

"Yes, sir. Now as to the people in the primary or A cell within the White House. It is headed by Captain Barbara Stoneham of the Air Force, who has top marks for discretion and a Cattell Scale IQ of 146. She has been attached to intelligence for some time. In addition, she is reported as unusually attractive and quite spectacular in her physical assets."

There was a general murmur of appreciation at that; few of the men present had seen their wives, or other female associates, for some time.

The major continued. "Captain Stoneham is backed by Captain Mary Mulligan, Army Intelligence, who for some time has been on TDY with the Agency. Her outward personality is quiet and self-effacing; she passes as the typical government virgin in her early thirties. She has a brain, too, and knows how to use it.

"The third critical individual in the group is Raleigh Hewlitt, originally a language specialist who is now acting more or less as Zalinsky's appointment secretary. He has a top rating for the careful handling and translation of classified material. We don't have an IQ readout on him, but Captain Stoneham has had him under close observation for some time and she reports that he has been underrated. Which is good to know. When our safe house that this cell has been using was raided, he covered by leaping into bed with Barbara and conducted himself admirably."

"In line of duty of course," Admiral Haymarket quipped.

Pappas actually allowed himself to smile. "Someday, sir, I'd like one of these desirable field assignments. The relationship between those two is continuing, and I can understand that too."

The joking over, he became serious once more. "In the case of Zalinsky, an independent report from the other cell we have operating in the White House proper confirms that fact that Hewlitt has a certain working relationship with him, a rapport which could have been very useful to us. With Rostovitch that's entirely out the window—far out."

"Wait a minute," General Gifford cut in, "if Rostovitch does take over and Hewlitt tries to carry on as directed with him, he won't last ten minutes. I mean that literally."

The admiral drummed his fingertips against the tabletop. That was a sign they all knew and they waited for him to speak. "If Hewlitt strictly followed his orders," he said finally, "and talked to Zalinsky on the basis that it was privileged information for him alone, and assuming that Zalinsky isn't stupid—which I'll buy—everything will be at a standstill while he's recuperating, if it's rapid."

He stopped when another message was passed to him. He read it and then looked up. "All bets are off. Zalinsky's having his gallbladder out; that's definite. Things won't hold still while he gets over that."

"That means Rostovitch," Wagner said.

"Has Hewlitt encountered him yet?"

"We don't know, sir, not yet."

"All right," the admiral declared. "I want the closest possible watch over the White House and our people there. Get Mark in there on the double, I don't care what else he's doing. Set up the machinery immediately to pull out as many of our people as we have to protect their safety; God knows they've earned that. Ted, keep Counterweight on the ready, but don't trigger it until Ed gives the word; that's in his department."

"Yes, sir," Pappas replied.

"Carl," Haymarket continued, "do we have enough people in Washington to set up a diversion on a considerable scale if we have to?"

"How considerable?"

"A White House demonstration large enough to commit most or all of the security people that Barlov has. I realize the danger, but it may have to be done anyway."

"If you want it, you'll get it," General Gifford said. "In answer to your question, yes we can do it. It'll take a few hours to set things up; after that we'll be able to go anytime on short notice."

"Good, do that. Issue strict orders that the demonstration is to be angry but peaceful. No one is to throw any rocks or start anything that would give them an excuse to shoot."

"Right."

"One more thing, try to scale it so that Barlov will apparently have his hands full, but not to the point where Rostovitch will think it necessary to commit any of his own people. We don't want that."

Higbee raised his hand. "I want in on this," he said. "They'll need a cause, something which will apparently trigger them, then all of the slogans—things like that. It's got to look just right; the spontaneous overflow of emotion by people who are badly frustrated, but who can't really do anything about it."

"You guys set it up," the admiral declared. "Anything else?"

Higbee continued. "Barney, I think we need to note that our timing, which was entirely designed to keep Zalinsky off balance, has gone up the flue. Now we've got a whole new ball game."

The admiral nodded sharply. "True. My thinking right now is that we shouldn't pull Counterweight until we've gotten our exposed people out first. They know Mark, don't they?"

"As Percival, yes."

"Then go batten down the hatches and as soon as that's done we'll hit Rostovitch where it will hurt. Keep me up to date on this by the minute."

"The people we take, shall we hide them out?"

The admiral weighed that for three seconds. "No, bring them in here. If Hewlitt is the interpreter he is reputed to be, there may be work for him to do."

Pappas was already on his feet. "Under way, sir. I just hope now that we're in time."

It was all that Hewlitt could do to hold himself together as he walked out of the Oval Office; he could almost feel Rostovitch's eyes burning the middle of his back. His mind and his body urged him to flee, to escape while there was still life in him, but to do that at once would be an overt confession—and death. He sat down at his desk and fought to think, to clear his mind. He had gone one short round with Rostovitch and had won a temporary reprieve which could expire at any moment; he would stay alive only while Rostovitch checked on whether he had deceived him or not. When the answer came in, there was no doubt whatever what would happen then.

The answer—get out and get out fast.

He hardly heard the phone when it rang; he picked it up by reflex action as much as anything else. Then he heard Barbara's voice. "Hew, I don't feel well at all. I've got to go home."

She knew!

"Can I help you?" he asked.

"Would you?"

"Right now. Can you come here or shall I . . ."

"Wait." That was all.

Then in a flash he saw it—Rostovitch had ordered him to deliver a message. He seized the phone and called Major Barlov. "Colonel Rostovitch has given me an errand to do," he reported.

"Then attend to it at once."

"I intend to, major; I wanted to inform you that I will be gone until it's carried out."

"Waste no more time."

God was with him, it couldn't be anything else. But he could not abandon Barbara. He got into his topcoat in seconds, picked up his briefcase, and looked for her with desperate anxiety. The seconds tortured him until she appeared, actually looking thoroughly ill. He took her arm and led her out, every precious moment the answer to an unspoken prayer.

The cool fresh air of the portico reminded him how sweet it was to live, every step now had in it part of the ingredients of life. The gate was visible ahead of them, if only the phone . . .

They were passed through with a casual wave of the sentry's arm; it had never been so simple. By the will of merciful fate there was a cruising cab just pulling in; there were fewer and fewer available each day. Hewlitt had thought first of going to his apartment, but he knew at once that it would be wrong; he gave the address of the safe house—there might be help there. Then he realized that he had to go there anyway since he had Barbara with him.

During the ride she sat close to him, holding his hands and saying nothing. She still kept up the pretense of being ill, so much so that he began to wonder if any part of it was real. If that was the case . . .

He was losing his grip, and that he could not allow! He took a new hold on himself and once more tried to focus his mind onto a decision as to what he should do next. He had found no definite answer by the time that they reached the house. He helped Barbara out, paid hurriedly, and then guided her carefully inside.

Davy Jones was sitting at the bar talking to someone. There were two glasses and a bottle. *A bottle.* He remembered and read the warning. "Barbara is sick, Davy," he said, "can you give me a hand?"

"Of course, Mr. Hewlitt, right now." As he got up he spoke to his guest. "Sorry."

"I was just going," the man said.

With a proper combination of solicitude and respect Davy followed behind Hewlitt as he led Barbara upstairs; he maintained that pose until the front door was shut behind him and he saw that the guest had gone. Then Barbara turned. "I had to get you out," she said. "You're blown."

"Into Barbara's room—now," Davy said. "I've got orders for you."

They obeyed him; the moment she was inside Barbara pulled out a suitcase and began to throw things inside with a speed that Hewlitt had to admire; she didn't waste a motion. He knew better than to offer to help her; she was doing it better alone.

"Percival's coming," Davy said. "He'll be here any moment. Hew—you, Barbara, and Mary are being pulled out right now. We've already got the essential stuff from your apartment for you—forget the rest."

Hewlitt was still trying to think. "I bluffed Rostovitch," he said, "but it won't last for long. It may be gone already." He turned quickly to Barbara. "You're all right, aren't you?" he asked.

She didn't even pause to glance at him. "Of course. Slightly pregnant, but that's nothing at the moment."

The door opened without a knock and Percival was there. "Are you ready?" he asked.

"Yes," Hewlitt answered for them both, "but Mary isn't here." He remembered that he had only a few dollars in his wallet, but that could not be helped. Barbara snapped her case shut and waved help aside. "Where to?" she asked.

Downstairs the front door opened once more; Davy turned quickly, then relaxed when he heard Mary's quick steps on the staircase. She was with them seconds later. "Two minutes," she asked.

"No more," Percival warned.

Davy went with her as she literally ran to her room.

"Let's get started," Percival said.

"The others?" Hewlitt asked.

Percival nodded quickly. "Cedric is all right, so far at least. And the rest. But we've got to get you out as fast as possible." He glanced at his watch, then stood waiting for agonizing seconds to pass by. The house remained quiet, which was all that Hewlitt dared to hope for. After a half minute of eternity Percival started out the door. Barbara followed, carrying her own case; they were halfway down the back staircase when Mary came running after them, followed by Davy who had her case in his hand; apparently they had scooped everything into it in a matter of a few seconds.

When they reached the first floor Percival swung open the door to the basement staircase. Hewlitt remembered then that there was another way out of the safe house and he was desperately grateful for it. He followed Barbara down, being careful not to stumble in the semi-darkness. The feeling of being the hunted was strong in him now, and the urge to flee was fighting for possession of him.

It was victory when his feet touched the floor of the basement, even though he did not know where he was going. As he turned to follow Barbara toward the rear of the building, he heard a sudden noise from upstairs; he analyzed it instinctively and knew that the front door had been flung open. Then he heard a commanding voice and identified it as Major Barlov's. One glance behind him told him that Davy had shut the cellar door and was more than halfway down the steps with Mary still ahead of him. He gulped in air and resolved to move as swiftly and as silently as he humanly could. It was a matter of seconds now.

Percival barely paused before the door to a small partitioned-off storeroom; it was heavily padlocked with a chain wound around two posts; even with a key it would take precious time to open. As Hewlitt watched, Percival reached to the other side of the door, touched a hidden latch, and swung it open from what had appeared to be the hinged side. Barbara passed quickly through the opening; without thinking Hewlitt stepped aside to let Mary go next. At that moment he heard the door at the top of the basement stairs yanked open and the sound of someone running down the steps.

Hewlitt did what his primitive instincts demanded; he whipped his body around to do battle, and to buy time for Barbara to get away. Then he felt the ramming force of Davy's hand against his chest pushing him backward. As he yielded, because he could not help it, he saw the face of Major Barlov and knew that they were trapped. He stumbled backward, Davy crowding him hard, and realized that Percival was closing the trick door. For a bare moment Barlov was at the opening, then as the door came shut he heard the words, "Get going, you chaps."

His brain told him to obey the voice, the voice of Major Barlov. But it had been a different voice, one he had only partially recognized. He lowered his head and passed through an opening protected by a metal door and into some sort of tunnel as Percival thrust him against the side in order to get past. Then the metal door closed behind him. A flashlight beam cut ahead and he could see the two girls, Percival leading them, then a tunnel intersection.

They turned at a right angle to the left and were in some sort of an underground utility passageway; overhead and on the sidewalls there were multiple pipes and conduits. After a short distance Percival halted and pulled open what appeared to be an electrical junction box. From it he quickly took out several compact handguns, passing the first to Barbara and the second to Mary. "Can you shoot?" he asked Hewlitt.

"I'll learn damn fast."

Percival handed him a gun. "Keep the safety on," he directed. "Mary will show you."

"Can she use a gun?"

"She can drop a running man at sixty yards," he answered. "She has." Then he slapped a gun into Davy's free hand, took one himself, and was in the lead once more.

At a niche in the concrete sidewall there was a steel ladder going up; after the brief climb another door and they were inside a small garage. Without hesitation Davy opened the trunk of a commonplace-appearing sedan and stepped onto a couch which had been prepared on the inside. Percival waved Hewlitt toward the rear seat as he shut the lid of Davy's compartment. Obediently Hewlitt climbed in and was grateful when Barbara followed. Mary took the front seat as Percival slid behind the wheel. At the touch of a button on the dash the door began to lift open as Percival started the engine. Moments later the car came out into the sudden brightness of daylight, the door of the garage slowly closing automatically behind it. They came down a short driveway, turned into the thin traffic stream, and everything was suddenly commonplace.

Percival drove through the city with apparent unconcern. He held to a westerly direction until the last of the new housing developments finally had been passed and they were in the beginning of the open country. He turned once or twice onto semi-thoroughfares with the familiarity of a man driving from his office back to his own home and no one, so far as Hewlitt could tell, took the least notice of them. He looked up at the gas gauge and saw, as he had expected, that the tank was full. He sat back next to Barbara, holding the gun he had been given concealed inside his coat, and deliberately relaxed. When he had done that he said to Barbara, "I'm glad you're here."

She pressed his hand; it was eloquent enough for him and he was satisfied. They drove on, the car running smoothly, the day beautiful and clear. They continued for more than an hour and then at last Percival spoke. "We should be in the clear now," he said. "We know all of their emergency roadblock locations and they're behind us now as far as the city is concerned. They don't have any description of this car and they're still short of people; they can't make an exhaustive search."

Hewlitt swallowed. "What happens now?" he asked.

Percival kept his eyes on the road. "Things are all set up for us," he answered. "If nothing goes wrong, in a day or two you'll meet the First Team."

As soon as the preliminary information was all in, Ed Higbee saw the admiral. He sat down and waved away the inevitable cup of coffee, refreshment was not on his mind at the moment. "Barney," he began, "we've got a bear by the tail."

"Let's have it."

"I'll start with the good part first: Mark got there in time and pulled out four of our people who were in a critical position. It was touch and go, but they made it."

"That includes Hewlitt, the interpreter."

"Yes, sir, plus two of our best girls and the electronics man who was in charge of the safe house. The house is blown, but our people all have whole skins. Speaking of that, Hewlitt was called in to face Rostovitch and somehow he bluffed him out. God knows how he did it."

"God knows, and I intend to find out. Go on."

"Rostovitch is running the show, as we already knew, but there's a new angle. He told Hewlitt that *Magsaysay* has been sunk. According to Hewlitt, whom Mark considers to be thoroughly creditable, he was almost triumphantly factual about it."

Admiral Haymarket pursed his lips and leaned back in his chair to think that one over. The possibility of a bluff was immediately obvious to both men; so also was the fact that Rostovitch would be unlikely to volunteer a statement from which he might have to back down later on. Both men also knew that despite Canada's official neutrality, the enemy had been conducting intensive search activities by air over much of the northern Arctic under the guise of weather reconnaissance. And there were remarkable detection devices still highly classified in what had been the American arsenal, devices which could well have been independently developed or, more likely, compromised by espionage.

The admiral sent for General Gifford, Colonel Prichard, and Major Pappas.

"We have a new can of worms," he told them when they had assembled. He painted the picture exactly as Ed Higbee had given it to him. When he had done so, he turned to Pappas first. "When are we due for a communication from Commander Nakamura?"

Pappas shook his head. "In order to insure minimum risk, sir, no contacts whatever are scheduled. But we can query."

The general shook his head at that. "Precisely what they would like to have us do, I suspect," he said. "That is, if Rostovitch is bluffing."

The admiral passed a hand across his face, blinked his eyes to dispel his sustained fatigue, "Quote the odds," he invited.

Pappas, the human calculator, was the one to answer that and he responded. "Sixty per cent bluff, forty per cent truth based on present data."

"Hank?"

Colonel Prichard was ready. "I'll concur with that for the time being. It's close enough to an even split to cause us concern, that's for sure."

"Which opens the possibility that Hewlitt was fed the information and then allowed to break loose," the admiral said. "That would explain his supposedly outmaneuvering Rostovitch. To the best of my knowledge Walt Wagner is the only man who has even taken his measure before, and it wasn't easy."

"Make it sixty-five, thirty-five on the strength of that," Pappas contributed. "I have one recommendation, sir. Whatever we do, no request for a report from *Magsaysay*. I'll give you one hundred per cent that they've got every detection and listening device that they have trained continuously, waiting for her to break silence. And they'll read her out, position and all."

"Agreed," the general added.

"Do we gamble?" the admiral asked.

When it was silent for a few moments Ed Higbee realized that the question was mainly for him. He had his answer ready. "If we don't, we're dead."

"What about Counterweight?"

Higbee had to think before he was ready to commit himself on that. It took him a good fifteen seconds. "I think, Barney," he said at last, "messy as it may be, we've got to do it. We've just landed a punch; it's time for another."

"How soon?"

"Right now. We're still cocked?"

Admiral Haymarket smiled grimly. "We are. I concur. Pass the word to activate. How long will it take?"

Pappas, as usual, had the answer where scheduling was concerned. "It should be all over in two hours, sir." The words were plain enough, but there was a grim decisiveness behind them.

The admiral drummed his fingers for two or three seconds on his desk. "Tell Colonel Durham," he directed. "This is one time I want the chaplain in; we can use all of the help we can get."

The man who called himself Carlo was blessed with his own form of protective coloration. He was short and dumpy. His face was undistinguished except for his eyes, which were small and hyperactive; he was always looking about him to detect what was going on, like an animal forced to exist in a hostile environment. Constant suspicion was part of his stock in trade; he could trust no one and by keeping that fact constantly in his mind he continued to survive. The only joy he found in life was in his work; he was a professional assassin and he liked to kill.

As he sat in his security office he waited, as he had waited more or less patiently for weeks, for his next assignment. The same lack of normal emotion which made him an efficient death machine kept him from being bored; he did what he was told and collected his pay—if he had any other concerns he kept them to himself. He had managed to make himself comfortable in the United States of America because his needs were few and public approbation was not one of them. He had enough men assigned to him to meet his requirements and, although he did not trust them, he knew that they were competent. He did not practice because his skills had long ago been developed to a very high point and they remained there. He would respond when called upon; until then he was content.

His working room had a simple desk which he did not

need, but it was a status symbol and he made use of it in a casual way. He was seated behind it, looking about the room he had carefully inspected thousands of times before, when the door was violently flung open and he found himself looking directly into the barrel of a gun.

Like a cat awakened from sleep, he was transformed into combat tension within the fraction of a second. Then he saw the face of the man who held the gun and he saw death. It was a face that belonged to someone as unyielding and trained as himself—the eyes told him that.

Carlo did not move; it was the first step of his counterattack. If he tried for his own weapon it would trigger the tense man in the doorway, but doing nothing might throw him a hair off-stride. His own eyes were fixed now, for a hair was all that he needed—he had seen the ends of guns before.

The man with the weapon motioned him to rise. Carefully Carlo did so. He knew every angle of the room, the exact position of every object that it contained; his opponent did not. He stood by his desk, deliberately looking helpless, as lethal as a poised cobra.

The man motioned him to come forward. He responded at exactly the right pace, and recalculated when the man with the gun retreated a step or two to keep him at a safe distance. He entered the hallway and turned right as he was silently directed. Then he walked slowly ahead, listening intently to the sounds behind him. There was a corner coming, and that would be his first point of defense.

When he reached it and turned, another man, and another gun confronted him. No one man armed with a single weapon could take him out of a building, but two, one in front and one behind, was another matter. But when they were in a single straight line, neither of the men opposing him could fire without the risk of hitting his partner. Like a computer he continuously remeasured the odds and every step that he took was a conscious decision.

The silent men who had taken possession of him were trained too—highly trained. Carlo obeyed them, second by second, and kept up the appearance of a bewildered, middle-aged man of no athletic capability whatsoever. In the past that deceptive demeanor had cost several other men their lives.

Then he became aware that there were more and he knew that they were a team. They were skilled and they had been sent, as he had been many times sent, and he knew that it was not all for him. His men were together in one room and there was no way that he could warn them—not without paying with his own life, and he had no intention whatever of doing that. His best hope now was that he was wanted for questioning, that they would try and detain him, keeping him alive in the meanwhile. That had been tried before, too, by people who had not known Carlo and by one or two who had, but the result had been the same in every case: they had not been able to hold him and he had left dead behind him when he had made his escape.

There was only one door to the room where his men were gathered, waiting as he had been himself for something to happen. Carlo could not see as it was burst open and two alert men charged in. He heard the shots that were fired and from their sound and number reconstructed what was taking place; his men were good and not enough challengers could get through the doorway to prevent some of his people from opening fire. That meant casualties on both sides, and possible confusion. He watched with concealed intensity for the first hint of diverted attention on the part of the two men who had him in possession, but their eyes did not move from him and their pace did not change.

In the rear yard of the building he and his men had been occupying Carlo felt the texture of the soil underneath his feet and appraised the strength and exact angle of the sunlight. He hoped that there would be enough brilliance to cause the men who had captured him to react to it, but if they did, they did not show it. He was backed against the wall and then his opponents stood one on each side of him, well away and where they could watch him directly while he would have to view them at an angle.

Things were not looking too good.

Then others began to come out of the building, men of the opposing team and his own men, for the moment overpowered and two of them visibly bleeding. One of the attackers had been shot in the arm, but he appeared to be ignoring that. It was his left arm, which meant that the procedure had been correct, but the aim too hasty.

There were nine men in the attacking team; himself and

twelve of those assigned to him opposed. The morale of his own men was bad; they were confused and not as alert as he was. But there were enough of them to provide confusing targets, and he still had three potent weapons concealed on his body.

The man with the wounded arm was the leader of the attackers. With a single gesture, he signaled that the seized men were to be lined up against the wall, on the opposite side of the doorway from Carlo himself. They were turned face inward, forced to spread their feet, and to lean forward until they depended for their balance on their hands resting against the brickwork. In that position they were expertly searched; Carlo turned his head and watched in the hope that his own captors would do the same, but the maneuver was not successful. He saw his men disarmed and sensed what was about to happen. He had no plan yet, but his racing brain was still weighing every possible factor, seeking, searching for the slightest opportunity.

When his men were all disarmed, they were turned and inspected, one at a time. One man from the capturing team looked into their faces and motioned three of them aside. Then Carlo knew: two of his men had been replaced since the day that he had disposed of the student underground cell; the three who had just been picked out had not been with him on that small operation. This was the revenge squad, not purely for that, of course, but to reply to Colonel Rostovitch. He, Carlo, was to be sacrificed to make good a simple power play. The futility of it hit him and for a bare instant his alertness was clouded.

He had himself back in hand almost instantly—that was the kind of mistake he was waiting for his captors to make. He could not afford to relax for the tiniest fraction of a second or he would pay with his life for a lost opportunity.

Then he heard the first words that had been spoken since he had been surprised in his office three minutes before. In his own language, or in one which he spoke fluently, he heard the death sentence pronounced. "This is for the students you killed. You will now die exactly as they did."

He saw the fright on the faces of his men, the despair, and the dull acceptance of the inevitable. Then the guns began to speak. The first of his men screamed and hit the ground. The scream had been training, but it did not for a moment divert the attention of the men who held their guns trained on him. Time was growing short now and he would have to make his move within the next several seconds.

Six of his men died before he could think of a thing; he knew that no bluff, no fake would work with his captors —they were not amateurs.

The seventh man dropped, his face a sudden mask of blood. Damning sweat broke out on Carlo's brow.

The eighth man died with his face twisted in agony and hate. The ninth was his best torturer, who preferred to vary the manner of his killings. As Carlo watched he was seized by the arms and held hard against the wall. Then the leader of the attacking team drew his own pistol, turned it around, and measured the butt end against the man's skull. Carlo did not care how his men died, but that showed that these men had unexpectedly good intelligence, for that was exactly how his man had chosen to kill the student turned over to him. The gun rose, the arm that held it was cocked back, then it crashed down with concentrated power. The man's head did not crack with the first blow and the movement had to be repeated. When the execution was over, only Carlo himself was left.

And then his concentration broke. The ability to maintain a razor edge in the face of every desperate emergency had saved him time and again, but he suddenly could not stand the sight of death. He turned to face the men who held him at gunpoint and knew that his own weakness was in his eyes. For fear was beginning to build inside him, sickening, debilitating fear he could not control.

Sweat stood out on his forehead, and his lips began to move. He had killed so many times himself he knew every aspect of men facing sudden violent death and he found them all within himself. His brain, his expertly trained reflexes, betrayed him, fear took command of him.

"And now you." He heard the words and he opened his mouth to protest. But it was dry and his tongue would not move. In one last, frenzied effort to regain control of himself he snapped his arm inside his coat to get his own weapon, but he was too late. He felt the bullets as they tattooed his abdomen, but the pain was nothing beside the fear that seized him, and in the grip of that fear he died.

CHAPTER TWENTY-THREE

Colonel Gregor Rostovitch received the news with a cold and tight-lipped understanding. The death of the man Carlo he had expected for some time; the rest of those who had been killed were of no special importance. What did matter was that he had been challenged on a face-to-face basis, that was the message and there was no mistaking it. It was also, remotely, a threat to his own person, and he understood that too. The world was full of people who wanted to see him dead and he did not care. But he had been challenged and that he knew would be to a finish. The high diver, and those who were associated with him, had asked for what they were about to receive.

His mind was clear as he planned his response. The people against him had tried terror, knowing that he was probably the greatest expert in the use of terror anywhere on the international scene. And behind him he had awesome military power. Against him he had a so far unseen foe, which made the game more interesting. Also against him he had the clock and the calendar. The conquest of America had been perhaps one of the greatest coups in history, but it had unexpectedly also proven to be one of the most costly. The government he had left behind him was growing increasingly unstable and uncertain; unless he could return home as the new premier within a fairly short time, there could be very serious consequences. The Actor had about run his course and, wily as he was, his performance was beginning to pale. Gregor Rostovitch knew that he badly needed a personal triumph of his own to build his stature up to an apex. Now he had been presented with the opportunity to achieve one, which accounted for the fact that he was not enraged in the least. Instead he began to lay his plans with the grim satisfaction of a gladiator who knows that no man living can stand up to him and that another contest for him will mean another sure kill.

Not long after the first light of the morning had thrown its blushes into the sky, a light aircraft sat down on the concealed landing strip that served the headquarters of Thomas Jefferson. The pilot paused just long enough to allow three people to deplane, then he was off again at very low altitude, skimming over the hills on what could have been a hunting reconnaissance or a rancher looking for strays from his herd.

Some twenty minutes after that Senator Solomon Fitzhugh was escorted into the reception foyer, such as it was, of the Thomas Jefferson headquarters. The facility had not been designed to receive many visitors, and minimum attention had been given to the usual amenities. Nevertheless Fitzhugh looked about him and took it all in.

Mrs. Smith came out to receive him. "Good morning, senator," she greeted. "I'm very sorry that it was necessary for you to get up so early."

"That's quite all right," he answered her gravely. "I am by nature an early riser."

She sat down and faced him informally. "Senator, I believe that it has been made clear to you that this facility, and everything that goes on here, is supersecret in the strictest sense of the term."

The senator nodded. "It has."

"And as an American patriot you have agreed that under no circumstances will you reveal anything whatever about its existence until such time as you have been given specific clearance, from this headquarters, to do so."

Again Fitzhugh nodded. "I have assumed that obligation, and I am grateful that at last someone describes me as a patriot."

"Very well, senator, then I have something to show you before anything else. We are not much given to ceremonials here, we are too heavily engaged in other matters, but we do have something. Please come with me." She opened a door and passed through.

Senator Fitzhugh rose and fell in behind his guide. When he had passed through the doorway he found himself in a simple room with no furniture whatsoever except for a single American flag standing in one corner. On the wall there were some pictures. Some fifty people, men and women, looked back at him from their portraits, each with a name posted underneath. He stopped when he saw the face of his son and read the name GARY FITZHUGH followed by the dates of his short life.

"The man who directs our whole operation ordered this," Mrs. Smith said. "We all come in here every little while to look and to remember. The President knows of it too; when this is all over a suitable memorial is going to be built in Washington."

Despite himself Fitzhugh felt a growing lump in his throat. He looked long at the features of his dead son and then at the picture of the slender, quiet-appearing brunette which was hung next. He read the name and then looked at his guide. "She was your daughter, I believe you said."

Mrs. Smith nodded. "Yes, senator, my only child. I cannot have any more."

The senator bowed his head. "I am very sorry," he said.

"And I also, senator. But they did not die in vain. You will learn more about that very shortly."

"I understand that I may be here quite some time."

"Yes, but perhaps not as long as you might expect. Things are rapidly coming to a head."

She opened another door and, indicating that he should follow, led him down a lengthy corridor which penetrated deep into the underground complex. Then she paused and looked into the conference room. "This is where the First Team meets," she told him. "It is equipped with very advanced and highly protected communications facilities and many other features. It is much superior to both NORAD and the underground SAC headquarters. One major difference is that there are no press tours."

"I can well understand that."

"Good. Please sit down and you will be served some breakfast."

The tribute to his son, along with the others, had moved Solomon Fitzhugh, and he had something to say. "Mrs. Smith, I am very keenly aware that all of this was built without the knowledge or consent of the Congress, but I can see why it had to be kept very secret."

He drew an encouraging response to that. "Senator, I

don't question the integrity of anyone in Congress, but your colleagues in the Senate and the House represent a great many different shades of opinion; there are many of them who we would not trust to be here now."

A door at the end of the room opened and Admiral Haymarket came in.

For a second or two Fitzhugh did not react; then he began to stare in almost stricken amazement. The admiral came toward him. "Good morning, senator," he said. "I regard this as a much happier occasion than our last meeting."

Fitzhugh took hold of the back of a chair and tried to clear his head of disbelief. "But I thought you dead and buried!"

The admiral nodded. "We went to considerable trouble to create that impression."

Fitzhugh's mind whirled and a desperate hope came to him. *"My son?"*

The admiral closed his eyes for a second and shook his head. "Sit down, Senator Fitzhugh, and let me have your breakfast brought in. We have eggs ready the way that you like them. This, at least, we can do for you."

"I . . . I am astounded," Fitzhugh said.

"I can appreciate that," the admiral said clearly. "I assumed command of this operation, senator, on the direct orders of the President. I have the documents here if you wish to see them."

Fitzhugh was still stunned. "That . . . won't be necessary."

"Good. Here is your ration, I believe." He waited while the senator's breakfast was set before him. Then he sat down easily and rested an arm across the back of the chair. "While you're eating, I have some information for you. Our enemies, and I believe you recognize them as such now, have been making fun of our diplomacy for years and ridiculing our genuine peace efforts. But when we get tough, they understand perfectly. You remember Kennedy's actions during the Cuban missile crisis."

"Yes." Fitzhugh was somewhat uncomfortable, but he ate his eggs and listened.

"Well, we got tough yesterday. We closed in on their murder team that killed your son and the other students.

Forgive my referring to it, but I think you'd want to know. We disposed of them."

"You mean that . . ."

The admiral nodded briskly. "Yes, senator. Included in the group were two professional torturers and a well-known assassin. He was personally responsible . . ."

The senator shut his eyes for a moment.

"They won't do it anymore."

The senator picked up a glass of orange juice in a hand that shook a little. "Thank you for telling me."

"Now, senator, another matter. In a major operation, to which we gave maximum attention for many weeks and in which many people risked their lives in very hazardous assignments, we arranged for the escape of one of our most potent FBM's—Fleet Ballistic Missile submarine, that is."

"I know of this."

"Of course. Very recently the enemy boasted to one of our people that the submarine had been sunk. Our best guess is that there is a forty percent chance that this may be so, but we aren't sure."

"Can't you find out?"

"Yes, but that would require her to send out a signal and thereby expose herself to additional risk. If we transmit to her and request a reply, the enemy will know and will be listening too."

"I see."

"Therefore we may be playing with a bust hand; we don't know if our hole card has been stolen or not."

"There's no time that the submarine is scheduled to report in?"

The admiral shook his head. "Her captain is under direct orders not to transmit any signal whatsoever unless directed, or under circumstances that don't pertain here."

Fitzhugh rubbed a hand across his face. "I still can't believe that you're alive and that I'm sitting here talking to you."

"Well, you are." The admiral let him take his time.

"I have read the address you prepared for me," the senator began, thinking aloud. "If the submarine *has* been sunk, then it would be pure suicide to deliver it."

"Precisely." Admiral Haymarket nodded his approval.

"But if there is no broadcast."

"Then we're right back where we started and the war goes on indefinitely."

"The war?"

"Yes, senator."

"You see no peace ahead?"

"Do you?"

Fitzhugh thought for a moment or two. "No," he said at last.

"There you have it. If you prefer not to go on the air, I'll understand and we do have other resources. There's a celebrated war hero from Hawaii in the Senate and if we can get hold of him . . ."

Fitzhugh lifted his hand. "I have no one left to me," he said. "Only the memory of my son. This is the second time that you've invited me to cut my throat. I may do it this time."

Admiral Haymarket made it as easy as he could. "Why don't we cut the tape," he suggested. "Then we'll hold it pending your final decision."

"All my decisions are final, admiral," Fitzhugh answered him. "I'll make the broadcast."

The videotape was done the same morning. Once he found himself facing the familiar broadcasting equipment, Solomon Fitzhugh assumed the manner that was internationally known; once more he was the wise, powerful, and sincere senior lawmaker who carried great weight and authority. He had to be believed; conviction rang from his every word. His performance was masterly and as the admiral watched on the monitor in his office he gave silent thanks that he had chosen the right man. If Solomon Fitzhugh said these things, and sounded as if he meant them, then it would hearten the whole nation and help immensely to bring things to a rapid climax. Speed, in moderation, was essential now: *Magsaysay* could not remain at sea indefinitely, if she was still afloat, and each day that passed made the enemy stronger in the United States.

When the senator had finished, he asked to see the admiral once more. When he was shown into Haymarket's office he sat down limply and ignored the cup of coffee that was placed before him.

"I've delivered your speech," he said. "Exactly as it was

written—that was my agreement and I have carried it out. What do you want to do with me now?"

The admiral looked at him and saw an aging man from whom much energy had been effectively drained out. It was not the speech that had done it, he knew; it was the pressure the man had been under, the grief, the agonizing reappraisal of his position, the defeat of the personal philosophy that had guided him, publicly and privately, for years. For the first time since he had known Solomon Fitzhugh he felt for him.

A teletype in the corner of the office began to clatter; the admiral got up and stood before it, waiting for the message to be completed. When the machine stopped he tore off the yellow paper and brought it back to his desk. He studied it carefully and then handed it to Fitzhugh. The senator adjusted his glasses and read:

MY WARMEST AND MOST SINCERE APPRECIATION TO A BRAVE, HONORABLE, AND DEDICATED AMERICAN. YOU HAVE BROUGHT GREAT CREDIT TO YOURSELF AND TO THE MEMORY OF YOUR SON.

POTOMAC

The senator knew without asking, but he allowed himself to have a small added satisfaction. "The signature . . ."

The admiral understood completely. "The President," he said. "He was notified and was watching."

"He is all right then?"

"Very much so."

"Is he here?"

Haymarket shook his head. "I trust you completely, senator, but you have no need to know."

"Of course."

Haymarket became more practical, and very considerate. "You will be our guest here for a while, sir, I believe that was explained to you before you came."

"Yes, admiral, it was."

"Then one of our people will look after you beginning immediately. It may please you to know that we have brought your man from Washington and he will be here shortly to take care of your needs for as long as you are with us."

Fitzhugh recovered a little. "That is most kind of you, admiral."

"Nothing at all, senator. As a matter of fact he might have been in an awkward position if we hadn't protected him and we deemed it only good judgment. Now, sir, let's hope to God that our submarine is still at sea."

"Amen," Fitzhugh said.

When the amenities were over and Senator Solomon Fitzhugh had been shown to the quarters he would have to occupy for the time being, a harder and more factual appraisal of his work began almost immediately. This was Ed Higbee's show, and to him the rest of the First Team gladly deferred. Higbee saw the brief tape three times and then individual parts of it once again before he ventured an opinion. "It isn't perfect, far from it," he told General Gifford, "but all things considered it is damn good. I'm going to use it as is. If we tried to patch out the few soft spots, or asked Fitzhugh to redo the whole thing, we'd probably lose more than we'd gain in the process."

"When are you going to spring it?" the general asked.

Higbee glanced at his watch. "No good news story is improved by needless delay; it goes out tonight. The cut-ins on the major networks are all set up, and you can take it from me that it's been one hell of a job. We won't get full coverage, and we'll undoubtedly get cut off in some places, but in the main we'll get through."

"You said you had a gimmick for building the audience."

Higbee nodded. "There are still a considerable number of air-raid sirens left operational in the major cities around the country, and in most of the smaller ones as well. Stan Cumberland worked out a system so that we can set most of them off about five minutes before air time. When the American public hears that racket, you know what's going to happen: everybody'll be running to turn on the TV or radio to find out what it's all about. Then on goes the Fitzhugh tape. I'm counting on a lot of the local führers to think that this is their own people's work and to let it ride. It was pretty carefully written with that in mind."

"You should reach a good percentage of the country," Gifford said. "I like the air-raid warning idea—if it works, it's good."

Higbee punched a cigarette into an ashtray. "I hope to reach as many as I can for their own good, but I'm really talking to the Actor; you understand that. And to Zalinsky and Rostovitch. Zalinsky may miss it, in the hospital, but he'll get the word."

"I think everyone concerned should see the tape before it goes out."

"Barney had the same idea; I'll screen it at this afternoon's meeting and outline the plans. Then, unless someone disagrees, we'll go."

The conversation stopped there, the men at the top of Thomas Jefferson had long ago cultivated the habit of leaving out unnecessary things that were mutually understood.

It seemed to Hewlitt that the air had suddenly become much sweeter to breathe. The tension that he had been living under for weeks had been lifted; now he no longer had to hold himself in continuous check, guarding every sentence that he spoke, every gesture that he made. All playacting was ended. He was under a new kind of cloud, but the danger that it represented was simply the hazard of getting physically caught. He could get the breaks or they could get him, but so long as he remained free the air was wonderful.

And he had Barbara with him. He remembered very keenly what she had said while she had been throwing things literally into her suitcase and he presumed that he was responsible. In fact he hoped to God that he was, because she was his girl and if anyone was going to get her pregnant he preferred that it be himself. He had no illusions that he was the first man ever to make love to her, as he had never pretended that she was the first girl with whom he had ever been in bed. Somewhere in the dim past Mrs. Grundy had run screaming up the flue and people had changed their thinking about such things.

Of course she could be made unpregnant, and perhaps that would be the thing to do, but that decision should be hers and no one else's. The occupying authorities had put out an edict about that, but he doubted very much if anyone paid any real attention to it except to see that some additional precautions were taken.

The movement of the members of the little ex-White

House party had been handled very smoothly indeed. A Helio Courier aircraft had picked them up out of an almost impossibly small field and had carried them a considerable distance at night and at very low altitude with the aid of terrain-avoidance radar. Later there had been a much faster aircraft on an unspecified kind of disguised business and then a Land Rover ride up to the mountain hideaway where Senator Solomon Fitzhugh had been housed. In that retreat there had been a blessed opportunity to bathe, to sleep, and to savor a fresh sense of freedom.

Percival did not accompany them past the point where the Courier aircraft had taken them on board. He had left them without explanations other than a very brief farewell. "I've got a great deal to do in a short time," he had said. After that he had shut the cabin door and waved once at them before he had disappeared into the darkness.

Hewlitt did not know when he would be summoned for his promised meeting with the First Team, but he kept himself as prepared as he was able. He was considerably relieved when his luggage was delivered to him with almost all of the essential things that had been in his apartment. Everything had been tossed in evident great haste, but Barbara obligingly pressed a few items for him along with her own clothes and restored his confidence in his ability to make a presentable appearance. When he met the First Team, he wanted to look like the man from the White House who had faced Colonel Rostovitch and had outbluffed him, even if only for a few minutes.

When Mrs. Smith came for him, he was ready. He rode beside her in the simple car she had brought and talked with her about relatively neutral topics during the considerable ride that followed. He noticed that she had modified her appearance somewhat; she was still very much the same person, but the chic, perfectly turned-out look that had characterized her in Washington was replaced by a far less sophisticated outward image. She had transformed herself into what appeared to be a properly dressed, well-mannered Midwestern housewife, one who had three children to care for and when she was not doing that, belonged to the church women's club and subscribed to the *Reader's Digest.* Her manner changed, too, to match her altered appearance; she was simpler in what she did and more matter-of-fact. It was Hewlitt's judgment that she had blended herself remarkably well into the environment in which she was apparently now living and, despite the fact that she was notably attractive, she could pass all but unnoticed almost anywhere.

"We could stop for lunch," she suggested. "I believe that it would be quite safe unless we had a particularly bad break. Or, if you prefer, we can keep going for another two hours or so."

"How about yourself?" he asked.

"It's immaterial to me."

"Then I suggest that we go on. I'm in favor of avoiding any risk that it isn't essential to take."

She drove on; Hewlitt looked at her profile and wondered whether or not she had been testing him with that bit of business. If she had wanted to stop to eat, she would have known the proper place and would have pulled in without consulting him.

It was close to three in the afternoon when they turned off onto a side road and were out of sight of the highway in a matter of a minute or two. Hewlitt rode on, awaiting what lay before him. When they reached the boarded-up entrance to an old mine shaft, he was slightly surprised to find a hunter with a gun who took over the car without comment as soon as they had gotten out. The man drove away farther into the mountains and they were alone, apparently in the midst of desolation.

He knew better very shortly thereafter. As soon as they were both inside Mrs. Smith dropped her provincial manner and became what could have been a highly efficient executive secretary. "You are expected, of course, Mr. Hewlitt," she told him, "but we have an operation under way right now and your interview may be delayed for a little while. I believe that all I need to tell you is that anyone you meet here you may and should talk to freely and with total candor."

"I understand," Hewlitt said. "This is the headquarters, I take it."

"Yes, it is, and the knowledge of its location is one of the most vital secrets we have."

"I understand," he told her. "You can rely on me."

She gave him the fraction of a smile. "If we had not been

totally convinced of that, you would be in Canada right now."

With that she left him and he was alone for perhaps half an hour. Then a man came into the room who at first glance seemed to be, like Percival, a trim but otherwise undistinguishable individual. Then he noticed that part of one of his hands was missing. That meant an industrial accident or possibly a combat injury; Hewlitt cataloged the fact away in his mind and waited for what the man had to say.

He came to the point without formalities. "Mr. Hewlitt, my name is Pappas. I'd like to talk to you about several things if you don't mind."

"Certainly."

"I understand that you had an interview with Colonel Rostovitch."

"Yes, sir, I did."

"And after you talked to him, you returned to your desk briefly and then left the White House in Miss Stoneham's company."

"That's right."

"Did Colonel Rostovitch accuse you of being a member of the underground?"

"Yes, his exact words to me were, 'You are an agent; as soon as I finish with you, you will be taken out and shot.' "

"You have a good memory, Mr. Hewlitt."

"Thank you; it's an asset that's helpful at times."

"I believe that. However, you were not shot."

"Fortunately, no."

"Colonel Rostovitch is not noted for relenting on promises of that kind. I would be very interested to know what you said or did to cause him to change his mind."

Hewlitt didn't know who this man was, but the manner in which he spoke implied authority—not forcefully, but in a very quiet practical way that suggested maximum capability. "The answer I believe is Amy Thornbush," Hewlitt said.

"Who is she?"

"I don't believe that she is anyone," he replied. "The first time that I talked to Mr. Zalinsky he asked me if I knew Amy Thornbush. I remembered the name. Later it was mentioned to me once more. Since I was certain that I had not met any such person, I considered it possible that it was some sort of a code."

"Please go on."

"When I met Colonel Rostovitch he said to me very positively, 'You have been sleeping with Amy Thornbush.' That narrowed the field immediately—either it meant Barbara Stoneham or it was a recognition signal. At least those were all the possibilities that occurred to me at that moment."

"There were no other young ladies who had favored you?"

"Yes, there were, but the colonel's method of speaking implied a steadily continuing relationship, and there was no one else who would come under that category."

"That's all you had to go on."

"Yes, sir, at that moment."

"What did you do?"

"I gambled; I had to. There was a possibility, of course, that Barbara Stoneham was also known by another name, but since the colonel was aware that I knew her as Barbara, he wouldn't logically have thrown the other name up to me if he had had her in mind."

"You reasoned that out."

Hewlitt shifted his position and looked again at the man who was interrogating him. "I can't honestly claim that, I didn't have that much time. I liked the other possibility better and I bet on it."

"How?"

"I said to him, 'And so have you.' If it was a recognition signal, I gave it back to him."

"In your opinion, Mr. Hewlitt, is that why he let you go?"

"Yes, Mr. Pappas, it is. I realized that he could check up and determine within a very short time if I was in any way a member of, say, an enemy underground organization in this country, but it did buy me enough time to get out of the White House and into Percival's hands. Do you know Percival, sir?"

Pappas nodded. "Yes, I know him. I am fully aware of what took place after you and Miss Stoneham reached the safe house."

"I'm reassured that you are," Hewlitt said.

"One more point: were you able simply to walk out of the White House without any interference from the guards or anyone else?"

"Yes, sir. Major Barlov was very helpful there."

"Please explain that."

"Colonel Rostovitch said to me, 'Meanwhile I give you a message; deliver it.' I said that I would as soon as I was able. Then he said, 'We have devices of which you do not dream. We have used them. Inform them that their submarine, the one named for the Filipino traitor and that has the high diver on board, was found and sunk by us early this morning.' "

Hewlitt noted at once that Pappas paid particularly close attention to that answer, especially the latter part of it.

"That is a reasonably exact quotation of his words?"

"I believe, Mr. Pappas, that it is verbatim."

"Excuse me for a moment, if you please."

Hewlitt was alone for some time. He ran over in his mind the interview he had just had and reassured himself that he had quoted Rostovitch accurately. He was not likely to forget a speech like that, particularly with the references to the Filipino traitor—which Ramon Magsaysay had most certainly not been—and the high diver, which was most likely another code designation.

When Pappas came back he had with him another man; he was not unduly tall, but his shoulders were exceptionally wide and the tautness of his physique could not be concealed by the slacks and sport shirt that he wore.

There were no introductions; the newcomer simply said, "Mr. Hewlitt, would you mind repeating to me the exact words of the message that Colonel Rostovitch gave to you?"

Since the other two men were standing up, Hewlitt got to his own feet. "Certainly not. The message was, 'We have devices of which you do not dream. We have used them. Inform them that their submarine, the one named for the Filipino traitor and that has the high diver on board, was found and sunk by us early this morning.' "

"That is verbatim?"

"I'm certain of it, sir."

"Did you gain any other impression from his manner?" Pappas asked.

Hewlitt turned toward him. "Only that he was trying to impress me with his authority and the meaning of his message. Of the news he was giving me."

"Did you believe him?" the muscular man asked.

Hewlitt had not decided whether he liked this new man or not, he seemed a trifle peremptory. The fact that he had not as yet introduced himself could have been responsible for that impression.

"Not entirely, no," he answered. "In the first place Magsaysay was a distinguished patriot; a traitor betrays his own country. One untruth in a statement casts doubt on all of the rest. Then that bit about the high diver sounded like another code device to me—that's just a guess, of course. As to the submarine part, I couldn't evaluate that because I simply didn't have enough data to go on."

The new man relaxed visibly in his manner. "All this is very interesting, Mr. Hewlitt, including your opinions. Apparently you displayed excellent resourcefulness and your point about President Magsaysay is very well taken. As it happens, I'm the high diver, but you were right about Amy Thornbush and that was where it counted."

Hewlitt felt much relieved. "Thank you, sir. Pardon my asking, but I was told that I was to meet the First Team on this trip. Am I still programmed to do that?"

"You will," Pappas promised.

An air of expectation prevaded the conference room during the showing of the Solomon Fitzhugh tape. Those who saw it knew that Ed Higbee had already given it his approval, but when it was over they did not hesitate to express their own opinions. The consensus was very strong that the senator had done his best and that he would be believed as much as anyone who could be put on the air. That was enough for the admiral; in one of the few easy decisions he had made he O.K.'d the program to be aired that same evening.

"Some other things," he told the people around the table. "We have had some intelligence input from Europe that, in the main, tends to refute Rostovitch's claim that *Magsaysay* has been sunk. Part of it is reverse English—simply the fact that if they had done it, they would have trumpeted about it more loudly than they have. Hewlitt, the White House interpreter, is in here now and both Ted Pappas and Walt have interviewed him. Ted, what do you think?"

Major Pappas was ready as usual. "He's nobody's fool; based on what he told me, and he wasn't boasting in any way, I'm inclined to believe that he did outmaneuver Rostovitch at their one meeting. At least he didn't panic and blow his top, and that in itself is notable. One other thing: Rostovitch definitely told him, according to his story, that the high diver was on board *Magsaysay*. In other words, he was still unaware that she put in at Wainwright or that Walt was back on the job with us. So he missed one trick at least."

"Did you get anything else from the interpreter?" General Gifford asked.

"I liked his candor and the way he handled himself. I'm inclined to think he's pretty good—for an amateur."

"We might make a pro out of him if we need to," Colonel Prichard said. "I have a thought in the back of my mind and if it works out, he could be very useful."

"I suspect that I have the same idea," the admiral said, "but we don't have the time to go into it now. What I want next is to grease the machinery for a maximum feedback on tonight's broadcast. The more we know how well it goes over, the better we'll be able to set up the next moves."

Ed Higbee responded to that. "We've already got a very good net spread. I should be able to start giving you reactions minutes after it's over. There are a lot of good newspapermen in this country, and many of them are with us. They'll get the story."

"Fine," the admiral concluded. "We might as well catch some rest, because it's going to be a busy night."

The air-raid sirens that had been quietly hooked up at a hundred different control points began to sound at eleven minutes after ten, Eastern Standard Time. They did not all come on at the same time, because there was no need for a national hookup and establishing one would have entailed enormous difficulties. By individual timing they all responded within a time frame of thirty seconds, which was more than satisfactory as far as the plans that Ed Higbee had laid were concerned. By the hundreds of thousands, by the millions, Americans throughout the country turned on their radios and TV sets to find out what was going on. On many of the radio stations they were told to tune the proper channels on TV; the coverage was far from complete, but it was wide enough to insure the fact that the whole country would know what had happened before the night was over.

On the selected channels the regular programming disappeared, often in mid-sentence. It was a considerable technical achievement that the tubes remained blank for only a few seconds before an off-screen voice cut in. "We interrupt this program to bring you a special news broadcast." Those most potent of all words in broadcasting guaranteed attention; most of the persons who heard them thought that it was the enemy talking, but they listened to find out what new disaster was about to befall them.

The first surprise came when the unseen announcer followed with, "Speaking for the government of the United States, Senator Solomon Fitzhugh." Two seconds later the image of the white-haired legislator came onto millions of screens.

He looked into the camera and spoke. "My fellow Americans, I have news for you this evening of the greatest importance; I have been chosen to bring it to you because my sponsors feel that you will know my face and my voice."

Hundreds of occupying enemy personnel heard those words and assumed that the renowned peacemaker was once again allowing himself to be used. They knew the importance of propaganda and their own mastery of it; where they were directly concerned, they saw to it that the show remained on the air.

"Some months ago," Fitzhugh continued, "the United States of America was overcome by a superior force. Superior in numbers, in the timing of its operations, and in the degree of surprise with which it struck. The President capitulated, since the outcome was inevitable, in order that the loss of life and property could be kept to a minimum. I genuinely believe that tens of thousands of you are alive to hear me now because of that decision."

The senator appeared to glance about him for a moment, which was one of his familiar histrionic tricks, then he looked again steadily from the tube. "Our surrender was not complete, however. Actually we did not surrender as such; hostilities could be resumed at any time. Now they have been."

Those words caught his audience and guaranteed that the attention being given to him was at a maximum.

"Some time before the war broke out, our government

established a supersecret organization headed by the most competent and dedicated people that the President could find. The purpose of this organization, which was code-named Thomas Jefferson, was to provide a basis of resistance in the event that this nation were to be overthrown or occupied by force. It has been continuously active since that tragic event did take place.

"A few weeks ago it arranged to seize back from the enemy a completely armed and equipped ballistic missile nuclear submarine; this extremely potent weapon is now at sea in the hands of the United States Navy. It is carrying more than one hundred and sixty nuclear warheads and is capable of attacking any target of military importance anywhere in the world. The power of this single submarine is overwhelming. It can completely erase almost any nation on earth.

"At present the United States government, as represented by the Thomas Jefferson organization, has no intention of ordering this submarine to fire, for such an action would mean a fearful loss of life. But, on behalf of the President, whose spokesman I now am, I am authorized to say that this ship *will* fire, against the homeland of our enemies, unless certain conditions are met. Here they are:

"There shall be a gradual withdrawal of the occupying forces now in this country; they shall begin leaving as soon as practical and shall return home at approximately the same rate that they came over. Those who may wish to seek political asylum here will be given consideration.

"Through orderly process, and without bloodshed, the government of the United States shall be returned to the people. After this has been accomplished, we will be prepared to enter into negotiations with our former enemies to establish a new era of peaceful understanding and mutual cooperation. We pledge ourselves to extract no reprisals. Let this conflict be resolved between intelligent people who have no wish to destroy each other. We now have the power to carry out such destruction, but we have no desire to use it.

"It is fearful to think that in a matter of minutes we could wipe out almost every significant military facility that our present enemies possess and millions of people at the same time. We could lay waste to their entire country with nuclear salvos that would deliver ten or more separate warheads at virtually the same moment. Some might be stopped, but some surely would get through. And with each such salvo, the resulting destruction would be overwhelming, the loss of life staggering. This force we pray to God we will not have to use. But if the terms I have been directed to spell out are not met, then use it we will until they are. Thank you and goodnight."

Almost immediately through the nation, from coast to coast, in great cities and small communities, Americans talked excitedly about the broadcast and told those who had not heard what had been said. The lights burned long into the night. In some areas there was minor violence and the men of the occupying forces for the most part wisely remained out of sight. It was a turning point, the first great dawning of hope that all was not permanently lost. People openly wept, and a great many sought the sanctuary of their churches. Impromptu services were organized, on street corners and in cathedrals.

In the synagogues the sounds of thanksgiving were heard and then all was still once more. For the enemy force was fearfully powerful and one single submarine was all that challenged it. It was well that in that time of great emotional feeling only a very small handful of Americans knew that there was a good chance that the U.S.S. *Ramon Magsaysay* was manned only by a crew of dead men and that she lay rusting somewhere on the bottom of an unnamed Arctic sea.

CHAPTER TWENTY-FOUR

There was not a resident of Washington who did not know that he was sitting on top of a time bomb. The enemy operated from Washington and his presence there was in constant, inflexible evidence. The challenge to his power, and his authority, could be met with submission, but the people of Washington did not expect that. They had seen too much, and had heard too much more, to believe in any such utopia. The enemy would answer, they knew that, and the only question that held them in suspense was made up of three parts: how, when, and where.

Colonel Rostovitch did not leave them long in doubt. He had anticipated, very closely, what his opposition would do, and when the message did come, his response was planned and ready. The operational orders had been given out; his people had been alerted. All of them had been carefully chosen for their work and down to the last man none of them wanted in any way to cross, or even displease the fearsome man who was now effectively in charge of the country.

All during the following day announcements were made over every radio and TV station broadcasting to the general public that the answer to the Thomas Jefferson ultimatum would be given that evening at seven. Throughout the country some few dared to hope, but none in Washington. At a little after ten in the morning a squad of men sped through the streets toward Senator Fitzhugh's home. With speed and expert technique they set it afire and burned it to the ground; before midafternoon the brick walls that had remained standing after the blaze had been knocked down. His office, too, was systematically gutted and the woman who had served as his secretary for some fourteen years was seized together with her husband. More enemy personnel than had ever been seen before patrolled the streets;

people stayed in their homes. Those who had gone to work slipped away and came home early. The time bomb that was Washington ticked on toward its inexorable deadline.

In the hospital Feodor Zalinsky continued to receive the careful medical attention that his condition merited. Several times messengers came to his room, but he summoned none and required only that the television set with which he had been provided be kept continuously on. He was still in considerable pain and his recuperation was progressing more slowly than had been expected.

The White House staff kept as far from the Oval Office as possible and, when they had to go anywhere, they walked as quietly as they were able. Not everyone in the city knew the name of Colonel Gregor Rostovitch, but those who did trembled. With agonizing deliberation the hands of clocks throughout the capital marked the slow passage of time and measured off the hours and minutes remaining before the answer would be given.

When the time at last came near, in every home, apartment, and place of business the TV sets were on and glowing, the radios were set to hear what would be said. Regular TV programming was suspended, only test patterns appeared on the screens with, in many cases, the faces of a clock cut in at one corner. The tension mounted, minute by minute, as people stopped talking and waited. What Fitzhugh had said had been told and retold until it was already threadbare; what the enemy would say became all paramount, and nothing else, no matter what it might be, appeared to matter.

At precisely the time that had been set, the face of the enemy came on the screen of the TV sets. It was a specific face that few Americans had ever seen before. They did not know who he was, but they understood that he was a spokesman, nothing less and nothing more. His English was stilted and forced, but painfully accurate and precise. He enunciated clearly and not a word that he spoke could be misunderstood in any way.

"It is not necessary that much time be consumed by this matter," he said. "I speak on behalf of the greatest military power that the world has ever seen, a military power which is intact and of which the people of the United States have seen and experienced only the smallest fraction. It is a power which could utterly destroy, to the last tiny hamlet, this entire former nation in a matter of minutes. In such an attack no one would survive, no single structure would be left standing. The area that was once the United States would become a barren, radioactive, desert wasteland—and it would remain so as a lesson to the rest of the world until such time as we chose to make use of it.

"Yesterday a misguided, senile, totally incompetent former member of the humiliated American government dared to make a statement at the command of his masters. He will be dealt with. He dared also to lay down certain conditions to which we were supposed to yield. Those conditions will be met, but not as this utter fool proposed to us.

"He told you about a submarine which was supposed to be in the hands of a nonexistent navy. If you believed him, do not do so any longer. I told you of the power of our military forces; for us it was a simple exercise to find this submarine long before she reached even close to the range of our homeland. She was sunk many days ago and the bodies of some of those who attempted to take her to sea have been recovered and examined. Their names will be published.

"You have no submarine at sea, you have nothing but memories of an imperialistic, fascist, decadent government which was destroyed by the vengeful people from without and within. From now on the people will rule and we are the people.

"Hear this now carefully; there does exist an underground which, over a period of several months, has managed through desperation to kill a half dozen of our people. They, the people who comprise this conspiracy, will now surrender. They will do so at once. If they have not done so by this exact time tomorrow, and have not handed over the place where they are living, we will shoot one thousand hostages who have already been chosen. We will begin to collect them very shortly. For each day that the surrender is delayed, an additional one thousand will be shot. Their bodies will be left to rot and it will be forbidden to touch them until they decay."

Suddenly the speaker's face flamed into a fanatical intensity. "When ten thousand have died this way, if the total surrender of the imperialistic underground is not complete to the last man, we shall resume our nuclear testing and your cities will serve as our practice areas. This now lies ten days away. We will listen to no rebuttal, no counterproposals; we will speak no more of this matter until the surrender has been completed. If it is not completed by tomorrow night the first thousand hostages will die. You will now submit, totally and absolutely, to our will, or you will not survive. That is all."

Admiral Barney Haymarket listened, his chin resting in the palm of his hand. When it was over he turned to the assembled men around the table and asked, "Any comments?"

After a few seconds Walter Wagner responded. "I see two possibilities. One: get to their top people and hit them individually with everything we've got. That's the long shot—it might work but I have serious doubts. The other is obvious."

"Carl?" the admiral asked.

General Gifford was still thinking. "It was about what I expected. I can contribute one thing: they aren't bluffing. They couldn't because they have set too close a deadline, they'd have to call their own hand in less than twenty-four hours from now. If we pull a desperation operation and release their hostages, they will simply seize more and shoot them at random."

The admiral was in deep thought. "No one man has the authority to fire a nuclear weapon from a silo, an FBM, or any other place other than the President," he said. "I want to tell you all this now: I have been talking to the President based on what I expected to hear and he has authorized me to order *Magsaysay* to fire when and as I see fit. I'm not ducking responsibility—I've never done that in my life—but I believe any such order, if it is given, should come from us all."

Ed Higbee answered that. "Barney, you know that all of us will back you up in anything you think necessary. You've got the military experience to weigh the factors involved, and that's what we need here because this is a military crisis."

"Tell me this," Haymarket said. "If I do order *Magsaysay* to fire one missile, targeted as we have previously approved, do you think that it will influence the Actor to overrule Rostovitch? What will the public reaction be?"

Higbee thought. "Let's say that ten nuclear warheads hit on the other side, or assume that they shoot down four and the other six get through."

"Six, then."

"It will answer all claims that *Magsaysay* has been sunk. It will put us back into the poker game."

"You're forgetting something: the enemy knows perfectly well whether or not we have a ship at sea. We don't know, but they do."

The discussion stopped for a moment and there was a full five seconds of silence. It was broken by the unhurried voice of Major Pappas. "Gentlemen, we have an offer. I have been talking with Hewlitt, the White House interpreter whom we brought in here. He forecast quite accurately what we have just heard."

"That wasn't too hard," General Gifford said, "but what did he offer?"

"That if something of this nature was proposed, and we can get him back to Washington in time, he will talk to Zalinsky in the hospital."

Again there was a brief silence. Then Walter Wagner spoke. "That makes him a pretty gutsy guy. We could get him back all right, and get him into the hospital, but the guarantee stops there."

"Do you think he meant it, Ted?" the admiral asked.

"Yes, sir, I do, or I wouldn't have mentioned it."

"Let's get him in here."

"Now?"

"Right now. I'd like to see how he conducts himself."

Major Pappas got up and left the room. When he came back very shortly with Hewlitt, he made minimum introductions. "Mr. Hewlitt, this is the group that is generally known as the First Team. Admiral Haymarket is the commander."

Hewlitt looked at the well-known face and addressed himself to him. "I'm very happy to see, sir, that the reports of your death were grossly exaggerated."

"Thank you. Mr. Hewlitt, Major Pappas has just told us that prior to the broadcast you offered to return to Washington to talk with Mr. Zalinsky. You heard the speech?"

"Yes, sir."

"Does your offer still stand?"

"Yes, sir."

"Mr. Hewlitt, you had one good look at Colonel Rostovitch, which is more than I can say myself. What do you think of him?"

"Are you asking me, sir, if I think that he will carry out his threats?"

"Essentially, yes."

"Then I think that he will. He's as mad as Hitler."

"And as dangerous?"

"Yes."

"And anti-Semitic?"

"Violently so, I understand."

"How about Mr. Zalinsky?"

"I am a little more confident of my appraisal of him, sir, since I know him quite well. He is tough, extremely so in fact, but he is also a human being. And he has a first-class brain."

"You recall how he shot Major Landers."

"I'm not likely to forget it, sir; I was present when it happened. I would have killed him at the time with my bare hands if I had had the opportunity. Later I learned that Rostovitch wanted to get hold of Bob, and Zalinsky at least spared him that."

"How much authority do you think Zalinsky has right now?"

Hewlitt took his time before he attempted to answer that one. "I can't honestly say, sir, but I can offer one thought. I personally don't trust him for a moment, but I believe that he will see reason a lot faster than Rostovitch. And, despite his illness, don't count him out."

"In your opinion," Ed Higbee asked, "do you think that he can handle Rostovitch?"

"That's a very tall order, sir, but I would guess that in a showdown he could give him one hell of a fight. If he couldn't stop him, he could at least slow him up considerably."

"That may be the key," the admiral said. "We'll look into that. Thank you very much for joining us."

Hewlitt took his dismissal with good grace. As he left the room he wondered how many other Americans had stood before this same board. Not very many, he judged, and he had seen their faces. He knew Pappas by name and the secret that Admiral Haymarket was alive and the active commander. That, he decided, was more than enough for one day.

It was an hour later when Major Pappas came to see him once more. "Mr. Hewlitt," the major said. "We may take a very long chance on you; if we do, you may have to take an equally long one on us."

"Can you clarify that?"

"I intend to. As of this moment you know more than we dare to let the enemy find out. Principally, you know the location of this facility, something that we must keep secret at all costs. We trust you, you must know that by now; but if you were to be captured, you could be made to talk. You understand how I mean that."

"Entirely," Hewlitt responded. "I've been thinking along the same lines myself. If I were to return to the Washington area, I would represent a considerable risk."

Pappas sat down on the arm of a chair. "I'm glad that you see it so clearly. Since you do, here is the proposition. We propose to position you back close to the Washington area. If things develop so that we feel we need you to talk to Zalinsky, we will pick you up and smuggle you into the hospital where he is. After you have talked to him we will do everything humanly possible to get you out again. We expect to be successful in that, but we can't guarantee it."

Hewlitt saw the rest and understood. "If you can't, you won't permit me to be captured, is that it?"

Pappas nodded. "That's it."

Hewlitt thought. "Actually it would probably be the better way."

"That's how we saw it too. Rostovitch would never let you get away from him alive, and you might have a rough time of it along the way."

"How about your people?"

"For the most part they don't know certain of the vital facts that you do now."

"It would be quick, I take it."

"Instantaneous, and only as an absolute last resort."

Hewlitt considered the matter one more time. "It seems fair enough to me," he said.

Pappas got back onto his feet. "Then we'll ship you out pretty fast, but you'll have time for a good meal first if you don't linger over it. Personally I think you've earned it."

"Thank you, major. I'll try not to let all of you down."

"You won't do that. Come on, Walt is going to join us for dinner. You'll find him quite an interesting person."

The collecting of hostages began very early the following morning. As the intelligence reports of what was going on began to come in in increasing numbers, it became apparent that it was not an impromptu operation; people were not simply picked up off the streets or taken from their homes. A master list had been prepared and it was being put to use.

Among those taken as hostages were a certain Reverend Mr. Jones, his wife, Doris, and their son, Greg; their ministrations to Jews departing the country had been duly noted and their names had been entered as among those most suitable to be shot.

In the Oval Office of the White House Colonel Rostovitch watched the reports that were flowing across his desk and was satisfied. He had before him a list of the men who would be the executioners; each name that appeared was fully qualified for the task. He knew all of them either personally or by reputation; deliberately he deferred giving himself the pleasure of making the final choices from the list. He did not want to have too many of them; it would be better if the show could be prolonged on the nation's television screens so that the impact would be cumulative. In simple numbers one thousand persons was a statistic; seeing that many die, six or seven at a time, would serve to impress on every viewer the absolute authority and uncompromising ruthlessness of the program. For one thing was totally clear in Gregor Rostovitch's mind: that the side that was the harder and more unyielding always won. It had been that way when the French had been defeated, after eight years, in Indo-China. They had defeated themselves because their enemy would not yield. The Communist forces inspired by Ho Chi Minh had been inflexible, had followed the doctrine of talk, talk, fight, fight, and had eventually won the day. Every single one of the one thousand would die, publicly, and the executions would not stop unless the surrender message was received from Thomas Jefferson. And there would be an additional thousand the next day, and one thousand more the next. . . .

When he received word that a deeply distraught father had offered to die in place of his son, he brushed it aside. He issued a terse order that there would be no substitutes; in addition if any guard permitted a detainee to commit suicide, he would take that person's place.

The message to him from Admiral Haymarket and the First Team reached him shortly after nine-thirty.

Rostovitch, White House, Washington, D.C.

Final warning. If all hostages not released before 5 P.M. *this evening,* Magsaysay *will fire Poseidon multiple-warhead nuclear missile at your homeland. Estimate casualties minimum three million. Firing time nineteen hundred. If no response from you, second round will follow precisely at twenty-one hundred. If return fire received,* Magsaysay *will release greatest concentrated firepower in world history on irrevocable orders to destroy your nation. Your other enemies will finish up the job if anything remains. If this cannot be avoided, so be it.*

THOMAS JEFFERSON

Admiral Haymarket sat at the head of the table, where he had been sitting for the past several hours, getting up only to relieve himself and then returning at once. The First Team sat with him in continuous consultation, digesting the reports that came in, watching every move with total and intense concentration. Major Pappas kept his charts up to date before him and supplied data as they were required. When the message had gone off to the colonel he duly logged it and then posed a question to which he already had the answer. He double-checked everything as a matter of routine.

"Sir, you have final and absolute authority from the President?"

"Affirmative," Haymarket answered.

"Does Commander Nakamura fully understand that you are so empowered?"

"He does."

"He will then definitely respect the order to fire."

"He will. He is at sea for that purpose and he knows it."

"And technically the firing requirements have all been met."

"That is absolutely affirmative, Walt was there when it was checked out."

"According to the Navy regs," Wagner said, "I was not permitted to witness the actual check, but it was run and the captain told me without equivocation that he is fully prepared to fire and will do so upon receiving the orders from us."

"That being the case," Pappas said, still with no emotion in his voice, "I now recommend, sir, that you raise *Magsaysay* and pass the necessary first order to fire. If the enemy hears us, so much the better."

"Will she acknowledge?" Higbee asked.

The admiral answered him carefully and exactly. "If for any reason she cannot follow the order, then she will so advise us at a precise interval of time after we contact her. If she can, then she will give no response. Her position shortly before firing is extremely critical information. At the moment only General Gifford and I know where she is, other than the members of her crew. Two of us have to know in case anything should happen to me."

"Have you communicated with her?"

Once again the admiral was very careful with his words. "No, Ed, not recently. Two messages have been sent, but no replies have been received. I stress that none would have been given except in case of malfunction. We have a schedule for reporting such information. Our listening watch has been uninterrupted and she has not put out a thing."

"Pardon me, Barney, but like Ted I want to hear everything that is vital at least twice. If we send a signal to her, will she receive it?"

"Nothing is ever absolutely certain, Ed, with the usual exceptions, but it is as close to one hundred per cent as our best technology can make it. I will say this: she knows what is going on, she positively will be listening, our signal strength can reach her where she is with absolute ease, and her reception equipment is redundant several times over with independent power sources and all supportive gear."

"I then second Ted's recommendation that you notify her of your intention to fire."

The admiral looked around the table. "Gentlemen, you now know how Harry Truman felt when he faced the decision whether or not to release the bomb against Hiroshima. I want your individual votes: do we or don't we back up our message to Rostovitch. Shall I order *Magsaysay* to fire?"

"Yes," General Gifford said. "In your absence I would give that order."

"Hank?"

"Go," Colonel Prichard responded, "and may God help us."

"Ted?"

"Yes, it's down to the wire."

"Ed?"

"Agreed, we go."

"Stanley?"

"Is there any visible alternative?"

The admiral shook his head. "None of which I am aware."

"I just wanted to ask to make absolutely sure. Fire."

"Walt?"

"The issue is already decided, sir, and there's no question about it. I know Rostovitch better than any man here. Our hides won't satisfy him; he will keep this country in continuous terror and bloodshed for, at the least, months to come. That's the real consideration."

A message came in from Philadelphia. The units there volunteered to surrender themselves as the Thomas Jefferson personnel; they had enough supportive gear and communications equipment to make it look good. It would save the main operation. Acceptance was urged.

"As long as this country can produce men and women like that," the admiral said, "I'm going to fight for them with everything that I've got." He pressed a button before him and an aide came in. "Prepare a signal to *Magsaysay*," he directed. "First order to fire. Do you know the details?"

"Yes, sir. Will you please personally review the message, sir, before it is sent."

The admiral nodded. "I will. That's required and I know it—I made the rule."

"Yes, sir."

When the man had gone the admiral asked one more thing. "How about Hewlitt, the interpreter? I haven't heard about that."

Ted Pappas responded. "He was positioned, sir, a short while ago. Mark has him in tow. He reports that Hewlitt is calm and ready."

"Good. When shall we put him in?" He looked toward Ed Higbee.

The former journalist glanced at the clock. "Anytime between now and two-thirty this afternoon; after that it would be too late. Let Mark call the shot; he's got to handle the operational end."

"So ordered," the admiral said.

As he moved about through the rooms and corridors of the White House Major Barlov revealed no changes in his demeanor—he remained a disciplined officer well qualified to hold a field grade assignment and to carry the responsibilities assigned to him. Many of the White House regular staff were at pains to avoid him, which suited the major perfectly; it was precisely what he most wanted them to do. The two secret service agents who had been part of the Hewlitt-Stoneham cell continued to watch his movements closely and to report their findings through fresh channels of communication which had been set up for the purpose. It was a high tribute to the major's level of efficiency that not once, even for a single moment, did he betray himself in any way.

Although Rostovitch was, for the time being at least, sitting in the Oval Office, Barlov knew that the real center of his operations would still be in his own headquarters and that he had no intention of moving them. Zalinsky was not out of things yet and Rostovitch would keep a door open through which he could make his retreat if such a temporary expedient became necessary. Barlov was still in full charge of his own department, but when his telephone rang and he learned that a newly captured prisoner was to be brought shortly to the White House to be interviewed by Rostovitch there, he knew at once that there had been a significant change in the signals.

With cool composure he appraised the situation and tried

to guess the identity of the person in custody. Within a few seconds he arrived at a conclusion and issued some orders. Then he made a phone call of his own and inquired about the nondelivery of some wanted supplies.

The first small group of demonstrators materialized outside the White House before another half hour had passed. No great stir marked their arrival, but the major sent a man to watch them nonetheless. Pesently others came, so that when a car pulled up with the prisoner and his captors, the line of marchers was already of sizable proportions. Silently the major gave thanks that the Americans, who had never been too well known for their skill in such matters, were proving efficient this time.

Barlov went himself to receive the prisoner. It was not the person he had anticipated, nor the most likely alternate; this meant that the demonstration being staged outside might be futile and a trump card had been wasted. For that the major blamed himself, but at the same time he knew that the bet he had made had been right and that the odds had been with him.

But if the prisoner had been brought directly to be seen by Rostovitch himself, then despite appearances he was probably someone of consequence. Barlov wasted no more time in conjecture. "We will take him," he announced coldly. "He will be held and produced for examination on the colonel's order."

The man in charge of the small detachment shook his head. "We must take him to Colonel Rostovitch ourselves."

"That is impossible," Barlov reported. "The rules on White House security are rigid and no exceptions are permitted for any reason whatsoever. We will take the prisoner; the colonel will be notified at once."

The major's rank insured his victory in the small contest; he summoned three of his men and watched approvingly as they took over with convincing authority. "When the colonel is through with him you will be notified," Barlov said. "We will await his pleasure." He gestured that the prisoner was to be taken away.

Outside, the leader of the demonstration knew that he and his people were taking a considerable chance. Protests against the occupying authorities were not allowed; his group had been summoned because a diversion was urgently needed and one had to be put on even at great risk. He did not know the purpose; the instructions he had been given and had passed on to his people had been explicit: their conduct was to be nonviolent and peaceful, giving the enemy the minimum excuse to arrest them. In all probability, he had been told, he and his people would be ordered to break up and clear out, but if there were no conspicuous leaders, it could possibly end there. No resistance was to be offered.

Only one thing had not been foreseen. His full group had been on the job for almost fifteen minutes, but it was still unaccountably growing. At least fifty people in the line of march were not known to him and more were joining them every minute. The placard he held himself read: WE PETITION EQUAL RIGHTS FOR JEWS. It was deliberately mild and in a cause that was centuries old, but it had not been conceived of as being a popular rallying point. Perhaps it was, or perhaps it was simply a case of frustrated Americans seeing a cause and wanting desperately to be part of it; but whatever the motivation, recruits were arriving in a steady stream.

By that alchemy through which people know what is going on without possessing any visible sources of information, more and more came to march silently up and down the sidewalk on Pennsylvania Avenue until their number was more than three times what had been planned.

"Let me carry the card for a while," someone said to the leader and took the handle away from him.

"It could be dangerous," the organizer warned.

The other man became confidential. "I don't think so. You know about the submarine. I don't care how much power they've got, they can't take what she can dish out and you know it."

The man in charge of the demonstration understood—Americans were finding heart and they wanted to be part of the resistance too. He only hoped, fervently, that in their eagerness they wouldn't push things completely out of hand.

When the coded knock came on the door of the Oval Office, Rostovitch barked, "In!" and looked up for a moment. The sound had told him who it was and that his business was more than casual. "Well?" he demanded.

"Another of the underground agents has been caught," Barlov reported. "Your orders were that all such matters were to be reported to you personally at once."

"Correct," Rostovitch chopped. "A man?"

"Yes."

"Where do you have him?"

"Directly outside, in case you wish to see him. Your people delivered him to us for that purpose."

"Good. What is that commotion going on outside?"

"A meaningless demonstration; we will take care of it. Please do not trouble yourself about it."

Rostovitch put one hand over a telephone. "You require help?" he asked.

Barlov quickly shook his head. "We will handle it; that is our job." His voice was unexpectedly hard; he wanted it clearly understood that he knew his business.

That pleased Rostovitch. With the next thought his eyes brightened; a captured enemy agent could be made to supply information and the time for that was never better. With a gesture of his left arm he indicated that the man was to be brought in.

Three of Barlov's men were controlling him; they held him, one on each side, while a third kept watch with a drawn pistol. They almost literally threw the prisoner into a chair, then the man with the gun took up a steady watch directly behind him. It was efficient and ruthless, as it was meant to be.

"What's your name?" Rostovitch demanded.

He was mildly surprised when the man answered him quite calmly, "Frank Jordan."

"You are a spy, an underground agent."

"I'm a cabdriver."

Rostovitch half rose out of his chair and shot out words like bullets. "You are a spy!" Then, deliberately, he relaxed and let contempt come into his voice. "And a nigger to boot."

"Don't call me a nigger," Frank said.

Rostovitch, with the calculated insult, had found the first soft spot. *"I say* you're a nigger!" he hurled at the man before him.

To the colonel's real surprise Frank kept his composure. "And I say that you're a goddamned jerk."

Rostovitch jumped to his feet. The man standing behind the prisoner raised his weapon to strike, but Rostovitch waved him down; he was not ready to have this man killed —not just yet. First, the information.

"And," Frank added, "you're a frigging coward to boot."

Rostovitch walked slowly around to the front of the desk and then leaned on it with his hands behind him. He waited a moment, then spoke with deceptive calmness. "You do not know who I am."

"You're Zalinsky," Frank said.

Rostovitch was amused. "Zalinsky a coward, maybe yes; he is very good at making ladies' sweaters." Then he hardened abruptly. "But *I* am not Zalinsky."

"You're still yellow," Frank taunted him. "When you talk to an unarmed man sitting in a chair, you still gotta have another guy backing you up with a gun. That's because you took one good look at me and got scared that maybe I could beat the shit out of you."

Barlov interrupted at that point. In a completely factual voice he said. "Shall I have this prisoner taken outside and shot?"

Rostovitch's eyes narrowed, then he shook his head as he studied the man before him. A sudden new idea was shaping itself within his mind: it was born of colossal pride and the accumulated frustrations that he had had to accept ever since the blind, stupid fools in San Francisco had let the submarine get away. Here before him was a momentary way to redeem all that, and to mend the partially shattered fragments of his fearsome reputation.

At that precise moment, as though he had been reading his thoughts, Major Barlov ventured to ask another question. "Excuse me," he said in the language he knew that Frank could not understand, "how many of my men do you require for your personal safety?"

Rostovitch glanced at him. "Explain," he said.

Barlov remained calm. "I am about to dispatch some more men to deal with the disturbance outside. But I cannot leave you alone with this prisoner; you must be protected at all costs."

Although it seemed obviously unintentional, that was another insult, another prod at the colonel's wounded pride. "Major," he said, "more than fifty men have tried, from time to time, to lay their hands on me. Are you aware of the outcome?"

"I should not care to try it," Barlov replied.

That was better.

The colonel held out his hands to be inspected. They were like the ends of twin battering rams, scarred, disfigured, and lethal. "I require no protection," he said. He did not add that he carried weapons concealed on his person, a habit he had not broken for years.

"Very well," Barlov replied, "I will send my men to take care of the incident outside, they are needed there. But I cannot leave you alone with this man; I will remain myself."

The colonel could not protest because Barlov was obviously doing his duty, but he was further annoyed. He looked at the prisoner and made a point for Barlov's benefit. "If I chose to kill you with my bare hands, you might last as long as thirty seconds," he said. "But I have no time to amuse myself in this way. *You work for the agent Hewlitt!*"

Frank said nothing.

Rostovitch waited just long enough to determine that no answer was coming, then he came suddenly forward and started a powerful, openhanded smash against the side of Frank's face. As he whipped his arm down, Frank without warning kicked him violently in the shin. The impact almost knocked Rostovitch off his feet and caused his own blow to miss. Barlov leaped forward, but the colonel waved him away.

One more time Rostovitch tried to thrust down the boiling acid of frustration and recover his composure. He forced his voice into something approaching normal speech. "Why do you challenge me?" he asked.

"Because you called me a nigger, you horse's ass, and because you ain't nearly as good as you think you are."

Rostovitch's rage descended to an icy calm; he realized that he had nearly been goaded into forgetting himself, and his whole lower leg burned with pain. He was used to pain, but it had not lost its power to annoy him. Barlov remained silent and motionless, ready to do whatever he was directed. Rostovitch knew that he could have the man before him dead in another fifteen seconds, but that would not reveal any information. Worse, Barlov would not forget what he had seen and heard. "This man has been searched?" he asked, attempting to make it sound casual.

Barlov was stung. "Thoroughly. He would not have been permitted in your presence otherwise."

There was another hidden barb in that, although the answer had been completely respectful. Rostovitch let his fingertips feel the contour of the knife that was concealed against his leg. "Leave us," he said to Barlov in English. "Attend to your men. You will return when I call you."

Barlov looked at him and knew that he meant exactly what he said. He allowed the slightest suspicion of a satisfied smile to touch the corners of his mouth. Rostovitch noted it and approved; it was a testimonial which told him that his image was intact.

When they were alone Rostovitch looked at Frank for several seconds. "I give you one last chance to save your life," he lied. "If you tell me enough, fast enough, I may relent. I am not Zalinsky, he is in the hospital. *I am Rostovitch!*"

"Now ain't that a great big surprise," Frank said, and calmly stood up.

The colonel began slowly to walk around him, measuring him with his eyes. When he had finished, the slight exercise had eased the biting pain in his leg and put his mind back into proper focus once more. "You have perhaps heard of me," he said with deceptive mildness.

Frank looked at the skull-like face and casually surveyed the total picture that the formidable colonel made. "You ain't much," he said.

Rostovitch struck like lightning; his left arm shot out aimed directly, with two fingers extended, at Frank's eyes. Instinctively Frank drew back, then Rostovitch's hammer-like right fist slammed into his unprotected abdomen.

Frank's body knifed over from the blow, for a moment he was bent half double. With his hand held edgewise and open, Rostovitch swung down with concentrated force toward the back of Frank's neck. The blow landed, but on the top of the skull and well before it had gained its maximum power; despite the sudden shock of pain and loss of wind, Frank was already jerking himself upright, his right arm bent with his hand almost resting on the top of his own shoulder. Using the power of his torso and his leg muscles for a maximum effort, he smashed the top of his elbow against the underside of Rostovitch's jaw. He felt a renewed stab of pain as the blow hit; he saw Rostovitch's head snap back, but the jawbone had not broken. Any ordinary man would have been knocked senseless with a shot like that.

The colonel fell back one step, shook himself, and smiled with the fixed expression of a carved mask. Then he kicked.

He did not telegraph it, but he was too far back for any other attack and Frank had anticipated him. He spun sideways, letting the kick hit the side of his hip and deflect; then with his own left foot he kicked, with limited power but great speed, against the back of Rostovitch's left knee, unlocking the joint.

Rostovitch fell, but when Frank lunged after him he rolled backwards in a complete circle, his head sidewise against his shoulder, and came back up onto his feet again. Frank was still down; Rostovitch aimed a cool and driving kick against his left shoulder and sank it fully home.

Frank flipped onto his back, turned himself with astonishing speed, and aimed his feet toward his opponent. Then he too swung over backward, favoring his shoulder, and gained his own feet.

"A cabdriver," Rostovitch spat out, almost under his breath. "A cabdriver! You expect me to believe that?"

"You wanna go somewhere?" Frank asked. He stood still, working the muscles of his left shoulder, loosening them and easing the strain of the hard kick he had taken.

Rostovitch attacked again; he seized Frank's left wrist with both of his hands, lifted it up, and then almost whipped it out of its socket. As he snapped downward Frank dropped with the motion; bent over he spun halfway around to the left and grabbed one of Rostovitch's own wrists with his free hand. Jerking upward he thrust his injured shoulder into Rostovitch's armpit. Shooting both of his own arms out he forced the colonel to extend his own arm—the leverage was against Rostovitch then and despite his strength and all of his training, he could not help himself. He knew that he was trapped in the Judo throw *Seoi-nage*, but once the shoulder was in his armpit, all he could do defensively was to attempt to throw his whole weight backward and pull his opponent off balance.

He had only a fraction of a second in which to do that; before he could drop his body Frank straightened his legs, lifting him off the ground, then bent forward rapidly with all of the power his body could command. Despite his more than two hundred pounds of hard, muscular weight, Rostovitch was thrown over Frank's head and slammed hard onto the floor flat on his back.

He had barely landed when Frank followed up with a driving stomp into the solar plexus, enough to force the wind from Rostovitch's body and to render him momentarily helpless.

Despite the fact that there was almost no breath left in his body, Rostovitch attempted to fight back. With intense determination he managed to roll over, then attempted to thrust himself against Frank's legs. He managed, and bit into the flesh until the blood flowed freely. Frank broke it, but only by literally tearing himself away. He was breathing heavily now, fighting dizziness as well as intense pain. But he retained his balance and when Rostovitch attempted to get up, he kicked once more and caught him with partial success in the groin.

That doubled Rostovitch up once more. Frank waited, grateful for the opportunity to gulp air and to gather his remaining resources. He was an extraordinarily powerful man, but in Rostovitch he had met an enemy of almost inhuman toughness. He looked, and saw the small, almost concealed hand gun that Rostovitch had had hidden. He leapt forward, hands outstretched, and locked them around the weapon. Then it became a test of strength and Rostovitch was like steel. They wrestled on the floor, without science or skill, until Frank felt the point of Rostovitch's elbow thrusting into the base of his throat. That meant death and he knew it; in one supreme effort he rolled himself sideways, bending the hand backward against the gun until he felt the wrist snap. Then, his strength all but spent, he hammered his forearm across Rostovitch's throat.

The colonel gasped and his eyes opened wide. "That's for calling me a nigger," Frank panted, not caring whether he was heard or not. Once more he raised his right arm, the edge of his hand hard with his fingers bent slightly backward at their base, slightly curved forward at the joints. In that rigid karate position he smashed it down, with the concentrated remnants of his strength, across the bridge of Rostovitch's nose.

"And that," he gasped, "is a present . . . from the Marines."

He lay still after that for several seconds across the man he had felled. Gradually his wind came back and the well-springs of his body recovered a little from the savage beating he had taken. When he had the strength to do so, he lifted himself up a little with his arms and battled to regain control of himself. His shoulder, his leg, and his chest were all racked with agony, and his vision was not entirely clear. When the focus began to come back he looked down at the man who lay underneath him. He studied the features and saw that the nose had almost disappeared from the face; the narrow bone that had given it shape had been driven back into the skull. When he saw that he knew that Rostovitch was dead.

It was a full half minute later before he managed to draw his legs up closer to the rest of his body and get unsteadily to his feet. He knew that he had only minutes more to live, if that, but he no longer cared. He saw the small hand gun lying on the carpet and considered picking it up. Then, realizing the futility of it all, he kicked it aside. He had sold his life for a good price and he was satisfied.

When he was able to walk he made his way unsteadily to the door and knocked.

CHAPTER TWENTY-FIVE

As Feodor Zalinsky lay in his hospital bed he could not decide whether he had more pain from the healing incision in his abdomen or from the thoughts pounding in his brain. At least physically he knew that he was on the mend, and perhaps some of the annoying problems that had plagued his body in the past would now be over. That much was good. Mentally things were getting progressively worse. He had been keeping very close watch over his television set, but the steady flow of dispatches from the White House that he had been receiving had dwindled rapidly during the past twenty-four hours. In plain language that meant one thing: Gregor Rostovitch was taking over.

The constant parade of medical attendants in and out of his room he accepted as necessary; since he was in their hands he cooperated with their demands and endured their ministrations without complaint. In return for this they had given him what was obviously expert care from the beginning and had even gone so far as to prepare certain foods which he sensed were not part of the usual hospital routine. The guard that had been stationed in his room he had ordered removed as unnecessary and at times inconvenient, such as when he wished to use the bedpan. The man sat outside, across the hall in a chair that had been provided for him, and thereby allowed Zalinsky some partial feeling, at least, of privacy and quiet. He rested as best he could and thought, more often than he wanted to, of his home and family that were so distant in both time and kilometers.

When three more medical people came unannounced into his room he looked up to determine what new benevolent discomfort they were about to inflict on him. Then one of them pulled down a surgical mask and said to him in his own language, "Good afternoon, Mr. Zalinsky, how are you feeling?"

Zalinsky lifted himself on his elbows, looked into the face of the man who had spoken to him, and said, "You have just assassinated yourself."

Hewlitt shook his head. "I hope not, because a lot more depends on my talking to you than just my own personal welfare. I asked, how are you feeling?"

Zalinsky fell back onto the pillows propped behind him. "I am progressing, or so I am informed. Perhaps in a week I shall be better. I now ask you a question: is it true that you had an interview with Colonel Rostovitch in my office from which you walked away a free man?"

Hewlitt nodded. "In part, yes. I did talk to Colonel Rostovitch; he accused me of being a spy."

"He was right, of course. How, then, did you get away?"

"He accused me also of sleeping with Amy Thornbush. I remembered that you had mentioned that name to me and I guessed what it might mean. So I gave it back to him and walked out while he was checking up on it."

"Your life expectancy is now shorter than the needles that they plunge into me here. Why have you come to see me?"

"Because of what Colonel Rostovitch has done and what he proposes to do."

Zalinsky rolled his head on the pillows to loosen the muscles of his neck. "The hostages, I know. But you should know what kind of a man he is, the high diver should have told you."

"He did, I spoke with him yesterday."

"That is impossible unless you used radio; he is on board the submarine."

Not to the slightest degree did Hewlitt reveal the electric feeling that those words conveyed to him. He kept his face, his posture, and his voice unchanged. Percival stood on the other side of the bed, but there was no way he could pass the information, and Percival did not understand the language they were using.

"Mr. Zalinsky," Hewlitt said. "I have known you now for some time. You are a very tough person, I have never underrated you there, but you are also a practical man with common sense. You can run steel mills."

"If you are asking me to countermand Colonel Rostovitch, you have undertaken a hopeless task. I am the administrator; I run the country, yes, but its internal security is entirely up to the colonel, and he reports directly to the premier."

"So do you, isn't that so?"

"Yes, but the colonel . . ."

"Mr. Zalinsky, I have come to tell you something. Colonel Rostovitch received a message, only a few minutes ago, from Thomas Jefferson. Do you know what it is?"

"What is Thomas Jefferson? Of course I know!"

"I mean, do you know what the message said?"

"It has not yet been transmitted to me."

Hewlitt was not certain, but he thought that he detected a hint of bitterness in that. The message probably would be relayed on to Zalinsky—but it might be delayed.

"I have been told what it is," Hewlitt said. Then he quoted the context exactly, translating it for the benefit of the administrator.

"You are very important to this Thomas Jefferson, is it not so?"

Hewlitt shook his head. "No, Mr. Zalinsky, I am not. I have nothing whatever to do with decision or policy. I was sent to see you only because we know one another."

"What is it that you want from me?"

"Mr. Zalinsky, like every decent human being, I do not like to see people die in war."

Hewlitt was only beginning, but Zalinsky interrupted him. "Then is it easy, surrender as you were directed; give up your few and save the great many."

"You don't fully understand, Mr. Zalinsky. We do not want people like Colonel Rostovitch keeping watch over everything that we do, and doing the things that he has done in the past. Mr. Zalinsky, I do not want one thousand of our people to die, but much more I do not want to see three million of your people die. And more than that if the *Ramon Magsaysay* unleashes her full power. You will have no country left."

"And neither will you."

Hewlitt nodded. "But at the moment, we have much less to lose than you do, because our country has been largely taken from us. Think, Mr. Zalinsky, and count up the nations that you can call your enemies who would rush in to finish the job if we lay you flat on your back."

"I am precisely in that position now," Zalinsky said. "It is visible to you."

"Very well, suppose that you had personal enemies in this building who knew of your condition, where you were, and that you were not only unguarded, but that there was no one to avenge you if they struck. How long would you last?"

Once more Zalinsky propped himself up on his elbows. "All right, I am a sick man. I cannot defend myself. In my office sits Gregor Rostovitch. Do you believe that he will remove himself simply to please me if I call him and suggest it? You met him, you should know." He reached for a glass of water; Hewlitt handed it to him.

"I don't want you to call the colonel, I want you to call the Actor," Hewlitt said. "He is balancing on a tightwire right now. Let him release the hostages in the name of humanity and the whole world will approve."

"And Gregor Rostovitch will sit in his chair within a month."

The phone beside Zalinsky's bed rang once softly. Reaching over with some effort the administrator picked it up. "It will be the message," he said.

Hewlitt contained himself and kept his face impassive, but with an effort. He had been making his play, and it was the one time that he did not want to be interrupted for any reason.

Zalinsky listened to the instrument and then his face visibly changed color. "There is no possibility of a mistake?" he asked in his own language. Once more he listened; then he spoke a few brief words and hung up. After that he pulled bedclothes up under his chin and surveyed Hewlitt with renewed interest. "Your timing," he said finally, "I admit that it is superb. You will know very shortly anyway so I tell you now, Colonel Rostovitch is dead. Is it now that you are going to kill me?"

Hewlitt repeated back the news, in English, as though to convince himself that he had heard correctly. "Colonel Rostovitch is dead, you absolutely affirm this?"

"I have just been so told."

Hewlitt kept his face as composed as it had been. He had gambled before and he had won; he was prepared to gamble again. "Mr. Zalinsky, I will tell you the absolute truth: we will not permit the hostages to be killed and we have very strong ways to prevent that. But the most merciful thing is for you to give the order that they are to be released. There is no one in this country to challenge your authority and I know you—you would not do this thing that Rostovitch had planned because you are too good a manager—the price to your own people would be unthinkable. You are the man who shut down the steel mill while you put the machines where they had to be; this is the same thing. You are tough, but you are not, and never will be, insane like Rostovitch."

"You knew that Rostovitch was to be killed then?"

Hewlitt saw a sudden ray of light. "I came here to see you. Before you knew what was to happen, you told me that I had assassinated myself."

Zalinsky looked at him, then eased himself back onto his pillows. "If I am to die," he said, "return to me what I did for your Major Landers and let it be very quick and painless. I am not a man of great physical courage; at least I do not wish to be exterminated."

Hewlitt continued the role he had unwittingly assumed. "Mr. Zalinsky, I have specifically given the order that you are not to die, that your recovery is to continue with the best care that we can give you, and that you are to be treated with consideration, if you will do this one thing that will redeem you before the whole country that I represent. It is the only possible decision. Otherwise, our submarine will fire. And you know that it is not sunk; you told me so yourself a few minutes ago."

Zalinsky raised his arms and rubbed his face. Then he picked up the telephone and called for Major Barlov once more. When he had him on the line he asked for a further report on the death of Gregor Rostovitch. When that had been done, he said, "Very well. List the names of the hostages and then let them go for the time being. I will make a decision within twenty-four hours."

"You are a very great man," Barlov said over the line.

"Are you one of them too?"

Apparently Barlov did not presume to take that seriously. "Excellency, I venture to say to you that I feared greatly for our country; the power of the submarine, it is terrible. Of this I know. And my wife and family, you know where they live."

"And mine also," Zalinsky said. "But it is the jackals I consider now—if we get into this, they will gather to devour our flesh and there are a great many of them."

"As I said, excellency, you are a great man. You see things to which others are blind."

"Give the necessary orders in my name."

"Yes, excellency. What shall I do with the man who caused Colonel Rostovitch to depart from us?"

"You have him in custody?"

"Yes, excellency."

"Be careful that he does not escape. If he were to escape, I could not avenge my dear friend Gregor as I wish to do."

"Your wishes will be carried out, excellency. I shall keep you informed. Speed your recovery."

"I am feeling very much better already; I will be back into my office soon." He hung up, then turned to Hewlitt. "What is now to happen?" he asked in English.

"I heard the conversation," Hewlitt said, "and I say the same. Speed your recovery."

He turned and left while he was still in command of himself.

The conference room at Thomas Jefferson was usually extremely well ordered, a reflection of the man whose desire to keep things shipshape had characterized his many years in the Navy. For almost twenty-four hours that standard had been abandoned as the room became a strategy center, plans headquarters, restaurant, message command post, and very nearly a dormitory. The members of the First Team occupied it almost continuously, and there was a steady flow in and out of the second level of command and all of the support personnel who worked directly with the managers of the operation. Occasionally used coffee cups were cleared away and accumulations of discarded notepaper were removed, but the atmosphere in the room became continuously heavier nonetheless and there was no fault in the air conditioning.

The admiral sat, and he paced up and down. He consulted charts, conferred with his colleagues on a hundred different points, and read incoming messages with almost savage eagerness the moment that they were received. Like the good commander that he was, he gave careful thought to the idea of surrendering himself and his colleagues. He explored the idea fully and rejected it: it would betray the President, the country, and the whole complex organization that had been so painstakingly constructed to meet the exact emergency with which it was now confronted. To throw all of that away would be to sentence the entire country to serfdom for the indefinite future, and that was not the purpose of the command that he headed. He had the *Magsaysay;* at least he was determined to carry on with the assumption that he did, and with that single but almost unbelievably potent force available he was in the game to win. In warfare there were no second prizes.

He left the room and returned in a blackened mood. He called over one of the service personnel who was emptying ashtrays and pointed. "It's all out of toilet paper in there," he declared.

"I'm sorry, sir," the man answered. "I hope that there was something else available."

"What did you expect me to use—a moonbeam?" Haymarket barked.

The man didn't blink. "If you accomplished that, sir, I would like to shake your hand."

The admiral relented and smiled; there was not a man or a woman in the underground complex who had not been handpicked. "Fix it, will you?" he finished mildly and went back to his work.

He was passed a message, read it, and at once called for attention. "They're putting Hewlitt in," he reported. "Mark is going in too; I don't agree with that, but I can see arguments both ways."

Colonel Prichard, who headed up all of the internal operational projects, looked concerned. "We can't afford to blow *him,*" he warned.

"Totally agreed," the admiral answered, "but Mark knows what he's doing; if he went in, he had a reason."

Walter Wagner was thoughtful for a moment. "If they try to capture both of them, we could be in trouble," he pointed out.

General Gifford shook his head. "They won't take Mark. He is equipped to prevent that."

"And they won't be able to stop him?"

"No."

That was that and Wagner subsided. The admiral wanted to ask Ted Pappas once more what he thought of Hewlitt and his chances of success, but he held himself in check because he had already put that question three times and had gotten a precise, careful, and exactly similar answer each time.

Another message came in; Admiral Haymarket read it and swallowed hard. "Who is Asher?" he asked.

"A Washington ex-Marine cab driver; his name is Frank Jordan," Colonel Prichard answered.

"How good is he?"

"A pretty good man, I'd say. Not the lightning brain type, but far from stupid. I've never met him, but the reports on him are very good. Loyalty unquestioned. Why?"

The admiral read the message one more time. "He's been captured," he announced. "He was taken directly to the White House."

"That means Rostovitch," Wagner said. "Write him off and pray for his soul."

"Can we help him?" Prichard asked. "We still have people in there. Several of them are top shots."

"How much does he know?" the admiral asked quickly.

"Not too much. He controlled Hewlitt for a while and helped to set up the safe house. Both of those are blown. He knows Mark, but only as Percival."

The admiral made a hard decision. "We can't help him," he said. "It would cost at least a man to do it and we'd be right back where we started. God bless him."

General Gifford looked up. "I'd like the room cleared," he said.

Immediately, and with complete understanding, all those present who were not actually members of the First Team abandoned their usual posts; when the door had been closed behind the last man through, the general waited a few seconds and then spoke briefly. "You told me privately that Barlov, the director of White House security, was with us. To what degree is that true?"

The admiral looked around the table. "This is not to be breathed to anyone under any conditions," he said, then he waited to let that sink in. The men he was facing were of very high intelligence and unquestioned dedication, but even with that he hesitated. Then he told them. "He is a

British agent, one of the most valuable that they have."

"Then we have to assume that he can't blow his cover, no matter what the opportunity to save our man," General Gifford said.

The admiral nodded. "There was a classic sea engagement once during which the British Navy sank a German heavy cruiser. When the admiral in command heard, he was badly shaken. The executive officer on board the German ship had been a British agent much more valuable than the ship and its crew."

Stanley Cumberland said, "I remember reading about that."

The admiral touched a signal which indicated that the room was once more open to those who had legitimate business inside. Then, for the next half hour, he was as restless as any of his immediate associates had ever seen him. He paced the floor, unwittingly frustrated because it was not a deck, and kept his brain at constant flank speed. If there was an angle anywhere, anything whatever that he could do, he would find it. Two or three times he stopped to say something, then at the last moment thought better of it and went back to his pacing.

"Sir."

The man who handed him the message looked him in the eye first, which indicated that it was something very important. Haymarket took it, said the shortest silent prayer of his life, and then read what it contained.

He looked up and about the room, then read again. The words on the paper could not be mistaken, and he knew better than to ask if the transmission had been accurate. There was no mistake in the signal.

All this took him no more than a few seconds; when he looked up a second time he saw that the room was still and that all movement had stopped. They were waiting.

"Gentlemen," he said. "I'll give this to you just as I have it here. It's from a source inside the White House which is five by five in every way." That meant, as his hearers knew, that the information was considered totally accurate and the source unimpeachable. *"Asher interviewed by Rostovitch. Conflict followed, Rostovitch repeat Rostovitch killed. Asher badly beaten, but alive in custody."*

There was a stunned silence. Then Ed Higbee said, "My God!"

The admiral stood still, his hands at his sides, the signal still held unfeelingly in his fingers.

"Is it true?" Major Pappas asked, making sure.

Slowly the admiral nodded. "It must be; there is a veracity code that's watertight. We'll check, but I believe it right now."

Stanley Cumberland spoke in measured words. "Assuming that the message is accurate, then it is up to Hewlitt. If he knows this, or finds out in time, and if he is good enough to take advantage of it, then, sir, I'd say that things look better."

Again the room was quiet, then the precise voice of Major Pappas was heard once more. "Sir, I recommend that you advise *Magsaysay* at once. Then I would advise passing the word to all field units as rapidly as possible. Some of them might decide to do as Philadelphia suggested, and without consulting us for permission first."

"So ordered," the admiral said. Very calmly he returned to his chair at the head of the table and sat down. "I agree with Stan," he said. "Things do look a little better now."

The Reverend Mr. Jones sat quietly, his arm around his son. He had been talking to his wife for some time, speaking of the mercy of God and of the certainty of the salvation of Christ. When he had reenforced his faith and pressed her hands in loving understanding, he had turned to enjoy, in the fleeting time that remained, the company of his son. He had already ministered, as much as he was able, to the others insofar as his own human endurance had permitted. Many of the hostages were bitter, many wanted to be left strictly alone, some had the attitude "They can't do this to us!" and were waiting for some responsible part of the American military to come and rescue them by force. The Reverend Mr. Jones knew better than to disillusion those people; it was their rationalization and made it perhaps much easier for them to spend the final fearful hours.

He looked at Greg and saw with great pride that his boy was trying to smile back at him. In this period of intense soul-searching he knew that Greg was an average American boy, but that still made him a pretty fine future citizen.

There was no doubt whatever in his mind that he would be with his wife and son in Heaven, but what they would have to go through first was an image that he tried to thust out of his mind.

Greg was not equal to it and he knew that he had to help his son. "Greg, I want to talk to you," he said. "You know that this sort of thing has happened before many times in the world's history."

Greg nodded that he understood, and swallowed very hard.

"Sometimes," his father continued, "when things look blackest it is time to count blessings. You may not think that there are very many right now, and I'm forced to agree with you, but there are some things to think about nonetheless. Some very important things. I don't like to bring this up, but at one time, and not too long ago as history goes, people who were held like us faced fearful things that we have escaped completely. Remember this, Greg, there are no lions. There are no torture chambers and all of the unspeakable horrors that they contained. There are no Roman circuses to see men and women die in a hundred different terrible ways. There is no crucifixion that Christ endured—and so many others after Him for His sake."

"I know, dad," Greg said.

Jones could not help it; he tightened his arm about his son and fought desperately to keep back his own tears. "Son, I love you with all my heart and soul; I'd give my life for you in a moment if I could. I want you to know that just having you for my son, in these years, has been one of the greatest joys of my life. And our Savior loves all of us this same way too, so we have nothing whatever to fear when we pass into His hands."

Greg's face began to tighten as he fought to keep himself under control. Then he failed and the tears came openly. "Dad, I don't want to die!"

Jones flung both of his arms around his boy and lifted his eyes to ask for the compassion of Heaven. Then he could control himself no longer. He was racked by a great heart-wrenching sob that he was totally unable to control and then he felt his wife's hands on him and knew that she was trying her best to comfort him. "Remember what you just told me," she pleaded. "Remember!"

Reverend Jones lowered his head in shame because he could not remember. He was gripped by sudden desperate and uncontrollable fear—not for himself, but for his son. For all the promise of him, for all of his youth and good health, for all of the healthy and normal interests that he had, for all the years that he had labored in school for the not too outstanding, but better-than-average marks that he had brought home. For the hope that when he had matured a little more he would one day take a wife who would bring him a lifetime of happiness. For the prospect of grandchildren sometime in the future and the pride of having given a fine young citizen to society. And for the years of companionship that should have remained to them. And for the wonderful, irreplaceable, God-given girl who had consented to become his wife and share the restricted hopes of a minister of the Gospel and the limited outlook for anything more than a very modest scale of living all their lives. All of it piled up on him until he felt like crying aloud, as One had done before him, *"My God, my God, why hast Thou forsaken me?"*

He fought; with all of the spirit and conviction that he possessed he fought to find himself once more, to thrust from him the fearful, brutal, insane injustice of it all, and to remember that there would only be a few minutes of acute distress and then the gates of Heaven would open before him. He remembered the Jews who had died under Hitler, and the thousands who had gone to the stake for the sake of their faith, or in spite of it. His dear ones did not have to face death by fire and the frightful agony of having their flesh burned from their bones. There would be a firing squad, only a few moments facing the guns, and then the face of God. . . .

A man came to the door of the huge room. The Reverend Mr. Jones did not see him at first, but he sensed the sudden change around him and looked up to see what had caused it. When he saw the man in uniform he shot out his own hand and gripped his wife's fingers until the pain almost made her dizzy, but she said nothing and gave no sign.

The man had a paper in his hand and that meant that the time had come.

"Dear God in heaven, grant me the grace and the strength . . ." he began, speaking aloud without realizing it.

The man raised his voice and half-shouted, half-spoke in English. *"You can all go home."*

Doris Jones did not comprehend the miracle, her mind was too numb from the torture it had undergone. Greg did not believe the words, and looked at his father for the strength to resist this last, utterly cruel jest.

The man in uniform began to motion that people should go out the door. "A mercy," Mr. Jones thought, "a mercy to make it easier for them to get into the trucks or whatever they have waiting." But when, halfway in the exodus, he at last led the way through the door so that his little family could have the last split second of comfort, there were no trucks waiting, no long gray buses, nothing but a rapidly gathering crowd of the curious who were staring at them.

A sudden blinding light caught Mr. Jones in the face and made his stop. Then he heard the voice of a man who thrust a microphone before his face and asked him, "Who are you, sir—what is your name, please?"

In the stunned condition of his mind he hardly knew how to answer; he stammered out "Jones" and then recovered himself enough to add, "I'm . . . the pastor of . . ." and he could not remember the name of his own church.

The man with the microphone picked him up very fast. "You have been comforting the others, haven't you, reverend?" he said and made it a statement that somehow had to be replied to.

"Yes, the best that I could."

"Your prayers have been answered, sir, you know that now, don't you?"

The Reverend Mr. Jones didn't know, for he was far from sure as yet, but he nodded his head and looked again at the swelling crowd that was pressing in for a closer look.

"Sir, this is not for just one network, the whole nation is watching and listening. Please, tell us what it was like."

"I'd . . . rather not do that." The emotions he had felt were still locked into his mind and he did not yet believe that deliverance had come.

"Sir," the man said, "you have all been set free, because of a nuclear submarine. A fearful weapon of war, yet so far it hasn't fired a shot. Have you anything to say to that, sir?"

Those were the first words that the tortured minister really heard, but he did hear them and at last understood.

He raised his head and answered. "Yes," he said, "I do." With shaking fingers he placed his hands together. "Let us pray."

Across the whole breadth of the nation he was heard by uncounted millions of people. And some of them bowed their heads, in their own homes or wherever they were, and waited for his words.

CHAPTER TWENTY-SIX

Senator Solomon Fitzhugh sat in the quiet confines of Admiral Barney Haymarket's office and looked across the desk at the man he had once regarded as an adversary in what seemed to be the dim past. The admiral himself gave no evidence of even remembering those days; instead he relaxed to the point where he took off his reading glasses and rubbed his eyes with his fists as though to clear away some of the fatigue that had settled into them during the past several weeks.

When he had finished, he turned his attention to his guest. "Senator, I'm sure that you've been keeping up with the dispatches that I've had bucked on to you, so you know that, thanks to the grace of God, we've at last got a victory on our hands."

"More or less yes," Fitzhugh said.

"I invited you in," the admiral continued, "because I wanted to fill you in a little more and also to advise you that you may have a further and very important role to play."

Fitzhugh looked at him. "I have been regarding myself more or less as a discard at this point. I publicly reversed myself on a position that I have been maintaining steadfastly for years. I doubt if my constituents . . ."

The admiral raised a hand to stop him. "I don't have a poll available to prove it," he said, "but I would guess that your popularity, on a national basis, is at an all-time high. And that's damn good, because we're going to make use of it."

"Another speech?"

Haymarket shook his head. "Considerably more important than that."

He got up and poured out two more cups of coffee, setting one in front of the senator almost automatically. "Let me lay it out for you so that you will understand exactly where we stand. We are entering into a new phase of things which is a lot different than international diplomacy is supposed to be—it is strictly a face-saving period. If—and I say that very seriously—we can pull the chestnuts out in such a way that not only no one gets burned, but also certain people are made to look good in the process, we may be able to trade off a little prestige for some very big stakes."

"I'm not sure, Admiral Haymarket, that we have very much prestige to barter with right now."

"That's right, senator, but we can manufacture a little, and that's what I'm trying to do. You know the Actor; in fact I understand that you were the audience for one of his most brilliant performances."

"You could put it that way," Fitzhugh admitted.

"All right; now here is how it stands, senator. By the way, what do your friends call you?"

Fitzhugh was edgy about that. "Solomon, sometimes."

"I see. Anyhow, through private channels which were set up for the purpose, and with the approval of the President, I've been in touch with the premier. Not in my own identity, but as the commander of Thomas Jefferson. Some horse trading has been done. His government is not stable at the moment and usually at such times over there heads roll. To protect himself, he has had to make some moves. He has agreed through a series of apparently unimportant steps to start pulling his people out and in turn I have promised to call the *Magsaysay* home."

Solomon Fitzhugh considered that and then shook his head. "I don't know, admiral," he said, "once the *Magsaysay* is no longer a threat to them, then won't we be completely at their mercy once more?"

To Fitzhugh's surprise, the admiral seemed to be delighted. "Senator, I agree with you totally, and I'm particularly pleased to hear you express that opinion. If you'll pardon my saying so, I believe that you're beginning to see the advantages of keeping our powder dry. Here's the rest of it: I agreed to pull in the *Magsaysay* with appropriate fanfare, but with a very secret proviso. Before she leaves her present station, another of our FBM's must be allowed to replace her. We had three in Holy Loch when this all started, and one of them has already quietly slipped away.

The British know; they had to since Holy Loch is in Scotland and the ships were technically impounded there. We are letting them have the propaganda victory, but our basic strategic position is essentially unchanged."

"He simply let you do that?"

"Yes, to save his own neck and his government. You see, it can remain a secret permanently because the new ship on station isn't going to fire—we both knew that. He's far too smart to bring that down on his head, and there wouldn't be any winners in a nuclear showdown."

Fitzhugh fingered his coffee cup while he thought. "Why are you telling me all this?" he asked. "When I asked you about the President, you told me very pointedly that I had no need to know."

The admiral leaned back, coffee in hand. "I was just coming to that. In the plainest language, with Rostovitch dead and his own economy almost on the brink, the premier's got to get out of a serious overcommitment here before the walls tumble down behind him. Nelson won at Trafalgar, but he got himself killed in the process. The Actor prefers to be around for a while to enjoy his position, his girl friends, and the other amenities of life."

"So?"

"Very simple," Haymarket said. "He has suggested that since the occupation has achieved its purpose, he is now ready to talk with his old friend, the esteemed peacemaker, Senator Solomon Fitzhugh."

The admiral expected a reaction to that and he got it. "Dammit, it wasn't too long ago that I was very rudely told that the premier wished to hear nothing more from me. I was given to understand that if I did not comply, my toys would be taken away from me. In those words!"

"I know—but that was before we had a nuclear submarine aimed right up his backside. *Magsaysay* and her overwhelming destructive potential made it a new ball game."

"Does the President know?"

"Yes, and he has approved. Understand clearly that the deal has already been made; your part will be to show up overseas, accept the protocol, talk about your long-standing devotion to the cause of nonmilitarism, and help the Actor to put on his show. In due time the two of you will issue a joint communiqué. When that's all over, he will start pulling back his forces and you, naturally, will emerge a national hero."

Solomon Fitzhugh shook his head. "I'll go if it *will* help the cause of peace. But the hero part will come when you and your associates come out of hiding. Everyone knows about the First Team now."

The admiral finished his coffee very casually. "No, senator. I'm going to come back to life and really retire this time, but otherwise all of the personnel of this operation are going to remain unheralded and unsung. We always hope for a better world, but we don't have any guarantees —not yet. So we are going quietly to break up except for a few maintenance personnel and go on about our separate businesses, but our organization will still be there if it's ever needed again. The same goes for all of our backup people, and you have no idea how many there are."

The senator was not fully satisfied. "Consider history . . ." he began.

The admiral firmly shook his head. "You take the bows, senator; you've earned them. Publicity isn't our business, in fact in our kind of operation it could be fatal to us. You go and make the Actor look good, then you can come home and run for President."

"I don't want to be President," Fitzhugh said.

Two hours out of port the U.S.S. *Ramon Magsaysay* rendezvoused on the surface with a supply vessel which passed over several packages of soft goods. The men of the submarine received them gladly and with their aid prepared themselves more suitably for an appearance at a United States naval facility. For a short while the captain disappeared from the bridge; when he returned he was in proper uniform and, what was more, he had been well fitted and his decorations were correctly displayed. Underneath him his ship rolled slightly in the water, a welcome change from the monotonous steadiness while submerged. As he walked back and forth on the small area available, he drew in deep lungfuls of air and glanced up every few seconds at the sky. When the lookout announced landfall he pulled down the edges of his coat and began to check that his ship was fully prepared to enter port in a smart and proper manner.

He passed some orders and verified a number of things to the point where Chief Summers remarked that he had never seen the old man in such a testy mood.

It did not last for long. The New England coastline grew nearer and then the familiar outlines of the New London–Groton area. The *Magsaysay* cut cleanly through the water, her speed exactly right to ride the tide in. The navigator passed up a message that she should make her berth within two minutes of her ETA.

"Improve that," the captain replied.

At the proper time smartly uniformed members of her crew came on deck and formed an impressive line of sea-going fighting men. The captain looked them over from the bridge with an eagle's eye, but he could find no fault. He nodded to the Officer of the Deck and once more adjusted the edges of his coat.

Those who were waiting on the pier, from the three-star admiral on down, watched with a mixture of pride and well-founded emotion as the narrow black submarine came slowly in under her own power, her crewmen lining her rail in the finest tradition of the Navy. From her first sighting the television cameras had been on her, now as she drew closer they trained on her deck and then panned up to her bridge where only heads and shoulders were visible.

It took longer than many present had expected for her to berth, for she came in well away from the pierside to avoid fouling her screw and was properly snubbed in with the minute slowness that the very careful operation demanded. Then at last the short brow was put into position that led from the dock over to her deck and *Magsaysay* was officially in port.

Following the orders that he had been given, Commander Ishiro Nakamura, the son of a central California strawberry grower, came down from the bridge. Under the direction of Chief Summers a small formal party took its place on the quarterdeck on each side of the brow and a pipe sounded. "*Magsaysay,* leaving," came from the ship's speaker system.

The captain crossed the brow as the television cameras recorded his every movement and then tightened in on his handsome dark fatures as he saluted the vice-admiral who stood waiting for him.

The admiral held out his hand. "Welcome back, commander," he said. "How was your cruise?"

Commander Nakamura shook hands with proper dignity. "Routine, sir," he reported.

In response to the summons he had received Hewlitt crossed the hotel lobby and took an elevator to the fourteenth floor. As he walked down the corridor he was aware of the fact that one area had been sealed off—not obviously, but any casual visitors would have been stopped and asked their business. A few months earlier he might not have noticed this; now his sensitivity to such matters had been considerably sharpened. He was not surprised, therefore, when he had to produce an identity card before he was able to stop in front of one door and knock.

Feodor Zalinsky himself opened it. Hewlitt had not seen him since they had had their meeting in the hospital and his appearance was a surprise. He was a good ten pounds lighter, possibly even a little more. He had on a new suit which had some pretensions of fitting him. His face too, had changed. It was essentially the same, but there was a different cast to the features. As a first guess Hewlitt decided that he looked less harried.

"Come in, come in," Zalinsky said and there was a change in his voice too, the built-in challenge which had characterized it was at least modified. Hewlitt entered, glanced at the view out of the window, and then sat down.

"I have discovered that you make very good beer," Zalinsky said, "and I like beer. Will you have one with me?"

As he accepted, Hewlitt noted the fact that Zalinsky was speaking his own language; apparently the enforced English practice had been discarded.

At the small wet bar with which the apartment was equipped Zalinsky poured out the two drinks in pilsner glasses and then set one of them in front of his guest. Then he dumped himself into a chair and tasted his brew. "From time to time many different peoples have tried to conquer China," he observed, "but it was too big and cumbersome; they could not digest it."

Hewlitt nodded.

"This country, it is hopeless. I do not know how you run it yourselves."

"Sometimes we can't," Hewlitt conceded. "We make a mess of things every now and then."

"I could give you some very good suggestions," Zalinsky said and then took a long drink from his glass that left foam on his lips. "But I do not have the time for all that; I am going home."

Hewlitt shifted his position slightly, and waited.

"You may have in your mind many reasons for this: the submarine, the Thomas Jefferson business, the death of Gregor Rostovitch. I do not deny these, but the whole truth is not there either. We could have answered the submarine if Gregor had not gotten so far ahead of himself with the hostage business; there are too many other people in the world who would have recoiled from that, and we would have been left outside the church. We could have pretended to negotiate for a period of weeks and each day that passed . . ." He shrugged his shoulders and left the remark unfinished. "Anyhow, that is all over, you still have your high diver and there is perhaps less work for him to do now."

"I hope so," Hewlitt said.

"I will tell you this," Zalinsky continued, "long before the submarine left San Francisco I advised my government that the occupation of the United States was a great mistake and that we should withdraw as soon as we could. We did not have the multitudes of skilled people that it would have taken and not very many of us can speak English; it is not a natural language for us. So when the submarine appeared on the scene, I urged that we use this fine excuse to get out of an impossible situation."

Hewlitt drank his beer.

"So anyhow, it is finished. A little sooner than it would otherwise, perhaps, but we would not have been here too long no matter what happened; it simply wasn't practical. We cannot occupy your country indefinitely, and you could not occupy us, for many of the same reasons."

Once more Hewlitt nodded.

"So when Gregor, as you so picturesquely say, bought the farm, I forgot my pain long enough to call the premier and tell him for God's sake not to lose the chance to save his own neck. This is not to be repeated, yes?"

"If you say not, no."

"You will keep your word on that, I am aware, although it is not all that important; others will figure it out."

"I suspect that they already have."

Zalinsky shrugged his shoulders and finished his beer. "I regret that I did not meet the man who defeated Gregor Rostovitch; he must be a giant."

Hewlitt shook his head this time. "Not really, although he is very powerful, there is no denying that. Most of all, he was angry and with a just cause—that helped."

"You have him where he is safe?"

"He's fine, thank you."

"It is amazing that you rescued him so easily; you must have had some help."

Hewlitt looked him in the eye. "I believe we did," he said.

"Now, anyhow, I am going home. I will be glad to get back. After a little rest and a chance to see my family, I will probably be given another factory to run. There are times when I am tired of factories."

That gave Hewlitt an opening he had been waiting for. "Mr. Zalinsky, I don't think that you should go home. We talked once about suspicion—this time I am suspicious, they will want someone to blame besides Colonel Rostovitch and you will be the obvious choice. You have given me advice, I now have some for you: ask for political asylum and stay here. It will be granted, I have already asked. Your family will like it here. We are a funny people, but as soon as you ask for asylum they will accept you and you know now that this is a nice place to live. You speak English and you won't have to run a factory—you can teach political science."

Zalinsky smiled grimly for a moment. "It is a temptation, but the premier wants me to come back so I will, and if there is punishment for me, I will accept it. But I do not think so; you see the political climate in my country changes as the seasons do; it is spring at the moment and sins are being forgiven. I like it here, but it is not my own country—you understand that."

"Yes, of course. But if you arrive and find that there is a blizzard, come back."

Zalinsky changed the subject. "You were a good helper even if you were a bad spy. But that is forgivable; you had no experience and no training—dangerous for an amateur."

"I tried hard," Hewlitt said.

"Too hard, I could see that. But I did not tell Gregor because I do not like messy scenes myself and he did not appreciate any help. I missed only one entertainment—the night you were driven into bed with the Barbara girl."

"It was not too difficult to accomplish."

"This I can believe, but I would liked to have seen it. One complaint I had with this job was lack of amusement. Would you like some more beer?"

"No thank you, Mr. Zalinsky."

"Then I give you a present as I leave—I will state that I was completely fooled and never suspected what you were doing. They will believe it and it will be all right." He got to his feet. "You do speak my language very well."

Hewlitt shook hands with him for the first time. "I'll be down to see you off," he promised.

Andrews Air Force Base was shrouded by a thick low overcast which hung in the air like a pall over the whole area and gave to everything a monotonous gray appearance. The wintry gloom penetrated all of the installations. It was the kind of a day when people had found it difficult to get out of bed and looked forward with more than average anticipation to being free to go home again and enjoy whatever creature comforts awaited them there.

Hewlitt tried hard to keep the mood from affecting him. An episode was ending, but to him it had seemed more like an era. He had gone into it as a White House functionary, accepted for his particular skill and well established in the minor role he had been assigned. Because his work had entailed a few minor and impersonal contacts with the President, he had enjoyed a very limited amount of prestige which had been ladled out according to the strict and stifling protocol which had regulated the government structure. He had worked in the White House, but he had still been classified far down the totem pole as one of those who did not matter.

He mattered now. In the morning papers one of the most important national columnists had given him a major write-up and had printed some of the facts relative to his service with the Thomas Jefferson project during the tenure of Feodor Zalinsky. It was not the first such publicity that he had received. Furthermore, the writer, who was noted for doing such things, had concluded with the firm recommendation that here was a man who was needed in a far more important level of government. He had already had a number of phone calls, one from the majority leader in the Senate, who had seriously proposed that he consent to fill out an unexpired term in that august body that had fallen vacant. The appointment, he had been firmly assured, was his if he wanted it; he was suddenly a popular hero.

He had no particular desire to become Senator Hewlitt, but he had agreed to think it over. One thing recommended it: he had a lot of ideas now and the opportunity to put some of them to work appealed to him. And he was certainly old enough to hold the job even though the bulk of the Senate was made up of more senior men.

He was touched on the shoulder and turned around to find Percival there. He had been expecting him and held out his hand. "How've you been?" he asked.

"All right. There's been a great deal to do."

"I believe that. When you're through, are you going to continue in the business?"

"I'm not sure, Hew. It's been quite a tour of duty, I'll say that, but I'd like to get back to my family, for a little while anyway, if I can."

"I didn't know you had one."

"Three kids, and I don't want them to grow up without knowing who their father is."

Hewlitt opened his mouth to speak, then he saw Barbara coming. He waited for her and then put his arm around her in protective greeting for a moment when she stood beside him. "Where is he?" she asked.

"He's not here yet. They're bringing him in through the back way to forestall any last-minute problems that might come up."

He looked at the familiar sleek lines of the four-engined jet transport that was fueled and waiting for its scheduled transatlantic flight. By order of the President, which in this instance probably meant that Admiral Haymarket had been responsible, Feodor Zalinsky and his immediate staff were being sent home in one of the official aircraft as though he had been an honored visitor. It was a bit of stage setting to support the "negotiations" between the premier and the senior American senator who was already overseas.

Hewlitt turned to Percival. "You're sure that this won't blow you—put you in any danger?"

Percival shook his head. "Under the circumstances—no. I've had advice on it."

"I would expect so." He left it at that; his conscience was clear. Before he could take up the next topic in his mind he saw a car coming, a single vehicle that was flying a flag on its front fender that gave it permission to be on the flight line. He watched as it pulled up, and the two secret service men who had been in his small White House cell got out. A few moments later Zalinsky appeared, wrapped in an overcoat which added little to his appearance. Hewlitt noted that; it was good stage setting for his return home, marking him as the humble people's representative who still chose to wear the nondescript garments which had been his when he had left. Once more he realized that Feodor Zalinsky was not dumb.

He went over a few paces to meet him and was surprised when Zalinsky spoke first. "Good morning," he said in English. "It is a lie, the day she is terrible."

Hewlitt shook hands with him again. "I hope that it will be a lot better at the other end, Mr. Zalinsky."

"It is necessary that it be, it will be my own country."

"Then have a happy homecoming."

Zalinsky abruptly changed the topic. "I see that you have the Barbara girl and the other man."

"Yes, you asked to see them."

Zalinsky began to walk over to where they were. He addressed himself first to Barbara. "We have also women in our country," he said, "but you are of very good quality."

She smiled for him. "Thank you, Mr. Zalinsky."

"It is my sad fate that it became necessary for me to drive this man here into your arms."

"Thank you very much," she answered him.

Zalinsky thrust his hands into the pockets of his coat. "If I had been constructed higher and less round, I might have wished it differently," he said, "but that for me is a fairy tale."

He paused and studied the aircraft he was soon to board. "If I insult you I am sorry," he added.

Barbara put her hands on his shoulders. "That never insults any girl," she told him, "and if they pretend otherwise, they're lying. Or they don't deserve to be called female."

"This is enlightenment I hope for my own country," Zalinsky said. "For us Queen Victoria is still a very young person. And now this man."

Hewlitt did not know how to make the introduction; Percival solved it by taking a step forward and offering Zalinsky his hand. "Since you admire Barbara, we have something in common," he said.

Zalinsky shook hands with a slight embarrassment. "You are very intelligent," he said. "I know of you for some time."

Percival did not comment on that point. "I'm glad that it's all behind us, Mr. Zalinsky, and I'm glad to meet you. You have done certain things that I personally appreciate."

"It is good that we say this and then stop," Zalinsky answered.

"Agreed. Come back with your family, as a tourist, and let me show you around. You haven't even seen the Grand Canyon. We have quite a nice place here."

"I do not consider that possible."

"Mr. Zalinsky, very few things are impossible anymore as long as we are living. Things change. People are changing. If you wish it, it can be."

Zalinsky stared at his feet, then looked up once more. "It is time for me to go home," he said. "I leave you now here." He pulled his right hand out of his pocket, chopped a small gesture in the air toward each of them, then turned and walked toward the aircraft.

When he was on board, Barbara said, "I'm going into the terminal for a moment," and left them.

"Will I be seeing you again?" Hewlitt asked.

"Very possibly," Percival answered, "especially if you accept that Senate appointment."

"You know about that."

"Yes, it came down through channels. Do you care for some advice?"

"Shoot."

"Take it; I think the admiral would be pleased."

"Him again."

"Quite a man," Percival said.

"By the way," Hewlitt began on a different topic, "I don't really know who you are."

Percival smiled. "It must have been annoying, but you understood the reasons."

"Absolutely. And if you don't want to say any more, stop there. We've just won a skirmish, but the real war isn't over yet."

Percival became sober. "I'm glad you see that, Hew, because unfortunately it's so. I wish to hell that it wasn't, but it is. I know too much about it; the public knows too little."

"Why don't you tell them?"

"Maybe you can help do that—in the Senate."

"Maybe."

The piercing howl of awakening jet engines cut them off for a moment; they watched as the transport turned toward the taxiway and began to roll forward.

When it was far enough away, Percival said, "I'd better get back to work now, Hew, I've still got a lot to clear away." He held out his hand. "The name is Mark Goldberg; I'll drop you a line if you'd like when I have a new duty station. I'm a lieutenant commander in the Coast Guard."

"I wouldn't have guessed that," Hewlitt said.

"Our service doesn't get the publicity, but we do our job. We're a pretty proud outfit in our own way."

"You're a good proof of that," Hewlitt said.

"It's not the man, it's the mission." He saw Barbara coming back. "Keep that to yourself, my ID I mean; that goes for everyone."

"I will."

Five minutes later Hewlitt was alone with Barbara. "I hate to see Percival go," he said. "I like him."

Barbara agreed. "You'll see him again. I'd met him before. I reminded him of that, if you remember."

He recalled immediately the scene in the safe house. "So you did," he acknowledged. He made a mental effort at that moment to put the whole business behind him. "Come on," he said. "I want to go somewhere and do something—anything. You name it."

She didn't answer him until they were in his car and he had the engine going. "Hew, I want to ask you something first. I started to make a decision, then I realized that you ought to be consulted."

"About your pregnancy."

"Yes. Let me make something very clear—you're not on the hook in any way."

He rolled the car out of the slot and toward the exit driveway.

"Furthermore," she continued, "I'm not the least bit interested in the morals involved; we've outgrown that, I think, and you were literally forced into bed with me."

Hewlitt took over. "I don't want your pregnancy to enter into this. If you want it terminated, then by all means have it done with my blessing. And I demand the right to pay the bill if the Air Force disallows it."

She laughed a little. "I did incur the problem in line of duty," she reminded him.

He drove out of the lot and picked up the main street of the base. "I realize that you have to make up your mind, and that you can't wait forever. Now let me explain something: I'm not going to come galloping up on a white horse, leap off with plumes flying, and then ask for your hand before the whole court assembled while you blush violently and hide your face in an ecstasy of embarrassment."

She looked at him with interest. "Why not?" she asked.

"Because there's a drastic shortage of white horses."

"Oh, I see."

He waited until they had cleared the base.

"Barb, this whole damn thing we've been through has got me off balance. I can't quite get it into my head yet that for practical purposes it's all over."

She came closer to him. "Me too."

"Now I've been all but offered a seat in the Senate and it has more than four years yet to run."

"Then that answers the question," she said.

"No, it doesn't. If I take it, assuming that I can get it, then I want you with me. And none of this we-were-secretly-married business either; I don't like that kind of fraud."

"No one does."

"If I don't go into the Senate, and do something else instead, then, if you're game, I still want you with me. But either way, if you're willing, let's have the baby."

"All right," she agreed.

He turned and looked at her. "Since that's decided—another topic. Can you put up with me?"

"Pretty well."

"Care to perhaps be a senator's wife?"

"No, but if I must, I will."

He discovered that he wasn't watching his driving. For perhaps half a minute he carefully concentrated on what he was supposed to be doing, but his compelling interest was elsewhere. "I want you," he said. He was glad he had put it simply; he couldn't stand maudlin sentimentality.

"I want you to have me," she answered him.

Sentimentality or not, that called for action. He pulled the car halfway onto the shoulder strip and didn't give a damn if it was still blocking traffic or not. "Come here," he said.

He had held her before, they had been in bed together many times, but this was different. For a short while he satisfied his hunger for her, as much as he could in a public place, and ignored the barrage of honkings that was building up behind him. If he was blocking the lane he had earned the right, and he was putting it to good use.

When he was for the moment satisfied he released hold of her and put the car once more into gear. "Let's go and have a good meal," he proposed. "After that we can decide when, where, and how we'd like to get married."

"Fine," she responded. "As a matter of fact, I'm hungry."

"You've got a right to be." He let a car pass him and ignored the glare that the other driver aimed his way. A thought crossed his mind and simply because she was his girl he wanted to share it with her. "I wish we could tell the admiral," he remarked.

She looked at him sideways, then shook her head to reset her hair. "He already knows," she said.

CPSIA information can be obtained
at www.ICGtesting.com
Printed in the USA
LVHW040017170420
653809LV00001B/81